NATIONAL BESTSELLER

"*Hummingbird Salamander* features ecoterrorists, evil corporations, a race to defuse doomsday weapons, gunfire, fisticuffs, action sequences and hair-raising escapes. But . . . VanderMeer introduces all this genre fun mostly to subvert it . . . The secret interconnections of the spy novel map onto the secret interconnections of the natural world. And the unfurling plot mirrors the unraveling ecosystem."
—NOAH BERLATSKY, *Los Angeles Times*

"The sheer delight of a new novel from Jeff Vandermeer . . . is that you never know what you're going to get. With *Hummingbird Salamander,* he delivers a crackling page-turner, a canny eco-thriller cut from the same cloth as such 1970s cinematic classics as *The Conversation* and *Three Days of the Condor* . . . A philosophical exploration and a warning, delivered in a package of sheer reading pleasure."
—ROBERT J. WIERSEMA, *Toronto Star*

"This is an astonishing book, topical and madly compelling. A timely, unsettling novel of obsession and descent—a thriller equal parts ecological and psychological, whose puzzle warns of a natural world on the edge of ruination. There's an urgency to it, but it's not preachy. Jeff VanderMeer shines in revealing our current dystopia."
—CHUCK WENDIG, author of *Wanderers*

"[An] inventive and surprising page-turner, maybe the purest demonstration yet of VanderMeer's knack for dressing up fascinating philosophical conundrums in the clothing of a taut, breakneck thriller."
—*The A.V. Club*

PRAISE FOR *HUMMINGBIRD SALAMANDER*

"*Hummingbird Salamander* reads like an existential James Bond novel crossed with a David Attenborough documentary . . . Sentences pulse like irregular heartbeats. Long stretches of Jane's narration shatter into action with shootouts, chases, and dramatic confrontations. The result is that, like Jane, readers can never let down their guard for a moment . . . It's tough to integrate science into fiction without falling into didacticism, but *Hummingbird Salamander* manages beautifully."

—**LEIGH ANNE FOCARETA**, *Pittsburgh Post-Gazette*

"Action-packed, memorably voiced, and rich in detail, the novel uses the thriller format—bureaucratic espionage and private investigation—to spiral inwards to a story of personal and ecological disaster . . . Like much of VanderMeer's work, *Hummingbird Salamander* is an attempt to imagine, not an end of the world, but a *transformation*."

—**JAKE CASELLA BROOKINS**, *Chicago Review of Books*

"*Hummingbird Salamander* is a profound and incendiary thriller hurtling backward from the end of the world. Jeff VanderMeer's tale of ecological and personal obsession inhabits that strange, surreal space where the natural world and human ambition collide—a space almost no other writer has chronicled with as much reverence and imaginative lucidity. The result is a detective story unlike any I've read before, futuristic in bearing but deeply relevant to this present, dangerous moment."

—**OMAR EL AKKAD**, author of *American War*
and *What Strange Paradise*

"Riveting . . . VanderMeer is a marvelous craftsman. Every word here feels carefully chosen; every sentence has a purpose; every plot point causes ripples felt through the rest of the story . . . Switching genres with aplomb, VanderMeer knocks his conspiracy thriller out of the park."

—**DAVID PITT**, *Booklist* (starred review)

"An existential mindfuck cleverly disguised as a thriller. Though the plot never stops rocketing forward, this astonishing novel continually shifts and expands in scale, until the puzzle the narrator is tasked with solving at the outset becomes an almost Matrix-like invitation to open herself up to a new and shattering understanding of her world, and ours. Visionary, dark, beautiful, and strange, *Hummingbird Salamander* is that rare novel that coaxes you into imagining the unimaginable."

—**KRISTEN ROUPENIAN**, author of
"Cat Person" and Other Stories

Ditte Valente

JEFF VANDERMEER
HUMMINGBIRD SALAMANDER

Jeff VanderMeer is the author of *Hummingbird Salamander*, the *Borne* novels (*Borne*, *The Strange Bird*, and *Dead Astronauts*), and *The Southern Reach Trilogy* (*Annihilation*, *Acceptance*, and *Authority*), the first volume of which won the Nebula Award and the Shirley Jackson Award and was adapted into a movie by Alex Garland. He speaks and writes frequently about issues relating to climate change as well as urban rewilding. He lives in Tallahassee, Florida, on the edge of a ravine, with his wife, Ann VanderMeer, and their cat, Neo.

HUMMINGBIRD SALAMANDER

JEFF VANDERMEER

HUMMINGBIRD

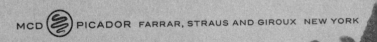
MCD PICADOR FARRAR, STRAUS AND GIROUX NEW YORK

SALAMANDER

MCD
Picador
120 Broadway, New York 10271

Descriptions of the hummingbird and salamander life cycles were created by
Dr. Meghan Brown Smith and are used with permission through license with
VanderMeer Creative, Inc.

Photograph of Chinese salamander on title page and part openers by Pan
Xunbin / Shutterstock.com. Images on pages 129, 217, 323, and 357–372 created
by Jeremy Zerfoss, © VanderMeer Creative, Inc.

The Library of Congress has cataloged the MCD hardcover edition as follows:
Names: VanderMeer, Jeff, author.
Title: Hummingbird salamander / Jeff VanderMeer.
Description: First edition. | New York : MCD / Farrar, Straus and Giroux, 2021.
Identifiers: LCCN 2020050640 | ISBN 9780374173548 (hardcover)
Subjects: GSAFD: Suspense fiction.
Classification: LCC PS3572.A4284 H86 2021 | DDC 813/.54—dc23
LC record available at https://lccn.loc.gov/2020050640

Paperback ISBN: 978-1-250-82977-1

Designed by Abby Kagan

Our books may be purchased in bulk for promotional, educational, or business
use. Please contact your local bookseller or the Macmillan Corporate and
Premium Sales Department at 1-800-221-7945, extension 5442, or by email at
MacmillanSpecialMarkets@macmillan.com.

Picador® is a U.S. registered trademark and is used by Macmillan Publishing
Group, LLC, under license from Pan Books Limited.

For book club information, please visit facebook.com/picadorbookclub or
email marketing@picadorusa.com.

mcdbooks.com • Follow us on Twitter, Facebook, and Instagram at @mcdbooks
picadorusa.com • Instagram: @picador • Twitter and Facebook: @picadorusa

10 9 8 7 6 5 4 3 2 1

FOR ANN

HUMMINGBIRD SALAMANDER

[O]

Assume I'm dead by the time you read this. Assume you're being told all of this by a flicker, a wisp, a thing you can't quite get out of your head now that you've found me. And in the beginning, it's you, not me, being handed an envelope with a key inside . . . on a street, in a city, on a winter day so cold that breathing hurts and your lungs creak.

A barista leans out onto the sidewalk from your local coffee shop to say, "I almost forgot."

The before of those words and the after, and you stuck in the middle. "I almost forgot." Except the barista didn't forget, was instructed to make it happen that way. "Time sensitive."

You turn in surprise to receive what someone has left for you, but you don't refuse it. Bodies don't work that way—a person hands you something, you take it. A reflex. You worry about what it is later.

Or who wants you to have it. Because the barista doesn't know. No one in the coffee shop knows. From the night before. A different shift. No chain of evidence. The barista retreating into the coffee shop sudden, like a monster grabbed him in its jaws and pulled him back inside. As if he never wanted to talk to you in the first place, except someone paid him. Who? How much? No answer.

You're left holding an envelope, breath like a chain-smoker's, trees all around stripped of leaves and imprisoned in concrete. Your hand is all that burns, attacked by the cold, the sound of your nail ripping the envelope flap almost urgent.

Do you have a secret admirer? That feels both new and old, like the snooze button you hit three times that morning as your husband mumbled on the bed next to you. Your usual routine has been dull and kind of fucked up for too long.

Inside the envelope, along with the key, is an address and a number. The number is 7. The key is a trap, but you don't know that yet.

On the back of the envelope, someone has scrawled "If you received this, I am already gone. You're on your own. But not alone."

Maybe it's the heat in your body giving itself over to the cold in a rush, something to do with absolutes, but you can't withhold a surge of raw, rough emotion. *Not alone.*

The idea of going on to work feels ever more muffled, distant, under all your layers. Yet you crumple the envelope in that cold hand, a smolder at the presumption in those words.

Standing there on the sidewalk. Black slush of snow pushed to the sides of the street. A dead robin in the gutter, one torn wing spread toward the drain like an invitation to the underworld.

Another winter morning in a city in the Pacific Northwest.

Where, exactly? I won't tell you.

Who am I? I won't tell you. Exactly.

But you can call me Jane.

Jane Smith. If that helps.

I'm here to show you how the world ends.

PART 1

HUMMINGBIRD

DIORAMA

[1]

I went to the address in the note because I didn't want to go to work. The car came for me, dark and chrome and sleek, its shadow leaking across the windows of fast-food places, gas stations, and tanning salons. The radio whispered panic about the elections, and my driver, unsolicited, had already imagined, in a soft voice, black drones congregating at night to listen in on our conversations. Yet I knew from my job that this was old news.

I had no reason to remember the driver. Back then, I thought I was smart, for all the details I caught, but there was so much I never saw. He had a beard. He might have had an accent. I remember I feared he came from some place we were bombing. We didn't talk about anything important. Why would we?

The driver might have believed I was a reasonable person, a normal person. Just a little larger than most. I dressed, in those days, in custom-made gray business suits because nothing store-bought fit right. I had an expensive black down coat. I didn't think much about where the softness came from, at what cost. My faux heels were decoys: comfortable, just worn to preserve some ritual about what women should wear.

My main indulgence was a huge purse that doubled as a satchel. Behind my back, my boss called it "Shovel Pig," which was another way of calling me shovel pig. Because I frightened him.

"So, what do you do?" the driver asked.

"Manager at a tech company," I said, because that was simple and the details were not.

I stared out the window as he began to tell me everything he knew about computers. I could tell his greatest need, or mine, was to sit alone in a park for an hour and be as silent as a stone.

The downtown fell away and, with it, skyscrapers and gentrified loft apartments, and then, after streets of counterculture, zoned haphazard and garish, the suburbs took over. The driver stopped talking. So many one-story houses with slanted roofs and flat lawns, gravel driveways glinting through thin snow. The mountain range like a premonition twisted free of gray mist, distant but gathering.

I hadn't done a search on the address. That felt too much like being at work. Didn't make my pulse quicken.

■ ■ ■

When we reached the gates with flaking gold paint, I knew why I had a key in addition to an address. Emblazoned over the gates, the legend "Imperial Storage Palace." Because I have to give you a name. It had seen better days, so call it "Better Days Storage Palace," if you like. I'm sure, by the time you found it, the sign was gone anyway.

We glided down a well-paved road lined with firs and free of holiday decoration, while the base of steep, pine-strewn foothills came close. The light darkened in that almost-tunnel. I could smell the fresh air, even through the stale cigarette smoke of the backseat. Anything could exist in the thick mist that covered the mountainside. A vast forest. A tech bro campus. But most likely a sad logged slope, a hell of old-growth stumps and gravel the farther up you went.

The lampposts in front of the entrance lent the road only a distracted sort of light. The vastness of the storage palace, that faux marble façade, collected weight and silence. The murk felt like a distracting trick. What was it covering up? The pretentious nature of the Doric columns? The black mold on the plastic grass that lined the stairs?

Nothing could disguise the exhaustion of the red carpet smothering the patio. The threadbare edges, the ways in which pine cone debris and squirrel passage had been smashed into the design.

Beyond the shadow of the two-story complex lay a wall of deep green, merging with ever-higher elevations. The pressure of that pressed against the car, quickened my pulse.

This was the middle of nowhere, and I almost didn't get out of the car. But it was too late. Like the ritual of accepting what is offered, once you reach your destination, you get out of the car.

Too late as well because the world was flypaper: you couldn't avoid getting stuck. Someone was already watching. Somewhere.

"Should I wait for you?" the driver asked.

I ignored that, lurched out of the backseat. I am six feet tall and two-thirty, never mistaken for a small woman any more than a mountain for a valley, a heavyweight boxer for a gymnast. I need time to get up and depart.

"Are you sure I can't wait?" he asked across the passenger seat out the half-opened window.

I leaned down, took his measure.

"Do you not understand the nature of your own business?"

The driver left me there, a little extra "pedal to the metal," as my grandfather would've said.

Sometimes I am just like him.

Inside, gold wallpaper had turned urine yellow. The red carpet perked up as it ran past two ornate antique chairs with lion paws for feet. Beyond that lay a fortress outpost in the cramped antechamber: a barred cage jutting out and a counter painted black, from behind which a woman watched me. Beyond that lay the storage units, through an archway. A legend on a sad banner overhead read "Protecting your valuable since 1972."

"What do you want?" the woman asked, no preamble. As if I might want almost anything at all.

"What do you think?" I said.

Showed her the key, as I wiped my shoes on the crappy welcome mat.

"Which one?"

"Seven."

"Got ID?"

"I've got the key."

"Got ID to go with that key?"

"I've got the key."

She held out her hand. "Identification, please, and I'll check the list."

I considered pushing a twenty across the counter. That idea felt strange. But it felt strange to let her know who I was, too.

I handed her my driver's license.

She was much younger than me. She had on a lot of black, had piercings, highlighted her eyes to make them look bigger, and wore purple lipstick. Practically a uniform in some parts of town.

She might've been a brunette. I remember her expression. Bored. Bottled up here. Doing nothing—and I wasn't making her life less boring.

"I've come a long way," I said. Which would be true soon enough. I would've come a long way.

"If you're on the list, great," she said, finger scrolling down a single sheet of paper with names printed impossibly small.

"Yes. That'd be great," I said. Struck by how meaningless language can be. Yet I remember the conversation but not her face.

The woman found a line on the page with a ballpoint pen, gave me back my ID.

"So go in, then," she said.

Like I was loitering.

"Where?"

"Over there."

She pointed to the right, where another door waited, half disguised by the same piss-pattern wallpaper.

I stared at her for a moment before I walked through, as she picked up a magazine and ignored me. Somehow, I needed a list of life choices that had led this woman to be in this place at this time. To take my ID. To ignore me. To be sullen. To be anonymous.

I wouldn't see her on my way out. The cage would be empty, as if no one had ever been there.

As if I had emerged years later and the whole place had been abandoned.

■ ■ ■

All those rows of doors. So many doors, and not the usual rolldown aluminum. More like a sanatorium or a teen detention center: thick, rectangular, the smudged square window crisscrossed with lines and a number taped on as an afterthought. Not all the doors had been painted the same color, and teal or magenta made the institutional effect worse somehow. The smell of mold was stronger. Sound behaved oddly, as if the shifting weight of clutter behind the doors was making itself known.

What did I know about storage units? Nothing. I'd only known our mother's, a place we'd rented to appease our father, who didn't want to become a hoarder. But, just maybe, if you drove all the way to the outskirts of the city, to the edge of the mountains, what you kept here you wanted at arm's length. And what you wanted kept at arm's length could be precious or fragile as memory. Even a bad memory.

Nine through eleven followed one through three. Had I missed a passageway? It was a warren, with several crossroads. Perhaps the storage units went on forever, the space wandering beneath the mountains in some terrifyingly infinite way. A moment of panic, at the thought of getting lost, as I kept walking and didn't find number seven.

But I found the right door.

Or the wrong door, depending on your point of view.

[3]

"It was all meant to be" is a powerful drug. Crossing that threshold into Unit 7, I couldn't have told you what was preordained and what was chance. Or how long it might take to separate the two.

All I saw at first was the emptiness of some square stripped-bare cliché of an interrogation room. A modest wooden chair stood near the back, under flickering fluorescent lights in the ceiling. A medium-sized cardboard box sat on the chair.

I stood in the doorway and stared at the box on the chair for a long time. Left the door open behind me, an instinct about doors slamming shut that wasn't paranoid. The trap could be anywhere. It was so still, so antiseptic, inside. Except for one moldy panel of the back wall. I don't recall dust motes even. Like a crime scene wiped clean.

But I checked the far, dark corner, the ceiling, before walking up to the chair. I did that much.

Just an ordinary cardboard box. The top flaps had been folded shut. Lightweight, when I gave it an experimental nudge. No sound coming out of it, either. No airholes. Nothing like a puppy or kitten, then. Immense relief in that.

I put down my purse, pulled back first one flap and then the other.

I think I laughed, nervously.

But there was no moment of misunderstanding, of recoiling in horror. A small object lay in the bottom of the box. A curio? Like the horse figurines my mother used to collect. Which is when it struck me this might all be an elaborate joke.

A tiny bird perched down there. Sitting dead. Taxidermy.

A hummingbird in midflight, attached by thick wire from below to a small pedestal. Frozen wings. Frozen eyes. Iridescent feathers.

Beside the hummingbird, I found a single piece of paper, with two words written on it and a signature.

Hummingbird

.. .. ..

Salamander
—Silvina

Oh, Silvina, thank you for not scrawling "Find me" across the bottom of your note.

Thank you for knowing that wasn't necessary.

[4]

A man who could've been the brother of the first driver took me home, at the wheel of a car more anonymous and darker than the first. The landscape seemed compressed, moved past more quickly, so we were back in the city sooner. Or I just wasn't paying attention.

Hummingbird. Salamander. One there, one not, and the one not there the creature I knew so well from childhood.

The overturning of rocks. The swirl of the river and the sway of the tiny river plants. The deep-green moss. All those expeditions so long ago.

I sat silent in the backseat with the box guarded by my knees, arms engulfing it gently. So I wouldn't crush it. Dead, but somehow alive, able to be wounded. I didn't dare open the flaps to stare at it for fear the driver would see. I had no thought. Nothing at all. Or maybe I was held by the outline of memories I'd left behind. The look of rage on my grandfather's face. The slack, pale form of my brother by the river.

No therapist ever told me I should forget my childhood, because I hated therapists and had never seen one. But I knew that forgetting was best. Let the dead stay dead. Make dead what was still alive. Move forward.

It wasn't the box or the storage unit. I don't know exactly what tried to pin me back there, trap me, except the sense of not being in control.

[5]

Early afternoon. No one would be home. I had already taken care of my boss and texted in sick. I set the box on the kitchen counter, next to my purse. Tossed my coat on the living room couch, came back to the counter, hesitated . . . then opened the box and removed the hummingbird.

I regarded it from a precarious kitchen island stool, on the edge of that expanse of wood and marble. Spotless stainless steel, double sinks, a cutting station on wheels, a sparkling black-and-white stove, a smart refrigerator I'd deliberately fucked up so it couldn't report back.

Somehow, the hummingbird dominated that space beyond its size. Beyond even what I could've thought it meant at the time.

The hummingbird had a fierce aspect, jet-black feathers, smoothed out and yet bristling. Even the beak, long and slender, made me think of a blade or a needle meant to draw blood. I imagined a dozen of its kind circling someone's head like guardians or a crown of thorns. Hard to imagine this species sipping delicate from a flower, but I didn't know much about hummingbirds. Our neighborhood didn't have them, nor any school I attended, and they'd been rare on the farm. We didn't plant a lot of flowers.

The thick wire attached to the dead bird had the look of dull silver. The stand had a glossy look, almost a deep red. On the bottom I found the letters "R.S." Plain, crudely carved. By the maker or by Silvina?

Taxidermy registered strange to me. The language of taxidermy made no sense. I didn't like bars or restaurants where they signaled "macho" through deer or bear trophies on the wall. Macabre. Pathological. But this—this came from a different impulse. Secretive and elusive. The bird's body caused a disconnect. The stillness, and then the way the eyes weren't blank but staring at me.

The distance across the counter widened, and the silence grew unbearable. Who was "Silvina"? And why had she given me a hummingbird? And where was the salamander? Because the salamander felt personal. As if this woman I didn't know had done her research and understood the salamander didn't need to be there, in the storage unit. That just the word could awaken a recognition or impulse.

Some things remain mysterious even if you think about them all the time.

Salamanders. Hiding under logs and river stones. A creature that did not want to be found.

I drank a glass of water, had an apple and then a big bowl of leftover chicken salad, rummaged for gum in my purse after. Tried to shake off whatever had gathered within me, but the hummingbird stared at me defiant. It was what I had to work with.

I resisted the idea of using my phone for an online search for "Silvina" and for "hummingbird." A search for "R.S." yielded nothing useful and, three pages down, "arse." But adding Silvina's name to "R.S." concerned me. A stabbing unease at the thought of exposure. I needed context more than data. Didn't want to open up a channel that could lead back to me. A client breach around search terms months ago didn't help rationalize the risk.

Was the hummingbird code for something? Or just the first of two bookends? That space between them yawned like the abyss, and the space in my head felt deliberate, like Silvina wanted it to be there.

[6]

Before the school bus brought my daughter home, I put the hummingbird back in its box and hid it under a couple old blankets in the trunk of my car. I knew enough to act normal and ask my daughter about her day. To close myself off while receiving, in the usual way, the eye roll and shrug as she took off her sneakers.

"Fine. Swell." Always "Fine," along with something terse and sarcastic. "Swell." The swell of teen angst. The swell of irritation with parents. Her chaotic grades reflected a creative child with an erratic attention span, no patience, and so much talent it hurt to think about.

Backpack tossed in a corner with the discarded shoes.

She had no sense of caution, would jump from a tree to our rooftop on a dare from the kid across the street. She'd cost me thirty-two hours of labor, a breach birth through C-section. I didn't mind the scar; it joined the others. I just wished she'd be easier sometimes. I used to get texts from her, but not lately, except for "Ready for you to pick me up."

A grunt. That's how my daughter acknowledged the mound

of gifts we'd snuck under the tree after she'd left for school. She scrambled up the stairs to her cave. I'd barely gotten a glimpse of her wide, open face and the thick dark eyebrows I loved so much.

Soon enough, my husband would pull up in a late-model tan sedan. A car chosen to be tidy and respectable and solid if seen by his real estate clients. But he was fooling himself. I had married a shambolic mountain in human form. He always made me feel I was a reasonable size.

No matter how often he shaved, he would always have a shadow of a beard. He smelled fantastic. He had hardly ever raised his voice to me.

■ ■ ■

Once upon a time, I could still imagine he'd burst through the door at the end of the day and I'd greet him with a smile. He'd bring me close, one mountain to another. Plant a rough kiss on my neck, my cheek, my mouth, pull away to stare at my face. Then, reassured, barrel through the house in search of our daughter, making a production of not knowing where she is, so when he finds her she will be exasperated with his theatrics, his need to track her down for a mighty hug even as her scowl dissolves into a half-grin.

Then he will make dinner, like he always made dinner. Because I could just about cook an egg. Had taken steps never to get better at cooking, throughout my long, bumpy career as a woman.

My husband in the kitchen never looked like anything other than a cheerful Kodiak trained in the glories of French cuisine, a glass of Malbec held careless in one hairy paw and a knife in the other. I always felt he would knock over everything that I hadn't and maybe start a fire and burn the house down. But instead he just used every plate and utensil in the kitchen and made a mess.

After the mess, I will sit down at the kitchen table to a

meal of something delicious—pork chops with asparagus and roasted potatoes? We will talk about our day, me, my husband, our daughter. Or I would and he would. Together we will tease out of my daughter the things that were important to her. Or some version of them. After, I do the dishes and maybe help my daughter with her homework. Before bed, we play a board game or watch something stupid on TV.

I still remember. When there was a time that was still plausible. The *bigness* of that.

The sheer expanse of that.

■ ■ ■

You'll never get their names. I can't bring myself to, not even surrogates. The moment I type their names, they'll be lost to me, belong to you. I think I know when you'll read this, but I can't be sure.

Even then, there was too much neither of them knew about me. Only the cast-off interference, the things that caused distance or created it. A kind of shadow or smudge. Not a clear view.

The face that stares back at you from the mirror later in life is so different than when you're young. There's a winnowing away and a shutting down. A sense of something having been taken from you and you don't know exactly what it is, just that it isn't there anymore. What opens up to you instead is experience, is cunning, is foreknowledge. Nothing you sought.

How much a mind could take in before it began to resort to metaphor or to turn away from the truth. That was how you measured privacy: by how you became lost in the torrent.

I couldn't see the future, but it was hard not to bring my work home with me. To anticipate surveillance. To foretell that I might have to confuse the watchers, distract and fool them, to pursue this mystery. I knew what made us visible. But, even careful, I was too naïve to see what spilled out from us into the night.

I made it through the end of dinner without confessing to a hummingbird, a salamander, or a storage unit. Maybe because Silvina wasn't the first secret I'd kept from my husband.

[7]

I rarely drove myself to work, but some paranoid impulse made me loath to call a service. I left before the family woke up. They were used to it, and I felt I might crack if I had to be home for breakfast. The hummingbird seemed to weigh down the trunk as I drove. The elevator up bucked, complained, but that was probably more about me than the bird.

Everything in our offices had been designed to project "security" or "secureness." A lobby as inoffensive as the inside of a drone. Sound-muffling gray carpet with glints of sparkle. Cubicle partitions that gleamed obsidian. Abstract art providing muted color on the white outer walls. Passion? No threat of that. It remained wrapped up in plastic in a closet somewhere. We were purely of the mind. Except when we weren't.

I meant to let that seamless place neutralize the box on my desk. Smother it. Or I thought it a lark, a diversion, a way to stave off boredom. Can't remember—that's the scary thing. I can't remember what I thought back then.

No one commented on the box as I walked to my office. It looked like the size that could house a table lamp. I'd brought lamps in before, to push back against the generic feel of the workplace. That would be reasonable, ordinary. Turn what was in the box into something else. Even if I didn't know what was in the box yet. Not really.

My boss stuck his head in the doorway a few minutes later. Let's call him "Alex" because he resembled an Alex. Reasonable and solid. Flickers of humor a few times a year. A lightbulb that couldn't quite remember how to turn on. Nothing memorable about his blue suits, white shirts, and red ties, but nothing shabby, either. He should've looked like a human flag, but chose faded tones. So instead Alex looked like a flag that had seen better days.

I knew of his arrival moments beforehand due to strong aftershave. Glasses were an affectation or he left them off most times because he was self-conscious. Before security, Alex had founded a VR company that had gone bankrupt.

"Feeling better?" he asked/said.

"Great! Much better!" I knew what slop he wanted shoveled at him and with what energy.

"Hit the gym this morning?"

"Still a little under the weather."

"Fair enough," he said. That and "No worries" he used to hide a multitude of sins. I forgive you. You are forgiven. Don't let it happen again.

"Did you go?" I knew he wanted me to ask.

"I did," Alex said. "Benched a shit-ton. Pull-ups and . . ."

I zoned out. Ever since he'd found out I'd been a bodybuilder, I'd gone from the going-to-fat creature to the gym-rat anomaly. Maybe he thought I was a freak. Or maybe he just couldn't let go of one of the only personal things he knew about me.

"Sounds great!" I said when he'd finished. Months later.

"All right—see you around. Strategy meeting late Pee Em."

Punched the doorway like a jock, I guess, then gone. The doorway always got abuse from him.

But I wasn't free yet.

"What's in the box?"

"Larry," from the office just around a dead-end bend. We had a free-floating hierarchy. Equals, except Alex always invited Larry to go fishing in the spring on his boat. Ruddy Larry. Red-faced Larry, with the mane of brown hair that didn't fit his face. Larry, who'd stood too close at the Christmas party last year, so I'd had to pull away. Just by accident. A well-calculated collision with my shoulder.

"What's in the box?"

Because I hadn't replied and Larry was like a crappy can opener.

"A dead body."

Larry laughed. "Looks too small for that."

I shrugged. Didn't offer more. Stared at him. Never once thought the hummingbird was an office prank, and I didn't now. Not their SOP.

"Another lamp?" Larry asked.

I said nothing.

When Larry got flustered, his face looked like someone had strapped an invisible cage full of rats to his head.

Gradually, his form receded from my doorway.

· · ·

I never much understood the point of the world of men. How they fed off each other. How they motivated themselves. I mean, I got the *purpose*, but I navigated that world the way an astronaut would an alien landscape. Trying not to breathe the same air. Which was impossible, of course.

When I started out, I had been one of only two women in the company who were not on a secretary track. The idea I'd be a manager seemed absurd, but the money was good. I had no experience.

For a long time, I thought of myself as a secret agent, embedded there, in the company, except the only handler I reported back to was my other self. In the conversations of my fellow employees, I would gather intel to get a sense of whether I was in the loop or being left out of the loop, and whether it mattered. A new catchphrase from Alex I'd not been in the room to hear. Or perhaps my peers had talked about some new management strategy while on a hunting trip together. I would never know what information they conveyed at the urinal, but had no interest in piss-stained intel.

Down in the park, far below my window, after Larry left, a lone bird fluttered up against the gray sky. Back then I couldn't have told you the species or why you should care their numbers had dropped fifty percent in the last three years.

What did our company do anyway? Here's a clue: Alex once said that we "sold orchards to apples." Apples always needed orchards to survive. At least in our business they did. A kind of scam, but also like detective work—figuring out how companies worked instead of how they said they worked. Found the security gaps. Sold the fear of security gaps. There would always be security gaps.

The internet was a colander. You were the water. The metaphor changed by the week. It didn't always make sense.

[8]

"*I want to be lost,*" Silvina wrote once. "*I want to be so far beyond anything that there is no map, and the compass spins wild. And when I come back, if I come back, you need to know I've changed, and with that change it means I carry 'lost' with me everywhere, even in the heart of the city. That I am lost forever, and that's how we need to be. So the systems can't find us, can't wreck us. So our heads are clear.*" (One of the first things I found later, but you can have it now.)

The context? At the age of twenty-one, Silvina went upriver, toward Quito, following the path of the famous naturalist Alexander von Humboldt more than a century before. Fleeing her aristocratic parents. Silvina, born in Argentina, but exiled to boarding schools in the United States. Silvina returning. Silvina headed to Ecuador, not home. Smart enough to want to have some distance from her family, their influence. Or afraid of her father.

Spurred on by the light sensitivity and sound sensitivity that plagued her from around age nine. Silvina *physically* needed to be away from cities, from towns, from people. To be healthy. And so often was not.

"Those of us who are different know the world better, know it how it truly is. We can't edit out parts of it. The horror and the beauty most ignore. When your senses are acute, you can't escape. And you see the disconnect we have from . . . everything."

She had had a vision in her head of that journey to Quito, I'm sure. Of what it might mean. A vision as pristine as what the naturalist had discovered more than a century and a half ago. Perhaps she found part of that. She met with indigenous activists and the more liberal Church leaders. She toured ecological success stories. Islands in the path of a hurricane.

But, mostly, what she found instead was the future. Oil companies and mining had devoured part of the route. Foreign to her for many reasons. The moment when she realized she couldn't run. Couldn't hide. What she hated would always be in front of her.

"The point of being lost is this dislocation. This point of entry to the real. Some never lose it. But most do. You have to shock it awake. Be in real danger. Create real danger. An unknown."

Idealistic? Maybe. But I found it moving.

Even if I'd never been lost that way, or suffered that disconnect. At best, we plotted sometimes to buy a mountain retreat deep in the forests. Build a house in the wilderness, connected to town by a dirt road. Emergency generator, childhood knowledge of semi-rural life. Woodsy, roll-up-your-sleeves self-sufficiency. Except, we'd have good internet access. Except, on the weekends we'd drive down to a local pub and eat farm-to-table and drink microbrews made from the neighbor's clean well water. Free of mindless conformity. We'd do it debt-free, pay off the credit card, a burden that had always made me nervous.

We talked about it, never did anything about it. Deep down, we liked the comfort of our generic house. Experienced amnesia about the cost. It was easy, like sinking into the cushions of a comfortable leather couch. Of which we had two.

We lived in a generic version of reality. The house we settled on in a suburban neighborhood had few differences from the other houses on the block—and the block after that. Call our neighborhood "Meadow Brook" or "Canopy Trail" or "Lake Shores" or any other name that fucks with your head if you think about it too long. Because there isn't a meadow or a canopy or a lake. Anymore.

"It was hard to remember what to forget," she wrote. As if she could read my mind.

I think about the Quito part of her life often, even now. That tiny cross section, a matter of two months or fifty-nine days. How it changed her. What it stole from her. What she could never reveal.

What it helped make her into.

[9]

I called my assistant "Allie" into my office. Let's say she wore a lot of black, had piercings, highlighted her eyes to make them look bigger, and wore purple lipstick. She might've been a brunette. Sometimes she wore dark, floral-print dresses with thick socks to fend off the cold outside. I didn't put her in front of clients.

Or maybe I did. And maybe she was brash and bold and not a waif at all. Let's say she was tall. No, short and stocky. She was white. No, she wasn't. She's been erased. I erased her. It was the safest thing to do. Make up whatever you want to about her. I did, because I had to.

"Add the Better Days Storage Palace to your research list," I told her. "Key word 'Silvina.' Anything you can find on a

Silvina connected to the storage palace." I made sure to look her in the eyes; my only tell is when I look away. Some people find me impassive. I think it is more that they focus on my body, not my face.

But even as I said "Silvina," it felt like overstep. That I wasn't meant to say the name aloud. Not yet. The name lingered in the space between us. Did I think Allie would be immune because she was young and unimportant? Had I never heard of collateral damage?

"Priority?" Allie asked. We had deliverables for a million-dollar contract with a client in just a week.

I hesitated.

"High-priority." I did not elaborate, even though Allie didn't gossip or overshare.

"That'll mean overtime," Allie said.

"That's fine."

"And it might jeopardize—"

"I don't care." Then reconsidered my tone. I never raised my voice to Allie. Except when I did. "I mean, you can have overtime, and also delegate to someone in the intern pool. I'll get Alex to authorize."

Allie nodded slowly, and I could see she was uncomfortable.

"What account?" Usually, that's what I led with. The anchor.

Forget it, I wanted to say. *It can wait.* But I couldn't. "Low-priority" might mean a week to know more. I didn't think I could wait that long. Somehow felt I needed intel, context, as soon as possible. For threat assessment. At least, that's how I rationalized it.

"Potential new client. I can't talk about it yet."

Allie nodded. "Got it." But did she?

I didn't yet see that giving Allie this task might sacrifice her to something. An idea, a cause, she never signed up for.

Or did I? Wasn't that *why* I gave her the task? To put the act at one remove from me?

Imagine you analyze security protocols for a living. You help minimize breaches. You actually think you might be good at it. But something comes at you from an unexpected direction. It takes you a while to understand what this thing is, what it means, how it could change everything.

In the gap, you're lost.

[10]

I was a wrestler in high school, a weight lifter in college, a semi-pro bodybuilder for a handful of years after that. Wrestling saved my life, in a way, even though it was just three of us folded into the men's team. All the away trips. All the bus rides in the dark. Traveling far from that farm. The number of times I had to stay late for practice that reduced the hours in my room at home. The way we bonded. Even if I don't even know where they live now.

I became a wrestler because I loved a certain kind of aggression born, in part, of joy. My body was made for the task: the training and the matches both. Competition was the only thing that put my body to the test, kept it in the state it was meant to be in, and back then if sports could be perpetual, always 24/7, I would have loved that.

Except I couldn't. Like bears are always injured, exist in that state, I was always injured. Shoulders or ankles or something. But to me back then . . . that was a state of being. To be joyful was to have the signs of having stretched myself, and injury told me who I was supposed to be, just as soreness told the older me now.

What wasn't born into me was the anger I channeled into physical activity. How I snuffed it out, even if it smoldered deep. Never quite gone. Waiting.

But trying to be a bodybuilder missed the point: I'd gotten away. I was gone. Whatever I needed wasn't performative. Couldn't be fixed posing on a stage. Needed to stay grounded, personal.

Now I go to fat, then come back again. I don't care.

So I went to the gym at lunch, to work out the tension. Lunch hour traffic, along with overcast skies and sludge, made me wish I lived somewhere warmer and more remote. Except, heat is not my friend.

I came to rest at the bottom of the hill in the potholed strip mall parking lot. Took my hands off a steering wheel I'd been holding on to too tightly. The parking lot smelled of gasoline or motor oil. I favored a parking spot in the middle, under a streetlamp.

I'd found the place ages ago after becoming disillusioned with the antiseptic gym near our house. I liked that it was a little out of my way. A dive gym, and across the street a dive bar I might, daring, frequent once or twice a month when I came here after work. Oldsters and shady types in this gym, abutting a neighborhood once middle class, now a crucible for meth busts. Pure intentions, but maybe I was slumming.

The trudge to the smudged glass doors tattooed with dust and the logos of extinct energy drinks. Inside, the thin, sharp line of some cleaning product, punctuated by years of accumulated sweat and the pungent ache of WD-40 lingering on some of the machines. Free weights rusting through their silver paint like something ancient becoming visible. Old-style Nautilus equipment the owners kept fixing with off-brand parts. Benches with split upholstery. Hardly a mirror in the place. No TV.

An old black man named Charlie was there most days, custodian and security both. He had a flag from Antigua on the wall behind his favorite chair. I thought he owned the place, but we didn't talk much. Usually, Charlie was working out when I got there. A nod of recognition was enough.

Most everyone left me alone. When they saw me on the bench press with numbers of like 360 or, once, 420, the men faded away. When they saw me deadlift. That's when I became more visible *and* invisible to them. But all I really cared about was no one saying anything stupid to me.

Imagine me at the gym every other day, locked into my thoughts. Putting on my armor, if it was the morning. Taking it off if evening.

Imagine how as I do the pulldown or squats I can't stop thinking about a box with a hummingbird in it. Even as I try so hard not to think about it.

Because I've brought it with me. Because I plan on hiding it in a locker. Even bought a special lock to make it safer. I can't keep it in the office. I can't keep it at home. I can't bring myself to open a bank safe box for it—that feels like a tell. It might not be safe in the gym, either, but I haven't figured out yet that it isn't safe anywhere.

Imagine me trying for a few new gym records while Charlie watches over all, impassive. Because it doesn't make a difference to anyone but me. Exerting myself until I'm so sore, I don't even feel the soreness.

But after, at least, I feel a lot better. Always do, before it gets worse again.

[11]

The first time I saw Silvina wasn't in the photographs in a file. Not really. Not in a true sense. In all the photographs, Silvina looked stiff, uncomfortable. Resembled a corpse, propped up in a chair or leaning against a balcony railing. Back problems plagued her, and she didn't like her photo taken, or she didn't like the photographers. Or she'd told them not to and they did it anyway.

First time was a grainy video, twenty seconds, in an old nature documentary uploaded to the internet. The lighting was bad on purpose, in deference to her sensitivity. I can't remember how many days after I found the hummingbird I found the video. The shock of wild black hair I noticed first. How she didn't like to tame it, or pulled it back in a ponytail rather than deal with it. Then, that she didn't know where to put her arms—on the chair, crossed in her lap. Silvina had large hands, strong, rough, calloused.

She kept looking down, away from the camera lens, so I almost couldn't see her face. But right at the end, she raised her head, and I saw the tight cheekbones, the firm set of the strong jaw. Determined, dangerous.

Her eyes were so dark, they registered as black. Set across a face a little too narrow in a charming way. Slightly sad, distant expression, even when she smiled. But the smile broadened her face, too, and then she was kind of beautiful.

In her practical clothes just one level better than army fatigues. If not for the floral pattern of the shirt, she could have been the spokesperson for some people's army. When she crossed her legs, you could see she'd tucked her khaki pants into hiking boots. A silver bracelet on her right wrist, but no other adornment. Reading glasses on a chain hung down over the shirt, as if she was an old lady in a rocking chair.

Later, I would learn the bracelet was from her mother. The one thing she wouldn't give up from her past.

Silvina didn't smile in any photograph. Just at the end of the video clip. That was right after the thing they accused her of, that followed her around from then on. Whether she'd done it or not. Before the trial.

For a moment. I froze that moment—in that other moment we haven't caught up to yet. Replayed the clip. I watched her smile. It kept breaking my heart. To know I'd never see her as she really was, underneath. That maybe the smile came the closest.

Except, that was a lie of the heart, of the head. She was who she was all the time. I should have known that already.

Back at the office, I was supposed to start reviewing workflow and organization of a natural gas pipeline company. Clients knew me as a "vulnerability assessor" or "vulnerability analyst." If I could figure out how to compromise their security systems or flaws in the human element, I could learn how to save them, too. Analysis, and then an actual hacker would do the force work. That's what Alex called it, "force work," as in "blunt force trauma," as in "use the force." You had to make the client feel insecure to force him to be secure. Reflexive security, most of it. A twitching lizard's tail. Except the hackers preferred to be called "penetration testers."

But, instead of working, I decided to use Larry's office. I'd ghosted a spy onto his machine for a while that helped me unlock it. Because it wasn't just how they shut me out. Maybe that was most of it, but I liked to mark Larry's office as my territory. Honed my security skills. But, also, it felt *good*, and I liked to feel good sometimes.

Larry was out with a client for the afternoon. Safe, because his office was around a dead-end corner, out of sight, and few ever willingly went to his office. Once there, you'd spend a half hour getting unstuck. He was a talker who rarely said anything.

A useful experiment to search for the hummingbird on Larry's computer. I couldn't put that on Allie. That might be the kind of random that would wind up lunchroom talk. "*And then she made me waste an afternoon clicking on this* bird." Later, I could check Larry's computer remotely to see if the search had triggered any attention. In the past, my meddling had died the death of any seemingly idle, innocent search. Lost in a wash of other data, protected behind our firewall.

I found the hummingbird so quickly, it surprised me. A half hour down all the hellholes of the internet, into obscure ornithology and eccentric research. But, no: an image search, adding the word "endangered" on a hunch, and there it was.

No mention of a "Silvina" associated with the hummingbird, but a few names of scientists and an article on poaching in its South American range. Along with a vague mention of wildlife contraband seizures in Miami.

I hit print and leaned back in Larry's chair, yawning.

There was Larry, in the doorway, staring at me.

I jumped. Sat up with an awkward sproing of springs.

"Oh, shit, Larry! Gave me a fucking heart attack."

His face was a stern anvil. But the swearing confused him. I didn't swear in the office. Whatever he'd been about to say he put on pause, turned his head a bit, like now I was a stranger. Reappraisal. I didn't like the light that had turned on behind his eyes.

"So this is what happens when I'm out," he said. Flat, dead tone.

"Sorry—my printer died," I said.

Not good that Larry could check if that was true. I clicked on delete and the hummingbird page disappeared from the screen. No time for search history, but what was Larry going to do? Complain to management that I'd read about a hummingbird on his laptop?

"Your printer died."

Larry now blocked the doorway. When expressive men become still, emotionless, I start thinking about takedowns and choke holds.

"I've gotta ask . . . how'd you get on my computer? In the first place."

"I was in a hurry, and you'd left it unlocked." Saying sorry felt like it would be an admission of intent.

"Did I? Did I really? Is that even an option?"

"Why, you worried about that porn you watch?" I smiled like it was a joke. It wasn't.

He blanched. Off-balance.

I snatched the pages off the printer, stood towering over him in the doorway. I could've picked him up and set him back down and gotten out. But he moved.

"Maybe tell me next time you want to use my computer," he said. "And I'll be sure to say no."

I brushed by him without a word, making sure to knock into his shoulder. Went back to my office feeling exposed, embarrassed, locked myself in. Got an important piece of the pipeline thing done and off to Alex for his approval. He liked to weigh in on the important stuff, even though it wasn't his level of detail.

Waited past five, when I could be sure Larry had left.

This was the day they all went down to the bar two blocks away and got shitfaced early. No way was Larry going to miss that.

[13]

Were companies units or loose, ever-shifting alliances of individuals? Still didn't know. But I'd learned on the farm that animals were not individuals, not persons, but groups. Categories. Mother, father, grandfather told me this, every day, growing up. It was the most constant, repetitive lesson learned from the grown-ups in my family. In both word and action.

This was the way of the world at large, perhaps with more callousness. On the farm—or, at least, on our farm—you respected animals, but they also gave you eggs or milk or meat. Your goats had names, but one day you would slaughter them. You scratched the pigs on the coarse hair of their backs until they grunted with pleasure, you knew their personalities and habits, but then one morning your father would be helping put them in the back of a stranger's truck and they'd be gone forever.

On top of that, I had a decade of what Silvina called "indoctrination." From raising a daughter who we encouraged to love YouTube videos with cute animals without once thinking about the context or source. Animated movies where birds talked and smiled like people, and maybe the animal was the villain, or maybe not, but it, too, talked and made faces and in every way tried to be part of the human world. That had distanced me from anything useful I might've known about animals. Something not tested or something foundational where you should seek the exception. Something toxic from the monoculture.

"Using 'us' when thinking about the environment erases all the different versions of 'us,'" Silvina once said. "Many indigenous peoples don't think this way. Counterculture doesn't always think this way. Philosophy, knowledge, policy exist that could solve our problems already."

So maybe at first the frisson of mystery and intrigue came from reading what I'd printed out while idling in the parking garage, doors locked, before heading home. Alert for every possible Larry approaching.

"Hummingbirds are aesthetic and aerobic extremists," read one site. "Their tiny bodies hover akin to flying carpets; did one just zip by? Hummers evolved high in the Andes Mountains with progressive colonization of lower altitudes and expanded latitudes, especially to the north, and eventually to the far reaches of Canada and Alaska. They remain restricted to the Americas, with the vast majority of the 300+ species residents of South America."

"Information isn't story," Silvina wrote. "No animal should be condensed to a summary in an encyclopedia." But all I *had* was information at first. And a dead bird's body. Because that's all she'd given me.

"The naiad hummingbird (*Selastrephes griffin*) is of moderate size (less than 12 cm body length) with an especially long migration that delights the most diligent of birders across its range. Although difficult to find and observe by humans, the brilliant colors and patterns of the males are adaptations to catch the eye of their mates."

I had a large female specimen, then. Pitch-black. No-nonsense.

"They are fine athletes whose stunt repertoire includes backward flight, treading air, and maneuvering precisely in gusty wind. And whose migration between the Pacific Northwest and Argentina equates to several back-to-back ultramarathons."

I tried to imagine traveling that far as an adaptation, through so many different kinds of terrain. This was an epic journey—and one only allowed due to incredible specializations. The changes a human being would have to undergo to inhabit such places without equipment. Wouldn't they change your point of view, too? Wouldn't you become someone else?

Like many species that have northern-skewed ranges for breeding, *S. griffin* is a snowbird and migrates closer to the phylogenetic nexus of hummingbirds in South America. *S. griffin* winters (December–March) in the Andes (where, of course, it is actually summer). Oxygen is limited at these altitudes (> 2,000 meters) as well as during the bird's migration; nonetheless, *S. griffin* maintains extraordinary metabolic rates that are enabled by adaptations in the hemoglobin protein that binds oxygen to iron. These changes to the heme group are inducible during their migration and winter in the Andes but are not present during their summers at lower elevations in North America.

But it wasn't just the journey. The flowers. The nests. All of it, once I had time to really immerse myself. Caught up in a way I hadn't expected, not just because of the mystery. But the *data*, after all. Who wouldn't be moved by the details? Maybe it was just me, or maybe it was the flush of the first real intel.

Status: Unknown. The last documented observation was in the Stein Valley Nlaka'pamux Heritage Park, British Columbia. Ornithological groups are seeking information, photographic sightings, or recorded calls.

Not just rare, then, but presumed extinct. Last seen in 2007. I felt a pang of emotion, as if this was a twist. But a twist that you could have seen coming. And after the pang—it took no time at all—that emotion began to recede from me. Couldn't hold on to it. Self-inoculation.

That month the southern white rhino and a species of pangolin had gone extinct. Wildfires in five countries meant animals were crawling to the side of roads to beg people speeding by in cars for water. People were poisoning vultures and shooting bats out of the sky, scared of pandemics. To care more meant putting a bullet in your brain. So, like many, I had learned to care less. Silvina called it "the fatal adaptation."

Alone with my thoughts, this was all unsettling, destabilizing. Excitement, joy, sadness, unease, in the briefest period. Even now, I can't truly explain the nexus of that, and how it rippled through me.

So I focused on the why.

Why would a person named Silvina leave me *this particular* taxidermied animal? I saw the route the hummingbird took as evidence. Northwest. Local during part of the year. They might even have flown right through our neighborhood. In the middle of the night—headed somewhere that cared enough to put out sugar water or plant wildflowers.

What sort of person would send this kind of message?

Sometimes a founder's psyche became reflected in their company and, thus, in how they handled security. But this wasn't about what happened subconsciously. This was a person who couldn't afford to be direct. Or who didn't trust me but, for some reason, had to tell me something. Bound by the rules of a game I couldn't see clear yet.

Usually, a *message* wasn't passive. Usually, on some level, a message so dramatic called out for action. But Silvina hadn't asked for anything. Except, I thought, to follow the clues.

There, in the parking lot, I loved that hummingbird, with a fierce and protective love. But resentment flared up, too. I could neither get rid of nor keep the hummingbird. Silvina had made some essential decision for me and it came with baggage.

The taxidermy Silvina had given me was illegal, contraband. If caught with it, if I read the law right, I could be prosecuted.

I should have destroyed the hummingbird. Could have tried to find a way to save myself. Remained frozen instead.

Not because of the mystery of the word "salamander," but because of the blank spaces between hummingbird and salamander. The more I stared at the piece of paper, the more those lines of . .   . .   . . ate at me. Something watched me from those coordinates, and if something watched me, I was already involved.

Code or symbol, distress signal or warning?

[14]

The week that followed seemed like another country. Perhaps because the country I had lived in didn't really exist. Or not the way any of us thought it did.

Things like family dinners. The repetitions that spoke to how much we loved routine.

Pork chops and asparagus and small golden potatoes with a crisp skin soaked in butter. I had seconds, and then thirds.

"Long day?" he asked.

"Yes, and I forgot lunch."

That came as such a surprise, he leaned back in his chair. Even my daughter looked up from her devices.

"Distracted?"

"Yes."

A bird in my locker at the gym. Tiny lie, growing larger and larger. Tiny Larry, growing larger and larger as he feasted on fallout from our encounter.

"Yeah? Why?" My husband was a bear, but when it came to prying he was more like a burrowing badger. He had his reasons.

The box pulsed and glowed and shook, wanting so much to open and fly away into words.

"She has difficult decisions to make," my daughter said, saving me.

"What do you mean?" I asked, too sharp.

My daughter shrugged. "You always do."

Is that how it seemed to her? I laughed then, but now it makes me sad. The look she gave me. Did she know something I didn't?

My husband nodded, as if she had explained my day to him and there was nothing I could add. Eat more asparagus, cut into the crisp skin of a potato. Take another sip of Malbec.

I made a note to tell my daughter more about my job, not hold back the way she did about school. Let her know things— like how few women did this kind of work when I entered the job market. How few worked in management at my job. I truly meant to.

I asked my husband about his day because I didn't want to risk talking about mine. He went off on a story about a stubborn potential client he'd shown six perfect homes to, mugging for our daughter so she'd laugh, and I was safe again.

I made it through sitting in the living room playing card games and our daughter going upstairs for a shower and then to bed. Through more rituals with the familiar beast I loved, this bear I could hug, cuddle with, bite the ear of.

The presents under the tree belonged to the future, and still do.

[15]

Somewhere along the way, for reasons I misremember, I had bought a go-bag. Maybe a paranoid moment at work. Or at home. Left it stored in my gym locker. A thick lump that lay in the bottom compartment and moldered there. Didn't think about it much. But I'd bothered to buy it pre-made. With a credit card my husband didn't notice because I'd never told him about it.

That didn't mean I meant to leave without my family. I think I just wanted to protect them—from the thought, the impetus, the raging landscapes of the nightly news. Protect them from the idea that I believed such a future might come to pass.

So when I pried the hummingbird's eyes out sometime during that first week, I stashed it all in the go-bag in my gym locker. I worked on the hummingbird in the unisex bathroom, with the door locked. Sitting on the ancient, cracked toilet seat. Using the tip of a nail file and a toothpick. Took an obscene amount of time and I cringed every time I thought I might be crushing the hummingbird.

Ghoulish, wrong, a violation . . . but a security situation with a client and a camera situated in the eyes of a teddy bear had made me think of it.

Scrutiny with a magnifying glass had revealed evidence of a prior excavation. The hint of glue leaking from one bird eye as I'd examined it close, shook it for some dislodged rattle.

The adrenaline rush at what was revealed, like I'd achieved something. As if I had some sense of why Silvina had chosen me.

Hidden behind, etched, delicate and tiny, into the sockets, still hard to make out even with the magnifying glass.

Two numbers: 23 and 51.

Combination or code?

I did a visualization, which helped sometimes. Tried to look down on myself, there in the crappy bathroom. Feverishly prying eyes out of the hummingbird. This hulking, bulky shadow doing brutal things to a delicate bird. Everything about that act wrong.

What were that person's assumptions? What might this person miss?

One was this: the number could just be some taxidermy reference. Some manufacturer's designation. Nothing to do with Silvina.

Still, I wrote the numbers down on a slip of paper, stuck the paper in my wallet. Stuck the wallet in my purse. The next day, I would glue the eyes back in because I couldn't bear the thought of the hummingbird without them.

Left the mystery alone, did not tug on the string of it. But, all the while, the string was tugging at me.

[16]

Things I learned, I couldn't undo or forget. Things that hurt me in the knowing of them.

The hummingbird had gone extinct because of poaching, habitat loss, and climate change. The wildlife trafficking cartels manufactured need—they told those inclined to buy that this or that animal was good luck or the next hip thing for the rising newly rich. They pried open the coffers of countries that would look the other way. They dealt in volume, so the inconvenience of a shipment or two caught at a border meant little to them.

They'd played off specific Latin American traditions about love potions, and what had been a few hundred birds, caught and killed for the purpose in Mexico each year, became thousands and thousands, smuggled around the world. Stuffed into little plastic pouches. Sometimes well cleaned enough, not just dried, to wear as the centerpiece of a necklace. A rabbit's foot. A dead animal. But people wore dead animals all the time.

Their route became more arduous and terrifying because of unthinking development, their normal rest stops on the way to their summer habitat taken away one by one. They had to fly farther between food and water. More died along the way. While in South America, the warming climate meant their preferred habitat moved higher and higher up the mountainside—and became more degraded. With more competition from other species seeking cooler temperatures. A susceptibility in a smaller population to disease had created micropandemics that didn't help. Spiked use of pesticides and herbicides everywhere had taken its toll.

Finally, it was not so much that this fierce bird had given up or given in but that the numbers were too few. Even if some birds could now winter in Southern California due to climate change. It was still too long a migration for too small a group.

I had a vision of that last small expedition, the last group, setting out. Maybe it was just a dozen, maybe less. Tried to imagine it as Silvina had. Trying their best to overcome those obstacles. Each one of those individuals on an epic journey. One they never came back from.

But: the joy. Even then, there must have been moments of joy and of contentment on the journey. Sanctuaries and times of plenty. It wasn't just a winnowing. It was a life. I held fast to that. Even if it was selfish, for myself.

17

All the other usual things. Precious as any amount of money, but worthless until they're gone. Until you really feel the loss.

My husband's sister, her husband, and her son came over the next evening—they lived three hours away. Just far enough they didn't visit often. So we were supposed to put them up that week. He knew I could only take a couple days before claustrophobia set in, but I would be gone by weekend.

The son always brought out the tour guide in our daughter, so they often were outside. The husband talked seldom and his sister talked too much, though I liked her well enough. They just wrong-footed you with their extremes. She was in pharmaceuticals. Kept mistaking what I did for what she did, because we both used "strategy." Kept asking myself what strategy had led me to mutilate a dead hummingbird.

The banal inconvenience of not being able to relax in my pajamas in the evening. The "holiday cheer" I loathed from past experience, of pull-out beds and futons and close quarters in the bathrooms. Past slights between siblings that came out between my husband and his sister that made me roll my eyes because my husband didn't always know how good he'd had it, family-wise. Dinners laced with too much wine and beer because, underneath it all, we were not always comfortable with one another.

The sister's husband was a conservation biologist. That could not be easy. At the time, though, the biologist exasperated me. Such a narrow focus. All the wonderful things in the world. All the ways life was better even if the world wasn't. This stutter-step of disaster after natural disaster was just a blip next to LED lights, driverless cars, a possible end to poverty through gene-edited crops.

Mulled wine and stockings over the fireplace. Crisp smell of the six-foot fir that had been cut down so it could be adorned with plastic and glass baubles that polluted the house. As the tree died in celebration, there in our family room.

Maybe I was withdrawn during their visit. Maybe gregarious and lighthearted on the outside. Who knows? My daughter was a dervish, though, I know that. She could not stop moving. When not playing host, she could not stop assisting me with chores or in the kitchen or out shopping for the holidays. Her energy, even now looking back, had a febrile quality, like she was making up for some lack in me.

The fireplace. Hot cocoa. The warmth that hits you in the face and the hands and the stomach. Surrounded on the U-shaped couch, after a heavy dinner of turkey and sweet potato casserole and stuffing, by people in Xmas sweaters and the TV spouting sports off to the side, sweetly raucous.

Can it have been true? Can it?

Every day, off to work I went, gym first. Then my husband, who was on holiday break, would text about something before I had even turned on my computer. I needed to pick up an item for the family on my way home or confirm dinnertime, or whatever was on his mind. Wrapped up in his arms, the clutches of his family, even sitting there at my desk.

This normalcy should have pushed the hummingbird farther and farther from me. Pushed the idea of Silvina away from me. To have this secret life, but no fear of it swallowing me. Even if Silvina's world had begun to encroach on mine. Instead, it had the opposite effect. I was thinking about it all the time.

"Are you happy?" I asked my husband late one night, around the kitchen island, the teenagers asleep, the adults half comatose from leftovers, in front of a television talent show.

He kissed me, smelling of his sandalwood aftershave, and sweat. Because he knew I meant was *I* happy. As if he had to monitor that for me.

But, deep down, I knew I was going to follow the thread. I just didn't realize how far that would take me.

18

Oh, the flowers, Silvina. The flowers and all of it. Videos entranced me, watched on a burner phone from the go-bag I didn't realize would have other uses.

This creature that was everything I was not. We could not be more dissimilar, and yet, inside, I felt a welling up of sympathy for the toughness. For the miracle of this creature. Was this a gift Silvina gave me, too? How the world opened up? How it kept opening up.

The hummingbird went into a kind of suspended animation, or "microhibernation," each night due to the high number of calories it needed. "Torpor" was a word I'd never considered, as in "Torpor decreases their metabolism by 90%, their heart rate by 15 times, and their body temperature from over 100 degrees Fahrenheit to the ambient temperature."

Torpor. They ran hot, so very hot, but then got so cold, like icy jewels there in the mountain. Clinging to a branch. Hidden by foliage. Dreaming of what? Did they dream of anything? They died, in a sense, every time, and the sun resurrected them. The nectar was life. Miraculous, and as I learned more and loved them more, I loved Silvina more and more. What I felt must have been what she felt, although how could I know?

The flowers, too. The flowers. The words connecting hummingbird to blossoms that I hadn't known, like "nectarivorous."

As is the lifestyle of hummers, *S. griffin* maintains a symbiosis with flowering plants, and particularly those in the family *Solanaceae*. In the Pacific Northwest, it is often associated with upland larkspur (*Delphinium nuttallii*), but also utilizes columbines, fireweed, and heaths. Each flower provides a sugary snack that satiates the small tank and the high burn of the hummingbirds, but only enough so that frequent visits, to many flowers, promotes pollination.

Larkspur! Columbine! Fireweed! The "small tank," the "high burn." All of this new information lit tiny fires inside. I took such delight, and delight didn't come easy to me. But it did here.

They feasted on a particular kind of flower, "*Solanaceae* flowers in the *Schizanthus* genus (commonly called 'Poor man's orchid,' or, in Spanish, 'maripostia') that occupy stream valleys at mid-elevations in the Andes." These flowers contained powerful alkaloids hallucinogenic to humans and had affected so much of the birds' evolution. Remarkable details. Their very *head shape* had adapted to "better carry pollen between immobile flowers, and, in turn, the flower cups have adapted to fit the hummingbird's bill."

> The forked tongue of *S. griffin* efficiently laps up flower nectar. The coevolutionary pairing has also impacted the flowers, as their color, size, orientation, and nectar content are adaptations to better seduce birds to visit and then disperse the flower's gametes to a fertile mate. *Schizanthus* flowers will release the entire anther (a male reproductive segment) onto the hummingbird's head to promote successful pollen transfer for these ornithophilous plants.
>
> The flowers never select or meet their mates, those partnerships are at the whim of the avian matchmaker, but the female *S. griffin* is most intentional about selecting her mate. Females have complete agency, and mating males must win their affection by being artists of many talents—a singing, dancing, and beauty competition all in one.

Singing, dancing, beauty competitions. How to process this ethereal touch, this intel so at odds with my job, my life?

Hadn't the hummingbird been a kind of miracle?

Hadn't it diminished us not to see this as a miracle and protect it?

19

The next day, or the day after that—some of it blurs—my spy on Larry's computer sent an alert. A malicious attack. Rebuffed by security. A closer look revealed the attack had been a distraction while an unknown entity had rooted around in his files. Masked which files, exactly.

Evidence of this second thing pulsed on the screen like a dangerous lure. In theory, anyone sophisticated enough to breach our security should also have been able to erase evidence of information extraction. This intruder hadn't. Instead, the trail stood out in stark relief. A hellmouth. I wouldn't follow it. This time, it wasn't the convoluted path back. The answer to the question "Who?" wasn't worth walking into a trap.

I sat back in my chair, feeling light-headed. Did I need to inform Larry or Alex of the breach? But I couldn't, not without admitting I'd bugged Larry's computer. I went round and round, rationalizing . . . no action. And, in the end, I decided Larry should be okay. IT did routine checks on employees to make sure their information hadn't been compromised. If this was truly malicious and weaponized, IT would find out soon.

In the middle of me thinking this through, Allie walked in with her report on Silvina. As she handed me the folder, I felt a twinge of concern for her.

"Have IT check your laptop for malware," I said.

Allie stopped short at that. "Why?"

"Just do it. The latest batch of clients makes me think it's a prudent precaution to check for intruders more regularly."

"Okay," she said, drawn out, slow, staring at me, as if for some secret sign or symbol telling her more. "There wasn't much, by the way."

"Much?"

"About Silvina. Enough, maybe. But more about her family than her. Her family's not just rich but influential—the storage palace is just one property they own in the area. Vilcapampa

Enterprises. They run it like a family business, but it's international. Operates in forty countries. Which made me think they wouldn't blink at having a data scrub done."

The kind of task we performed for clients. To protect their reputation. A scrabbling panic that maybe Silvina knew me through the company I worked for. Dim, depressing thought. But, later, when I checked: no. Not true.

"Possible," I said, dropping the folder on my desk. Trying in my awkward way to seem casual. "Thanks again."

But Allie wasn't done.

"I didn't know you were asking me to research a terrorist."

Then I did look up. "What?"

"Animal rights activist who fought against wildlife trafficking. Murdered people down in Argentina. A bombing. At least, that was the claim. She even had a manifesto."

I could understand her confusion. Usually, the moral ambiguity or ethical confusion came from a different impulse. Robber barons and tech bros. Wall Street. The killing a remote sleight of hand. Indirect.

"Manifesto?"

"Yeah. Read something like 'Liberation for the Earth, at any cost. Liberty or death—death to those who oppose.' I translated it from Spanish. Very uplifting."

"A lot of talk, maybe?"

Allie folded her arms, considered me. "Like I said, she went on trial for murder. For terrorism. Acquitted, but still . . . And she had followers. May still have followers. Like a cult. Even people, from what I could tell, who might not like someone digging into their private business."

I considered that, nodded. "Got it. Thanks again." Wanted to leave it at that. Tried to put on a poker face.

But I was stunned. I hadn't known. Hadn't guessed. Because the hummingbird was so beautiful.

Terrorist? Murderer?

"Should I send flowers?" Allie was still standing there.

"What?" I couldn't tell if she was being sarcastic.

"To the family."

"Why?"

"Because. She's dead. Recently."

That came crashing through.

But *why* did it hurt? Hadn't the note told me that? Hadn't Silvina herself told me, in her way? Yet, somehow, I'd thought the task would be *finding* Silvina. Literally finding her. Not tracking her ghost.

"And there's this," Allie said, handing me a black-and-white photograph of a man standing on the bow of a yacht. He had a kind of weird bowl-cut for his dull brown hair, clean-shaven, and had a hooded look about the eyes and a small nose. Wearing a short-sleeved button-down shirt with a flower design, cargo shorts. Prominent gold chain around his neck. Something in the thin mouth, the curl of lip, made me dislike him. If not for the clothes, he would've had a chameleon-like look. You might not notice him in a crowd.

"Who's this?"

"Ben Langer."

"Am I supposed to know who he is?"

"You always talk about 'the credible threat.' About 'collateral circles.' Well, this name kept coming up. Ben Langer. Works for an import-export company that Silvina tied to wildlife trafficking. Also has a hand in illicit biotech and drugs. Langer might be doing the dirty work for that organization."

"Good point," I said.

"Langer is an opportunist of the worst kind. A sociopath at best."

That seemed like belaboring the good point. Half our clients were sociopaths.

"And?"

"What I mean is: Silvina's friends are dangerous. Silvina's enemies are dangerous. This whole thing is fraught."

"Fair assessment," I said.

I set the photo down on my desk. Wanted to turn it over, but resisted the impulse.

"That's that, then, right?" Allie asked, arms still crossed.

Projecting irritation. But unsettled underneath, the irritation for putting her in a bad mental space. Crime was meant to be invisible in our systems.

Should I stop? It seemed antiseptic to me. We were just gathering data. Passively. Not interviewing past associates. Not being obvious. So I felt confident in my answer.

"Keep digging," I said. "It's low-risk. This is all information on the surface."

"*Keep digging*," she said, in a flat voice. "You want me to keep . . . *digging*."

"Yes. Keep at it. There must be more than a photo and"—I flicked through the folder—"a paltry dozen pages of information."

Allie said nothing.

A mention of a corporation run by her father caught my eye. "Check property. Shell companies, the rest."

"No," Allie said.

I put down the file.

"No?"

"This isn't about work," Allie said. "Larry told me."

Larry doesn't know shit. Larry isn't your boss.

"Larry doesn't—"

"What about the pipeline account?" she asked.

"Spend an hour on this. It won't kill you."

"Then tell me the client, because Silvina's dead."

I sighed. Okay, I would go through the charade.

"The Vilcapampa companies. As you noticed, many of them are local. Silvina's death may create an opportunity."

Was that crass to say? She must have thought so, from the stare she gave me.

It occurred to me that I hadn't tried to bind Allie to me. That I hadn't done the things that create loyalty. Because that felt like a trick. A trap. And now it turned out I didn't know her at all. Didn't know the first thing about her personal life. Had rarely taken her to lunch. The kind of interest I'd taken was important to me, but maybe not to her. Was that what I was paying for now? Interoffice politics? Larry talking to her probably felt like sympathy or empathy.

"An hour or two," she conceded, but I wondered if she would. She walked out.

Funny—I'd wanted her to be independent. I had wanted her to question me. And now . . .

Only later did I wonder if she'd found something more, something she hadn't put in the file. That had unnerved her.

[20]

Strength lived in my body so directly back then that I could mistake it for armor. It shone out of me like a drug and flowed back into me like power. It made me drunk in a way, made me take chances. Or gave me reasons for excuses.

Worse, I was too proud of having studied criminology and psychology, in investigating Silvina. As if that meant I could exist, even flourish, in a world of mysteries. I knew in college that bodybuilding probably wouldn't pay the bills. Or I wasn't sure. It was more like: how do I make the strength of my body at least more than a hobby?

I had a vague idea of joining the police force, maybe one day become a detective. I could snap any number of men over my knee. I might stand out, but I would also look like someone who shouldn't be messed with. Be one of the boys. Pretend, at least. But what you face doesn't always work like that. Whatever's indirect. The thing your strength might not match up against, any more than a boxer understands how to fight a wrestler.

But underneath that: even if you didn't solve a case, even

if I didn't make it to detective, I would be the one who had the most information and most control. If you couldn't make sense of a death, no one could, not really. Except, perhaps, a priest, and I didn't veer existential or religious. No one in our family did. My brother came closest, but even in him it was more a kind of spirituality, a sense of awe at seeing the stars in the night sky. "The rogue immensity of the cosmos." Like he'd never understand the world, but that didn't bother him.

Psychology was criminology's cousin, and perhaps something in me also wanted to find a way to understand our grandfather's situation. The way I despised him, and yet there were moments I wanted to conjure the pure, blunt, uncomplicated menace of the man.

But, over time, the passion I'd had for being the one to solve cases had dulled, the anger and the sadness behind it.

The verdict in my brother's death was drowning.

I never believed it.

[21]

The only obituary Allie could find ran in a niche leftist Buenos Aires newspaper with an online presence. Just a few sentences with no photograph. The feeling of a cover-up or data wipe persisted.

Autotranslated from Spanish and cleaned up by Allie, the obituary noted that she'd died a week before, but didn't list cause of death. "No mention of embezzlement online," Allie wrote in the margin.

An ardent defender of the environment and animal rights, Vilcapampa, 54, was the daughter of a notable industrialist and businessman. Born in Buenos Aires, she grew up Florida but moved to the Pacific Northwest for college. In the 1990s, Vilcapampa was arrested on charges of conspiracy to commit murder in the disappearance of five alleged wildlife traffickers but was released due to insufficient evidence. She moved back to the United States soon after to manage several of her father's companies. She was suspected in further crimes in the early 2000s, including embezzlement from one of her father's companies, but nothing was ever proven. Recently, Vilcapampa had been under investigation for alleged ties to bioterrorism groups.

The mention of "bioterrorism" earned a raised eyebrow from me. I knew how activism became terrorism—in part, the shifting goalposts of changed laws. But how had Silvina's eco-terrorism morphed into bioterrorism? Banned from her country of birth after the latest round of amorphous accusations. But the U.S. had let her stay. Why?

Somehow, the father had managed to have his name kept out of even this brief mention. Fear on the part of the outlet or pressure applied?

Allie had also found a local traffic report that named "Silvina Vilcapampa" as a "hit-and-run" victim seven days before. Police were looking for an SUV or minivan. "Nothing else local," Allie wrote. "No funeral I can find." No idea whether she had been buried or cremated. No follow-up to the initial mention. I found that suspicious. Normally, the paper would have run some kind of follow-up, under traffic reports or the police roundup. More meddling by the father?

I tried not to imagine the violence of a vehicle hitting a human body, turned the page.

Six or seven years ago, Silvina had begun a kind of community outreach, through an arts nonprofit created by Vilcapampa Enterprises. Trying to reconcile with Vilcapampa senior? She'd briefly funded "eco-artists" who'd formed their own community called "Unitopia" on an island made with recycled plastics, out in a lake in the wilderness. This struck me, after having seen the video, as ludicrous. The kinds of things that the Silvina in the video would label "bourgeois." But a big deal to whoever Silvina thought she was at the time.

Then that came to a halt as quickly as it had begun.

Her whereabouts unknown the past four or five years. Activities unknown. Purpose unknown.

I could feel my blood pressure spike. The message and storage unit key took on a heightened intensity.

Surely no one cared about Unitopia these days? Still, at lunch I went to a shitty little internet café, put on protections, checked to see if their website was active. Rather than upset Larry again.

Static, but still there. Mostly just a gallery of shots of the space. It had the slick, seamless feel of something put together by a branding company. Because it had been.

A floor plan that almost looked more like the schematic of a spaceship, or cathedral, with a long, wide space with circles and half circles for rooms branching off to both sides and leading eventually to the crux of it all: a huge dome in the back that housed the visitor center and a presentation about the environment billed as "planetarium-worthy." But the sneak peek video didn't exist anymore. Just some text about how Unitopia had been inspired by a diagram by Humboldt, the naturalist. A symbolic peak, showing the richness of the world's habitats, altitude by altitude. From valleys to the oxygen-starved summit. The idea of wilderness integrating humans into it. The holistic view. "Unitopia." Silvina's word for it, not Humboldt's. Her contribution to a lost canon.

Then I noticed in a photograph of the center a peculiar presence: taxidermy. Very ordinary, bear heads and more benign plastic models of sea life.

Did it mean anything?

Screw it. The more I dug, on a public computer, the worse things could get. But I was curious. Since the project had received city money, I wondered if there were line items for the budget or a proposal with vendors. Like, who had provided the taxidermy.

Sure enough, "assorted animal models" appeared in an old PDF proposal, with a company name, "Animal Magic," that was easy enough to find online, although now bankrupt.

Animal Magic was a blanket company that provided a number of services, even animal mascots for birthday parties. They had a list of third-party vendors, if you looked hard enough.

Only one was a taxidermist: Carlton Fusk, based in Brooklyn.

I leaned back in my chair, in that humid, claustrophobic space, surrounded by the pecking and clicking of people searching for god-knows-what.

Was this a valid clue? Or was this just a coincidence?

Too early for me to know the difference.

But, deep inside, I felt a thrill.

My head felt clear, working on this mystery, like I'd been fuzzy before and hadn't realized it.

That was enough to make me want to pursue it.

Which required me legitimizing it.

[22]

I stopped by Alex's office: another glass cube with a minimalist desk, shockingly offset by a whaling scene in a gold Victorian frame and, in the corner, a stubby, faux Doric column with a bowl of gummy bears on top. Like usual, it smelled of his spice cologne. Reeked of it.

He gave me a cheery smile, looking up from his laptop. He wore the glasses that performed no known use for him.

"You know, Allie's up for a raise," Alex said.

No preamble, as if he'd come to my office.

"Oh really?" The hierarchy was shifty in our company, but I was responsible for her performance review.

"Yeah—she's hitting it out of the ballpark. Thanks for keeping her on the straight and narrow." All these dead words we used.

The message was clear. Allie had complained about the Vilcapampa research.

"I agree," I said.

He looked pleased about that, as if he'd expected an argument.

"So, what do you want?" The largesse would be of use to me.

What I wanted and what I needed—were they the same? Maybe some part of me wanted Alex to say no. Needed Alex to say no and stop me. Because I wasn't going to stop myself.

"I know it's short notice, but I need to go to that conference in New York."

Alex frowned. "I thought we'd decided to skip it this year."

"I took another look. Seems important for some of what we're working on."

Alex took off his glasses, chewed on one stem. You could see the accumulated bite marks had torn the plastic off, revealing wire underneath.

"Kind of a rebuilding year. And you've got the pipeline project."

"Allie's doing great on the pipeline project. Like you said, she's hitting it out of the ballpark."

He considered me. A full-on, taking-my-measure look. Like, was I playing him somehow.

"Allie says you've got her on a wild-goose chase, since you mention her."

He'd brought her up first, but whatever.

"I haven't let her in on the details, but I think the Vilcapampa companies are a good possible client. They're international, but have local affiliates. There're hundreds of subsidiaries. The backing behind some popular brands. Like you said, a rebuilding year. Some of their reps will be in New York. Could be worth millions."

Didn't mention Vilcapampa Enterprises owned the knock-off brands, mostly, the second- or third-tier ones that mimicked the brands people knew and loved. Didn't mention that Vilcapampa had their own in-house security analysts. That the closed familial hierarchy meant even if I'd been serious, getting an in, getting an audience, would be tough.

Alex considered that a moment. One thing I'd never done, or been good at, was generating business. He had me on record as saying I didn't think that was an analyst's job. But, mostly, I stood out like a sore thumb. My body made men uncomfortable. Women, too.

"Yeah, she said you were researching that. I have to admit, I wondered why. Still, seems like short notice and the pipeline thing can't really—"

"Tell you what—how about in return this year Larry takes my place on your yacht retreat?"

Flash of anger. I could see it there, plain. There was a way he had to control his body's reaction to me calling him on that. How we both knew I'd never get that invite, ever. Then it was gone. But I'd expended capital, and I wouldn't know how much until the punishment. Maybe the punishment would even be disguised as a perk.

He wouldn't look at me as he said, casual, "Oh, what the hell—go. Have fun. Just don't order room service or book a room with a gold-plated toilet."

That was my cue to laugh. But I didn't.

[23]

"Work toward a better world, but never forget what world you live in."

Strange, this compulsion. I lived within it, but also studied it from afar. I would be in a meeting presenting charts, ideas, diagrams to a client and they would have no idea I was somewhere else, in another world. And neither would I, at first, and then I would have the peculiar feeling of continuing the presentation while spying on my own distractedness. Muscle memory of so many other presentations carrying me through. Click of the key to advance the slide; the transition from statements to the questions I only asked when it was safe.

The nylons that signaled "familiar" and "safe" to the client. The high heels, with their wide, pragmatic soles. The stiff, siege-like quality of my dark gray business suit, that kept them far enough away that they could not peer into my thoughts.

But my thoughts kept spilling out, strange and stranger. I kept having a dream. Every night. The hummingbird flew down like a tiny god, to the back deck of our house. Some fairyland version, glowing phosphorescent in a cascade of emerald, sapphire, and hot pink. As if revealing a true self as it descended steep from on high. Looking the whole time as if being moved seamlessly by an invisible hand from an invisible point in the sky to a hovering position above me.

The hummingbird gave me what I can only describe as an imperious or even contemptuous look, hovering there weightless. It pierced me. Found me wanting.

Then, with a slight leftward tack, the hummingbird veered off, disappeared, and I woke with a start. Sweating. The ticking of the bedroom clock, too loud.

In the neighborhood we had an unidentified drone. Not a delivery drone. One of the new small ones. Could perch on a branch so you almost didn't register the presence, because you thought it was a bird. Then, I loved drones. I loved how I could order something and it would be there immediately. I would toss the plastic in the recycling bin and never questioned the magic of how I had received yet another gift. We could do drones well, but we could not stop pouring plastic waste into the ocean.

And, still, I was lost in the dream.

24

In a rush: of a sudden, the end of the week. Gasping from that. Yet also euphoric. Trying to be calm on the outside. I locked my office as I left Thursday night. Didn't want Larry in there. But he could get in if he wanted. Anyone could.

The weather had turned a sour lukewarm with pockets of chill, unfamiliar for the season. Glittering gutters. Tinkling gurgle of water passing through shards of ice. Now we had flood warnings instead of sleet warnings. Flowers bloomed that should have waited until spring. I took my own car, telling my husband short-term parking was more convenient than him having to take me. Not that his grumbly offer had been convincing; I'd sprung conferences on him before, but it always unsettled him, and him being unsettled made our daughter grumpy. Even if most days she would've hardly known if I was home or not.

On the way to the airport, I had two stops to make. First, the gym. It wasn't to work out. Just to check that the hummingbird was safe. Maybe that was me not thinking straight. Maybe it was me worrying too much. I guess I thought I'd get a few sets in, too, in my street clothes. Settle my nerves.

The box was there. The hummingbird was in the box.

The new thing was Charlie coming over to talk. Instinctively, I put my body in front of my locker so he couldn't see the box.

"What's up?" Thought I'd broken some gym rule.

"Someone followed you here," Charlie said. "Two men—in a black SUV in the back of the parking lot."

I laughed. That sounded ridiculous. Why did it sound ridiculous? A pinprick of alarm, but I didn't know the source. The information or my reaction?

Then I took a look, frowned. No one in the parking lot. "I don't see anyone."

"No—last time. This time, who knows?"

"Are you serious?" Like Charlie was paranoid. Like some quirk of his past was surfacing. Me playing amateur psychologist to deflect.

"Think I'm talking to you for fun or something?"

"No, I don't."

"Somebody is onto you."

"I haven't done anything." Blurted out.

He chuckled, like I'd told a joke. "You must've done *something*."

"No one's following me. No one's there, Charlie."

It came down to this: I wasn't ready to believe some online searches had spilled over into the meat world.

Charlie looked at me like I was naïve, then shrugged. "Okay, then. No one's following you."

He went back to his chair, picked up the newspaper, gave it a stiff shake to straighten the page he was reading. Didn't speak to me again. Wasn't going to waste more time on a fool like me, said the economy of his body language.

In the end, I left the hummingbird in the locker. Because I'd extracted what I needed. Because I didn't have time to do anything else with it.

Next stop was the coffee shop, where I'd gotten Silvina's message. I hadn't gone the whole week. "Safe" or "unsafe"—these weren't the words. But something had been broken and it didn't feel like a sanctuary. Or even a respite.

Only one reason to go back. And I almost didn't, except I checked the whole way. No black SUV following. No one following that I could tell, trying to remember all the bullets in PowerPoint about tailing someone from a past conference. Old-school stuff. New to me.

I slid into a chair at a rickety table facing the register. Returning to the scene of some crime. Except I didn't know what the crime was yet.

Did I have a heightened sense of my surroundings? Yes. Was my heartbeat rapid? No.

The barista who had given me the note stood behind the counter, trying to ignore me. Half expected he wouldn't be there. Different shift than usual or just disappeared. A gangly young man. A shadow beard. He wore a long-sleeved T-shirt and jeans, with a coffee shop apron over that. Though the place wasn't much warmer than outside.

When he was free of customers, I beckoned to him. For a moment, he looked like he might flee out the back. Then what? Would I try to retrieve him?

But, instead, he asked a bored-looking woman with a nose ring and fiery red-orange hair to take over. He slid into the chair across from me, smelling of clove cigarettes. A kind of confused defiance lit his features. As if trying to get behind a cause but didn't know what he'd signed up for.

"I told you already—the envelope got dropped off for me along with the money. No one remembers who dropped it off."

I pulled out a hundred-dollar bill. With the way inflation had spiked, who knew how much it would be worth in a month.

"I just have a few questions. Not really about the envelope."

He looked at me. Pity or distaste. At what? Me playing amateur detective?

"I have to serve customers again soon," he said. But he pocketed the hundred.

"You've seen me in here a thousand times, right?"

A pause before he nodded, as if it was a trick question. Let's call him "Clove," because I'm tired of typing "he."

"And you've seen a lot of other people in here around the time I'm in here who are regulars, too?"

"Yeah." With a "So what?" subtext.

"Any of them stop coming around the last month or two?"

Clove thought about that a moment. "I think so. I think some of the regulars dropped off. There's a new coffee shop down the road."

"Any of them women?"

"Some. Maybe."

"Any of them look like this?"

I slid Silvina's photo across the table. Not a great shot, a little grainy and ten years old, but close enough.

Clove picked up the printout. Exhaled, inhaled. Was he more nervous now? Put the photo down.

"Took a moment. She wore dark sunglasses a lot and had blond hair, but I think that's the same face."

Silvina, disguised. From me or whoever pursued her? Or just hiding from the light?

"How often did you see her?"

Again, Clove paused, reset.

"I can't say when she stopped coming in, or if she has. I just know I haven't seen her in a while. I couldn't say how long, though. A lot of people come in here."

"Was she ever in here when I was in here? If you remember."

"She always came in the morning. Early. So, yeah, she would've been in here."

Was it excitement or fear that spiked the adrenaline?

"Did she have a favorite spot to sit?" I asked.

"Oh, I dunno. Maybe."

"Are you saying she took her order to go instead?" Old trick with clients: put words in their mouths they had to react to, dislodging information.

"No."

"Then where did she sit?"

He pointed over my shoulder.

I swiveled to look, turned back to Clove. "That table there? By the window?"

Clove nodded.

I felt for a moment like I was back in the river by the farm, drowning. That I would be stuck in that moment forever.

But I managed to ask, even though I couldn't breathe, "How long has she been coming in?"

"Off and on? A year, maybe."

I was sitting in my own favorite spot.

According to Clove, for a year before her death, Silvina had come to the *same* coffee shop and sat in the best place to watch me. Without me noticing. Never striking up even a casual conversation.

"Did you peek?" I asked him. Random interest. Maybe I wanted to punish him. I was leaning in, invading his space.

"What?" Clove's expression suggested pornographic thoughts.

"Did you peek? At what was in the envelope?"

"No. I wouldn't do that." As if I'd accused him of a serious crime.

"Not even a little, tiny peek?" Tempted to share the message, ask his opinion. But that would be further contamination. What if men in a black SUV pulled up later and asked him questions from this same seat?

Clove shook his head. Grim-faced. Hands clenched in his lap.

Time to put him out of my misery. On a hunch, I took out the photo of Langer Allie had given me.

"One last question. Do you recognize this man?"

"No, never seen him." No hesitation.

"Fair enough." Skeptical.

But my sin was worse than disbelief.

My sin was the thought that Langer would've been in disguise, too smart for the man in front of me to notice.

25

The nests of the hummingbird are another miracle. They occur high in hemlock, Sitka spruce, western red cedar, Douglas fir. The birds are so small that the needles act like branches, and the nests, skillfully woven, are only three centimeters across.

S. *griffin* uses its bill as a crochet hook to incorporate lightweight lichen, moss, and downy plant material into a hammock for her young. Nests are attached to the needles with cobwebs. One or two uniformly white eggs are incubated in the nest for several weeks. The female coats each egg with a bacteria-rich fluid she excretes, which protects her brood from harmful diseases that can colonize the young as they emerge from the eggs. The baby's beak—a fraction of the size of a human baby tooth—cracks open the shell, and the hatchling immediately seeks nutrition from the mother, which she dutifully provides through regurgitating flower nectar and protein-rich insects.

The young spend less than a month in the nest. In that short time, they must grow and learn critical behavior from the mother. At month's end, they fledge and prepare for their ten-thousand-kilometer migration to a land unknown.

Or had. For many thousands of years. Now they were so rare the one in my locker was worth upward of a quarter of a million dollars. To the right collector.

If you could put a price on life in death.

And, apparently, you could.

PANORAMA

[26]

I did and didn't enjoy air travel back then. The quiet, cool cocoon, the ice in the glass just so, the smooth camaraderie of seasoned travelers broken only on occasion by the person to whom it was all too new. The freedom to be alone, to think alone. The spotlight from above that pearled the scented air. Pointing at only the important things. The sense of being motionless once at altitude. Outside of time, outside of history. Even with weather delays, in first class you could almost forget the world was fucked.

But, even there, the seats weren't always wide enough to be comfortable. Depended.

I had always been big—big-boned, broad-hipped, "shoulders like a linebacker," my father would say, as he pulled on those shoulders and said "Straighten up." The "son" implied. "Learn the clutch, not the automatic." "Go hunt with me." (I wouldn't.) Until the day, sometime in college, when something my mother said made me realize he was just saying and doing all the things his father had said to and done with him. And I had a vision, down through history, of a series of dad-robots saying and doing the same things and other sons and daughters being caught up in those ghosts.

From then on, I never let my father pull my shoulders back. I didn't like the idea that my grandfather's ghost was there; I always hated him. Maybe, too, that's why my father drank so much, and it had nothing to do with the farm or my mother's condition. At first.

My mind roved so much on that flight. Hummingbird, salamander, life on the farm, my brother. Settled on Silvina, on the file, on her family.

Silvina's parents were still alive, back in Argentina. I looked at the photos before the rest of the data—an old trick. The data always made the photos conform to a certain story. Sometimes the photos wanted to tell a different story.

The patriarch, Matias Vilcapampa, first glimpsed from a fairly recent picture, in his early seventies, with a great mane of silver hair and a ruddy, brooding, pockmarked face. A terrible flare of irritation to the eyes as he did nothing to soften his expression in the company photo. Perhaps even took pride in his anger, expressed. Yet in the bags under those eyes, an undecided quality to the set of the jaw, I decided I saw weakness or vulnerability or confusion that signified loss. Something the anger was meant to draw attention from or solve.

He fled repressive regimes in Argentina only to wash up in Miami even more absurdly wealthy and come back after to his native country with more influence, more millions, than his ranch-owning grandfather ever could have imagined. The empire he'd created during this time focused on mining, oil, and other dirty industries. Vied for wells and veins in African and Central Asian countries and then preyed upon the South American countries with the least regulation.

In Argentina, as if not to soil the nest, he stuck to cattle ranching, even gave to environmental organizations. Everywhere else: a major exploiter, extractor, and polluter, with his own private army of bodyguards, and ruthless tactics from a corresponding army of lawyers.

What did Matias do for recreation? A big game hunter, a trophy hunter. The glazed, open eyes of a giraffe, lion, water buffalo, bear, accompanied him across a grim progression of

photographs. And in these I imagined the confusion was miti-
gated or canceled or briefly gone. Because there is, at the very
least—and Silvina would call it less than least—a certainty of
purpose, a calm in the aftermath. In death.

I knew this man. So close in kind to my clients. This was
how they postured, how they showed off the size of their balls.
Common knowledge that we tried not to think about: that some
of our clients had their own security teams. People who were
ex-military. People who would do things for their bosses beyond
fixing their security systems.

Confirmation as to why there was so little information about
Silvina's death. Men like her father snuffed out controversy;
it was the default. There, in the relative safety of my office, I
imagined his reaction to my prying.

He would have been ashamed of her for decades, fighting
with her about her life for decades. Even as the family name was
a sham, a shame. A claim of indigenous blood, but from what I
could tell, it wasn't the original family name. It was a name he
had invented when he became a businessman.

Had there come a point where Matias couldn't take Silvina's actions any longer?

I went on to the information about the mother, Catalina.

Catalina, amid rumors of Matias's mistresses, was easy to
diagnose, even before I turned to the text. Much like my own
mother, although hard to talk about. She looked worn and
haggard and her gray hair had thinned, and none of the lavish
sequined dresses could distract from the fact that something
in their life was leaching the life from her. Or laughing at her.
Skip to the part where your husband spent most of his free
time posing with dead animals.

Beloved she was to many for being the face of her husband's charitable giving. Their endowment of libraries and
university buildings. Some small controversy about the name
"Vilcapampa" and what it meant to indigenous communities
affixed itself to the charity. But, in the end, no one cared.

To many, they were not bad people, not even close. Pillars of the community. They believed in the future. They believed they were contributing to the future even as they took the future away. I had probably pumped gasoline into my car that came from the Vilcapampa Oil Company. Had components in my phone made from rare earth minerals extracted by various Vilcapampa mining concerns.

Just as I had traveled out to their storage palace, which appeared to be the farthest and least extent of their empire. The most visible vestige of an effort to branch out. A receding tide in time—gashing the earth and extracting things from it was the expertise.

The storage palace must have been one of the companies Silvina was tasked with managing because who cared what happened to it. As far as I could tell, it operated at just twenty-five percent capacity currently, so must serve as a tax shelter. Or, just gotten lost in a spreadsheet somewhere. The Vilcapampa business empire was so vast.

Wondered which others had been on the list for Silvina to manage. What that list added up to.

But, mostly, I wondered what the ghosts looked like in Silvina's family. What were the words and phrases carried forward. What version of "drive a clutch" or "shoulder turning"? How far apart had we been growing up? Her accustomed to the newly aristocratic wealth, no matter how she would reject the trappings. Me in the lower middle class and living on a farm to boot. What would friendship have looked like? Couldn't imagine it.

And how did Langer fit into that? Just as an enemy or was it more complicated than that? At first, I thought Langer wasn't too far off from Matias. In the sense that Alex knew just which of our clients would hit it off over dinner. Even if they seemed to come from different worlds. Something always bound them, and that binding didn't bear too much scrutiny. If you wanted to pretend you lived a moral, ethical life.

Langer's sketchy background, pieced together, didn't help much. Grew up in New Hampshire out in the woods. His father had collected guns and Nazi memorabilia. Even had a cannon—it was there in the estate sale after the father died. Langer moving from business administration in college (flunked out) to a stint in the army (also brief). Peace Corps for a two-year tour, then ex–Peace Corps, too—Sumatra. Divorce while in Guatemala, no kids. Moved on to Ecuador, Chile. "Go overseas no matter what" seemed to be his mantra. Special ops? Then just regular ops—stumbling into import-export that happened to include wildlife trafficking? While also belonging to left-wing anarchist groups. An on-the-nose rejection of his conservative father.

It would be a long time before Langer came into focus, like some deep-sea creature glimpsed briefly through the murk.

I thought of Allie's warning, thought of my search on Larry's computer, then put it all aside with a rum and Coke.

On the way to New York, in blanketed dark comfort.

The last time I flew anywhere.

[27]

The conference had a small, tight feel. Insular. Familiar logistics. The jokes familiar, the words "disruptor" and "drone" meaningless—the first from repetition, the second through transformation, camouflage. The new, shiny thing, the way biotech advances could dovetail with new ways to view security. That kind of hum and babble that spreads like a wave, but isn't reflected in programming locked in months before.

The hauntings we could rationalize, become full-throated here, conjured up by panel titles on subjects that might be obsolete or irrelevant soon. "Smart Phone Virus Displacement in Reporting Tools." "Home Security Exfiltration Tactics in Totalitarian Regime Change." "Future Opportunity in Zoo-notic Viruses Sector." "Wireless Trail Cam Lamprey™ Remote Access." Nation-state infiltration, third-party nihilists, ransom-ware, Defcon.

This treadmill that kept changing under our feet. Growing fangs and spikes. Even as it paid the bills. Turmoil in national politics, failed nation-states overseas, conspiracy theories that infiltrated facts, and the undercurrent, never expressed directly, about the delicious unpredictability of that. The fact that the repressive tendencies of our leaders helped our profession. Cynically, the subtext spilled out. The seemingly somber debate. The truth we never uttered: that the Republic could become a husk and our borders a quagmire of death and discomfort . . . but this only strengthened our job security.

Year thirty in the same once-glamorous hotel in the once-glamorous country now stagnant. The lobby out-of-date and cheerless, modernized with its "unique boutique scent." Rooms subdivided smaller and smaller until if you lost the room lottery, and you were me, your feet felt the texture of the wall opposite when you lay in bed. Shovel Pig consigned to a man-tel too narrow. Both of you teetering. But they had superfast wireless.

Little in New York felt glamorous anymore. An eruption of the real had overtaken the unreal that week. Everyone felt the depression of that. Wildfires had consumed states in the heartland. Cyclones another. Earthquakes from fracking were omnipresent. Oil spills from pipelines that didn't bear thinking about. Pandemic, a rumor gathering strength.

Speculation. Snippets in the corridors as I oriented myself to location. The kind you didn't want to hear, but heard any-way. Most on a loop from past years. Because we didn't want to believe. As you pitched your product.

"Ice caps mean there's opportunity for resource extraction . . ."

"You can't count on fossil fuels forever, so plastics . . ."

"What I would do is invest in waterproof equipment, always . . ."

"My boss has a couple bunkers for the end-times . . ."

"Time to think about getting out . . ."

Stench of gasoline followed us up into the conference rooms. Stitching hum of drones outside delivering packages. The walls of the main ballroom had been fitted with neon catchphrases too depressingly banal to relate. A bird had gotten trapped there, site of the opening remarks, but we all took video, thinking it might be a drone instead. Some kind of stealth marketing by a competitor.

Most people in New York City had started wearing masks, to keep the pollution out, but also to protect privacy. The keynote was about that, on a technical level, as the trend spread worldwide. What came after facial recognition software? What lay on the horizon for all of us? Wondering idly who here was a spy for a foreign government. Or a local government.

Incoming: *>>Dad wants to know if you miss us.*

I was sitting in on a panel about biotech surveillance that made my skin crawl. As the panelists ignored anything ethical in their pursuit of a better, less detectable spy.

Me: I miss you especially now, during this boring bit.

>>Dad wants to know if . . .

All the things Dad wanted to know. Sneaky. She'd never have texted me otherwise. Even as he sent me a message and wasn't above letting our daughter deliver it. I didn't blame him.

But what I chased this time didn't feel like a betrayal.

Later, as I listened to the last speaker of the day, I wondered if we should give up and let the torrent overwhelm us. That in the roar of rush-hour traffic, the sheer numbers, existed a kind of anonymity. We always made security about privacy, and we stressed the impossibility of being "unhackable." That we were managing quality of life for patients with a long-term, low-fever virus. Everyone boasted about their bulletproof approach, but it was just a construct in their heads.

I said all of that to someone in the hallway after a panel. They ignored me. I wasn't on any panels myself because I had registered late. But in this business, it seemed vainglorious anyway. Or unwise.

"Still working for that piece-of-shit company?" a voice said.

I turned, and there was a man from a direct rival. Colorful shirts, broad collars. Former tech bro chastened by a bankruptcy. He'd never be a CEO again.

"Yes, I am still working for that piece-of-shit company," I said, in a monotone.

"Well, if you ever want to work for a real company—"

"I'll kill you and eat you and use your bones for soup," I said. Don't know why. Just felt reckless.

I gave him my best wrestling snarl and then licked my lips. He looked confused, maybe even frightened, turned away at the same time I turned away.

Only to fall into another unwanted conversation.

"Do you fake it to make it?" an older gentleman said to me, staring up from eyes in a bald head that topped out around five foot three. He, like me, could remember the idea of the Commodore 64. Floppy disks. Dial-up. But, unlike me, he might remember punch cards, too.

"Everything I do is real," I said, peering down at him.

"I'll bet, I'll bet," he said. "But does it matter?"

"Dark web," I said, as a joke. "Dark web." Just because I could. Just because we used the term so much to scare "civilians." Dank web.

He nodded like he knew what I meant. Like a meaning lay below the "dark" web. Like anything I said would be prophetic.

But he made me feel like an eclipse. I made an excuse to pivot to the refreshments table.

Fake it to make it. Email accounts full of emails we had created. Business correspondence. Personal correspondence. The things so false that they might at least confuse the intruder, force them to engage, that they might never peel back that layer to find the "real stuff," as the keynote speaker put it. Dramatic re-creation and forging. Some even employed movie writers to choreograph the story arc.

All the faces around me felt so gray and featureless. Scentless bodies, rapt, in the falling-apart banquet chairs, lashed together like life rafts, in row after row.

How had I become part of this?

[28]

With distance, I can see that the problem had a larger scope and that, eventually, I'd bought into systems that despised me. We were assholes and opportunists and sociopaths, a lot of us. We thought we were on the right side of things. But what did it mean that our clients resembled ghouls and grave robbers? I knew their families, or photos of their families. Stock sentiments for what looked almost like stock photos. I knew their habits when we took them out on the town. Their fears and doubts, revealed after martinis or boutique whisky. The altruistic pompous speeches about intent meant as much to reassure themselves as impress us. They shared the familiar things, the timeworn things that make up wanting to be comfortable with one another. While before we met, we knew their criminal records and what porn they were into, had to wipe images from our minds to pretend to be like them. And maybe we were like them, because we served them.

I couldn't always see past the seamless smiles, no matter how fixed, to the crimes. But the system was fixed, and I helped to fix it. What I believed was bulwark or siege defense morphed into the predatory. I allowed systems to flourish without consideration of people. Efficiency, and, especially, the word "proactive," lived in our heads always. Another was "optimization."

Most of the rest are fuzzy, or pulled one by one from my mind like hooks from the mouths of a row of fish. Until I'm floating in the dark water, released, but wounded, floating to the bottom, light lost in the murk above.

But I'd rather live here. It's more secure, for one thing. For another, I can't hurt anyone here the way I hurt people before, from afar. Pried into their private lives in the name of "monitoring threat" or "better serving need." What is need but a perversion in the end? I did receive the damage, too, but mostly it streamed out from me.

The blessing now is Silvina shining out from my eyes, obliterating the past.

[29]

Someone made a joke at the reception, early that evening, that disaster was the greatest security. "Savior of privacy." The places that Wi-Fi couldn't cover. If you were underwater, nothing could find you, went his joke. You couldn't interpret that without replacing his smile with a grinning skull. Consumed by the fire, you might rise as a phoenix. Or you might just be a pile of crumbling ashes.

The organizers had decided to make it a masquerade party. We were all to wear masks, supplied by companies that made designer versions. Various filtration systems. Others mimicked quarantine masks, but were specific to the subindustry devoted to subverting facial recognition software. Peacock iridescent. Some even with feathers. Others black and soulless as VR tech. A few had miniature waterfalls running down the cheekbones. Soon companies would be able to produce masks that were living creatures, had a hologram of what looked like a localized dystopia for your face. I chose a plain, neutral, unassuming mask.

We were a legion of fools in masks. A rhapsody of masks. A

rhapsody of fools. Just added another layer. What got through and what did not. Next year, there would be no conference. A few years later, businesses hawking wares would have changed. The old ones washed away by the shock of realization: the physical laws of the universe didn't give a fuck about them. Wouldn't protect them just because they existed and sold things.

Somehow, I managed to find the person I was looking for in that morass, after she texted me her mask type. Let's call her "Jill." I had contacted her well before getting on the plane, to give her enough time.

"Jill" approached me, wearing a pink-red parrot mask with three eyes for three types of filters. I couldn't even see her neck, so it was more like a parrot head. I was talking to someone wearing a parrot head.

The reception was work for her, so we didn't talk long, promised to catch up after. But the wonderful thing is, we knew we never would. We just had this understanding in the moment. Might do lunch next time, or might not. We didn't need more.

Our companies didn't collaborate on bids, but I'd met her at the conference four years ago and we had liked each other. She also went to the gym a lot.

"Here they are," she murmured, coming close to reach up on tiptoe to hug me and placing the objects in Shovel Pig.

"Thanks," I said. "It's a huge relief."

Jill smiled. "Happy to do it. I might need something someday." But she wouldn't, and I'd never see her again. I watched her pivot with envy, the seamless transition into the next conversation, across the room. Not my strength.

Now I had White SIM cards for a powerful crypto phone. More like a stripped-down version of my laptop that couldn't be traced.

Meanwhile, my "real" phone kept reminding me of home. *>>Dad wants to know if the hotel is fab.*

Fab?

>>*Dad should just take my phone and buy me a new one.*

>>*Dad is thinking about a fence for the yard.*

My daughter missed me, I think. This was the real message. But there was another message, about my husband, I didn't quite want to see.

I wound up calling my new phone "Bunker Hog," to go with Shovel Pig. "Bog" for short. Lost in the Bog. No one ever got out of the Bog.

It made sense at the time.

I put on my stoic face. Made the approaches I needed to, spoke to the people I needed to. The ones Alex talked to on a regular basis. To establish a presence, an identity, a sense for Alex of how I had moved through the conference. How I had represented the company in real time.

Alex, as if reading my mind:

>>*How's it going? Did you get to the gym? Knock 'em dead!*

Ignored that. So little thought put into his text, why bother?

I just wanted it over. I can do small talk, but it wears on me. I become clipped, sullen, resentful. Confused technocrats reeling in my wake, the ones who didn't know me staring, blank-eyed, at the bulky woman in the business suit.

Drowning in a sea of middle-aged and old men. Looking across the rows of faces for someone like me . . . and finding no one.

Imagine how little this helps me forget Silvina. Imagine how I maneuver Shovel Pig so I am even larger crossing to the station where lies in wait the white wine and the red wine.

Imagine that I am thinking about Silvina's trial and whether she was really a murderer . . . while wondering how many people in that room have committed some sort of crime.

Imagine, too, that I'm trying to figure out how the salamander relates to the hummingbird, across a sea of connect-the-dots.

The thought of Silvina staring at me in the coffee shop. Observing me in the day-to-day. Recruitment, except she'd died too soon?

Imagined Langer there, too, in spirit, no matter what the barista said. A ghost after scraps. His presence kept pressing in like a face through a dirty window.

[30]

A quiet corner in which to lurk, even if I'm not good at lurking. That's all I wanted. A cave in which to hang my hat. What Silvina would have liked. Silence. Stillness. A light was out in a mold-smelling corner of the lobby, next to drab drapes. I watched the video of Silvina on my secret, "impenetrable" phone. Rewatched it. While I wondered why Allie hadn't found it. Or, maybe more accurate, why she hadn't given me the link. Yes, you had to dig for it. But not too far. Self-preservation, maybe.

In the video, Silvina railed against something called "Contila." Which sounded like a new designer drug for a skin condition, but which I knew was Langer's import-export business linked to wildlife traffickers.

Contila had members in South American countries, but also ties to organized crime in the U.S., Russia, and China. A man named John Hudgens had run Contila from a shell company in Miami, and then, as things got hot, Canada and then Mexico. Silvina had taken a special dislike to Hudgens, had been the one to provide authorities with the intel that made him have to move operations. Then Hudgens had died in the bombing, along with four others.

If Silvina was an indistinct smudge on the internet, Contila had only Interpol alerts and not much else. Vague stories about bribes at border crossings and containership checks at ports of call. Hundreds of endangered animal seizures they could have been behind. With Hudgens gone, someone else in management took over, but that name was buried deep in Interpol files or they truly didn't know who ran it.

Langer was Hudgens's "manager," which to me meant an enforcer, promoted to some position that didn't have a name after Hudgens exploded. The guy Hudgens turned to and said, "This has to happen," and Langer did the dirty work or hired someone to. He'd been questioned by the feds, too, but they'd had to release him. Why?

It was hard to think of Silvina as "terrorist" or "murderer" compared to the people she'd been fighting.

That gap between the murder trial and being handed a note by a barista. Not just the four or five years of total absence, off the radar. But the rest of those fifteen years, about which such sparse information existed. Except Silvina had managed properties, stolen money from her father, given civic responsibility a go. Unitopia. Which just felt like a bad joke about storage palaces.

And what was this, from the video?

"The trees were whispering to me. The trees in the darkness wanted to tell me secrets." As if there were some truth to my daughter's cartoons.

And what was this, later?

"We have killed so much that perhaps we thought killing a little more wouldn't matter. If it could save us for another year, another five years. Out of sight so we never saw most of it. Or, if we saw, we disbelieved the extent or it had already happened. Like roadkill. Like an accident. Not purposeful, or the purpose having fled. Not the order of things as we had imposed it."

And what was this?

"'Progress': a word to choke on, a word to discard and then

pick up again, hurl it in the oven like coal, watch it spurl out its own name in black smoke from the chimney of the hunting lodge. I embrace it, and I repeat it, and yet I know no word I or any other human could use will ever be the right word."

And what was the next thing?

Around every corner something incendiary might lurk. Something personal. But also something searching for a polemic to leap into. To give it a body, a voice.

My point is that, in looking at everything I had about the Vilcapampa family, my initial analysis was the usual story of a daughter's rebellion from a tyrannical father and a weak mother. That Silvina decided to become the opposite of them. To an extreme.

But even if I had already begun to create a version of Silvina, I still didn't really have enough data points. This veil. This descent into speculation. As if the systems that I used, and that used me, deformed her. Kept changing her.

And me.

[31]

In the past, I had slept with strangers at conferences. Never knew the last names. As anonymous as I could be, to set the expectations.

Or, once upon a time, I did those things. I liked the *idea* of meeting strangers at conferences. I liked the bar, and maybe for the same kind of calm as the flight in, and the soft clunk and crunch of the ice in bronze-brown drinks that fooled me with a sophistication I thought I couldn't find elsewhere. Sudden flood of mint or basil from the bartender's stand. Rosemary. A kind of shock, an infiltration. Yet kept the job at bay. That fuzzy golden aura enveloping me. The glow pushing from the inside to the outside until I shone like the sun.

Most hotels had more than one conference going, so I would

hang out near attendees for the other conference. Textiles. Medical. Pharmaceuticals. Entomology. Who would I be this time? A homicide detective? A veterinarian. A flight attendant.

The other main conference was construction, with an emphasis on innovative use of drywall, textures, and roofing. Perhaps I was in that business instead. This wasn't me out of control. This was me in control.

I'd describe the hotel bar, except it was the usual. What I preferred. Dark-lit, not stools but high seats with backs. Some of the security conference attendees, gleaned from their lanyards, sat in the surrounding gloom at tables like murky islands with little flickering butter-white candles. Nothing much droned on, music-wise, beneath it. Like something flat moving around under the sparkly blue bad idea that was the carpet.

Even from the bar, I could hear their murmurs spiked with drunken exultations. The usual banter, among mostly men, with what I called "an appreciative audience." They could swing their dicks around as much as they wanted back there. I wasn't going to enter that fray.

I guess as I sat there, nursing a water after that drab day, I kept thinking about the significance of taxidermy. Of numbers found under a dead hummingbird's eyes. Of Silvina and the video. It still felt like distraction or adventure. How exciting that she'd been an ecoterrorist. How exciting that she'd been tried for murder. How *exciting* that she'd had to fight extradition. How exciting that she came from a rich, important, fucked-up family . . . instead of just a fucked-up family.

I am not a pretty woman, the way people think of beauty. I had a kind of jock-like, horsey charm when younger, I guess. But a man approached me soon enough. They always do. It takes a particular type not to be intimidated, but it's more common than you might think. All it really takes is ego.

He pointed at the seat next to me. Which I liked. Sometimes they put a space between me and them.

I didn't say no, so he didn't go away. Sat down, and his shoulder touched mine for a moment. He had some muscle behind him. About my height, a little shorter maybe, dark hair, strange blue eyes I couldn't quite get used to. Almost like he wore special contacts.

He motioned toward the bartender, made a joke about the "boats of Brooklyn" because of the flooding. But some instinct told me he wasn't from New York. Too much melody to the voice. Smell of a rich, clove-infused beer had confused me, until I realized it was aftershave.

The man ordered us both a Rusty Nail without asking. But it was a drink I liked. My father had adored it, to oblivion, in the rural way stations that served as bars, but his sins didn't pollute the taste for me.

I expected the man's hand to be clammy, but it was firm, warm, dry.

"Here for the conference," he said.

Telling me, not asking. Generic enough. Didn't care about specifics.

I nodded. "You?"

"Yes." Not "Yeah." Not another nod. A very precise and almost formal yes that made me realize his approach had also been precise. No wasted movement. Not a lot of motion with his hands. He was like the opposite of a hummingbird. But neither was he a salamander.

"Worth it?" I asked him.

He shrugged. "I find panel discussions boring."

"Like watching drywall harden," I said.

He laughed. "Yes, like that."

I put his age at somewhere between late thirties and midforties. Something about the wear and tear that registers right away even if you can't tell how you see it.

He had a wide but not unpleasant face. I remember thinking, with envy, that if he were an actor, he could be anyone he liked.

"My name is Jack," he said.

"I'm Jill," I said.

That surprised Jack into a half-smile, and he turned to take me in. I didn't look away.

A nice nose and mouth and jaw, the hair long enough to be thick but not an unruly mane. Eyes that wanted to be more direct than that mouth, and a hawk-like inquiry there that should've gone with narrow features. A sharpness. I had a glimpse, in that gaze, of sudden acceleration, of a plunge from on high. A velocity bearing down on an uncanny valley. The cry of some creature caught unawares. I don't know how else to describe it. I knew that he, like me, was playing a role. That Jack wasn't here for the drywall conference.

Fine by me. I liked that. Hawks, even in disguise, are so unlike bears.

Our drinks arrived.

"To extreme weather, experienced from the inside," Jack said, and we clinked glasses.

How much nicer, Jack continued, to watch the raindrops run down the windowpane. I can't remember how he said it, but so skillful, or the way he said it, conjuring a picture of the two of us already in aftermath, in bed, looking out a gray window. The undertow of his voice. A way you could get drawn into it, or caught in it. A rich, layered voice, and the more I imagined him beneath the suit, it was athletic, in shape. At odds with how fast Jack drank the first Rusty Nail. But he didn't order another right away, or put any pressure on me to finish mine.

"Do you like magic?" he asked.

That made me laugh, it was so unexpected.

"Depends on the magician," I said.

The kind of upturn to his mouth that said, *Fair, but I have some new tricks.*

"Do you have hobbies?" he asked.

"I wanted to be a homicide detective," I confessed.

"Really?" Eyebrow raised, faux surprise. Like this was part of me coming on to him.

I nodded. "Oh, yes. Studied psychology, sociology, criminology. But then I discovered statistics."

He considered that a moment, with clear disbelief.

But it was true: I'd found criminology duller than I'd thought and the required statistics classes more interesting than I'd imagined possible. This aggregate data. The ways in which eccentricities of human behavior persisted through software and how you could, with your own bias, skew surveys and studies to suit your interpretation. Maybe I liked the illusion of constraint. The restraint.

"But . . . even if I believe you . . . 'homicide detective' isn't a hobby," he said, with that smile I liked too much. "Not really. You can't come home from work and say, 'Now for my hobby.'"

Laughed outright at that one.

"True," I said. "Real hobbies?" I pretended to think, then said, recklessly, "Taxidermy."

"Is that right, Jill?" he said, and the way he drew himself up put a tiny bit of distance between us physically, made me think I'd made a mistake.

"What about your hobbies?" I asked.

Jack shrugged. "I get bored easily. Move on to the next thing."

Message received.

"What do you sell?" I asked.

"How do you know I sell anything?"

Well, Jack was selling himself, at the moment.

"I sell security," I said. "Now that I'm not a detective."

I don't know why I told the truth, except "security" could be so many things.

"That's my business, too," Jack said. "In a way. Not the way you mean, though."

"How do you know what I mean?" A little irritated. He'd sounded dismissive. And the more I looked at Jack, the more I saw the imperfections. A hint of a belly. The way his features resembled those of a local weatherman. How he might be a bit older than me, but had worked carefully to conceal that.

"No offense," Jack said. "I guess I think everyone sells security in some way. You're selling this idea that you're dependable, honest. Trustworthy. But most of us aren't. It's just a matter of whether it manifests in the job or not."

Manifests. Trustworthy. A strange kind of hitting on. In that moment, Jack didn't look like he much cared for the task at hand. He was sitting sideways—the better to see me, I'd thought. But also that way he could survey the entire length of the bar. Some other women had come in, were sitting at the far end.

Then the moment passed, and Jack said something witty about bars and bartenders, and I laughed and I described my frustration with conferences in general and I had my second drink, which was my limit. And we both kept the conversation going, as if it was necessary for whatever might come after. But we didn't particularly care about the conversation. It existed there, in the air, between us. All those words. A cloud of them. Maybe I sounded risky or exotic or eccentric. Maybe I didn't care what I sounded like.

At some point, conference-goers kept bursting into the bar in groups that made it hard to hear yourself talk. The music rose in volume until it wasn't just a mumble under the carpet. Someone spilled a drink, broke a glass.

At some point, Jack leaned over and whispered a room number in my ear, his arm around my shoulders. And then he was gone, as if a ghost torn apart. Too delicate, under the gaze of all those people. As if he'd never had a thing to do with them.

I didn't usually go up to a man's room. I was happy enough with my bar ritual. How it got me out of myself. How playing a role helped me somehow. I didn't want to. I wanted to. The drug of the unknown. That was simple. Aftermath wasn't simple. I'd been good for three years. Why now?

I made Jack wait. I had a third drink, downed some bar snacks, ravenous. I went to the elevator, to the seventh floor. Wandered, confused, down dim-lit corridors, lost in the maze of a dark fairy tale. I didn't mind—that was part of the story. This difficulty, this disruption. Which heightened the intensity and the risk.

But I never found his room.

I never found the room because the room number he'd given me didn't exist.

In the moment, you tell yourself he got it wrong because he was drunker than he looked, or he'd gotten confused and come from a different, adjacent hotel. You don't want to think that he blew you off, but that's what comes next.

Relief, disappointment. How you wander back down to window-shop the closed avenue of tacky stores on the street level.

How you look at the stiff mannequins in a clothing store and will them to move, to become something other than what they are.

How you're drawn back into your own shit no matter what the distraction.

[32]

What went on between my parents when I was at school or out, I don't know. Can't imagine. I want to think there was an affection there, an intimacy, they could not display when I was around. I want to believe that both could be more present.

My father went around with a perpetual frown, as if he thought the world was making fun of him. As if, in living, he'd stolen something from God, and every breath was a kind of trickery. He could be known to smile at the right joke or something absurd that had happened on the farm, but that was it. That was when I liked him best, if I liked him at all.

In those days, growing up, the farm might be tolerable and even "something special," as he called it. But the frown became over time a kind of cynical wince. The look of a man who thinks he understands the world and how much it wants to fuck with him. A sourness that creeps in when you have no more hope of being successful. My dad had degrees in animal husbandry and agriculture; knowledge, smarts, were not his problem.

Toward the end, as we hurtled toward bankruptcy, that's when Grandfather became an anchor. The "indispensable weight," as Dad's neighbor, another struggling farmer, called him. To us, he was just the agony of bursts of temper and bursts of static. I hate that one of my enduring memories is Grandpa, before he lost his mind, taking us to a Sears lingerie show and leering at the models. I was twelve, my brother three years older.

The cutaway of that, two years later. Cut away to: seeing my brother's lifeless face framed by mud. Framed by the riverbank.

My father's failure with the farm is one thing. My mother was another: easy to diagnose, hard to talk about. It had started with a forgetfulness I might understand. Because you saw it in others. A slack gaze, a misunderstanding of relatives. A need to be taken care of. These might be things that came premature, but fell into familiar categories.

But as if familiar wasn't her forte, the tiny, spiteful woman who had come from a strict religious upbringing into the evils of my father's agnosticism found ways to express whatever was going on in her mind that ventured into strange places.

As she became someone else, my mother wrote herself another history. Maybe she wanted her altered state to roam as far from us as possible. To stray and linger, in unequal proportions, to her illness.

Maybe it just happened because it was always going to happen. But that didn't make it any less catastrophic. I lost my brother, then I lost my mother, more or less, even as my father turned bitter and my grandfather, before the end, was no better than a thin, flailing beast. Sometimes my father summoned the nerve to lock him in a shed during his rages. Calmed into "thin milk," as Father put it. Calmed so he could be let out, but muttering and sharp and surly and nothing like a person. Not what I wanted a person to be. Sure to make Father suffer for what he'd done. So Father shut him up less frequently.

Sometimes I felt his flailing, his rage, was Mother's made manifest, in the body, in the world.

Mother's rants were worse for being written down, for being quiet until read, because, when read, they seemed intent on burning up the world, on tearing it down with inchoate rage. The sharp marks, ripping the paper, so violent. That her vacant gaze made it seem as if something had been summoned into her. I never knew what she was going to hand me. "*Con*-flagration," Dad would say, when they argued, and list the words around that, defining her—or that he would cast a spell, bind her, understand her.

Most of what she wrote was about my dead brother. But also about me, as if I had died, too.

I missed my brother, and here, in the letters, our mother had created this further life for him. Had written to him as if he were in college. As if he had gone on to get a job with his degree, begun to raise a family. As if he had been corresponding with her, telling her all the details of his days. Time became a miracle in these letters, so he might age a year in a month or not age a day in eighteen months.

While I, in these letters, these accounts of some parallel world, remained single. I remained single and always had a new boyfriend. I would appear at family reunions and be disruptive. I drank too much. I did unforgivable things. The Devil himself could not have come up with some of the accounts my mother did; at the end, she had more imagination than during the whole rest of her life.

It hurt, but it always hurt more that my brother was gone, so I read whatever she sent me. The delicate, curving handwriting in meticulous blue ballpoint pen on onionskin paper. Tucked crisp into sturdy envelopes. Sometimes trinkets fell out with the letters. Pressed flowers. Charms to add to bracelets I didn't wear. Once or twice, money. I received it all, all that damage, just so I could hear about my brother, alive, in some other place and time.

I kept reading them until my mother died. And then I felt the lack, but still felt the hurt. Maybe that was my cue to live another life than the one I'd chosen. I don't know. Except I had the example: you could be whoever you wanted to be.

When we moved from an apartment to the house, I didn't give my dad the address. Made it clear we were done.

But I kept my mother's letters.

[33]

I blew off the conference the next day. I luxuriated and wallowed in a huge room service breakfast of scrambled eggs, waffles, bacon, toast, hash browns. After a workout in a gym so small my ferocious intensity to wreck every machine drove out the one flabby, middle-aged man using the rower. The hunger and the fear in his eyes as he drank me in repulsed me and yet perversely made me push myself harder.

Then I went to find Carlton Fusk.

The way I'd always planned to.

Brooklyn was flooded from recent rain, but, oddly, not near the water. I had decided to check out a few other taxidermy stores before pouncing on Fusk. Maybe out of caution, but also to get a sense of what the average taxidermy store was like. Establish a kind of baseline to judge Fusk against, I guess.

But most of the stores had converted to selling other things. People didn't buy dead animals as much anymore. At least, not in Brooklyn. One place had become a kind of sad "man store," devoted to hair-care products and aggressive-looking outdoor gear for the faux tough who never went camping. They had a dead ostrich chick taxidermied, along with a lion cub. Every animal in there was a dead baby of some kind, even the owner behind the counter. The door near the back drenched in cologne. I crossed two other stores off after that, without visiting. Knew what they'd be and why.

"Roadkill is fine," proclaimed one storefront. "Roadkill is just fine." Another advertised "intricate detail," including "smaller birds," and I went in because a goldfinch or similar on a pedestal got my attention. But it meant nothing in the end. Why should it? Typical taxidermy store wasn't a thing, I concluded. It was more like used-book stores: the spaces and what they contained gave insight into the owner's mind more than some "industry standard."

I could only take so much of this kind of exploration before I was ready for Fusk.

As soon as I walked into Fusk's (let's call it) "The Low-Budget Bordering on Shithole Taxidermy & Antiques Shoppe"—the low-grade stench of mold hit me. That and some kind of furniture varnish. But also, I realize now, the smell of death, which meant Fusk must perform his "art" on-premises. Maybe in a basement, so a hint of reek rose from the floorboards.

The clutter was of the hoarder level only respectable in an antiques store. Someone I assumed was Carlton Fusk coalesced as a smudge of shadow in the back, seen behind the far counter through stacks of boxes, overflowing shelves, and floating dust motes.

The place made me sad. My hangover made me sad. How "Jack" had ditched me colored my mood, too. I kept telling myself I shouldn't care because I'd never intended to sleep with him. Yet sad manifested as reckless, I guess. I could cover my tracks leading to the shop all I wanted. But I didn't have a set plan for what to say or do once there.

I lingered in the front area, staring at window displays so covered in dust, you could tell they hadn't been changed out in years. I felt clammy. My hands sweated. Velvet-upholstered chairs. Porcelain dolls slumped over small tables inlaid with mother-of-pearl. It struck me so palpably that this could've been a scene out of the living room at the farm in the last years I was there that I felt sick. I had to look away. As if my mother had lived in the window display since her death.

Slowly, I made my way through the junk to the corner devoted to taxidermy. A desiccated bobcat. A fox with a strange gleam to the eyes and a sparkly lacquer to the fur that I realized after a moment meant someone had petted its back so much the fur had changed texture. Deer antlers. Spent shotgun shells. I guessed the best stuff was behind the back counter.

Books on taxidermy and related subjects, too. I picked one up as cover, pretended to read it. Then actually began to read it. *Oddly Enough: From Animal Land to Furtown*, from the 1930s. Even a glance told me it was perverse, wrong, possibly evil. Something an anthropologist studying cultural bias might study.

"We, as the fur bearers of the world, in order to be enthusiastically welcomed to your fur industry, must live a determined double life. First, we exist as 'an animal' following the vigorous paths planned by nature. When we depart from this existence as ambassadors of the wild, we will then live our second glorious and commercial being . . . a life as a fur."

Did the hummingbird on a pedestal exist separate from this philosophy? Silvina would say it didn't. That "fur" was a separate religion from "taxidermy." Yet, somehow, that paragraph made what had been done to the hummingbird more grotesque.

"Transpose what is done to an animal onto a human," Silvina said in the video. "If it is disgusting, wrong, unethical, immoral, then you know what the truth is."

I took the book to the back, to the guarded high counter. The man behind the counter had craggy white hair and a ruddy, deeply lined face, wore a plaid lumberjack shirt and jeans, with a vest over the shirt, in an unironic way. He was almost my height, and, if I'd had to guess, mid-sixties, and had spent most of his life outdoors. He had a sleepy left eye.

"You're Carlton Fusk," I said.

"Yeah, that's me. The one and only. That all?" he asked in the gruff voice I expected. Smoker, or ex-smoker.

"No."

"What else?"

"I have a question about taxidermy."

"The book's about fur."

"The question's about taxidermy."

"Sure. I know something about taxidermy." Said like we were somewhere in Upstate New York and I was a clueless tourist.

"You ever seen something like this?"

I unfolded a color printout of a photograph of the hummingbird, from the internet café.

Fusk took the photo from me without breaking eye contact. Then looked down with caution, as if I might be dangerous. When he was done looking, he let it fall from his hand onto the counter. For some reason, I'd thought he wouldn't give it back.

"And there's this," I said, pulling out a photo of the "R.S." on the bottom of the hummingbird's stand.

A flicker of interest? Maybe.

I pulled out my photograph of Langer. "And what about him?"

Fusk's bad eye widened. Then went slack again.

"You a cop?" Fusk asked.

"No. Detective. Private eye." I said it without thinking. I couldn't tell you why, except it seemed like the truth. Pursuing a mystery made me a detective.

"Identification?" Fusk asked.

"I don't have to give you that."

"Then I don't have to answer your questions."

I sighed, like this scene had played out before. Even if my heart beat fast.

"I'm out-of-state. You don't have to answer, but then I'll liaise with the police department and maybe you'll have to talk to them instead."

A huge adrenaline rush as I said the words. Overwhelming. I had to steady myself, as if a wave was about to knock me over.

Fusk considered that. I'd never play poker against him, but something shifted in his expression. I'd shifted it with my threat.

Then he turned to the shelves behind him, found a book, turned back to me.

It was a second copy of *Furtown*. In much better condition.

"The one you've got isn't a first edition," he said. "This one is. It's five hundred bucks, not thirty. You should really get this one."

I started to argue that I didn't care what edition I had, then understood.

"Sure."

Five hundred dollars. Why didn't I hesitate? Why didn't I walk away? Because: I had five hundred dollars on me. In fact, I had a thousand. Just in case. I hadn't known what I would need or when I would need it. Withdrawn from the bank before I'd left the West Coast.

I counted out the bills on the counter, let him pick them up. Then he slid the book across to me, took the other one back. I wondered if *Furtown* had been a big seller back in the day.

"After, I never see you again," Fusk said.

"Sure." Easy enough to say.

"Okay. But I'm taking a break. You like coffee?"

He put the closed sign up, led me through the back and up some stairs and into a second-floor living room with a wrought iron balcony looking out on a closed-in courtyard full of unexpected fruit trees. Somewhere beyond the living room was a little bedroom and a bathroom. I realized later I had followed him like "private eye" was some kind of armor against calamity.

He brought two lawn chairs onto the balcony. There was no coffee.

I held out the photos again. "So, what can you tell me?"

But Fusk didn't answer. He'd taken a gun out from under an overturned pot next to his chair. So casual. Like he'd done it a lot over the years. And yet beatific in its purpose, that action. I saw a light in his eyes that showed me how he'd been much younger.

The adrenaline left me, and I felt so ancient and so weary. My mind didn't want to focus. All I saw was the gun. Heavy and dangerous-looking, with six chambers. Old, but clean and well-maintained.

He could have shot me. I would have done nothing. That's how helpless I was back then.

"Listen to me and really hear me," Fusk said. "Understand this: I don't know who you think you are, but if I ever see you again, I will use this thing. Get out of here and never come back. Don't ask questions. Don't show people these photographs. I'd say take another case, except you're not a private eye."

I didn't argue, like a switch had clicked off.

Stumbled out of my seat and stumbled back into the living room and stumbled down the stairs and stumbled out into the shop and then through the front door, out into the light of the street.

I didn't stop until I had walked another four blocks and had no real idea where I was, caught my breath, tried to slow everything down.

A coffee shop looked like a kind of haven. I sat down heavy in a seat, ignoring the frown of the barista cleaning tables.

I kept picking up my regular phone to call the police. Putting it back down again on the table. I ordered a Red Eye. I drank it quick, even though it scalded my throat. Should I call the police? And tell them what? That Fusk had threatened me after I impersonated a detective? What kind of offense was that in this state? How would this tip my hand to people who might be watching? To whoever had tracked my search on Larry's computer.

Had I given my real name? I couldn't remember. Had I done anything that Fusk could trace back to me? Didn't think so. Couldn't be sure.

I was still clutching the book about fur. Even though the words were meaningless now.

[34]

A layover in Chicago on the way back, because of bad weather in our path. The kind you can't fly through. Also, once we landed, some mechanical issue. So we would have to change planes. Another delay. Well, that was the way of it with miracles like flight. The magic had become tawdry, tattered, excruciating.

By the time I had had a couple drinks in an airport bar, my panic had faded and the encounter with Fusk taken on an almost daring, swashbuckling tinge. Memory fucks with you when it tries to protect you. A third bourbon and Coke, and part of me thought I'd been calm when Fusk pulled the gun. That I'd expected something like that. That I could've subdued him in close quarters if I'd needed to, with an MMA or wrestling move. Cheers—have another drink.

Fusk, I decided, had been the kind of encounter I'd been seeking at the hotel bar. The purest distillation of it. The kind that's dangerous but not dangerous. The gun probably hadn't even been loaded. I'd tell my grandchildren about it someday. How foolish their grandmother had been.

Which made guilt well up, and I texted my daughter. Direct, not through my husband.

>>*Headed home, kumquat. How're you? School good? Dad picking you up on time?*

Nothing for several minutes. Then:

>>*Not much. It's all cool. Dad's out in the yard a lot. Patrolling. See you soon.*

Smiley emoticon back. I knew not to push it. Didn't think to ask why my husband was out in the yard. "Patrolling." He hated yardwork. We had someone for that.

Two hours to kill and I felt brave enough for risk again. Time to analyze Vilcapampa property holdings. Had to get ahead of this thing. Had to carve a path forward.

Didn't I?

. . .

The Vilcapampa "umbrella," or "octopus," looked straightforward because it was so crude at times. A classic autocratic, top-down, family-run company that happened to produce net revenues of just under one trillion dollars a year. Blunt, in how organized, at least from public records. The senior Vilcapampa served not just as the founder and owner but also as CEO. The CFO was his younger brother. The ruling board was riddled through with other relatives. Anywhere Vilcapampa could promote from within the family, he did. This had clearly hurt them in some areas, as the expertise of those appointed didn't match up with the responsibilities.

Wince-inducing: there was even a Vilcapampa Institute in Peru that traded off the faux indigenous connection to "help" traditionally oppressed Indian groups in the mountains, near ancient Incan ruins. Just enough distance from Argentina that the institute could, with apparent impunity, help launder monies from the less savory of their side businesses, as far as I could tell.

In addition to the main corporation and its subsidiaries, there were, as always, a flurry of shell companies and investments in other corporations. (Incorp Corp, Inc., was my favorite.) Which was where the crude and the blunt became a knot.

I wasn't yet ready to undo the knot. I just needed to know what company names Vilcapampa had operated under in the Pacific Northwest, to get a sense of other physical locations that might hold the clue to a hummingbird, a salamander.

The easiest thing was to locate the properties Silvina herself held or leased. What was in her name? The storage palace, until recently, because so unprofitable, no doubt. The history there was fraught. Her father had basically bought the whole mountain, fenced off most of it, and had briefly intended to continue an abandoned mining operation near the summit. Except permits had been difficult to get due to community concerns, and he'd withdrawn from the effort after a year or two. Contented himself with some halfhearted logging.

Which fit a pattern: whenever Vilcapampa Senior seemed on the verge of being in the public eye, the shell companies would retreat and he would move on to something else. But he rarely parted with the properties, clearly preferring they lie derelict than be sold to anyone else. In 2007, perhaps at Silvina's initiative, a lot of money had been sunk into trying to create a second storage palace farther up the mountain, and they'd even broken ground. Perhaps to salvage the initial investment. But then the 2008 recession hit, and Silvina or her father had decided to abandon the idea. Leaving just a storage unit business in the foothills that dipped in and out of the red. Tax shelter?

Shortly thereafter, it felt as if her father had lost his last scrap of patience with Silvina. Or he'd discovered the money she'd stolen from him. I couldn't tell which came first. Or if the company had recovered the funds. Nor even how much money Silvina had stolen. It must have been a lot, because from then on she had to provide for herself.

I also found an apartment that she'd owned until a year before and then sold. Occupied. Had been rented by Silvina to a series of what looked like college students. No clues there.

But: where had Silvina lived while surveilling me? No record of it.

After another drink, another thought: that she could have been watching the house. That she could have known all kinds of facts about my family.

The veering, the drift—it told me I was rattled. I bore down, there at the bar, holding court with my fourth drink. Ten in the end. Ten companies I could find with connections to Vilcapampa. Thirty properties. I scanned the lists trying to visualize the parts of town. The neighborhoods. The purpose of each. Some were leased as gas stations or hardware stores. Others as restaurants. A fair amount of commercial property. But also apartment complexes.

It wasn't until I wrote the addresses down, until I looked at the full list, that it hit me.

The numbers. From behind the hummingbird's eyes: 23 and 51.

And right in the middle of Silvina's properties: 3215 Avalon Boulevard.

That had to mean something.

Registered to a tenant that didn't exist. *Alexander Humboldt.* Clever, but not clever.

It wasn't that I suddenly became sober. It was that I was exuberantly, profoundly drunk. Maybe because it made me forget about Fusk. Maybe because it felt manageable: checking out an apartment in my hometown.

I felt like I'd won the lottery.

But, really, it was what Silvina wanted me to find.

THE DAMAGE

[35]

I knew the risk in giving myself over to Silvina's mystery. I did, on some level, *know*. But on another level, this drift felt more like depth to me. I wasn't drifting; I was being pulled deeper, and, with each step I took, I learned more, and thought that just around the corner . . . it would end. I would have the answers and, tug of disappointment, life would return to normal.

Knowledge was power, right? That's what Alex liked to say, because he liked to say simple things. But the truth is, I enjoyed the sensation as much as I enjoyed badly lit bars and unfamiliar men, as if losing your balance was a kind of pleasure. That sweet retreat from control and yet you knew someone was in control.

Because Silvina was always there, far ahead of me, even though she was dead. Beckoning me on, and me too stupid, or too smart, not to follow.

As the plane landed and I turned my phone back on, I remember thinking: what world was I returning to? Would this be the time something had happened to make it unrecognizable?

On the familiar route from the airport to the house, the weather had turned warm and humid even though it was winter. In a day or two, it would freeze again. Bees would die in confusion. The plants that had bloomed out of season would fade and decay. Alerts popping up that a pandemic raged in far-distant places.

Almost dusk, but enough of that dark gold, late-afternoon light. Staring once again out the window, observer in my own life, I saw the holding pond around the corner from home. The crosshatched branches of a beaver's lodge, there, where the creek became something human-made.

I hadn't seen it before, the pond or the lodge. Not really. It had registered as dead branches, just something clogging up the system. And maybe this time, too, for the last time. I can't recall if I passed that way again; it wasn't the usual route. But that time or the next, I saw it as a home. As someone's home. Something's home. Right in the middle of our subdivision. And how had that happened? Weren't they supposed to be out *there*, in the parks, in the wilderness? That was the agreement. Not here. Not with us. Beside us.

I think now, so late, too late, of the neighbor's lawn service, using leaf blowers to release herbicide all over their lovely roses. How all of that invisible death didn't disappear into the air. How it coated us, all of us, and that holding pond. How it masked us from ourselves. How it shone through us and we didn't even know it.

Soon, my illness would get worse. I would notice what Silvina had noticed as a young person: how many dead things haunt us in our daily lives.

"As purses, handbags, shoes—even as heads on walls. Or as roadkill, unless it's a fox or something we haven't seen a hundred times before. The mind renders them as setting. But now I saw them everywhere—an ongoing, everyday exhibit of dead animals and their parts. A horror show. A vast extermination of lives and minds."

Does analysis colonize you? Subject matter become the subject. Truth or cult.

As my illness progressed, over time, I would see also the complexity of what we took for granted in our landscapes and hidden lines of connection would attach to me until moving through the world was like being wrapped in chains. But it was the links, the chains, that made you free. Once you saw it all, you could never go back. Everything was alive. Overwhelming. I was overwhelmed eventually. Overcome.

Silvina wrote that even through the poisoned landscape, we must love it. We must love what has been damaged, because everything has been damaged. And to love the damage is to know you care about that world. That you're still alive. That the world is alive.

How did I not see the damage for so long?

[36]

Husband and daughter—glad to see me, in their separate ways. Husband with the long, all-encompassing hug. Daughter with a wave from the kitchen, where she was having breakfast cereal for early dinner, some weird perk of it being a school holiday or a lenient dad. The relatives had left in my absence. The house had a reassuring silence to it. I could find almost no trace of their former presence.

"Held down the fort?" I said.

"Fortress secure," he replied, hands on my shoulders as he regarded me closely, as if looking for contamination. Had I slept with anyone? I felt a pang of guilt. That I could never stop that thought in him.

"Glad to be back," I said.

"Conference good?"

"Boring. I went to bed early both nights." Which was true, as far as it went. Still drunk, trying to hide it with breath mints and a considered precision to my movements.

"Got some good intel?"

That word again, like a trap.

I shrugged, taking off my shoes. "Nothing earth-shattering. The usual." I had Silvina's apartment, 3215 Avalon Boulevard, burning a hole in my head, distracting me. Tomorrow I would investigate. The office wouldn't expect me in right away.

He followed me up to the bedroom, helping me with the suitcase, even though he knew I liked to carry it up the stairs, just to feel it in my calves.

As I was unpacking, he turned to me and said, "Listen, there's something I have to show you." The tone felt urgent, even if I was already on alert.

I stood up from the dresser drawers, from that family heirloom from the farm that smelled of people and places I'd deserted or had deserted me. With, I realized, an almost pathological number of photos of me, my daughter, my husband. To erase it.

"Can it wait until tomorrow?"

"It won't take long. Out in the yard."

"I heard you were thinking about a fence. And doing yardwork or something."

I said it like he'd been thinking about building a hill out of mashed potatoes in our living room. But it's true it was unlike him. For some reason, he had always treated landscaping like bringing his work home with him.

"Yes. To a fence," he said. He wasn't smiling.

There it was, at the fringe, evidence that wasn't a phantom SUV or a sullen Fusk. In that wooded corridor between our house and our neighbor, haunted by the ghosts of garter snakes, rabbits, and deer. It was a quiet place, I'd always thought. Too silent for a wood. No thought for why. Now the stillness deepened.

"See why I brought you?" my husband said.

"I understand," I said. The last of the energy I'd brought from the plane dissipated into the ground. Even if it had been a kind of poison in me. A dizziness in the gathering dusk, some nausea.

A flattened patch of earth, the grass yellowing. Behind a large oak tree. Perfect vantage to surveil the house. A single cigarette butt. A beer bottle, Belgian import, that might not have been related. A couple shoe prints in soft dirt. Deep imprints. Someone was very large or had stood there a long time. A tree branch had been snapped off and shoved into the ground. Boredom? A message?

"Drifter," I said.

"Drifter?" my husband echoed, incredulous. "Did you just say 'drifter' like we're in a fucking western or something? A 'drifter' in suburbia."

He didn't swear at all unless intensely upset.

"When did you notice this?"

"I don't remember—a couple days ago. But from those shoe prints overlapping, he could've come back since."

"Why didn't you call me?"

"Didn't want to bother you." Hands in his pockets, staring at the ground like a kid.

"And yet it bothers you so much I'm on the receiving end of . . . whatever this is."

I let out my breath. I had been threatened with a gun less than twenty-four hours before. No stamina to keep being mindlessly reactive. Which just made me feel even grainier, like I needed a shower.

"Has a homeless man been seen in the neighborhood?"

"No, Jane. This feels more like someone watching us."

"Because of the cigarette butt?" Incredulous.

"You tell me." Resentful.

I relaxed, because I could tell part of the problem from his tone. He'd reverted to an older accusation, one I could accept. That I was the one who knew security, that I should be the one on top of those things just as he was always on top of cooking meals.

"We can extend the security system out here," I said. "It's probably just someone passing through. Some transient spending the night. Or, happy thought: it could be a neighbor whose wife doesn't want him smoking."

I didn't think it was any of those things.

"We're putting in a fence," he said. "I don't care how it looks. You call someone."

Through my fatigue, irritation. He didn't understand my job, that I *managed* security. I wasn't out there in a uniform installing home security systems.

"Could be one of *your* unhappy clients, too, you know," I said.

It just came out. Didn't mean it, except I did. He spent too much time helping a colleague off-load homes in a subdivision plagued with housing code citations. Just because they were old friends.

"Really?" he said. "Really?"

Not really. But we'd never have the real. That was the sadness that came over me in that moment. Struck me—hard— that the distance between us had increased tenfold since I'd left for New York. And it was all my fault.

He stalked off. He'd drop the subject. I'd drop the subject. We would click back into place on the tracks, like it had never happened, a space I could inhabit like an actor. If I wanted to.

Because we had a reservoir of love and goodwill? Because we, like most, were creatures of habit?

I never discovered the answer, because there was also the world beyond us, changing and changing again.

[37]

I met my husband in college. He'd been on the football team, third-string defensive end. More specific: on a bus to the pep rally for a crosstown rivalry that spanned multiple sports. This big, hulking guy with great hair and a wicked smile.

"Hey, Dandelion," he'd said. Absurd. No one had mistaken me for a dandelion even as a kid. But he managed to convey by his tone that he thought I was hot, that I was not a dandelion, but that he wasn't making fun of me.

"Hey, Bear," I said, from within the cocoon of my fellow female athletes. Like we'd known each other for years. "How're things? I haven't seen you in a while."

"You know—the usual," he said. "Was in prison for a while. Then lost a bet. Had to board a bus. To go sit on a bench."

"Bus to lift a bench, Bear. Like always."

"How about you? Did you ever get certified as a psychic?"

"No. Turns out I'm terrible at seeing the future."

"So am I, Dandelion. That's why they got me to play football."

"You'll grow out of it," I said.

"No, I'm done growing. Sick of it. How about you?"

He sat next to me on the way back. He'd lost a sibling, too. I don't know how the subject came up. But it did. Talked about it intensely, in the back of the bus. Talked about it honest. Then rarely if ever talked about it again, all through dating for three years, engagement, and then marriage. Because we didn't have to. He already knew how I was feeling around the date of my brother's death. And I knew how he was feeling.

I didn't have to keep pulling out my insides for him. Explaining any new thing might pull all the stitches out, without warning. Neither of us would ever "get over it." Neither of us would expect the other one to pretend to.

But we were different. His family had gotten it right. His sister's death didn't pull them apart. It brought them closer together. Maybe I kept his family at arm's length because *that* was too painful. Maybe I resented how much time they'd had to say good-bye.

"Hey, Bear."

"Hey, Dandelion."

I never thought anyone would call me Dandelion. I never thought I'd be married, or to a bear. Never thought I'd have a kid. All I had focused on for the longest time was escape. Escape velocity.

We hadn't used those terms of endearment in a long time.

Would it have made a difference if we had?

[38]

I stayed out there by the oak tree for a while. The dead leaves obscured the man's path to the observation site. A sour smell permeating the undergrowth, a kind of sweat smell that registered like sickness. Like my mother's last years. I felt I had smelled it before, but the memory of my mother snuffed it.

I took out my key chain, flicked on my little flashlight, examined the ground in a semicircle out from the oak into the corridor of woods. The faded glow of dusk couldn't quite claim this territory. I already knew you couldn't be seen looking out from behind the oak. But here? I'd never realized how much of a shadow you'd be. You could stand there for hours and no one would ever know you were there. Never disturb you. The line of sight to the street—at a right angle to our house—was negligible. A thicket of high bushes. But once on the street, you'd have to get into a car. Or you'd have to walk four or five blocks to a public park. Either you'd have to look normal, like you belonged, or someone would notice you.

Somehow, I wasn't up for canvassing the neighbors just yet. Not over evidence so flimsy. I had to take it seriously, but how much energy should I put into it?

I came back to the oak. I stood there, behind the tree, and stared at my house. Tried to see it as an intruder might. A generic, usual house for an upper-middle-class family. A comfortable swing my daughter had used when she was younger, hanging off a far branch of the oak. A garden hose attached to a sprinkler. A nub of a deck with some molding plastic lawn furniture. That umbrella stand we rarely used.

Ah, Silvina, it was everything and it was nothing.

How the swing and the old tire in the yard became reduced to the stilted, broken shapes of skeletal animals as the dark leaked in. How the lights of the house made mockery of the curtains, so silhouettes came clear, like a shadow puppet play. There, on the second floor, even now: my bear husband in his study, pacing, still angry. There, my daughter's room, and her sitting upright receiving the bright blue glow of her phone screen. The first floor: dull rectangles in which could be seen the kitchen table, the living room couch.

What would you learn about me while I wasn't home? It wasn't that cold, but I shivered. What was a watcher but a warning? Forget a deep character study. He wasn't out there taking notes on habits, personalities.

But I struggled to visualize what he *had* been doing. What information was being pushed toward? Why was it important to have eyes on my house in this age of electronic surveillance? Visual verification? Of what?

Still grasping, gasping, vaguely drunk. I wanted an enemy I could grapple with, draw close, choke out.

I didn't want to acknowledge that Langer might've been in my backyard. That might've taken me the rest of the way from defiant to scared.

The little bird drone watched me from a branch halfway up the oak. Noticing that came as a shock. My husband had been told it was security provided by the HOA. Later, I would ask to see the surveillance footage, be told a glitch had erased it. Meanwhile, it just sat there, a dull pewter jewel with blue plastic wings. Staring at me. Sharing in the mystery.

Imagine you're all alone and out of nowhere someone starts talking to you. It might be from the past. It might be through a cigarette butt and a beer bottle, or a drone . . . or by aiming a gun at you.

But, no matter how, you're receiving and you can't stop receiving. Even when it becomes damage. Maybe you're used to damage. Maybe the damage is what lures you in.

[39]

Routine would save us, my bear husband and his dandelion wife. Say good night to our daughter, bound by that love shining down from us into her. Our shared half-smiles at how she shrugged out of it, turned away, but still acknowledged and shared in it. How we looked at the posters of pop groups on her walls and the microscope on her desk and the old Girl Scout badges pinned to a corkboard. How we saw her four pairs of sneakers, but also how she didn't waste time on jewelry or "accessories." How she did sometimes use her phone under the covers after lights out, but the strict curfew she gave herself of an hour. So that by midnight she was safely asleep and away from a screen.

That she set her own routine even if sometimes her discipline lapsed in other areas. We knew when to pick her up from after-school events because she presented us with a weekly schedule. An art class. Chorus. Debate. How she could also be aloof and remote, and I would wonder where she was off in her thoughts and if I should worry. How she could be gruff in her demands: that she didn't want to take the bus to a debate meet, wanted us to drive her, which was her way of saying she wanted us to be there. Then ignored us the whole time.

By these coordinates, we had set our lives.

By the coordinates, too, of my husband making the rounds of the downstairs, turning off lights, coming up to where I was already in bed with a book. His noisy ritual of brushing his teeth, putting on pajamas if it was cold. Of coming around to my side to give me a hug and then, ponderous, back to his side. And maybe we would cuddle later, but it was also okay to just be comfortable with another breathing, snoring human being.

All of these things happened as always the night I returned home from the conference. I could tell from the preciseness with which my husband went through the usual list that he meant to reassure me after our argument. So when he got into bed, I put my hand on his, reached over and kissed him, went back to my book.

It felt like it was going to be okay. Like I had kept my normal, everyday life. I remember I let out a deep breath and breathed in and was surprised by the surge of oxygen. Hadn't realized I'd been holding my breath, breathing shallow, waiting for the next surprise.

I'd run out of Silvina intel to read but couldn't pick up the mystery novel I'd started before I'd left. I needed to feel like I was making progress. On the hummingbird. On Silvina. So I was reading *Oddly Enough: From Animal Land to Furtown*.

Strange that a book come into my possession by chance, bought to bribe, laid bare so much. But it did. The introduction gave me such pause, I read through it twice, then skipped to the illustrations and skimmed while I pondered it.

"Let it not seem queer to see us dressed alike, humans and animals. It does not appear queer when the genius of your fur science transforms us to look alike despite the different origins of our families. As representatives, part of our mission shall be to applaud that genius."

Those words written by an Arthur Samet in the 1930s. There was no part of it I didn't recoil from and yet nothing in it existed far from my father's attitude making a living on the farm. This was just the extremist version—the one in which the animals enjoyed their slaughter. But no matter the complicity, we had slaughtered animals, too, for market. Not for decoration or fashion. And trappers had killed animals, often in cruel ways, for coats and other necessities in that often cold climate. So what, exactly, repulsed me?

"We praise your modern machinery and your art which converts our raw greasy skins into attractive fur pelts and thus

preserves us for a lasting existence in our second being. We ad-
mire your artistic design when you cut, sew and nail our skins to fit
the patterns designed to meet the demands of modern fashions."

Worse things than cattle led to market. Worse things than
being reduced to a piece of taxidermy. But how much worse and
why? Did the amount of suffering matter? Did wild or domes-
ticated matter? We interfered with all, left nothing alone, as
Silvina said. We could not leave anything untouched. And, for
some, the compulsion grew not to simply do the deed, as my
father did, but to be heroic for it. There, with the suffering, lay
a further crime.

"For those of you who intimately understand us will be able
to recognize us regardless of change of shape or color. However, to
those who are not thoroughly acquainted with us, the parts we
play in this story shall feature our distinguishing characteristics,
that will immediately identify us in any disguise . . . This is Our
Inalienable Right."

How did the wildlife trafficking cartels justify it? I hardly
thought they cared. But someone must, along the way. That a
family would starve if not for a dead pangolin? That if not me,
then *someone else* will do it. This is the way of the world.

Or, better: this is progress. The *new thing* murdered, wan-
ton and alone, gifted with credentials not yet earned.

An old bookmark advertising Carlton Fusk's antiques store
fell out while I was reading. I snatched it up, placed it safely back
between two pages. But my husband hardly noticed. Me and
eccentric books had happened before; I liked to read out-of-date
cybersecurity manuals. I found them comforting.

The bookmark had a black-and-white photo of Fusk, much
younger, beardless, but recognizable. Fusk proudly held a taxidermied armadillo. The legend read "If it's dead, we can fix it."
Even after death, we couldn't leave anything alone.

Fusk. The gun. Just an old eccentric who didn't want to be
questioned? Or something more? Hard to tell what was more
unlikely: Fusk reaching for a gun so quickly on impulse or

because the photo of the hummingbird had triggered that response. I began to feel the impulse to contact him again, across the safety of a continent.

I lay awake long after we'd turned out the lights, thinking about Fusk. Thinking about Silvina and her family. Unsure what part of the puzzle ate at me the most. The moon was bright that night, and I rose to stare out the bedroom window down into the wooded fringe. Which was veiled by shadow. When I began to imagine I could make out the singed tiny red circle of a cigarette, I went back to bed.

I dreamed not of hummingbirds that night, but of salamanders. Giant salamanders and flooded rivers and the slack face of my brother, staring at me, half caked in mud.

[40]

The next morning, headed for the 3215 address, I rechecked my car first. For surveillance devices. Found nothing. Hoped I had done the check right. There had been a lecture on current procedure at the conference, but I'd skipped it. I laughed and hit the steering wheel as I drove. Realized I couldn't be sure I hadn't done my check based on what I'd seen on TV shows.

The apartment complex was an anonymous block of concrete painted a pale blue. Staggered concrete balconies jutted out at irregular angles like gun emplacements, up the full five stories. The balconies cast shadows on the dull gravel path leading to a covered garage in the basement. A few scraggly decorative trees didn't seem up to the task. Stink of asphalt from something new around the corner. The established neighborhood beyond had been subdivided to hell and back, most of the trees cut down.

I parked down the street, up the hill from the apartments. Thankful the address wasn't in a gated community. Yet. The walk down to the apartments, I felt exposed, observed, but no one was around. It was midmorning. I should've been at work. But everyone else was.

My husband texted, the sound startling, shrill.

>>*The office called. Urgent. Asking where you are. Something's urgent there. Where are you?* Something was always urgent. Something that could always wait.

>>*I'm on my way,* I lied, and turned off my phone.

Silvina's property lay on the third floor, hidden from the street by a covered walkway beyond the stairs. The gate to the garage had a hitch, so it didn't close right away after a car went through. But the stairs, although more open, made me feel less like a thief. Just a visitor.

The blue door made me rethink what I was doing. Of course there was a locked door. What did I think would be there? An open archway? A welcoming committee? Some refreshments?

Because: what was I doing? I'd have to break in.

Fusk pulling the gun on me. Fusk telling me to leave well enough alone.

No.

I broke in. The method isn't important. I've done it since. Several times. Each time it feels less like crossing a boundary or a border. Each time, there's less resistance.

Inside, I tried to think like a detective, to *be* a detective. Trusted my first thought inhabiting that: everything I'm seeing has been staged. Just like in the storage unit. Maybe because there was so little of it. Hardwood floors, rich grain, and tiny pillbox windows, and the sliding glass doors to the balcony at the far end, and, before that, a living room with a fake fireplace and an open-concept kitchen, with the office and bedroom down a corridor to the left, beyond the balcony.

It struck me that if Silvina had lived here, or visited, she must have hated it. She must have loathed this place. Even if there had once been more here. Even if she'd found some way to make it resemble a cave. But she *had* lived here . . . why?

The blazing-white kitchen island eclipsed most of the rest.

The off-white walls faded into the backdrop. A coffee table in the living room and a couple more chairs. Generic landscape paintings on the wall. The smell wasn't new apartment or old apartment, but stripped apartment.

Over the fireplace, perched precarious on the mantel: three foxes, fur tattered and mangy. Old taxidermy, with clipped fiberglass paws. A male, female, and kit. Whoever or whatever they had fallen afoul of, death had come long ago. The male had a dusty bluish tint to his coat from overapplication of chemicals.

They had no eyes.

Did that mean someone had gotten to a clue before me?

My blood pressure had risen. I had expected, I guess, more evidence of a secret life. Some comfort in the mundane. Books, magazines, a better sense of her.

Instead: cautious, precise. Why had I expected the disorganized mind of a hoarder anyway? Because my mother had lived that way, and that's what the past meant to me. An accumulation of crap.

But I was already there. I would search among the non-wreckage to glean any possible clue. I put down Shovel Pig and got to work. I checked behind every painting. Nothing. I went through the few cabinets and drawers, entered a bedroom stripped down to the mattress.

No one and nothing lurking in the closet.

I came back into the common space, feeling an urgency. I picked up the foxes and rattled them. Solid. And still I was shameful, disrespectful, in my desperation to be thorough but to finish fast. I treated those bodies like objects. I tore the first two foxes apart, just in case. Massacred them again. Nothing. Nothing in them.

The third, the kit, remained in position on the mantel. I hadn't been able to bring myself to tear it apart, too. There was in its scruffy decay a kind of ancient, vulnerable quality combined with youth that overwhelmed me.

Something about the empty eye sockets got to me. And I saw.

Three sets . .   . .   . . from Silvina's note . . . and three foxes. It could be. It could not be.

Where did they stare? Where did the last one stare?

The balcony and a dead houseplant in a large ceramic container, flanked by faded falling-apart lawn chairs.

I slid the door open, went out on the balcony. The "railing" came up to my waist and was made of thick concrete. I didn't think I could be seen from the other apartments. No building taller nearby. Just a gridlocked grid stretching, stitched, farther down the hill.

The planter was enormous, the plant housed by it ridiculously small and dead, the soil dry, almost like sand. Even for me it was an effort to lift the planter, make sure nothing was hidden in the saucer beneath. An awkward, unwieldy weight, like trying to lift a concrete ball in a strongman competition.

I put it down again, dug with my bare hands through the porous soil. I had hoped to leave no trace, but that wasn't possible. I could discard the remains of the foxes, but there was dirt everywhere. My fingernails were caked with evidence of my own crime. I was a mad gardener, searching for roots. I don't know what I was.

My hands in the dirt felt real. As if I could've just done that for an hour, as therapy. But then I encountered something. Way deep down.

With difficulty, I brought the object to the surface. A small black journal, hardback, protected in its own clear plastic case.

A sound came from the street below, carried by the wind. Like a sharp cough. Just that. I froze. Maybe I was wrong, but I felt like I had no more time. Cleaned nothing up—what was the point, I'd been a disruptive mole—ran to the front door. Then realized I was disheveled, covered in dirt, and had left Shovel Pig on the coffee table. Next to the ripped-up foxes.

I stuck the journal in my waistband, on the side. Tried to

get clean in the bathroom, gathered my belongings, put the poor foxes in the bedroom closet.

Ran down the stairs. Only slowed to a walk out on the street. I didn't think anyone was following me as I headed into the office.

Something nagged at me. Something I'd forgotten to check in the apartment, but it eluded me.

As if I'd failed. That there had been something else I was supposed to find.

[41]

Larry had been the victim of a hit-and-run in the parking garage the night before. For once, he'd been working late. Details were sparse. It had happened in a corner not covered by a surveillance camera or the camera had been broken. The irony. He'd been seen arguing with someone right before. A parking attendant had called an ambulance, and, in the confusion, no one at the office had known about it until the morning.

Larry, in the hospital, with broken ribs and broken collarbone and a broken arm. Larry, not yet conscious, but his wife said his phone and wallet had been taken. The car ransacked after he was hit. "Cold-blooded," is how Alex put it. Alex had already been to the hospital, as had some of the rest of the staff. Allie was ashen. I didn't have to apologize to anyone for coming in late. No one cared.

I made supportive, sympathetic noises. I chipped in as a cup went around for money for flowers and a card. I said I'd visit later that day. But I wouldn't. I kept thinking of the watcher in the yard. Larry wouldn't be answering questions for a while. If I was right, Larry would just be . . . bait. As I tried to see things from the point of view of a private eye. Which meant, be paranoid. Which meant shoving aside the uncomfortable idea that

I was complicit in Larry's condition. Ironically, this wasn't the first lapse in garage security. I could be wrong.

I owed Alex and the other managers a conference report, but I was too on edge. I loaded up on coffee, as if I thought that would help. I kept typing the same sentence over and over again. "The conference focus on new protocols designed to thwart third-party service attacks . . ."

Silvina's diary burned a hole in Shovel Pig. In my mind.

"The conference focus on new protocols designed to thwart third-party service attacks revealed a flaw in overall security thinking . . ." Trying to find ways to shove references to Vilcapampa companies in there. As much to forestall Allie as Alex.

I wanted to quit, go home, have time to think.

"Opportunities for business partnerships include a shift toward examining the changed psychology of human security risks due to personal isolation and working from remote locations. The conference's partial focus on new protocols designed to accommodate concerns about zoonotic viruses reveals a flaw in overall security thinking due to the assumption that . . ."

But I couldn't. Couldn't go home. Couldn't stay in the office. Uncomfortable and itchy in my own skin. Allie kept coming in to talk about Larry, which made me twitch and wince, until I point-blank told her I had to concentrate on my report. Only to watch her face go cold. "I understand." No, she didn't understand. But I didn't understand her, either.

Alex came by to share new office protocols, in light of the approaching pandemic. I listened with half an ear. When he asked me if I was okay, I said sure, even got to the gym. Everything's fine. Be calm, Alex. Be still, Alex. Be gone, Alex.

I closed my door. I closed the blinds. Like a flag at half-mast, for Larry. Even then, I put Silvina's journal in a folder to disguise it as a client file. Began to skim and sample it. But I was too shaken to even do that right. I got bits, pieces, kept missing things and starting over. Allie, undaunted, would knock and bring me documents piecemeal to sign for expense reimbursements. A coordinated attack to punish me for not caring more about Larry?

But some things came clear to me, even then. One was the full extent to which Silvina experienced the human world as a torment and a kind of siege upon her senses. Right there in the journal, head-on, she addressed that moment of change as a child. That fundamental *shift*.

"I woke up one night to the sounds of traffic on the street below. I woke to the light through my window. And the sound never turned off. The light never turned off. They just intensified. Ever after. No matter where I was. And if I sought sanctuary in wild places, it was selfish at first. Because I couldn't tolerate life elsewhere."

How she said her father's friends tormented her for her "weaknesses." In how they talked. How they looked at her. The way they would go out trophy hunting at one of her father's lodges, in whatever country, and bring back the heads. How the heads piled up in their palatial homes in Miami, in Buenos Aires, and, finally, on the West Coast.

"I remember as a child walking down a hallway from my bedroom to get a glass of water and all those faces were looking down at me. A gauntlet of death in the shadows. If I'm dramatic, it's because I had nightmares from that. I didn't want to forget what that meant. Who it meant something to and who it didn't. In the daylight, everyone walked past these tombstones as if it was nothing."

How her father had the idea that she would grow up to be a model U.S. citizen, almost as if he planned to use her to legalize the less savory of his operations. How he would tell her that she, as the eldest, would be his heir, and then he would undermine that idea because she wasn't a son. How his favor fell to a younger son, and then also to Silvina's younger sisters. And no way to tell exactly what came first: Silvina's radicalization or that repudiation. How she had reported her father's "collector" friends to the police. At age thirteen. And as she entered adolescence, her father sent her on a tour of the places where he owned property, always absent himself. So that she went to school the way an army brat does: knowing she would be somewhere else the next month or semester.

"The first thing to realize is that you are all alone and you can rely only on yourself," she wrote. *"And if you can realize this is a good thing, not a frightening thing . . . that is a miracle."*

I couldn't imagine it, that state of being. Not without curing yourself of a fear of death first.

"There's no one they won't kill in time because you don't matter to them," Silvina had written in the margin, and I began to realize I was reading a composite, a hybrid: a journal, or diary, that had begun to be transformed into a memoir.

Also in the margins: hastily drawn diagrams. That resembled homemade bombs. What she'd been accused of. What she'd escaped going to jail for.

I stopped reading when I reached the diagrams.

Here was a woman who had idly drawn bombs in the margins of her notebook. Absentmindedly. Daydreaming. Accompanying an account of traveling in disguise by train at the age of twenty-one. The expedition to Quito. Her repatriation to her home continent. A state of mind.

As she tried to acclimate herself to a country where she'd never lived. As she set her compass by Humboldt, the European naturalist who had done so much good, but also had electrocuted four thousand frogs in the name of science.

I stared at those sketches a long time. Trying to imagine the reality or fantasy of them. But I saw nothing real there. Just a terrible sense of dread, such stress, that I could not live beneath the weight of it. The weight of her journal.

I read more, but my heart wasn't in it. I kept hoping it was misdirection. You're drawn to the visual, but maybe that was the least important part.

There was a monkey with a broken leg in the jungle outside of Quito. Javier, a guide, wanted to put it down, but she had them catch it. Make the monkey a splint, put it in a cage to recover. It's frightened in the cage. I don't know if she ever set it free or where. She never mentioned the monkey again.

On that same Quito expedition she had encountered the naiad hummingbird. Or had sought it out. Or had found them for sale in a local market as love charms, dead and dried out. I was reading too fast. As if I would find some key or some clue that would leap off the page to help me.

Allie barged in again. I closed the file, set it on my desk. Frustrated anyway by my lack of focus, or perhaps what I began to see as Silvina's lack of focus. Or a straight answer.

"Just one more," Allie said, with no apology in her voice. The sheet for the bar drinks with "Jack," which had to be filed separately as "Meeting with potential client." I'd made up a last name. "Fusk." Jack Fusk. No one ever checked. Just like no one ever cared about Larry taking clients to strip clubs.

But "hummingbird" had jogged loose another fear. Something about the torn-out eyes of the foxes.

Was the hummingbird still in my gym locker?

[42]

I parked up the hill from the gym, on a side street, then walked down to the strip mall. I didn't think I'd been followed, but I wanted some distance from my destination. I wanted to get the lay of the land from up high. A short walk, but a long one in terms of how at the top of the hill lay the rich neighborhoods. Then a strip of scruffy forest, hidden by a tall, wooden slat fence, that no one had developed yet, and then the parking lot.

Outside was a guy I knew vaguely, eating a burrito from the fast-food place down the street and smoking a cigarette. I knew he'd spend a half hour lifting heavy weights or working the tired heavy bag over in the farthest dark corner. Oddly comforting to see him.

But inside, all that evaporated.

One look at Charlie's face and I knew.

"Your locker was broken into," he said, in a flat tone.

"You didn't call me?"

I hurried over to the lockers, saw the broken lock, dangling. Everything was still there. Except the hummingbird. I'd known this could happen. I'd tried to steel myself to the possibility. But the absence was stark.

My locker wasn't the only victim. They'd gone down the line, busting off the locks. Saving Charlie a major repair bill: only a couple dozen people bothered to use locks.

"When did it happen?"

"I don't know. They jimmied the door in the night. I came in, stuff was all over the place. I just finished cleaning up."

"Do you have surveillance footage?"

The look Charlie gave me was incredulous. A lot of people used that gym because Charlie said he didn't use cameras.

"Here's the license number of that SUV I saw hanging around. Someone else saw it again yesterday." He handed me a scrap of paper.

"Thank you, Charlie!"

But I should've realized he wasn't looking at me in a friendly way. Or I wouldn't have said what I said next.

"Do you know people who could hide something for me?" I was thinking of the journal in my purse.

"Know people? Know *what* people?" With scorn. "No. Get the hell out. Take your bag of junk with you."

I straightened up. I was one step behind what was happening. Again. The panic returned. Hard to doubt his tone. Something about the contempt for my go-bag hit harder. Like he'd always been judging me.

"Charlie—"

"You leave *now* and you don't come back here. For a good

long time. I don't want any part of what this is. Remember—I *told* you someone was following you."

A gut punch. But it made me mad, too. Reflexive. Like, I didn't understand the old world was receding from me.

"No, I'm not going to do that. I've been a member of this gym for—"

"Leave or I'll call the cops," he said. "Trespassing."

"What the fuck, Charlie!" Call the cops . . . on the one who'd been robbed. Unfair. Like I was playing a role where I was the innocent.

"Cops or get the fuck out!"

I knew he'd do it. The expression on his face told me. The set of his body, like he wanted to punch me. And that's when I knew for sure Charlie owned the place. And it was all he had.

"Can I come back when—"

"Get the fuck out."

So I got the fuck out.

[43]

Halfway back up the hill, I realized someone had followed me from the gym. A glimpse back revealed a bulky man in a suit. Shitty haircut for dull brown hair, washed-out features. Very wide shoulders. Maybe fifty and a powerful build, only a bit gone to fat. Laboring on the incline. Built for a different kind of labor.

Quickened my pace, determined to get to my car, then slowed again. What if someone else was waiting at the car? Then fast-walked again. I had no choice. There was no one on the street, just a few cars passing by. I'd reached the part with the fence and the small woods. I got ready to use my phone to call the police. Hesitated. Realized just how complicit I was in . . . something. I'd broken into an apartment. For example.

I looked back, and the guy had gained on me. A kind of determined calm look on his hangdog face that irritated me. Like I was just all in a day's work. Like, this woman isn't going to be a problem. I couldn't tell if he was just trying to shadow me in his clumsy way or catch up.

I slowed again and could feel a kind of calm come over me. Something about the anonymous nature of it all. Something about still being in the dark. About having Silvina's journal to defend. How I told myself this was probably the guy who had taken the hummingbird. How I felt that loss like the hummingbird had been alive. Grave-robbing after the grave had already been robbed once.

Slowed still more. I could hear his heavy tread now. What if he had a gun?

But I was angry. A kind of rage building up and spilling over. Too much of this skulking around. Too much of it. The guy watching the house. Fusk with his threats. Larry in the hospital and me unable to connect the dots, recognize the significance. I was bigger than the man following me. I was more dangerous. Why should I be the one to run? Why bother? It was tiring. It was a role that wasn't me. Just something people thought I should be.

I stopped, pretended to dig around in my purse, as the man approached. Twenty feet, ten feet. I didn't look up. I don't know if I imagined him lunging at me or he'd just arrived in my space. But I hit him with my purse anyway. I hauled off and "went for the country mile," as Dad would've said.

Shovel Pig, full force, smashed into his face, and he staggered back, holding his head with both hands, bent over. I rushed him, pulled his head forward and down with my hands behind his head . . . while I brought my knee up into his chin.

That made a sound. I even felt it in my knee. When I hit a person, they don't forget it. I don't know any other way.

He dropped to the sidewalk, rolled over, tried to get up. I

kicked him in the chest, and he came to rest against the wooden fence, which buckled but held.

"Who the hell are you?" I screamed in his face. "And why the fuck are you following me?"

I had my pepper spray out and was threatening him with it. Which felt like anticlimax. But I don't think he knew what was happening yet. He looked around, in his rumpled suit, like someone was going to stop and save him. But it was quiet. Or no one wanted the trouble. Or the neighbors were used to this kind of trouble.

I repeated my question.

He looked up at me through a bloody eye. A trickle of blood from a split lip. His left eye already had a black circle around it.

"Stop looking for Silvina," he said. Local muscle? He had an accent like he'd grown up here. "Stop looking for Silvina. Or you'll pay." He had a good chin to be so coherent already.

I lunged like I was going to kick him again, and it felt good when he flinched, held up his hands. It was like being back in the wrestling ring. Me circling an opponent, looking for the opening. Them already down, at a disadvantage.

"How about this," I said. "You stop following me. You stop threatening me. And you stop stealing things from me."

Was that surprise in his eyes? Like one of those things I'd accused him of something he hadn't done?

"You won't like what's going to happen if you don't stop," he said, already readying himself for another assault. His gaze unfocused.

But my anger was banking. More cars were driving down the street. I saw someone looking up at us from around the corner of the parking lot down below. A distant siren that probably had nothing to do with us.

"Leave me alone," I said. "Or I'll go to the police. Now, get out of here."

I held Shovel Pig and my go-bag in one hand and the pepper spray in the other.

With difficulty, without another word, the man got up and staggered back down the hill, down the sidewalk. I'd torn his suit in the back. The white shirt beneath protruded like the inside of a stuffed animal.

My heartbeat was going to overwhelm me, so I steadied myself. Slowed myself down. Took some deep breaths. Watched the man disappear around the corner into the parking lot.

I started back toward my car, up the hill.

That's when I heard it. The sound of someone on the other side of the fence. Someone shadowing me. I stopped walking. They stopped walking. I started up again, they started again. I kept walking. Stopping again would be a tell. I was shaky, not ready for more.

Maybe just a concerned neighbor? How long had he been there? Every instinct told me it was a man.

I kept walking. The car would be close. I could sprint to it if I needed to. I could unlock the door fast, could get behind the wheel fast. Remember to lock the door as soon as I was in.

But then, the sinister thing. The thing that truly unnerved me.

I could tell that a *second* person had joined the first. I heard a scuff of shoe, an intake of breath, a strangled choke.

I stopped. Frozen. Looking at the fence slats as if willing myself to see beyond them.

A weight fell to the ground. Like a body. It had to be a body.

Someone lit a match. Someone stood there, breathing.

And as I stood there, I smelled cigarette smoke. A thin spiral curled up above the line of the fence. I had a sense of a darkness, of a presence that was chilling in its silence. Its precision.

Fuck. I was immobilized like prey.

What had I gotten myself into?

I wrenched myself out of my fear. Whatever got me moving. Not just pinned there.

I made for my car, all discipline gone, Shovel Pig smacking

into my side. Shambolic. In sheer, instinctual panic. I ran. I ran and did not look back and I got into my car and I shoved the key in the ignition and I roared out of there without my seat belt on.

The calm, even breathing of the person I couldn't see. The spiral of smoke. The firm, even tread. The sense of bleakness, of darkness, and the sound of the shoes or dress boots against gravel and dirt. A body at his feet.

It didn't seem credible that the man I'd beaten up had anything to do with that specter, haunting me, invisible, from the other side of the fence.

But what did I know?

Nothing.

[44]

Much of Silvina's journal described an epic journey down the West Coast. According to her account, she'd started at the border with Canada and gone as far south as Northern California. This was in the third year of her banishment after the trial. I would've been thirty-three at the time: oblivious, still learning the ropes at the company, not yet a manager.

I reread the story of her "expedition" over and over. Not just because it had been important to her. But because it was odd to see the familiar through her eyes and to realize how familiar it had been to her. That Quito had been where she had felt strange. That Argentina had meant little to her. And, after her trial, even less.

"For the first time, I felt, in a way, as if I was home," Silvina wrote. "In those endless miles of coast, in the cold and the fog and the rain, I opened up what was closed down. I received and kept receiving. It was sunless. Bridges would appear monstrous out of endless shadow, almost brutalist. The smell of marsh water would hit unexpected and the richness of cedar.

The hawks on the telephone wires felt like sentinels judging my progress.

"I would drive until I found a wilderness trail—through hills or along the coast. I loved lighthouses because they were always somewhere isolated. I didn't like to see lots of people when driving. How can we pretend we are alone, but I wanted to pretend I was alone. Until I wasn't.

"I saw deer and otters, a bobcat or two, and, once, a bear, in the distance. Just a smudge, a shadow. But that was enough. While in the trees, as I walked, so many birds, and under rocks and fallen branches a world of the small that carried on beneath our notice.

"I fell in with strangers sometimes. I could tell by the look in someone's eye when they said hello whether they approved or disapproved of me. But I spent time with the disapprovers, as much as the other, because I was curious. And sometimes, around a campfire, they would soften. Others, never lose a rigid, guarded pose, and I would make excuses soon enough."

She would stay in cheap motels and befriend strangers in bars and diners. Once, she stayed in a houseboat along a river delta for a month or two. A few times the folks she befriended in bars she would go home with. She described them, as above, with a miraculous miscomprehension. As if they were miracles, because most of the time she was out in the wilderness. As if, over time, she didn't know what a human really was.

"I wasn't searching for anything, and yet still I found it. I found a place to work and to live and to be at peace. A place to sever myself from the past and not to seek it out anymore. If I could exist only in the present, then my problems would be gone. Or would only ever be in front of me.

"I saw the naiad hummingbird at elevation, in the middle of the King Range, and I don't think anyone was within one hundred miles. This was the off-season, cold and blustery, and I wasn't really prepared, so I felt the chill too much and lost weight. But I was happy. The more my body reduced itself, the more my mind seemed to expand. The more I could experience what was around me. I did not bathe. I did not shower. I walked until I was tired and then tried to sleep inside my sleeping bag inside a tent. The food tasted like nothing to me.

"By the tenth day, animals did not appear to see me. I could walk by a deer and it wouldn't run. The otters playing by the creek gave me a first and second look, then continued with their day. Or so it seemed to me.

"Yes, on the twelfth day, I saw the hummingbird. Coming across it with the overwhelming scent of cedar all around and the mountainside rich green with moss and lichen, and the trees, full of lichen, too, and ferns, so their leafless limbs burgeoned with life.

"I turned a bend to see a puddle or a pond, something caused by rainwater, in the middle of the trail, and bent down over the water, to drink . . . the naiad hummingbird. A female. The iridescent black wings. Her sharp, long, thin beak.

"She didn't see me at first, her back to me, and I stood and watched as she stood there so defenseless, on the ground, drinking. Until with a little cry she sensed me and, alarmed, rose effortless and acrobatic straight up into the air and cursed me from above, hidden soon by the cedar.

"I hadn't eaten all day. I had drunk very little water. I felt light as air, and in the moment of seeing the hummingbird, I began to weep with the beauty of it, which I cannot convey. I cannot get across to you or anyone the emotion of that moment. Because of the hummingbird on the ground, not in flight, and knowing that not one person in a million had experienced the miracle of such a small moment.

"So you can imagine how I felt when, later, I identified the bird and realized how rare the species was and headed toward extinction, and what I had borne witness to wasn't just a minor miracle but, in fact, a moment that would replicate only another hundred or another thousand times.

"That in the history of the world, a naiad hummingbird

would only come to the ground to drink a finite number of times before they no longer existed.

"This thought was unconscionable to me. Unbearable. It ripped me in two. It destroyed me. And then remade me, and I became someone different than before."

Just reading it on the page destroyed me. Remade Jane. I was already in the grip of such exhausting emotions and impulses. Yet I let Silvina in again when I had resolved not to.

Because I had let the hummingbird in first.

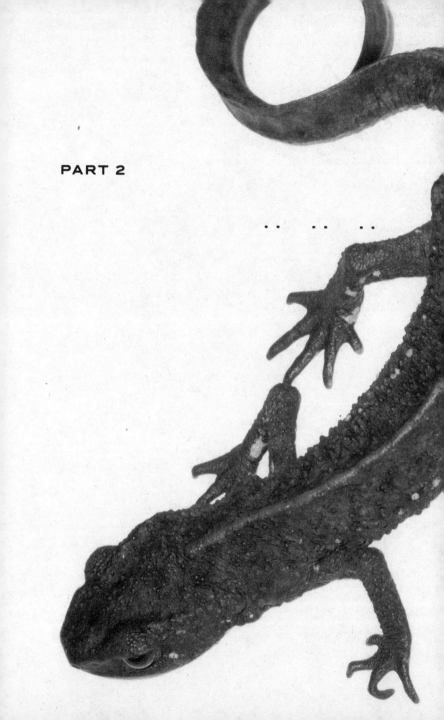

PART 2

THE TANGLE

[45]

I try, in these moments now of anticipation, of the possibility of the ecstatic . . . I try to recall the framework by which I made decisions after the encounter on the hill. It seems so far away from me and constantly receding.

Scared, angry, wanting to punch a wall for the hazy nature of the enemy. Wanting out, but not knowing what "out" was, and, perversely, not wanting to abandon Silvina. Underneath it all, too, an elation at flexing muscle, at knowing I was built like a truck and could defend myself. As if the idea of me as analyst was a kind of disguise or deep cover or adaptation, and the true me was shining through.

But that was a trap, too.

How in your altered state you miss details, even when you think you're calm. The world around you becomes a kind of blur. You turn off the radio because it distracts from the chaos in your head, only you thought it was the chaos in your head and with silence, you're still adrift. Spinning.

How you realize you're hyperventilating when you hit the first stoplight and you stare in the rearview mirror and notice there's a black SUV right behind you. Except there's a soccer mom type in the front seat and two kids in the back giving her hell.

But that jogged something loose. The scrap of paper

Charlie had given me had slipped my mind in the aftermath of the hill encounter. I took it out and, with one eye on traffic, looked up the vehicle license number.

It took so little time. Registered to a shell company, Offshore Shithead Corporation. A sigh of frustration, smacked my hand against the steering wheel. Trying to unravel that to a source probably would be pointless. Allie might've had the time and patience, but not me.

Fuck it. I pulled into a pharmacy parking lot, across two lanes of traffic. Ignored the honking. Ignored the pissed-off looks. At least no one followed me across.

There was only one direct lead. Even if it came with a threat.

I called Fusk at his antiques store. End of the day for him. Early afternoon for me. What else could I do?

Idling there as if I were a meth addict screwing up the nerve to go in and buy Sudafed. The Christmas decorations at the entrance were garish, incomprehensible, partisan. What kind of a country did we live in?

Fusk answered on the fourth or fifth ring. But said nothing.

"Fusk. It's Jane, the detective."

"Can't help you," came the rough rasp.

Hung up.

I looked at the phone. Recalled the photo of his wife and two kids right before he'd pulled the gun on me. Estranged or not, I had to think he was protecting them, not himself. Or mostly them. Which didn't mean he couldn't still be the villain.

I wondered if Fusk had actually read *Furtown*, with its psychosis and its warnings.

"For reasons man may never fathom, the raccoon is lured by shiny metal. When the trapper learned of this weakness, he ingeniously set his traps with bright metal. The moon ray appears to brighten the silvery tinfoil image in the crystal stream. Soon, the racoon appears and is attracted by the glint and steps into the

trap, to be held prisoner until the trapper appears with his final death sentence."

I called again. Different phone card. Still disguised, if someone tried to track it. The phone rang for a long time. Nothing. No one. Gone for the day or suspicious?

I cursed. Didn't want to go home without having talked to him.

>>*If you haven't picked up groceries, I will.*

Helpful husband. I looked at that ordinary text like it came from Mars.

There was an earlier text I'd missed.

>>*Will need help with homework tonight.*

Raised eyebrow. When had my daughter ever asked for school help from me? Never. That felt like a trap, too.

Not thinking straight. I was still missing details. Fusk could wait. I needed calm. I needed to go home.

Only then did I recognize that my hands were shaking.

[46]

But I had another problem: the go-bag. I didn't want to leave it in the trunk of the car. That felt like mixing sanctuaries or solutions. It needed to be separate—the whole reason I'd stored it at the gym.

A couple of Silvina's other properties I'd already looked into at the start of my research seemed promising. One was basically an abandoned shack, a twenty-minute drive away. On the edge of an environmental easement. Maybe it wasn't the clearest thinking, but I needed to stash my stuff somewhere.

The detour made me even jumpier, so I took a bigger risk. About ten minutes from the shed, I found a fringe of tall weeds abutting a few conifers. I pulled over, waited until there was no traffic, and I took every electronic device out of Shovel Pig, put them in a smaller purse, and shoved it among the weeds, out of sight. Then I rechecked my car for tracking devices. It was an older model, which I was thankful for. I didn't think it'd be easy to track from an internal GPS.

Then I went on to the property. The shed, more like a tiny house, had a fallen-in, slanted roof and a lock on the ramshackle door. Someone a long time ago had painted it jaunty bright reds, greens, and blues, as if to contrast with the yellowing grass.

Around back, a rusty shopping cart and just as I'd relaxed— the loud sound of a body, a crack.

I turned, fast, in time to see a raccoon run off. There had been reports of Japanese raccoon dogs roaming the area, escapees from a zoo. But, no, this was just the usual. As I watched, the raccoon slowed, stopped, watched me from the long grass. Funny. I couldn't meet its gaze. Not while breaking into the shed. *Furtown*'s atrocities against raccoons had been hardwired into my head.

How many of these run-down properties did Vilcapampa companies own? Too many, but maybe if you had that much capital, the small stuff became forgotten. Best way to live off the grid: in the amnesia zone of large corporations. Until the day they woke up and routed you with dogs or drones.

I doubted Silvina shared much history with the place. Maybe she'd known the racoon's grandparents. I scouted enough to confirm it was abandoned, used a cracked window to get in the back door, felt the smell and texture of abandoned, old, not-used around me, and hid the go-bag under a tarp. Put an array of rusty tools overtop like mulch. Then got the hell out.

Relief.

My phones were still in the weeds.

Just like me.

47

I drove home. Past fast-food restaurants and baseball fields, parks and the brief ache of that particular coffee shop. Drove through a grid and grief of traffic so predictable it lacerated me now, when I wanted to go fast and reckless. We all expected the slowness, even if it didn't slow us down. All of our minds drifting there together alone.

The needling pulse, the inability to resist, to analyze: *why* was Fusk so resistant? On principle? Because, in his circles he'd know Langer by reputation alone? Or because that hummingbird in particular meant danger to him? I had Fusk and *Furtown* and a journal full of memories. I had a man behind a fence doing violence to another man.

Even when the traffic lessened, I kept driving slowly—into our neighborhood. Drove like I was a solid citizen. Parked in the driveway and got out casual. Didn't bother going inside but walked to the backyard, onto the lawn. The swing seemed peaceful to me. I liked standing in that space and not seeing a soul. I let out a long, deep breath, looking up at the windows of our house.

Start over. Try again. Work with what you have.

I called Fusk using yet another phone card, yanked out of Shovel Pig's guts.

When he answered, I railroaded over his "Hello?"

"Fusk, next time I'll call from an open line, easily traceable, and whoever you're afraid of will know for sure I'm the one who called you. I'll do it. I don't care anymore."

Wreck the shreds of my anonymity to expose him. Burn down another part of my life. Because I had to. Because they already knew where I lived, so what did it matter? Except, it did matter. I was sweating, pacing. Decided to retreat toward the woods.

Silence. He didn't hang up, but he didn't say anything. I needed more. I could feel it. Luckily, I had more.

"Fusk, this is your life: your son doesn't write. Or call. He posts on social media when your birthday comes up. He definitely doesn't visit. Your daughter doesn't even bother with social media. Your wife's been dead a decade. You had some boom periods, but now you're about three months from going out of business. You like bondage porn. You visit prostitutes. You aren't a criminal, not really, but you know criminals. And that's just the start of what I know about you. Answer my questions or this could get worse for you. In a lot of ways."

Fusk breathed into the phone like someone on life support.

"Fusk?"

"I knew from the look of you that you had a mean streak," he said. Flat, neutral.

I almost laughed at that. The last thing I cared about was an insult from Fusk.

"Tell me what I need to know. You'll never hear from me again."

Almost in the woods. Out of the sudden sun. Out of sight.

"Promises."

"Truth."

"Won't matter," Fusk said. Matter-of-fact. Fatalistic.

"To who, Fusk?"

Something was in the spot where a vagrant had watched our house. Obscured by the branches of a bush, enveloped by a rush of dead leaves.

"I dunno. Wildlife traffickers. Anarchists. Lots of folks. You tripped a wire. I don't want to be in the cage with you."

"Because of Silvina Vilcapampa."

Now I could see it clear: next to the empty bottle, propped upright like an impromptu gravestone: the little bird drone. Smashed. I had to work on my breathing again. I was suffocating, my chest tight.

A loud, bitter laugh from Fusk jolted me back to reality.

"What's funny?"

"Silvina. There's a name to forget you ever heard."

"Tell me why."

As I stood there, looking down at the drone, the bottle.

Worse, this time it wasn't one cigarette butt. Instead, a half dozen, each a different brand. The boot prints that obliterated the former shoe prints looked melodramatic, like someone had taken care to push the tread into the drone and the leaves and earth beneath. Marking territory.

An irrational pity for the drone, the delicate cracked beak, the shimmering brittle brokenness of the wings. The vacant eye that had never truly seen as a bird sees.

"I don't think I will tell you why."

"Names—I need names."

Defiant. Despite the uptick in how my hand on the phone shook, how Shovel Pig felt double heavy on my shoulder. I could smell the cigarette smoke, cloying, on the leaves. Recent?

"If you're involved with the Vilcapampa family, they'll be tracking you already. They'll find you. You'll know their names soon enough."

"Silvina's dead. Why do they care?"

Said as I squatted beside the bottle and drone.

"Well, there you go. Your first clue." Contemptuous.

"I need to know about a salamander, too. Taxidermy."

The bottle had a price sticker on it that looked familiar. Maybe if I hadn't been distracted, if I had said something more into the silence on the phone, Fusk would've ended it there. Maybe I'm kidding myself.

After a long moment, Fusk gave me an address two towns over. The address felt familiar, but I couldn't place it.

"It's in a . . . The place is a kind of repair shop now."

"So?"

"R.S. runs it."

A pure spike of energy. That would explain why I hadn't found an R.S. who ran a taxidermy business. I'd checked antiques stores, too.

"What's R.S. stand for?" I tried not to let my elation show in my voice.

"Ronnie Simpson."

"And how do you know Ronnie Simpson?"

"How does anyone know anyone these days?"

"Suddenly a philosopher."

"You're the detective—figure it out."

"Anything else you can tell me?"

Stupid thing to say, but I had picked up the bottle, not thinking about fingerprints or gloves. Nothing unusual about it, and clear enough that I could tell nothing was inside.

"I can't ask the questions for you, Detective."

"Call me if you do think of anything." I gave him a secure number, to a burner phone I hadn't used for anything else, and tossed the bottle onto the ground.

"Yeah, right. You can be sure I won't." Then, with a click, he was gone.

Conclusion, staring at the heavy tread, the cigarette butts: someone was fucking with me. The drone was strangely like an offering. But it also told me whoever stalked me was sophisticated enough to take out the neighborhood surveillance.

Was Fusk fucking with me, too, with his claim about R.S.? The levels kept changing, like in MMA. You'd think it was a boxer's advantage and then the ground game would kick in.

I stood there in the woods for a long time, thinking. Going round and round. Trapped. Frozen. What did the world want from me? What did Silvina need? What did I need? A pattern of cigarette butts in a rough circle on the ground told me the answer. A bottle with a familiar sticker.

Wanting to break out from the trap.

So I tried. I did my best.

48

"There's no one they won't kill in time because you don't matter to them. There is nothing they won't take from you. Because they simply don't care."

A call with Fusk. An intruder in the backyard again. A missing hummingbird.

I had finally placed the address Fusk had given me: it was Unitopia, the environmental center funded by Silvina's family. I devoted a moment to kicking myself for not investigating it already.

"They'll use you against you. They'll isolate you. They'll marginalize you. They'll use lies and the truth. Whatever they need. Because they don't care."

But R.S. was for later. Because I knew in my gut the man I'd beaten up on the hill wasn't whoever was watching our house—and I had a hunch about that.

I got back in the car and drove to my local convenience store, just outside of our subdivision, at the edge of a highway. It doubled as a gas station. The usual. Windows plastered with advertisements for all the things we were supposed to want that were killing us. Nothing resembling a black SUV in the parking lot.

Inside, the clang of bells announced me. The place wasn't a favorite haunt—the kind of store you went to only if you woke up in the morning and realized you'd forgotten to buy eggs or coffee at the supermarket. It appealed more to motorists making a pit stop. It always smelled faintly of pot.

Stopped short a moment realizing there would be surveillance cameras.

But the woman behind the counter had already seen me. A weary, thirty-something Black woman, dressed in a business suit, which made me think a manager was subbing for a sick employee. A surgical mask hung slack around her neck, like the chain had issued them but hadn't told employees it was mandatory yet. Like most places.

"Hi, there!" she said, a kind of vacant hope in her voice. Up close, the caverns of her eyes made it clear she didn't get much sleep. There was a tear in the sleeve of her blouse. Her pink nail polish had chipped. Details were escaping her. I sympathized.

"This may seem like a strange question," I said, braced for resistance.

"I don't think it will be," she said, smiling. Practically beaming.

What did that mean? What did the smile mean?

I decided to ignore it.

"Have you had someone come in recently who buys a lot of different types of cigarettes?"

At least ten kinds protruded from the shelf behind her head.

"I did!" she said, with such enthusiasm it wrong-footed me again.

"Did he give you a name?"

"Nope." Again, so cheery, against the grain, that I wanted to coach her. Don't bother with this one. Preserve your energy.

"What did he look like?"

"Normal, except for the wig. White, a little tall. I didn't really notice because of the wig." Said puzzled, like she'd just realized she couldn't provide a description.

"Wig?"

"He had on a hoodie, and under the hoodie he was wearing a wig. Like a clown."

"Clown?"

"You know—a cotton-candy-colored wig. Like for a party."

I felt the beginnings of a stomachache. That detail got to me. It suggested someone with a sick sense of humor. It made me think of pranks, of derangement.

"Was he young, old, or . . ."

"Not really anything. I mean, I couldn't tell. But not in his twenties."

"What do you mean 'Not really anything'?"

She shrugged. "He aged well? Or . . . I just didn't notice."

"How long ago was this? When he came in."

She hesitated, and the smile had begun to fade. I began to get a floating sensation.

"Ten minutes before you came in just now?"

Ten minutes.

Floating became a falling. Nausea. Focused on the neon-red roll of lotto tickets, the calm rows of blue-and-green disposable lighters, the silver-wrapped caffeinated protein bars.

Where was this man now?

"He's your boyfriend or something, right? This is part of the scavenger hunt?"

But she already knew from my reaction. She went quiet, the look on her face as if a lemon drop had teleported into her mouth. Not in a good way.

"What do you mean?" But I knew what she meant.

"This man in the wig—he told me you'd be coming in and asking about him. He said you were old friends. That it would be funny to tell you. That you'd laugh about it."

The sound had come back to me, of one man scuffling with another behind the fence. Of one of them falling. Of the calm of the other.

"He showed me your photograph, too."

"What photograph?"

She hesitated again. "Of you at your daughter's birthday party."

Numb, I drove back to the house. A photo from my phone. A photo from my phone. How long had it not been secure? I resisted the urge to smash it against the dashboard and toss it out the window. I needed to know the extent of the damage. Better "they" not know for sure that I knew.

I turned the key in the front door, decided, paranoid, to go in the back door instead. Checked every room for signs of an intruder. Found nothing.

I stared down at the lawn from the master bedroom, then stepped away from the window. The sense of vertigo was intense. It was hard to get a grip on what was happening.

The woods down below on the fringe looked like a blank wall of brown with hints of dull green. It had begun to rain, a chill back in the air. I was sweating. I could hear the sound of my own breathing. What now?

It took an effort of will to walk downstairs. I had to check something, a stray thought, another bit of paranoia. But I had to be sure. Along the way, I picked up a poker from the fireplace, went outside, my limbs watery, letting the poker drag across the grass. A thudding in my ears.

Out to the woods. In the rain. The mist of it pearled on my clothes, sunk in damp and humid.

There was the bottle, placed upright again.

But no drone. Not a single piece of the drone remained, as if I'd imagined it.

Beside the bottle: unsmoked cigarettes of various brands formed a taunting circle around the bottle.

But there was a gun, too. A semiautomatic. Small, easily concealed. With clips beside it. Lying atop a white, starched handkerchief.

Messing with me. For real.

I was too shocked to be shocked further. And behind that a question loomed. I knew I could be dangerous. That I could get in someone's face. Could I pull the trigger, too?

My work phone buzzed from an outside pocket of Shovel Pig. A text. I pulled the phone out.

An unlisted number. Untraceable, as it turned out.

>> *I hope you like what I left for you.*

I looked at the words without them really registering. How long had my phone been compromised? Somehow, getting the text there, outside my house, was worse than if I'd still been in my car.

Me: Who is this?

>>*Can't you guess?*

Me: *No.*

>>*Are you sure you don't want to guess?*

Me: *Who is this?*

>>*I'm your brother. Back from the dead.*

Fuck. I almost dropped the phone. The shock. The sense of violation.

Then I took a breath. He wanted me flustered. He was telling me he knew all kinds of things about me. That was all.

Me: *Not funny, asshole.*

>>*No, not funny. Apologies. Well, if you won't guess, I guess you can call me "Hellbender."*

Hellbender. The Goliath of salamanders. Another unsubtle message that he knew my past. I don't know why I thought "he," but I couldn't shake the idea.

Me: *Leave me alone. Or I'll call the police.*

>>*Oh, by all means. Go right ahead. Shall I tell them about your contraband? Or about breaking and entering?*

The man who I'd beaten up on the hill wouldn't give me a gun, either.

Me: *What do you want?*

>>*I just want to help.*

Me: *Right. What do you really want?*

>>*I took care of the guy watching your house, didn't I?*

That made me pause. A jolt like I'd had to hit the brakes at a sudden stoplight. First one cigarette butt, then a half dozen. The almost comical layering of boot prints, erasing the shoe prints. And the weight behind the fence? Was the texter Langer or was Langer dead? But I couldn't bring myself to ask that.

Me: *I don't want help like that.*

>>*Hellbender thinks you do want help like that. Hellbender thinks you need help like that.*

Me: *Stay away from my house.*

>>*Oh, I have. If I wanted to be in your house, I would.*

Me: *Just stay away!*

I waited a minute. Two minutes. No reply.

A neighbor was mowing their lawn. A leaf blower sounded somewhere in the distance. A bird was singing from a tree above me.

I picked up the gun, hid it under my jacket until I could stash it in Shovel Pig. Along with ammo clips.

I don't know what army Hellbender thought I would be fighting, but it was a lot of bullets.

[49]

Staring at the gun, I felt my grandfather closer than ever. I had good reason to push his ghost away—and I worked at it the hardest when I was around my daughter. I couldn't relax knowing he lived within me. We called him "Shot" behind his back. He called me "Bullethead" to my face. He liked to shoot bottles and deer. He went off like a shot. He was shot. It rhymed with his real name, and maybe reducing him to triteness felt like containing Shot in a box. His father's father had established the farm, a homestead specializing in nothing and in doing everything ground down to nubs in a world of modern machinery and specialization. One hundred acres become fifty in a generation. As if Shot's anger kept choking the land. Shot's brand of stupid, which felt so unnecessary. My father wasn't stupid, but he let Shot make unwise decisions.

What made things worse: we were surrounded by normal farm families, doing normal, understandable farm things. Not given over to stupid schemes, like the time we tried to grow boutique crops for hipsters because some rep convinced Shot to "give it a shot." Or the idea we could lead tours of the farm and charge cash money. Or . . . so many things.

Even though Father was a grown man, Shot set the schedule forever and a day. Chickens, cows, crop rotations. Because he never passed all the knowledge down. Weak men know they're poor in virtue and take their self-knowledge as evidence others will plot against them. So they want to be the only ones who know things.

Shot drowned a chicken in a water trough more than once. For crimes unknown. Always some excuse. The inchoate argument that led him to the act forgotten in the memory of the dead eye and waterlogged feathers. The stink that rose soon after.

He sure liked to hunt, Shot did, and to get really drunk doing so. If you think that's a stereotype, you don't know the area, because that was kind of universal. There were places you didn't go because of drunk poachers, and you never ever thought about reporting it to the police.

When I went limp and he had to drag me, my father stopped him. But I'd already stopped him with the tactic. When I grew big and tall, muscle suited to me, Shot liked to joke that Father must've "done it with a cow, Bullethead." That was his level. Slapping, hitting, and mental abuse. Shot's idea of a good time.

By the time Shot dragged my brother to the water trough and our father had to stand in his way and physically restrain him, we all realized this sickness was transferable. Because Dad had begun to cross the line. Threaten to slap us. Punished us by overturning our cereal bowls in our laps if angry about something. To allow Shot's energy to break him down. And by then Mother just wasn't really there. And we had no defense for this new source of abuse, had spent our energy erecting barricades in the other direction.

Shot took his cues from an idea of nasty men, things he read in the old noir magazines he'd once collected or bad shows on TV. Where he was reading or seeing things from the villain's point of view. If he'd been a generation younger, we would've at least been spared the theatrical nature of his dysfunction. Maybe gotten something more original.

Then a kind of freneticness, or fit, would come upon him, and he'd be the one half in, half out of the water trough. Find it hard to move properly. Scream out for Father to help him. The convalescence meant we heard him more but saw him less. But if we didn't attend to him, in his bed, he would let us know about it when well again. Nor did he want to go to a doctor.

Shot made my brother read to him when an invalid. The racy, uncomfortable stories in those magazines. The ones with the ripped-bodice women on the cover and some steely-eyed private eye in the backdrop. Lots of leg and no sense. I meant to burn those magazines if I could, but I never summoned the nerve. What would it have mattered anyway? They already lived in his head.

I was beginning to feel my grandfather surging up inside me. All of that rage, that energy, and it had to have someplace to go. Just the parts I could use. If you could harness such a thing.

From a mythical place long ago and far away.

[50]

Back inside, I was still fighting the anger. How far had Hellbender infiltrated my life, without me knowing? I put the gun and ammo down on the kitchen table, and I took Shovel Pig and dumped her contents. I was shaking. I didn't realize the violence of the act until it was over. How much had been inside the purse. How upending it had been like pouring an ocean of "stuff" onto the table. How some of it fell off, so I spent the next few minutes picking it up.

All the flotsam and jetsam that accretes when you don't clean out a purse over time. Old receipts, worn and yellowing, from years ago. Coupons for canned food you never used. Extra school photos of your daughter you meant to send to your husband's relatives. Expired car insurance cards. Lots of gum. So many sticks of gum, I was just thankful little of it had come unwrapped and stuck to the inside of Shovel Pig. Perfunctory office prep: lipstick and some makeup I only used if we had a client meeting in-house.

All my various phones, burner and regular, and, of course, Bog. Some I had to pry out of their separate compartments to check underneath.

Paint swatches, cut-out articles of gardening advice I'd never used. A few folded-up documents from work, from long-ago projects. Two lanyards from conventions and three of those annoying pin-on types. The name tag from my first job, in fast food, that I'd kept for luck or out of nostalgia. Tampons. So many tampons, lost in crevices and various pockets. A couple exhausted AA batteries and my magnifying glass.

A worn paperback copy of a mystery novel I was slowly working my way through six months later. Stuff that had fallen apart and was hard to identify. A bottle of expired painkillers from when I'd hurt my knee. Keys to old houses and apartments, all on the same key chain, like I needed a museum of keys.

Condoms I immediately shoved back in their little zippered pocket.

Like all huge purses, Shovel Pig had also eaten many smaller, worn-out-looking purses. A couple hadn't even been used, and I couldn't understand why I'd ever bought them.

Why hadn't I gotten rid of them? Why had I kept *any* of it?

No wallet—I kept that in my front pants pocket at all times— but plenty of weaponry. In fact, the weaponry, once laid out in a row, was extensive in a way that made me laugh. Taser, pepper spray, a gutting knife from the farm I'd rescued because of the smooth bone handle. Brass knuckles in plastic wrap. Several more pocket- and penknives. Small flashlight that wasn't a weapon, but seemed weapons-adjacent. It was like a mini go-bag.

But although I searched every nook and cranny, every crevice, I couldn't find anything unusual. I stared suspicious at a puzzle piece, paranoid that someone had put it there, until I remembered it was a memento of a really fun family night.

No sign of surveillance. No bug. Nothing that bulged in the lining. Nothing restitched.

I shoved most of it back in, both relieved and upset. Something about all of that detritus of my life, so ordinary, but also all the garbage I'd been carrying around. Overwhelmed by it.

The smell of Band-Aids hung over everything. More than anything else, I'd had Band-Aids in there.

"Mom! What are you doing with that?"

Startled, pulled out of my own thoughts. I'd forgotten my daughter was already home.

• • •

Even with all that has happened since, I return to that moment so many times. In my dreams. In daylight. Now that I have no idea whether she is safe or not safe. No control over that. But, then, Silvina was in my head. Hummingbirds and Silvina.

My daughter stood there in the doorway of our house, a look of horror on her face. For a moment, I thought it was just me. That there was something terrible about *me*. Then I realized I was holding the gun.

I shoved the gun back in Shovel Pig, tried to be casual, even though that was ridiculous. Half the contents of my purse lay strewn across the kitchen table.

"Just cleaning my gun," I said. Trying to sound casual just made it weirder.

"Mom! Since when have you had a gun?"

"Awhile," I said. "Sorry—I should have told you. I didn't mean to startle you. It's just a precaution." Pathetic.

She was looking at me like I was an intruder. I felt small. I felt terrible.

"Does this have something to do with the man watching the house from the woods the other day?"

My heart. Oh, my heart stopped a moment, hiccupped, or something in my brain did.

"What man?"

"Don't lie to me!" The anger in my daughter just then brought Shot's ghost into her features. Made me angry at her, irrationally.

"We're dealing with it. Your father and I."

Her cue to drop it, but she ignored me.

"And what about what you hid in the trunk of your car? I saw you. I saw that. *What is going on?*"

My center of gravity shifted. I put a hand out to the chair next to me. Unbearably tired. Like I could sleep for a thousand years.

"I have no idea what you're talking about." In a sense, it was true.

"Don't bullshit me," she said.

"Language."

She sat down at the table opposite and glared at me. I said nothing.

"Fine, don't tell me. I know already anyway," she said.

Relief in her saying that, in a sense. This daughter who had always been, if I were honest, a distant and difficult beast. Never really knew what was in her eyes, even when she was very young. This baby with the furry head that went bald so quickly, only to sprout hair again, and then, magically, was old enough to be looking at me as if she were the adult. That almost teenager who scorned us and needed us. Who felt breakable and yet broke things so easily.

But she couldn't really know. So I gave in. Partway. Chose something not quite a lie.

"Something to do with work," I said. Not entirely untrue.

"Bullshit," she said.

I couldn't look at her as I said, "Language."

"Ever since you hid that thing in the trunk," she said, leaning over the table to fix me with her glare, "you have been in your own world. You have *not been my mom.*"

There it was.

"Work just got really bad," I protested. "It's tough being a—"

"No. That's not it," she said. "Don't feed me that bullshit again."

"Well, it's none of your business. I'm not going to discuss it with you." Blurted without thinking. My last defense. The only way to try to keep containment, to stop the drones from destroying us all.

"If you split up, I'm going to live with Dad."

My mouth opened and closed again.

What she was telling me. That she knew about my one-night stands. Thought I was having an affair, divorce on the horizon. That brief surge of elation that she knew nothing about Silvina crashed into such a wrenching sadness.

"Oh, baby," I said, and reached across the table for her hand. But she pulled back, out of reach. "We're not getting a divorce. We're just fine."

"No, you're not. You don't talk to him anymore. It's like the last time. Except this time you have a gun."

I leaned back, exhausted. Just wiped out by everything coming at me from all sides. Scared for my daughter, for a different reason, and ashamed. Such a grown-up look on her face. I didn't want her to have to be an adult yet. Even if part of me was impressed.

"It's not that way . . ." I mumbled, braced for the next accusation.

But a tiredness had crept into the anger on her face. A tiredness and, I realize now, a resignation. A retreat that made it clear how much it had taken out of her to say these things to me.

"Promise me the gun doesn't mean anything. *Promise* you really have had the gun for a while," she said.

I nodded. "I promise. It's true. I just didn't know how you'd feel about it."

"And will it go away? Will whatever *it* is be done with soon?"

No break in her voice, I'll give her that. No looking away. I withered under that full and damning regard.

"Yes," I said, grateful for the lifeline. "Yes, it's almost done. A couple more days."

But would it end soon? Was there a point where I could tie a knot and be done?

A text came in and I gave it a glance.

>>*Hello, Jane. Things going well? Or a little . . . sideways? Hope you keep the gun. You might find you need it . . . Let me know when you're ready to talk.*

My daughter frowned, gave me a long, appraising look, got up, and left without another word.

Relief at the avoidance. Relief that she'd left so I could study the journal. The regret came much later. The regret that I hadn't explained more, hadn't found some way to prolong the moment. To live in a moment more stable and more certain than any of what followed.

It struck me that she looked "off" for another reason. My daughter's hair was different. Shorter. She'd gotten a haircut since the hummingbird, the storage unit. I hadn't noticed, even though according to my calendar I was supposed to be the one to drive her to the hairdresser's.

I pulled the gun out again. Spent some time taking it apart. Just as I'd thought: a tracer, tiny, hidden inside the magazine. Something microscopic written on it. So I got the magnifying glass. The words read "Just checking."

I smiled. But I didn't laugh. The psychological profile of "Wig Man" wasn't good. Unpredictable. Or bored. Or full of himself. All of those were more dangerous than someone competent and balanced.

I put the gun back together, carefully placed the clips in secure compartments. Not much of a leap to accept Hellbender's gift. Shovel Pig had held a gun once, until the first time my daughter, age six, had showed curiosity about my purse and I'd found her looking inside. I'd gotten rid of the gun soon after.

But it wasn't like I'd never used a gun before.

[51]

Silvina's note to me lay deep within Shovel Pig, too. In a zippered compartment within a compartment, next to her journal. Somehow, I hadn't wanted to pull the note out. But now I did. Like a talisman. Like a balm. That direct communication. I sat there at the table feeling all alone except for Silvina.

Could this be as far as I was meant to go? From Silvina's perspective? What if the salamander was metaphorical or symbolic in some way? Then the journal was the last thing—the endpoint. Salamander was my business. But had become her business, because she'd done her homework on me. Something in that thought trembled on the edge of comprehension, of clicking into place, then faded.

The only "nature" expeditions I recalled as a child were those I took with my brother. He would tell me tales of mythic salamanders—that under the earth were long-lost cave systems, and giant phosphorescent salamanders the size of alligators lived there, coming up to the surface to hunt for food and to mate with salamanders from other cave systems before returning to the darkness. When we tired of overturning rocks to find some tiny specimen, he would lead me into the foothills above the farm and we would pretend to be searching for the giant salamanders.

Over time, there was mythology around them. Over time, we came to believe in their existence because of how it pushed every other thought out of our minds. There were maps for future expeditions. Folded paper picture books. Fake accounts of sightings. We kept it all in a secret compartment in a shed near the barn. Not because we thought Dad or Grandpa would destroy them, but because it was our secret. Our secret thing.

Imagine there comes a day when all of that, everything you've created, is gone. It's not because it's been discovered or thrown away. It's because the person you imagined it with doesn't exist anymore.

Imagine being frozen, and when you thaw, in another place, you can't be sure you made the right choice. How ever after the past calls to you and sometimes you want to join it in the black water, in the mud, among the snails and crawdads and salamanders.

How it's calling you now: to transform, to make a decision, to become one thing or the other.

Neither will make you happy.

[52]

I recall getting through dinner like a spy in deep cover who knows the other party suspects the deception. Being extra-nice to my daughter—and to my husband. Peppering him with questions about his day so there can be no questions thrown my way. My daughter mercifully mum about the gun and my husband putting her silence down to teen angst.

The texts keep coming in, but I ignore them until later. I can't think about them. I have to compartmentalize. I'm living in the moment but denying the moment, too. I can't think I can't think I can't think.

>>*You should respond, just so I know you're reading this. So you understand.*

>>*But, then, I have all the time in the world. Even if the world doesn't.*

What I can't see can't disturb me. Do I get rid of my phone

or use the phone to contain this demon? How far has the contagion spread? Are there cameras inside the house, watching us eat?

I "make" dinner by ordering out. Roast chicken with golden potatoes and broccolini. The chicken a little dry, but the potatoes are delicious, and he didn't have to cook. I am a very good wife. I am a very good mother. In these roles rejoice, for in these roles I can forget and forget again, for a little while. Keep the stress at bay. Take a couple Motrin and open a bottle of white wine. Drink just enough to keep the edge off. Drink less than I want to.

I go off to the bathroom to peek at the journal, with the one-page accident report shoved inside, but my daughter's knocking on the door soon enough, saying to hurry up. She needs to use the bathroom, but I think mostly she doesn't trust me in there for too long and I don't want to think of the reasons for that. So I come out, put on a smile.

What are we celebrating? my husband asks when I return, nodding at the bottle of wine. We never drink midweek.

I reply, with a look at my daughter, that we are celebrating the near end of a difficult project.

He seems relieved, so he noticed, too, that I have been AWOL, gone, not here. But what is "here"? Why is "here"? In the comfortable heat of the kitchen, as I clean up and my daughter beats my husband at checkers . . . as I scour the dishes and toss out a lot of single-use plastic.

>>*Looks like you had a nice dinner. You'll need your strength for the next part, no matter how it goes.*

As I let the water run a little too hot so my thumb pulses and burns under the flow. The smell of the roast chicken wholesome and enveloping, and me eating scraps because eating, too, is a way to forget. I don't want the clenched hands. I don't want the mystery. But I have it anyway, and no matter how I disguise it, I'm manic, I'm on fire.

I can't help but think of Larry in the company parking garage. I can't help but hope there will be some clue in Silvina's journal that will explain the plan. Why her ghost has reached out to me. Along with an emotion I can't identify that coalesces around this thought: if Silvina hadn't been killed, I would never have known she existed. Would never have received the rapture of the hummingbird. Would never have begun to wake up about the world. This terrible catalyst that has to *mean* something.

Right there, under my husband's nose, I am conducting a covert investigation. All he has to do is open the file folder and he'll see something's not right. Several somethings.

>>*Don't worry—they're safe. No one cares about them. Only about Silvina.*

I know he means my family. I know I don't trust him.

I am not a spy. Not a detective. Not caught and lost in some tangle or maze. Not lying against the mud and leaves watching over my brother's body. I am not I am not I am not . . .

But I don't know what I am.

[53]

"We're ghosts trapped in the wreckage of our systems. So why shouldn't we haunt them? Why should we not avenge ourselves upon them? Why be merciful?"

The office was a graveyard of abandoned cubicles, most employees off-site working on the pipeline project. The overhead lights in that emptiness shone hard but oddly dim. The smell of cleaners gave a lemon twinge to the corridors that felt off. A casual onlooker would've thought we were going out of business.

On the constant TV in the break room as I made coffee: the ongoing crisis of a cruise ship commandeered by climate refugees rejected by yet another port. A threat to security, but, then, wasn't everything? Europe was cocooned uncomfortable in a massive snowstorm that had killed three thousand people so far. The garbage in the Atlantic had slowed the Gulf Stream to a near-critical level. Some kind of contamination from the Far East would soon turn our skies green-gray, we were told. But none of this made us even blink anymore.

My office swelled with darkness, but I only turned the desk lamp on. I hadn't slept much. I'd ordered my daughter to check in via text every few hours. To keep an eye on her. To believe I had some control over any threat.

And, I had no hope of catching up on the pipeline project. My contribution was due in two days, but I needed seven. It felt almost a relief, that I couldn't do it. That other kinds of dread took precedence. What would I do when I missed the deadline? Alex would reprimand me, but I didn't think he'd fire me.

I hadn't been to see Larry. I would never go to see Larry.

Instead, I lurked in my office for the first hour, taking another, longer look at Silvina's journal and its spidery, hard-to-read handwriting. Even though I needed much more time than that.

I decided it felt more like a memoir, with all the thought that goes into what you reveal and what you don't. I also began to think about the journal in terms of chapters, even though Silvina hadn't divided it into chapters, and some sections would have to be moved around to fit my structure. But, otherwise, it could be mapped.

> *Chapter 1: The Moment*
> *Chapter 2: Early Life*
> *Chapter 3: Trapped*
> *Chapter 4: Rebellion*
> *Chapter 5: Awakening*
> *Chapter 6: Potential*

A classic journey, if you were a cult leader, if you had followers who called themselves "Friends of." If, maybe, you had planned something that would outlive your death. Despite wide gaps in the chronology of her life. As an analyst, that raised a red flag. Something was being hidden, but what?

"The Moment" was her alienation from the human world through how her body itself rejected that world. This was the anchor, the foundation. She wrote movingly of how her condition worsened with time. How as an adult she had to be so careful in sunlight. How her hearing had become so acute or fine-tuned that ordinary sounds felt like shards of glass breaking inside her skull, without earplugs. That in so many ways she kept receiving the world even when she didn't want to.

"Early Life" gave a baseline for what her life had been: privileged, all things provided, a future as a billionaire's daughter, meaning she could be anything or do nothing.

"Trapped" covered the phase when she tried to make it work with her family, overseeing properties in the U.S., but also covered her expedition to Quito, which was part of the trap.

"Rebellion" was her expedition down the West Coast, while "Awakening" was more abstract. "Awakening" tracked to Silvina holding her cards close and expanding her journal by way of ideas and hypotheticals and data about the environmental destruction in the world.

Finally, "Potential" gave a view of the future should this destruction be reversed, if we only had the political will and wisdom to do so. And it was in "Potential" that she returned to her early life—and, in fact, all phases of her life—to give examples that she then tried to fit to her philosophy. So that, in effect, the memoir transformed into a guide for living. A way of trying to use her life to get others to where she had ended up much faster.

Except, in the margins: all the sketches of bombs. Except also, the banality of much of it.

"The steps in place to make an impact" . . . *"How a pattern can be more than a sum of parts"* . . . *"The cause that leads to*

effect that cannot be seen but is felt" . . . *"A volcano that seems forever to erupt but never erupts. Then one day it does. And the surprise is not the explosion but the aftershock."*

Many of our clients engaged in "greenwashing": co-opting environmental causes to project an image of being sustainable. Too much of Silvina's language in the journal approximated that corporate takeover of the liminal. Not in how she spoke about her personal experience. But definitely in how that translated to anything approaching "revolution."

I tried to see me as Silvina might have seen me. Middle-aged mother, centrist politics, suburban life. Was the journal just another form of game playing? Of manipulation? Was I seeing things that weren't there?

A lack that nagged at me: never mention of any pets. No dog, cat, or even hamster. I don't know why that bothered me most of all. Didn't know what it said about her, or me.

I kept trying to imagine Silvina having lunch or playing a board game and I couldn't. And nothing in the journal made her any more real on that level. Not a single mention of a lover, a boyfriend, a girlfriend.

How much of Silvina didn't exist because she didn't want it to . . . and how much just wasn't part of her life?

Not sure if I'd made progress or just gotten lost again. I actually welcomed another text from Hellbender, the Wig Man, to put the journal down for a time.

I'd decided to keep the phone and not change the SIM card. Measures taken meant I thought he couldn't track me with it, but at the same time I must have felt the risk was worth the contact.

Me: *What do you really want?*

>>*Help you. I helped on the hill, or don't you remember.*

I shuddered. The sound of a body hitting the ground. I'd

read the paper, looking for a mention of a murder in that area, found nothing. Didn't know what that meant.

Me: *By spying on my family.*

>>*Just getting the lay of the land. Protecting you.*

Me: *Who did you kill?*

>>*There are a lot of dangerous people after you. Now one less.*

Me: *Do you know Langer?*

>>*Who doesn't know Langer?*

Cute. What if *this* was Langer?

Me: *Who do you work for?*

>>*I work for no man, but every man.*

Me: *So your boss is a woman? And you don't like it.*

>>*Nice try.*

Me: *Did you kill her?*

A pause, then:

>>*LOL! Silvina? No.*

I found "LOL" and a smiley face emoticon disturbing. So ordinary. I didn't want to normalize this "voice" on my phone.

Me: *Who are you?*

>>*Now, why spoil the surprise?*

Me: *I should destroy this phone card.*

>>*But you won't. You might need to contact me. In the event.*

Me: *In the event?*

>>*They find you before I find them.*

Me: *Them?*

>>*Don't be afraid to use the gun. It's not a trap. It's untraceable.*

Me: *Who's been killed with it before?*

No answer.

Me: *What do you really want from me?*

No answer.

Imagine a voice in your head you hate, but it's worse to get rid of it. Imagine you get used to it over time so you miss it if it isn't there.

When you find the world you live in unfamiliar, alien, it's nothing to slip into another.

[54]

Shot didn't just teach me how to handle a shotgun. Shot was a wrestler in one of his prior lives, after the navy. The kind of wrestler who became part of traveling roadshows, more spectacle than sport. He'd been an opponent on the semi-pro boxing circuit, too, and he'd sold clothespins and other house supplies door-to-door. Before he came back to farming. I always wondered what had qualified him at farming other than that our family owned a farm. A last-ditch thing—the last ditch he found himself in he raised himself out of for a time.

That great round, flat head with the broad features, atop an ever-dwindling body. My father said I looked like him, which felt like a curse more than an insult. In the barn, on the good days, Shot would show me exotic wrestling moves that mostly wouldn't work unless your opponent was complicit.

"You got to pretend you're a bigger bastard than them," he'd say. "Bullethead, you got to pretend you're" a this or a that. A neither or a nor. Different. No problem there.

Problem was my brother wouldn't pretend; he was just different. Or go along with the wrestling lessons. He had no interest, the kind of teenager elated by a library card. But that's why I bore the brunt of wrestling lessons. Late in a day, before Mother, or, in later years, Father, called us in for dinner.

There was a great lowing and mooing in the barn near dusk. An audience, of sorts. As he dumped me on my ass, made me enraged as he intended, so anger would be a friend to me.

"What's the point if you don't feel it," he'd say, and half beat his chest. "What's the point if it just gets away?"

But I never felt safer with him than in those moments.

He genuinely wanted to teach me, and he became a different person for an hour or two. Something of his past that meant a standard close to honor or regret or triumph meant he never hurt me then. Even if I did something wrong.

I could tell from my father's reactions that Shot had never tried to teach him to wrestle, understood on some level that my own father resented me for what I could not control. Maybe why he sided with the rest when my brother died.

We never knew Shot's wife, our grandmother. She'd died before we were born. No one ever talked about her.

But, then, it's not like we ever talked about much. Only me and my brother. Until we couldn't.

[55]

I went for a walk around the circuit that was the derelict, empty office. My mistake.

Another ghost lingered there, caught up with me.

Allie. She looked hollowed out to me. A sag to her shoulders I didn't like.

"Have you gone to see Larry?" she asked, clutching too many file folders as if for security.

Her eyes wouldn't meet mine. Her hand on the folders trembled. Almost imperceptibly. But I noticed.

"No. I haven't gone to see Larry." I was tired of the question. It felt frivolous, almost laughable. I must have sounded cold.

"Well, I did."

"Is he better, I hope?"

"Not really. I don't think he's going to be 'better' anytime soon."

"Well, I'll send him some flowers." That must have sounded cold, too.

I turned to go.

She reached out and grabbed my arm. Like a child. I could barely feel her grip. But I stopped, faced her.

"What's wrong?" But I knew. By then, I knew.

"Larry says he was *attacked*. That it was *planned*."

"That's terrible." My family was being attacked; I didn't have much left over for Larry.

"They asked him about *Silvina*. They asked about taxidermy."

"That's strange," I said.

But maybe it was normal, because I didn't feel shock or panic or any of the usual emotions. Maybe by then I realized I was too far in to quit.

"Is it?" Allie snapped. "You had a *bird* in your desk drawer."

Everybody knew things they shouldn't.

"I don't know what you're talking about."

She'd come close, defiant, like I was the cause and not another victim.

"And when Larry couldn't give them any information, they ran him over."

"Allie—"

"No. No. Don't."

"Allie . . ." But I didn't have much to say. I was in a different place, or the same place, a different room in the maze, and no time or patience.

But here it came.

"You asked me to look up Silvina's information *knowing* it might be dangerous. Not client-takes-you-to-dinner dangerous. Worse than that. And it's not for a potential account, no matter what you say. You haven't even reported a lead to sales. And I'm going to tell Alex, and Larry is going to tell the police what I told him."

I knew Larry hadn't told the police, calculating how much time must've gone by since Allie's visit. They would have dropped by my house or the office by now.

But Allie *would* tell Alex. I already knew he frowned on employees having "hobbies," by which he meant he was paranoid about employees doing a little business on the side. Would he think I was cheating on the company? Would he believe her?

"I'll fire you if you tell Alex," I said.

She drew herself up at that, gave me an appraising look, as if seeing me for the first time.

"I mean it," I said.

"No, you don't understand," Allie said, shoving a finger at me. "I quit. I am quitting and I am never coming back to this fucking place again."

Quivering with anger and fear. If only she could see how I was doing the same, deep inside.

"Allie."

"I left one last report on your desk. You're putting the whole company at risk."

She stormed away from me. Receding down the corridor until she was just a wraith, a trick of the light.

I think I made a motion as if to stop her, but only after it was too late. Too late in so many ways. I wanted—needed—to say something else, but she was gone.

Because I've lied to you about Allie. Just a little. I did care about her. I just hid it from her like something I needed to hide from myself. Because I couldn't be seen to care. If she faltered. If she failed. If I failed her.

Alex didn't know I felt a connection, a sympathy. Larry didn't. If they had, it might have gone poorly for her, was my reasoning. I tried to teach her what could be taught. Found excuses to give her the kind of work that would help her. So she would have it easier than I had in the business.

Irrational. Irrational that Allie leaving felt like my daughter rejecting me.

So I went back to my office with a different kind of doom in my mind.

What would Alex do? If she talked to him?

How quaint. How useless. How irrelevant. But it mattered at the time.

The report was on my desk, as promised. A photo of Silvina, like a mug shot, confronted me, and the signs and symbols of a declassified top secret report. With the stamp across the top, the agency unclear. Allie had dug deep for this, risked something to find it. Called in a favor I didn't know anyone owed her.

The gist, even at a glance, was clear. Bioterrorism. It was a report on Silvina's activities since she'd gone dark, since the trial. Names, places. Known communications. Known associates. Substances and supplies acquired with wealth stolen from her father, funneled through third parties and ever more shell companies.

Warehouses involved and trucking companies. Every last "associate" was rogue in some way. Rogue biotech. Rogue bioweapons. Rogues who liked to play with viruses. A list of names. I couldn't tell if Contila had branched out or imploded and these were all the nasty fragments.

Also, a mostly unredacted page or two from a federal agency interrogation of Langer, undated.

██████: Did you facilitate the sale of genetic contraband
    including █████ to one Silvina Vilcapampa on
    ███████ in the township of █████ in ████████?
Langer: No. I'm purely an export-import business.
██████: Don't be cute, Langer. We can detain you
    indefinitely if we want to.
Langer: I wish I knew what you were talking about. I buy
    and sell things. Legally. Illegal sounds like it would be
    a headache.
██████: What if it aligned with your political views?
Langer: I have no politics. That I am aware of. Not a nice
    thing to accuse someone of. Politics.

████████: Will you be so cute, I wonder, when you're
    languishing in a black site with a hood over your
    head?

Langer: Sounds relaxing.

████████: Let's make a deal. I'll stop threatening you if you
    stop cracking wise.

Langer: It's just how I talk. I can't help it.

████████: Did you post this rant from an extreme
    "socialist-anarchist" position in which you advocate
    the violent overthrow of government?

[Detainee provided with relevant documents.]

Langer: Got hacked.

████████: Did you get hacked when you browsed this
    website devoted to biological weapons?

Langer: Curiosity didn't kill the cat. Buying illegal shit
    did. Did I buy anything, ████████? Did I?

It went on like that, proving nothing except guilt by associ-
ation. Langer came across as a special kind of head case. Some
weird strain of altruism an overlay on his sociopathy. And I
didn't like the part where he called ████████ by his name. Felt
too familiar. The whole conversation, the more I thought about
it, felt overly familiar.

And I knew, as an analyst, that you could sometimes make
the data show more than one outcome or intent. But there was
a clarity—a damning clarity—to the supporting documents.
Showing how Silvina's purpose shifted from habitat stewardship
and land purchases to recruitment of underground biotech experts and geneticists. From acquiring wildflower seed and fund-
ing research into experimental wetlands restoration into the
kinds of things that kill people.

"Execution of mass-elimination plan as clear end-game,
given the scope of the knowledge base and the amount of
matériel," someone had written in the analysis part of the report. Parts of which were also heavily redacted.

Conclusion: she'd been trying to amass or even build biological weapons, with the goal of broad use against civilians. But no solid evidence that she was able to make the contacts and acquire everything needed. No direct links. Ghosts and more ghosts. Hauntings.

Still, I would have bet the government had been about to blacksite her anyway. Except she'd died in a car crash. Was it my delusion that I didn't believe it at first or was the report the delusion?

You could fake a death. I knew you could. If Hellbender wasn't Langer, then what if Hellbender worked for Silvina? I didn't know how paranoid to be. Had not been paranoid enough as an analyst sometimes, but also too willing to go down rabbit holes. The truth? Almost anything was possible when you dealt with humans, not systems.

I knew Alex was coming into the office. Alex wanted more of us to work remotely. I didn't want to see Alex. I didn't want to believe Silvina was an aspiring bioterrorist. I did and didn't want another text from Hellbender. I didn't know how to get out of these loops.

I left, even though I could feel eyes on me, a kind of communal judgment from those who had come into the office. How I wished I was small and anonymous-looking. But I wasn't, so I stomped my way to the exit, head high.

No one jumped me in the parking garage. No one tailed me. But, then, I had Hellbender in the front seat with me, trapped or trapping me on my phone.

Like some lucky talisman.

[56]

Unitopia. Allie's report had described the artists' commune as an artificial island in the wilderness. Unlike the bare bones of the blueprint, the finished structure, floating on stilts and pontoons, had a weirdly wilder, yet more elegant, feel. From the photos, it had looked clean, sleek, with glistening blue solar panels on roofs amid a snaking swath of bushes and trees and wooden walkways.

As for the wilderness, urban sprawl had caught up. The "lake" was an enormous converted holding pond, abandoned when another subdivision had been gouged out of the forest and a new holding pond created elsewhere. I was surprised to drive past chain stores and countless housing divisions labeled almost the same as the ones in our neighborhood.

Behind a half-built mall guarded by rusting earthmoving equipment, a potholed asphalt-dirt road led to a row of narrow fir trees and a parking lot. Five cars, other than mine, four electric, and a flatbed, along with an ugly-looking garbage compacter that didn't look up to the task of recycling. I already had the sense you get from a business park that never quite made it.

The smell when I got out of my car had a sourness to it, the breeze coming at me from the glorified pond they called a lake. It wasn't garbage, but it wasn't nice. Through the trees I could see the walkway led over water to a ramshackle "island" buttressed by large, repurposed faded-red buoys and a wall of reeds through which one- and two-story buildings stuck out at odd geometric angles.

A faded-green wooden sign by the walkway read "Unitopia." With "Once we were wiser" smaller below that. This was the land of fading promise I was about to enter.

But, in the end, it wasn't as sad as it appeared, just empty, deserted. Like a hippie version of a tech bro "university," with a closed organic coffee shop and lunch place. A shared common space composed of spliced-together dodecahedrons made of glass in the center. More raised pathways and more signs for businesses that either had failed or never taken root. Piles of tires supporting pylons made me wonder if flooding had been a problem. The geodesic dome of 1970s science fiction movies here felt cutting-edge, but also oddly comfortable.

But the smell hadn't gotten better, although I never found the source, and there was a creaking sway to the walkways that felt like being on a boat lashed to a dock.

Someone poked their head out of a bright orange door, then tried to pull it back in again before I could gesture to them.

Too late, and the man teetered there in the doorway like one day politeness was going to kill him.

"Where do I find the organic mechanic?" I asked.

The man winced. He had sleepy eyes and, despite the chill, wore the shorts, T-shirt, and flip-flops of a surfer.

"They don't do that anymore."

"But they're still here?" I asked. Assuming we both meant the same "they."

He winced again, and I realized it was just a tic in his face.

"Yeah, I think so." I noticed a joint behind his right ear. Which didn't inspire confidence.

"So . . . which way?"

Because it was a maze, and the arrows all seemed pointing different directions.

A shrug. "Any which way. Just keep going and you'll find it. It's at the end . . . You from the bank?"

I ignored that. Did I look like I was from the bank?

"What happened here?" I asked.

This time, the wince was real. A weariness that didn't match his age.

"What always happens," he said. "Shit got real. Then it turned to shit."

I nodded like I understood.

The actual artists' commune was at the end of the island, with nothing but the rest of the lake and forest beyond it. A wide dome painted rusted rainbow colors with little portal windows like a welter of eyes. The reeds alongside were intense. Moss and waterlogged trees with yellow flowers had usurped part of the walkway, so I had to step between two of them to get to the doorstep. Small solar panels had been stacked against a wall. Some kind of marsh heron stared at me with a cold eye from the far side of the reeds.

The sign for the commune read "Unitopia," which seemed like a mistake in hierarchy. You couldn't name both the island and a business on the island the same thing. The mold had overtaken the sour stench and a belch of swamp odor. The whimsical drawbridge between island proper and this seemingly detachable part was waterlogged, soggy. Leapt over it rather than trust it to hold my weight.

Leaving me in the open doorway, staring into the surprising light-filled interior. All those pinhole pricks of windows.

The front part was the abandoned visitor center, with a high ceiling and museum-like displays. A row of huge circular photos had been positioned at eye level along the outer wall to show views of different habitats. Some of it faded. All of it faux cheery in design. The flow of nutrients through wetlands charted as a metaphor for healthy life. Places you could pretend to take samples of water quality. Stations on high tables, with stools, that had once displayed brochures and had plugs for headphones and laptops for presentations.

I walked up to the main placard, the standard "Welcome to Unitopia" pablum. But next to it was another station where everything had been ripped out except a bit of wiring. The graphic showed sedimentary layers within the earth and the levels above, ending in sky. I read part, then took a photo to remember it.

What could be accomplished in understanding the miraculous in the everyday if we could truly see the hidden underpinnings of the world. Whether through truly immersive virtual reality or other method. Whatever the process to that end, however you were changed or contaminated or released or mutated or entangled . . . Afterward, you'd walk down your street and everything would be identical to what you'd see with your own eyes . . . except you'd also see the chemical signals in the air from beetles and plants, pheromone trails laid down by ants, and every other bit of the natural world's communications invisible to our primitive five senses. You'd also see every trace of pesticide and runoff and carcinogens and other human-made intercessions on the landscape. It would be overwhelming at first.

But once you got used to it, you'd look at the ground and it'd open up its layers, past topsoil and earthworms, down into the "deeper epidermis," so to speak, until you're overcoming a sense of vertigo, because even though you're standing *right there*, not falling at all, below you everything is revealing itself to you superfast. And maybe then, while still staring at the ground, even more would open up to you and you'd regress to the same spot five years, ten years, fifty years, two hundred years ago . . . until when you look up again there's no street at all and you're in the middle of a forest and there are more birds and animals than you could ever imagine because you've never *seen* that many in one place. You've never even seen this many old-growth trees before. You've never known that the world was once like this except in the abstract.

That sounded like Silvina, and the onrushing truth of that made me light-headed. Like I'd gone from being cold to hot, hot, hot. I knew, in that moment, that this place had meant something real to her. I knew this *was* her place, once upon a time.

A shame, then. How so little else lived here. The smell and how gutted it looked, with most of the stools gone. Dust coated everything. At the far end of this space, a doorway and a sign that just read "Organic Mechanic."

After a time, I walked through the doorway.

Once, Shot had an aquarium that somehow reminded him of his navy days. Sometimes old friends we didn't know would visit him and his behavior would be contrite, all right, and we knew we had nothing to fear. They'd hang out in his rooms, drinking until dawn. A low, muffled murmur and scattered laughter. A part of his life we weren't allowed to know. But we didn't want to know. Shot stood up straighter when they visited, had this look in his eye like he was a hero. I especially didn't want to know what he thought a hero was.

Over time, the aquarium went from ten fish to one, from lots of "stuff"—a deep-sea diver figurine, fake coral, rocks—to just one rock. The fish was a medium-sized bass-type fish. Slowly, the water got murky and the fish moved less and less. Soon enough, there wasn't anything in there but the fish, and, then, not even the fish. Nothing. Just a tank full of bad, sad water. He never let us clean it or help, even though the fish began to weigh on us. When it disappeared, he told us he'd killed it because we'd made such a fuss over it.

I don't know why that broke me worse than all the other things. I don't know why Unitopia reminded me of that, but by the time I walked into the back room from the visitor center, I was already sad for something lost. Nothing I did now could change that.

Imagine Silvina after the end of Unitopia.

Imagine what it might've broken. What, in the broken places, healed as resistance.

Imagine how, growing up, I didn't dare keep a salamander in the house although I wanted to, let alone a real pet. Just for a day or two, catch and release. Because all I could think of is Shot's fish.

Standing behind a carved wooden counter with the outline of a stylized mermaid's body across the front . . . was "Ronnie." It said it right there on her name tag. Which was good because I realized that, in the background research, I hadn't ever found a photo.

"Ronnie" was a slim white woman. In her mechanic's-style overalls. Rows of antique appliances behind her. So that was the "organic mechanic" part. No oil smell or anything else you'd expect.

This last dome was divided in half by the wall that housed vintage appliances, and an open, round door carved with vines led to a space farther back that looked spartan. A bench, a couple old chairs, some tools, boxes, and cans. Maybe someone else was back there, but I doubted it.

Ronnie had a wary look stitched on, which I doubted helped with customers. But, then, she couldn't have any idea who I was. I liked that her nails were ragged and torn and her hands smudged, as she cleaned them with a rag. So maybe she did fix things. I liked the openness of her face and the light blue of her eyes. In some vague way, I felt I'd seen her before. Otherwise, I didn't have an opinion.

"Are we alone?" I asked.

"That's a strange question, stranger, don't you think?" she said, putting the rag on the counter. The countertop was solid, so I couldn't see anything hidden behind it.

"I mean, I'm curious how many visitors you get, with the center closed."

Ronnie shrugged. "A couple a week. Most people call me. They don't visit. I do house calls."

"What do you tell them about Unitopia?"

Ronnie smiled. A tight smile. "What can I help you with?"

I didn't like how she'd started to bend at the knees. Was already in the wrong mood or mode.

I pulled out the gun, pointed it at her. It looked so small in my hand. I'd surprised myself. Had thought out so many subtle ways of questioning Ronnie. This wasn't one of them.

"Step away from the counter. With your hands where I can see them."

I held the gun tight-in to my body so no one passing by could see it past my bulk. Hell, they probably couldn't see Ronnie.

"I don't keep any money here. There's no safe or anything," Ronnie said, hands in that universal "Don't shoot" position. But calm, like she'd experienced this before or knew that it was coming. Or didn't believe I'd shoot.

"Money isn't why I'm here," I said.

"I don't think these parts will fetch much on the black market."

As if she hadn't heard me. I didn't appreciate the fearlessness. Defiance in the stance. Best to get to the point.

"I want to know why your initials are scrawled on the bottom of a stand for a piece of taxidermy."

"I wouldn't know," she said. A little too quickly. Not what she'd expected.

"A hummingbird. Skillful job."

"I wouldn't know." A cold, appraising stare. Like she was weighing the odds of a jail break.

"Silvina Vilcapampa." Another client trick. If you want a reaction, strip out the context.

A rapid blink, a wince, no way to hide it.

"You know her?"

No response.

"You served two years for breaking and entering. As part of sabotage for an extremist environmental group." Easy enough to get those records, once I had the name.

"They were going to poison a river for a mine."

"Did you do that for Silvina, too?"

No answer. But I realized it was probably before she'd met Silvina—the thing that had gotten Silvina's attention.

"And then you wound up here. Did Silvina set you up here? Did you run Unitopia?"

"No one ran this place," she said. "It was a commune of like-minded freethinkers."

"Who wanted to blow up things."

"No," she said, in a quiet voice. "We just wanted to be left alone."

"Actually, not true. You wanted people to come here. You wanted to make more Unitopias."

A wild, strange light turned on behind her eyes. "And why not?" Defiant. "Why did everyone have such trouble with that? Waystations for rebirth. Centers for resistance. Haven't you read the news? Do you think we couldn't have used it?"

"Except, on the side, you're also a taxidermist," I said. "Of extinct and endangered animals."

"No!"

"Then why are your initials on the stand for a humming-bird?"

With some difficulty, I'd managed to get my phone out with one hand and show her the image.

She shrugged.

"Why would Silvina give this to me?"

That lit up her features, but I couldn't read the emotion.

"She *gave* you this?"

"Yes. And a note saying I'm supposed to look for a sala-mander."

Such a complicated look on Ronnie's face. Hope mixed with anger or sadness or . . . ?

"She always was paranoid. Didn't trust people. Played games. Tricks. Tests."

"I don't care about that. Why me?"

A look I couldn't interpret again. Wistful, strange.

"Maybe it's an experiment. She was big on experiments. Like, looking at you, maybe it's 'Will some giant-ass, middle-class suburban woman with no clue about anything be moved enough by the plight of the planet to . . .'" She trailed off.

It took more than that to bait me.

"To what? What is this giant-ass, middle-class suburban woman supposed to do?"

"I don't know."

"But you know Langer, right? You must know Langer."

Something rigid about her dissolved; her hands wavered. Maybe it was just that she thought if I was asking about Langer, I wasn't with Langer.

"An asshole," she said.

"Seems like it."

We both relaxed, a little.

"What were you to Silvina?"

"I helped her. For a time."

This was like pulling teeth. Fusk all over again.

"I got that already. But she hated the wildlife trade, so why taxidermy? Why did she have taxidermy?"

"That was her business. Not my place to tell you." Loss? Something she'd lost.

"Where would I find a salamander?"

She shrugged, folded her arms, considered me a moment. Was that a hint of a smirk?

"There's a warehouse full of this stuff. Abandoned. Silvina's family owns it," she said.

I wasn't sure I liked how easily she'd given that up.

"Where?"

She gave me the address. Not as far as I'd feared. East side of town, about half an hour from my house, and forty minutes from the storage palace.

"I don't know anything else. That's literally the only thing I know. I've been out of her circle for a while."

"What circle?"

"Friends of Silvina. Rebel angels."

I'd seen "Friends of Silvina" in Allie's reports. That almost sounded like an organization. Hilariously innocuous, like a fund-raiser for fighting some disease.

"Are they still around?"

"I don't know."

"Did you leave because you realized what Silvina was *really* doing?"

It just came out unintended.

Her resistance stiffened. "How about we back up a step. How did you find me? And who do you work for?"

Like I didn't have a gun aimed at her.

"I found you through a taxidermist named Carlton . . . Oh fuck—"

Midsentence, she'd thrown an empty toolbox at my head, followed by a stool that smashed into my chest like a battering ram as she knocked the gun from my hand onto the floor. It made a terrible, sick sound, against the metal and stone.

No match for me, but I hadn't expected it, and, before I could recover, Ronnie had slid back across the counter and out the door to the back.

I snatched up the gun, followed, quick but cautious, into the back—just in time to hear a splash. There was a kind of hangar door in the middle of the back room, wide open, with nothing but a nub of pontoon and water behind it. Ronnie was getting away by swimming across the lake to the forest beyond.

At the lip where the slick black edge of Unitopia met water, I stood, braced with one arm and the other pointing a gun at Ronnie as she swam.

But I wavered, lowered my weapon. Couldn't do it. And why would I do it? I hadn't come to Unitopia to kill her. I just wanted information. Then I started to laugh. Then I stopped. It was comical that someone was doing the breaststroke across a lake to get away from me. But not so funny: the cold. No wonder she was swimming so fast. Perversely, I was rooting for her. The disruption I'd caused, and how clumsily I'd caused it. I'd been so clumsy.

No way to know where she was headed or how to get there. A search on my phone as I watched her disappear out of sight around a little island of reeds. In that respect at least it was wilderness—the island abutted a corridor of woodlands leading to a state park. By the time I got there, Ronnie could be anywhere.

I put my gun away. How useless it had proved. Because I hadn't been alert enough, had thought a gun was enough. But, also, I'd forgotten to take the safety off.

I was fairly sure Ronnie wasn't ever coming back to Unitopia. I was pretty sure I'd never see her again. I was positive she wouldn't call the police.

But now, at least, I had the address for a warehouse "full of taxidermy."

For whatever that was worth.

UNITOPIA

[59]

Maybe it wasn't wise, but I lingered in Unitopia. It had a sweet, naïve quality. No sense of threat, just of emptiness, of abandonment. I thought perhaps I would encounter the man who had popped out of the doorway before, but, no, not even him. And I had to slough off the aftermath of excitement, slow my breathing, try to take a moment to reset.

By then, the midafternoon sun had slanted and deepened in a way that made the holding pond resemble a real lake. The walkway had a bronzed look, under that touch, and the buildings a comfortable, lived-in feel. Even the geodesic monstrosity at the end. Perhaps I felt apart from this, from this idea of "sustainability," but I realized I could have gotten used to it. That it also felt like "sovereignty." And those portal views of other places—they had stuck with me. Maybe they would, in time, have become real views from other Unitopias.

Silvina, stateless. Belonging, in a way, to no place and no one. Perhaps, at first, Unitopia had felt like a way to create her own country.

Had people even lived in Unitopia itself? I didn't know. How sad if they had worked here for such a different future . . . but lived in a subdivision named "Lake Woods" or "River Creek." Revolutionaries trapped in a theme-park life.

The community Silvina could not sustain, but, also, didn't

seem to have the patience to sustain. Even though she'd poured so much effort into it, brought in green-tech experts and even biologists. On the cusp of trying to make Unitopia independent. Teetering there.

Something impossible.

No, in the end, easier to tear it down and start over. The soundless scream of social media these days. The system must be destroyed. It can't be fixed. Unitopia must have begun to seem like a Band-Aid applied to a gaping chest wound.

But how did you get from Unitopia to a kind of, for lack of a better term . . . weaponized taxidermy? And from that to bioterrorism? Or was that a pretty normal progression after you realize Unitopia is going to fail. That it's not enough or not in the right direction. So you set off in a new direction, without a map. Maybe you even say, "Well, I *tried* to be good, to play by the rules. I tried a *sustainable* approach."

On the west shore of the island, I found a relaxing nature park, along with a sign showing what you might see there. I sat on a bench and read about dredged reclamation and restored wetlands. Red-winged blackbirds in the reeds. Tanagers on migration. Marsh wrens. Great blue herons. The types of frogs. Even a rare sighting of a beaver.

But no hummingbird, no salamander.

When I got back to the parking lot, mine was the only car left. As if everyone else had fled along with Ronnie.

Texts I had missed made me wince, start up the car quick to get the hell out of Unitopia as if I could arrive somewhere else in an instant.

>>*Where are you? You're missing the talent show.*

The after-school talent show. I had it on the calendar. Just not in my brain.

Daughter: >>*Are you OK? Why aren't you here?*

The truth was . . . I wasn't really anywhere.

I was just someone who had a new lead to a mystery she couldn't have explained to a stranger in less than twenty minutes.

But I turned the engine off when I read the next texts. Not from Hellbender or my family. Alex. Coldly formal.

>>*The board has decided to terminate your contract due to erratic and irregular behavior and unauthorized use of company resources for private endeavors.*

>>*Your office belongings will be sent to your house. Do not come in to collect them.*

>>*If you require an explanation, HR will be happy to provide one.*

A weight pushed down on me. A weight left me. I slumped over the steering wheel like I'd been shot.

Then I called Alex anyway. I half expected he'd ignore me, but he picked up on the second ring.

Fusk all over again. I felt I had to hurry or he'd just hang up.

"Alex, I don't know what this is about, but just because I've been distracted lately doesn't mean that we shouldn't talk about this first. After so many years."

The voice that came back at me made me regret the call. I didn't need to hear that coldness.

"We have all the evidence we need of everything up to and including possible criminal behavior. The favor we're doing you is not bringing this to the police."

"I told you I was pursuing a client."

"That's not what you were doing."

"Well, so what if it was a bit of research on the side? You know Larry does all kinds of—"

"You don't get to say Larry's name," Alex snapped. "We know you're doing something dangerous. Rash. Stay away from the office. Security has your photo and name. Any attempt to contact me again and I will go to the police."

"Alex, I—"

"Don't worry, you'll get a severance package. Sort of."

"I can sue you over this," I said. Knew I sounded desperate. Alex took a breath. "You don't understand."

"What don't I understand?"

I felt a panic emanating from his voice. The anger came from fear.

"The 'client' you tried to recruit contacted us. That's all you need to know. And I never said that. Good-bye."

He hung up.

So not Allie complaining but the Vilcapampa family interceding.

It hardly mattered how. I'd gotten too comfortable, hadn't seen it coming. Any more than I'd remembered my daughter's haircut or her talent show.

Even as a rush of wild elation—or was it hysteria—came over me, and such a sense of relief. Like calling Alex had been about going through the motions. Just another thing I was supposed to do, another way I was supposed to react. And some minor-key satisfaction: I must be getting close. Someone in power knew I was getting close.

But, mostly, I was thinking of how I missed the hummingbird, the softness of the fierceness of its wings. Knowing I would never see one in real life. Already, the photograph wasn't enough and my memory wasn't enough and video online wasn't enough. Nothing would be enough.

That's what I thought of in that moment, god help me, sitting in the car after Alex hung up. To calm me down, to put things in perspective. The hummingbird and its vast journey, its tragic fate. Not my family.

Because I thought the hummingbird had to mean more. It wasn't a pointless regifting. Whatever snapped in Silvina, whatever made her too intense for Ronnie, Unitopia.

A little later another text came in.

>>*Bitch bitch bitch bitch bitch*

Well, that was Larry. Maybe Allie was wrong and he felt better.

Good enough to dump a paper bag full of dogshit on my front step.

[60]

The world that week seemed to be dying in flame and famine and flooding and disease. The things meant to help us were hurting us and the things meant to hurt us continued to get better at it. I told myself my job didn't matter. So I wouldn't enter a Möbius strip of might-have-beens. Tried to be calm. We had savings. We had assets we could liquidate. I could go freelance, as a consultant. I didn't really have it in me to think about job hunting. Didn't have it in me to tell my family, either.

I had Unitopia lodged in my skull. This concrete place that would breed so many new search terms. That would reveal a part of Silvina's mind I could cross-reference to the journal. Sparks of excitement, along with the stress.

Still, home was a nightmare. No evidence in the woods of a watcher, as if a hallucination. No evidence that I would be forgiven for missing the rehearsal. Dinner had a bleak, dull quality, made worse because it was the rare night I'd promised to cook. All I could do was stare at the woods and try to make my mind blank against a crescendo of conflicting thoughts.

Like: the address Ronnie had given me must be worthless, because she'd relinquished it so easily. Like it was where I was meant to go, because "R.S." had been given to me as a clue. So Ronnie'd been told to give me the address. Except, it was only by luck that I even knew who Ronnie was. Fusk was *my* investigation work, in the sense that Silvina hadn't put the initials "C.F." on the bottom of the hummingbird's stand. My twist on the incoming intel.

If the address was worthless, it wouldn't hurt to see it anyway. Intel wasn't just information—it was context, tone, texture, nuance. Maybe it would help. Maybe, at the very least, it would make me give up.

Because part of me wanted to give up. Part of me wanted to stanch the bleeding and find a way back to normal.

But all it meant, really, is that I was too far gone to come back to normal yet.

Blessed relief and release when dinner was over and we could go our separate ways for a couple hours. Once or twice, doing the dishes as inadequate penance, I opened my mouth to say something to my husband, sequestered in the living room with a glass of strong red wine. Then I would close it again. Futile. What would I tell him? About being fired? About wildlife traffickers. About a hummingbird, a salamander.

We migrated to the bedroom, with sullen, unreadable daughter off to her room. Something in her eyes: if we talked again, I would need better answers. I remember feeling relief: that my lie meant she wasn't ratting me out or writing me off. Whereas my husband suspected nothing. Or did he?

Wired to the moment, to the present tense, as I brush my teeth, put on my pajamas, as he flosses and puts on his boxers, takes up the half-read newspaper and grunts in satisfaction at his fullness from a dinner he didn't have to make. No questions from him, just the usual routine. While I'm making a conscious effort to take deep breaths, to be some semblance of calm.

Then I crash into the world again and I am no longer light, no longer able to keep it all at arm's length. Have to strangle a scream.

Surely he will notice? But he doesn't. He sits up in bed reading until it's time for sleep. Until we turn the light off and lie there on our separate sides.

He's snoring soon enough. But I can't sleep. I can't even begin to think of sleeping. I'm wired like a race is about to start, like a match is about to start, like a fight is about to start.

I rise up rise up rise up. The clock reads two in the morning.

I tiptoe best I can, seeming thunderous to my ears. To the closet, to put on some clothes, quietly go downstairs, retrieve Shovel Pig, take out the gun, close the front door behind me.

[61]

I needed to screw up my courage first. "Dutch courage," Shot would've called it. For what I planned to do. I kept telling myself it was stupid. Then finding ways to convince myself. This would be it. The last lead I'd investigate. I'd do this thing and Silvina would be out of my life. Whatever I found, whatever I'd already discovered that might be valuable . . . I'd send it anonymously to the authorities, to wildlife protection organizations. Whatever made sense. Then I'd find another job in the security business. Or somehow beg Alex to take me back. Like my old life just waited there, patiently, for me to inhabit it again.

First, I'd driven to within a fifteen-minute walk of the broken-down shed that hid my go-bag. I'd already taken out all the cards at the house, along with further precautions. I stashed Shovel Pig and all my phones save my work phone. Bog felt too valuable to risk, but I'd changed the work phone to make it harder to trace. I'd ditch it after.

Then I drove to the dive bar across from my gym, which wasn't too far out of the way. Back route through a residential neighborhood and parked a block away. Slipped in through the back door, sat in the velvet darkness on the long, low bench along the wall, derelict pool tables in a herd in front of me. Only three people at the bar. I waited for the bartender to come to me. Figured I was four or five quick steps away from slipping out the back door. That was how I was thinking. That someone might come for me.

I couldn't see the gym from my position, just the lonely parking lot streetlamp that I used to park beneath. Rationed my double Jack and Coke, ate some bar peanuts. It smelled like piss from the bathrooms, but the reek just kept me sharp, focused.

Ronnie Simpson. Apparently, an Olympic-caliber swimmer in addition to reformed ecoterrorist. Unitopia still in my head. A kind of sourness of regret. Maybe I still had a cage around my brain that Silvina hadn't pried open yet. Because I thought in that moment about the wasted potential. How with Vilca-pampa company resources behind her, Silvina might've done more good. Instead, she was dead, and all I could find of her were people like Langer and Ronnie.

My work phone beeped. A text.

>>*I don't have eyes on you. You just disappeared. Where did you go?*

Hellbender. Such a swell of satisfaction that he couldn't find me. That my precautions worked. That I had no need to answer.

But maybe I shouldn't have had the double drink. Because I didn't put the phone down. *You just disappeared.* The niggling thing in the back of my head. Something about the exact moment Ronnie had jumped me and fled, what I'd been saying. I hadn't put it together before, it hadn't registered. I could berate myself a lifetime, all the things I missed. All the stupid things I did notice.

Stared at my work phone for a moment. Tried to think through the potential risk. But everything was nearly over, right?

I dialed the number.

Fusk answered on the first ring, surprising me, and his hello was as steeped in whisky as my reply.

"Hey, you leathery old bastard."

"Who's this?"

"You know. The detective who wasn't. The one you said should stay away from Silvina. You were right."

"You're still alive."

"Sort of. Hey, Fusk, I have a question."

"You're drunk."

"So are you, so we're even."

I heard a husk of a laugh at that. Or maybe I imagined it.

Even from that distance, I could see the death-swirl of insects around the lamppost across the street.

A sigh, long, drawn out. "Ask your question?"

That made me sit up from my slouch. "Wait. Really? You're not going to hang up?"

"What's the point now."

A new refrain you heard a lot. And not just in bad country-western songs in bars.

"Fusk, did you know Ronnie? Actually know her, not just know of her?"

"I told you I didn't."

"One mention of your name over at Unitopia and she knocked the gun out of my hand and jumped in the water and I never saw her again."

"Oh yeah?" But something in his voice had changed.

"Yeah."

"So what if I did?"

Silence, through which I could hear a lot of police sirens and people chanting or shouting. Protesters? Protesting what this time?

"For Silvina," he said finally. "I didn't know it was for her. It was all under the table, you know? Ronnie was the one who came to me. I only found out later who she worked for."

I couldn't sit still. Had to pace my prison, cluttered as it was with pool tables. Circumnavigate those green, rectangular islands. Swivel, repeat.

"What, exactly, did she bring you?"

"A hummingbird and a salamander. Six years ago."

"What condition?"

"Pardon?" It must be hard to hear over the noise in the street.

"What condition were they in? Did they come in a cooler or dried out or what?"

"Both came in separate coolers. The hummingbird was in pristine condition. The salamander . . . I couldn't tell if it was fresh or thawed, to be honest."

I stopped pacing. "You mean you got the sense the hummingbird at least had been alive recently?"

"Yes."

"What kind of salamander?"

"I dunno. Big, though. Really big. More like an iguana."

I felt like an electric charge had gone through my body.

"Can you describe it?"

"Why does it matter?"

"Humor me, Fusk."

"Already doing that. Well, it looked like a salamander. Blackish brown. Yellow stripes. Don't know much about amphibians except they're a pain to prepare."

Racing stripes. Another thing to look up. But another thought made my head explode. The hummingbird. By then, they would've been extinct in the wild. Where had Silvina found a living one? Or was Fusk wrong, and it had just been brought to him well-preserved?

"But you must've looked at photos or done a search, right? You must have known it was probably as rare as the hummingbird?"

"Doesn't pay to look too hard. You should know that by now."

Wasn't sure I believed he hadn't known.

"And Ronnie. What did Ronnie say about the job? Anything about why they needed taxidermy made from them."

"Not at first. I just did the job, took the money, and Ronnie came and picked them up one day. About two months later."

"And then?" I prompted. "What happened next?"

"About a year later, Ronnie dropped by again. She'd dyed

her hair, which I thought was strange, and was wearing sunglasses in the store and a big hat. That made me nervous."

Ridiculous spy disguises. Friends of Silvina unused to some new focus? From the feds? From criminal organizations?

"What did she want this time?"

"She wanted me to sell the taxidermy I'd made. For her. I said no."

"Because you knew it was dangerous?"

"Yeah. I thought for sure they'd tried to sell it already and something had gone wrong. I didn't want any part of that."

"Do you know what she needed the money for?"

I could hear the shrug over the line. "The way Ronnie talked about it, maybe they'd been in the middle of some project where the money dried up. She asked me if I knew anyone who could unload them. At a discount. I didn't volunteer anyone."

I chewed on that, asked, "Has anyone else been nosing around since I was there?"

"A couple strange phone calls. A guy outside I figured was watching the place. I'm leaving soon. Closing the shop for a while." Or the shop was closing him.

"I've got a gun now." Just blurted it out. Cursed the drink, but who knows where the impulse came from.

"Smart. That's how you've lasted longer than . . ."

"Longer than you thought."

He laughed. "Yeah. The person who walked into my store wasn't going to last long. That I know."

I didn't want the grudging respect. Should've recoiled from that camaraderie. But instead I leaned into it.

"Where are you going to go?"

"Wouldn't tell you."

But I sort of knew. Upstate he had some land and a cabin where he used to hunt every summer. I cared. I didn't care. What was the pang I felt? The pathetic sense that I could talk to Fusk about things I couldn't tell my husband. And now Fusk was fading. Fusk was going to disappear. A sense of desperation came over me.

"Fusk?"

"Yeah?"

"Do you think Silvina was a good person?"

As if he were some kind of final arbiter. As if his answer would settle it for me.

Fusk put me out of his misery. He hung up. I never talked to him again.

[62]

A vault of night. An enormity and weight to it. Beyond the trains and the cars and the traffic lights and drones. Stars were all airplanes and the streaks like lights were really lives, far above. Unless they were satellites. I just knew they weren't stars. Something mysterious beneath or beyond the artificial. I was in a strange mood, almost an altered state.

The warehouse had a shallow, M-shaped roof with a tin-like texture, only thicker, and off-white walls lit only by a blurry yellow light out front. Woods to either side cocooning, enveloping. Nearest building was a gas station at a crossroads a quarter mile south. You could hear the highway, but distant. In theory, this was an incorporated part of the county, but not really. Enough little roads around and sudden elevations that it would be easy to double back and make sure you weren't being followed. So I did. Then eased into a dirt parking space. A fallen tree nearby made me think no one had been here in a while. Or taken care of the place in a while, at least.

Another text came in as I took bolt cutters to the lock, put my shoulder to the jammed door to make it give, hollow out a space for the likes of me. I dropped the bolt cutters, read the glowing words.

Any satisfaction I'd felt at leaving Hellbender blind left me.

>>*Jill, you need to tell me where you are.*

I couldn't move. Felt like I was suffocating, realized I was holding my breath.

Jill. Only one person had gotten "Jill" as my name the past three years. The man who had stood me up at the conference. The one who had given me a false hotel room number.

So that was Hellbender. Not Langer but some third party.

Tracking me all the way to New York. Wanted a look. A guy brazen enough to dress in a clown wig wouldn't mind getting close. A guy who'd done that so I wouldn't recognize him from the store clerk's description.

Jack. Not Langer. And he wanted me to know it. To make me answer.

I began to text him back, but a car had slowed on the street beyond. Something European and expensive, like a Jetta. So I pushed the bolt cutters inside with my feet, pulled the door shut until it was only open a crack, and watched.

They cut their lights, rolling to a quiet stop next to my car. Three men got out, hard to see in the crappy lighting.

But one of them I thought I recognized, even though the haircut was different. Something about his affect raised the hairs on my arm.

Langer. Not on my phone after all, but there in the flesh. He had a sharp, intense look to him. He didn't waste much motion. I hated him at a glance. Feared him, too. A kind of bulkiness built into Langer's pals that I read as heavily armed.

I retreated into the warehouse. It smelled moldy and like rust. The corridor or antechamber was narrow and long, with a weird fake stone veneer to the floor. I guessed the wings filled out into storage rooms only accessible from farther in. Like a corridor you'd lead cattle down, then isolate them through a U to either side. I put a door between us, then another. I could hear Langer and his men, faint, at the front door, being cautious. Maybe there was a back way out.

I felt foolish. Raw and inexperienced.

Too late.

Through a small window in the next door, I could see that the main space lay beyond. A dim-lit vagueness suggesting height.

"Jill." Langer. The man on the hill.

All the weight of that came crashing down on me, and it was like I woke up. Finally and forever woke up.

I called the house.

My husband answered on the fifth ring.

"Where the hell are you? It's the middle of the night, and you just—"

"Listen to me," I whispered, as calmly as I could.

"What is going on?"

"There's *no time. Get out* of the house. Take whatever you can gather in the next half hour. *Get out* and go up in the mountains or some property a friend is selling that's remote. Don't tell anyone. Someplace secure. And stay there. Just for a while."

"Are you crazy? That's just—"

I said his name. I said his name, and then I said, "The man in the woods was watching us because of me. Both of you are in danger. I'm sorry. There's no time. Don't tell anyone where you're going."

I hung up on him before he could reply. I never called. I always texted. No better way to make him understand the severity.

Then I texted Hellbender the warehouse address. I didn't trust him, but how could things get worse? Maybe the more people at this party the better.

Langer was through the first two doors. I'd just closed the third, wedged something that wouldn't hold long against it, and plunged through into the warehouse, phone held like a flashlight.

A sense of bulk, of heft, through the window, but it had been indistinct. What I could see, in the arc of white light from the phone, was the outline of a monster. A creature made of many, many parts. A great, heaping pile that ended only at the ceiling thirty feet above me and that spilled out to the sides so far that there was no way to get around it.

Dead bodies. Skins. The dead. Fur, feathers, scales. Dull glass eyes staring back at me. A confusion and chaos that made me take a step back, nauseated. The mold smell had intensified, and the chemical stench, and the underlying scent of the real: the traces of what they had been alive.

It made me sick. I didn't understand it.

I was facing a midden of taxidermy and cured and uncured skins. A great mound of snuffed-out lives, some common, but most rare and precious. A wall, or wave, and with my pathetic light I could only reveal parts of it. Was glad of that.

Behind me I could hear Langer close. But where could I hide? Nowhere. There were troughs and lanes through the damage, but indistinct, porous, like a trail overtaken by tall weeds with trees looming over top. Still a mountain of dead animals. Lemurs and monitor lizards. Tigers tigers tigers—so many tigers I stifled a cry. Some sights make the brain rebel, make a soul want to hide from itself.

But a survival instinct took over. A terror beyond thought that was instinct. I had no choice. The gun in my hand wasn't enough. I couldn't stand and fight. I had to plunge forward, hide in the morass.

So that's what I did.

[63]

I had never seen so many animals together in one place. I had never seen so many species. Even dead. Even dismembered or mutilated or destroyed in subtle and unsubtle ways. I had never known so much life, even dead. It almost killed me, all the incoming. All the death around me. Half extinguished any need to survive. Yet: I kept moving.

[64]

By the time the door opened and Langer and his friends entered the warehouse, I was hidden deep, cringing and shivering from the touch of so much unfamiliar texture. The smothered flat glossy feathers and furs against my arms and legs and face. The dead bright eyes I couldn't see in the gloom. The dull-sharp beaks rasping against me. Hooves and paws from the wrong directions, against my back. I was trying to adapt to the vastness of it as I heard Langer's voice talking to his men, so maybe he wouldn't realize I was here.

I couldn't process the smells, the dry and the moist of them, how there was a brackish scent of the sea and marsh. A hint of forest. Of how where they came from clung to them.

But the claustrophobia broke me down the most. I couldn't sit still in the middle of all of that. It felt like I was going to drown and suffocate at the same time. That I was in some kind of hell that pressed against my skin so I couldn't tell where my body ended and some other body began. I was drenched slick with my own sweat, and moving slick, trembling, trying not to retch.

Telling myself that if I could only tunnel through it *quickly*, I would be okay. That it was better to be fast in this horrible place. That the faster I got to the end and, hopefully, a door out, the less likely I would lose my mind. That Langer had yet to wade through the same hell. All while it rose and kept rising around me and above and over me and I was already going mad.

The rough heads of crocodiles on the floor tripping me

up. The coarse bodies of lions arresting my fall. I was nothing but an animal myself, scrabbling for air, for freedom. Nothing left in me but this impulse, this idea, of a door that might not exist. I couldn't stand it, not the touch of another skin, another fur. I couldn't.

But Langer heard me. I knew it from the uptick of excitement in his voice.

Then came whistling and burrowing through sharp, whizzing objects that cut through faces around me, shredded through flanks and through eyes and through stomachs and paws. A stitching and ricochet and almost it sounded like an odd rain. But it was bullets. Langer wasn't bothering to follow me. Wasn't bothering to ask me to come out. To come up for air. No, he was just shooting. Me, blind and burrowing through hell, as the bullets sank and lolled and spit past. Came at me from odd angles, clipped or bounced off tired antlers or tusks. The stench of glue. The sense of being hidden and exposed.

I had no way to fire back, could barely keep Shovel Pig from being wrenched from my grasp by a hundred hands, paws, forearms, snouts. And as big as I was, a sudden fear: that as I burrowed and the mound collapsed around me, it would bury me. So that I scrabbled faster, and in that moment didn't know what to fear more: the mound or the bullets.

A weird ping and an insect smashed into my thigh. A hornet or bee that made me cry out in pain as the blood flowed. Except it wasn't an insect—and then there was another that grazed my left arm, and I cried out again and became so panicked that there was nothing to me but fear and want and need, and you would not have known me from the folk around me, as if I had been destined for that place.

A wildebeest and a bear—there near the center of the mound, with some other monumental stag or antelope to create a space to breathe and a shield for bullets. Which continued to reverberate, to hum, to quiver and my only defense to lie against the comforting flank of the bear, to let the bear be my defense.

Until even that quieted, and I tried to slow my breathing so that I wouldn't be heard. Wished fervent that Langer would believe I was dead.

Except, as wary as he was of entering the mound, he was also careful about accepting silence. As I lay there, bleeding, I heard a great whoosh and growing crackle. It sounded like part of the ceiling had fallen in, but in a couple minutes I realized the true source: flames.

The mound was ablaze, from some accelerant. I was going to burn to death. Langer's cursing made me think the fire had surprised him, too.

"Come out," he shouted as the fire spread. "Come out, and I won't kill you."

His partners laughed. I knew it wasn't true anyway. I just wouldn't burn to death. Caught like a rat.

The heat increased, and I was sweating and coughing from the fumes set free from the skins and taxidermy. I could see an orange haze ahead of me where there had been darkness. A wall of orange intensifying to red. I began to cough worse, but I wasn't going to come out. I pulled out my phone, but I couldn't see right anymore, to know what number I was dialing, and something intense about the phone light made them start shooting again.

Except this time they seemed to be shooting not into the animals but behind them, back at the third door. I thought I could hear the lilting chatter of some other kind of gun.

A crack, another crack. Like the world was breaking open. A looming presence that made me gasp.

But from behind me.

I rose up to face this new threat and something smashed against my skull and I fell into darkness.

65

"Breathe. Draw breath. Take another. Isolate the shackling sound, the impatient light. Find a way to remove it. Another breath. Another chance to make it to the beautiful darkness. The bliss of silent places."

I was trapped in the pages of Silvina's journal, which had opened up and become an ocean of paper flooded with black water. It sucked me in and down until I came to the bottom and drifted there with all the dead animals. I saw their eyes now, or what had replaced their eyes. These glass stares, so false, and yet somehow real, too. I couldn't breathe, but I didn't need to breathe. I had gills or it just didn't matter anymore. The monkeys and the crossbills and the wallabies and the lizards and the box turtles and the frogs, so many frogs glowing iridescent way down there beneath the surface, in the bog. I could see an indistinct shape above and reeds radiating out and the faintest hint of moonlight.

I gasped and took on water. I waved my arms to swim and embraced the animals around me until their eyes were alive and quick with thought again. I did not care that they were rotting, that I was rotting. That we were all down below in some purgatory worse yet better than the warehouse. Had I brought them here? Had I led them here?

"Total Nature," Humboldt had written. Which meant no separation. No looking away. No way out but down.

I realized I was beneath Unitopia, looking up. That I was drowning underneath Silvina's creation, as surely as if Ronnie had put me there. Because she had.

66

I woke with a headache that kept trying to smash my skull in half. Staring up at ripped-apart foxes on a dim-lit mantel.

Silvina's old apartment.

I tried to move, but couldn't.

The man who had followed me up the hill flickered and drifted into view, and my axes aligned and I was right-side up again. Bound to a chair—an old plastic lawn chair brought in from the balcony. My hands had been lashed to its arms with police-grade plastic restraints. I had to keep shifting my weight because the frame wasn't going to stop my ass from smashing through the seat soon.

Two men stood behind "Hill Man." I didn't recognize them.

But I panicked at the way they were looking down at me and I thrashed, lunged, fell over in the chair, tore the seat, twisted an arm, my shoulder against the floor. A strangely numb shoulder. Throbbing. I'd been drugged.

Dust swirled up and I saw, close, drag marks on the floor I hadn't noticed before.

Still the men said nothing, just watched me.

I stopped struggling. The restraints wouldn't come off. The chair had collapsed around me in a way that felt like I'd trapped myself worse.

Something bounced off the side of my head, skidded past me toward the mantel. The fox kit's head. Staring back at me. Hillman had thrown it.

"No point," Hillman said as I tried to prop myself on an elbow and look up at him. Had to shudder back down. I could feel an icy cold burning in my shoulder, in my leg. Bits of molten coal hidden under the ice. I could see but not feel the bandage on my leg.

"You gave me something," I slurred.

"Painkiller. Hold you for now. Could've let you die. Remember that."

"This is kidnapping."

"We saved your life," Hillman said. "Langer would've let you burn alive and walked away laughing."

"Who set the fire?" I asked.

Hillman didn't answer, had found a stool or something from the bathroom, was perched on it, looming over me. Some satisfaction in how he sported a black eye, purpling bruises.

"You set the fire, didn't you?" Or Hellbender. "And Langer? Is he dead?" Like if I knew the answers, everything would be fine.

Hillman ignored me.

Up close, Hillman's face was more thoughtful than I remembered it. Creased brow, quick, green eyes, and some thought to the sophistication of a suit I hadn't ripped apart yet. He smelled of a subtle aftershave.

Hillman took out a long cardboard box. A coffin for a large doll?

"Boss said to tell you there was another clue, but he found it first. No one cares about these clues anyway. It's like something a kid would do. He says."

Hillman pulled something out of the box. My heart stopped or I stopped breathing, had to remember how again.

The salamander. A burnt umber color, with two wide yellow stripes down the back. Startling. Iridescent, almost bright gold. Tiny smooth bumps to the skin. Posed in a sinuous way, like a living river. Flat. Wide. Maybe as long as the box. But the small eyes and mouth gave the creature a vulnerable quality.

The salamander almost seemed to smile. Reassuring me.

Then Hillman set it on fire. I'd been so focused on the salamander, I hadn't seen him take out the lighter.

"No!" I screamed, and I must've lunged at Hillman, because one of the other two kicked me and I fell over again, doubled over in pain and frustration.

Hillman dropped the salamander into a large metal wastebasket . . . and watched it burn.

"So now there's nothing to investigate anyway, right?"

The salamander began to turn black, and a stench rose from it. One of them slid the balcony doors open to let in fresh air.

While I was bereaved, aghast, watching the face of the answer that had eluded me begin to melt, taking the smile with it. Watching my past melt away.

One of the other men had brought a laptop over, and Hillman retreated from the stool so the laptop could rest there.

Following that motion, I realized *someone else* was tied to another chair, just beyond my peripheral vision. Someone quiet. The positioning seemed purposeful. What I wasn't meant to see.

"Who's that? Who's that?" Afraid it was my husband. Afraid because it could be anyone.

But Hillman ignored me, and I heard the sound of one of the others moving the other chair until it was all the way behind me. Whoever it wasn't couldn't or wouldn't say anything.

"We're going to prop you up so you can talk to someone. If you give us any trouble, that man over there is going to shoot you with your own gun."

"It's not my gun. Who else is here? In the chair."

"Okay? Do you understand me? About shooting you?"

I grew still. Hillman looked like he was about to hit me.

"Okay."

With difficulty, I got into a sitting position despite the thicket of exploded lawn chair around me. Pieces cut into my arms while others dangled from weird angles.

The laptop was set on the stool, and I could see a face in motion across the screen. A familiar face.

Older than his photographs. White hair and a white beard. Hollowed out at the cheekbones so the eyes shone with an almost messianic glint. Who could mistake him for any other soul? The senior Vilcapampa, Silvina's father. The head of legions from hell. Maker of money across the globe, at whatever price. Beloved philanthropist.

"Jane," he said, smiling, his voice hollowed out, too. A smoker's voice. Those cigars.

But he didn't just say "Jane." No, Mr. Vilcapampa used my full legal name. Drawn out. The hollowness became gravel, then faded again. I couldn't tell if it was the connection or just his voice. I was too in awe of him. Not in the sense of worship or adulation. But in the sense of a mythical beast appearing before me so unexpectedly.

"This is illegal. This is kidnapping," I said. "Who else is in the room? Who's behind me?"

Like a stupid parrot. The kick in the side had dislodged more pieces of the chair. I still couldn't get free, but maybe if they kicked me some more . . .

Vilcapampa shrugged, ignored my question. "Perhaps. Was it legal when you broke into this apartment?" I was sick of hearing about that. "Anyway, it matters not." *It matters not.* Just the way he spoke. "You're an intelligent woman with a high-powered career. Why do you think I want to talk to you? Why should I take the time?"

Like this was a job interview or he was with HR and I was about to receive a reprimand.

"I don't know. I don't care." Which was true, in a way. He was like a cliff or a surging sea. A projection of masks. A force that had worn on Silvina like a geological event. The stench of the salamander scorched my nostrils. I hated him.

"Fair enough. As you say." His features became stern, turned that way sudden, but also in a rearrangement so swift it felt like acting. "I am a busy man, so I'll keep this brief. Silvina was a terrorist and a bad seed and a blight on our family's legacy. I have spent too much time cleaning up after her and defending the family name. I will not have scandal, now that she is dead."

"She tasked me with—"

"With *nothing*." The weight he put on the word hurt my shoulder.

"She wanted to make the world a better place," I said.

"No. She wanted to destroy the world."

"Silvina gave me that hummingbird for a reason."

Vilcapampa shook his head. "No. She gave you the hummingbird because she was unwell, deranged."

"Did you kill her?"

Vilcapampa's face went terrifyingly blank, as if someone had turned him off.

"No," he said finally, as if there was a time delay. "She made her own trouble, who she talked to, who she did business with. She was . . . She was . . . like a diplomat who wants peace but winds up running guns. No better than Langer."

I didn't want to hear that. I told myself it didn't make sense, that Vilcapampa was lying.

"You did business with Langer. *Your* people. And you took the hummingbird," I said.

He shrugged, but his gaze had moved offscreen, as if asking a question of someone I couldn't see. Another person I couldn't see.

"What we want to know is what *you* know. About Silvina's final project. What she told you."

"She told me nothing."

"You must know something. You're an analyst. You've studied the evidence, begun an investigation. You've followed the clues."

"No. I've been chasing shadows."

"I don't believe you."

"You're the one who made sure no one wrote about her death. You're the one who disowned her, gave her nowhere else to turn but criminals."

Even through the haze, I felt the sting of desperation. It was the desperation of knowing I'd never have a chance to talk to Vilcapampa again—and wanting to know so much more. I don't think the threats had even registered. But that was likely the painkillers.

"We could pay you well," Vilcapampa said. "To give us the information."

Maybe, if not for the painkillers, the situation, how far I'd come . . . Maybe I would've answered differently. Found some way to answer differently.

"I have nothing to give you."

Vilcapampa opened his mouth to reply, closed it again. Then began again.

"I thought you might understand the severity of this—and do the right thing. But, I can see that you don't."

"The world is so cracked open," I said. "The world is broken. She wanted to fix it." It was all I had. Yes, I was drunk, in a sense. I was not myself. But I meant it, and there it was laid bare: the reason behind the reasons, that meant I still had hope.

"That warehouse was *Silvina's*. The animals in it were what she sold to bankroll her crimes. First she stole them, then she sold them. Or tried to. Do you understand?"

I had no answer. The pain was becoming less under ice and more the coals. All I could say, again, was, "Who else have you kidnapped? *Who is sitting behind me?*"

Vilcapampa drew closer to the screen. I could see the fissures around his eyes. I could see that he wore foundation and concealer for age spots. I could see the ferocity of his gaze and the certainty of it. Almost too much ferocity.

"I thought I owed you a meeting and a reasonable conversation. For who Silvina was, before. But I was wrong. Now it's time for a different approach. For the old-fashioned, time-honored ways. Good-bye."

He nodded to Hillman, who snapped the laptop shut.

That was all I would ever see of Vilcapampa. In this life or the next.

"Are you going to let me go now? You can drop me off at—"

Another kick in the ribs and a matter-of-fact look. Just the usual from Hillman.

"Tough luck, but we have to find out everything you know. By whatever means. Doesn't trust you any more than he trusted Silvina. It's not up to me if you're alive at the end—it's up to you."

"*Did* he kill Silvina?"

"You mean, did I kill Silvina? No."

Hillman sounded insulted. Like I'd said something absurd, and I believed his answer. Even with an undertone I didn't understand.

He nodded to the two men and they went into the other room to get something. I heard one drop something heavy, metallic, and curse. A sinking feeling to match the ache in my head and my side. I thought I knew why Vilcapampa had risked talking to me direct. Because I wasn't getting out of here. No matter what I gave up.

"Nothing personal," Hillman said. "Really, I mean that."

"It's all personal," I said.

Hillman nodded slow, lips pursed, like I'd said something profound.

"Why not just let me die in the fire? You're about to find out I don't know anything."

Hillman ignored me. "We already moved your car, wiped what we could. No one will know you were there. Or us. It's all on Langer. And maybe you tell us what you know, you get your life back. Or, your choice, you flat-out disappear like Langer got to you. Like you took on Langer because you feared rendition."

"Retribution."

"What did I say?"

"Rendition."

"Is that important?"

"Clarity. About who you are." Which I had none of. Clarity. I was just saying things through a mist that swept through like needles.

Hillman shrugged again. "Here's one answer, but you won't like it."

Grunting, he turned my messed-up chair around until I was face-to-face with a bloody mask of a face, the body beneath it slouched in a torn dress shirt and black trousers. He had no shoes, just black socks.

It took a moment. But then I recognized him.

Alex. They'd interrogated Alex. He was breathing. I could tell because of the blood bubbles popping around his mouth. But I didn't think he'd ever be able to see out of his left eye again.

"A kind of premonition, you think? A kind of prequel, you think?" Hillman said.

A kind of bloody sack of meat. Who'd known nothing.

Hillman opened his mouth to add something. But I never found out what he would've said next.

Because I'd sprung to my feet and bull-rushed him.

Maybe if I'd made a move for the door, he would've been ready. But I didn't. So I plowed him under. Something snapped inside of Hillman and he screamed and his leg collapsed under him. And his collapse knocked Alex over.

Just as the goons came back into the room, struggling with a plastic tarp. One had had to put his gun down. The other had no clear line of sight.

By then I was lunging through the screen door to the balcony, breaking the mesh out of its frame.

I didn't think. I hurled myself over the balcony, as another fucking mosquito of a bullet clipped me in the left arm. I went over the side snarling like an animal, feeling all my weight in the fall and trying in that split second to protect my vulnerable spots, hands still tied, entangled in pieces of chair, but most of it mercifully left behind at the balcony door.

Just a wrestling move. Just a dive and roll. Choreograph it in your head as you tumble. Something I'd practiced a hundred times.

The fall took forever. The fall took no time at all.

Did I care if I died this way?

I was going to die another way, if not.

Screaming from the heat of the smoldering salamander clenched in my hands.

But I would not let go.

[67]

My brother's name was Ned. Yes, let's call him "Ned." We lived in the wildest part of, say, Oregon. That's where the farm was: out in the boonies. The place that eventually gets broadband and chain stores and isn't much different from the rest of the world. But people who don't live there don't understand that.

Ned was the earnest, open type, with a strong jaw and a shock of thick brown hair and striking blue eyes. He'd tried wrestling, too, but sports couldn't much hold his attention. He wasn't built that way. On top of all the rest, no matter how Shot tried to cure him of it, Ned was thoughtful, introspective. He considered things before he spoke and he didn't waste words, and you could already see in him, as a teenager, the man he would've become. Because he was that man even at fourteen. I wondered sometimes if my mother had had an affair.

To watch the girls in town look at him as he walked by . . . this was something I'd never have from the boys, and yet I didn't begrudge Ned. For one thing, he didn't even know he was beautiful. No, the only thing I begrudged Ned was a kind of secretiveness that came with the introspection, built in. He kept things to himself.

But even then, in the last years, as the divide increased between us, because of our age, because I wasn't a boy, our expeditions kept us close. That and surviving Shot. Or "Shit," as we also called him.

Ned's fascination with things under rocks as a child only intensified and sharpened as a teen. He could have a kind of lazy aspect because he didn't act right away, but things under rocks brought out a laser-like attention. It coalesced around more than just salamanders. But I noticed the salamanders more because he had to work for them harder and harder. They became a rare treasure around the farm as creeks dried up, or maybe it was the herbicides and pesticides to protect the crops. Or maybe the new development by rich folks up in the heights, and the runoff from that. But in the little hidden ravines where creeks ran at the bottom . . . we still would find them.

This could be Sundays with the forest beyond the farm as our church. Or we'd finished our chores after school and Shot was off at a bar getting drunk. We had to do things we liked while Shot was getting drunk, to store up kindliness, laughter, nice memories, as a kind of barricade.

Ned had learned of the megafauna of the Trinity Alps of California, and even though that was far distant from the farm, he hoped for some local sighting.

"Those places we can't get to—the gorge, maybe."

The gorge bordered an abandoned quarry, so I didn't think so. But I never said that.

Ten feet long, the Trinity Alps Giant Salamander had first been reported in the 1920s by a trapper. Basking in the headwaters of a remote river. Brown-black, strong, and broad. Never caught. Not a single photograph, even with sightings through the 1970s. But Ned fixated on the expeditions of Captain Hubbard in the 1950s. Which found nothing. Except the vast, unconquered wilderness that exists there today.

I knew why Ned clung to these mysteries. It was the same reason I lost myself in a stack of old Nancy Drew novels, and, when those ran out, the Hardy Boys. Then you didn't have to think about where you were or sullen, terrible dinners with your mother half-insane and your father absent enough that Shot could do whatever he wanted. Verbal abuse. Being slapped around. Pushed into walls. Punched in the gut. It was easier to ignore when I got into wrestling just because I didn't have to explain the injuries anymore.

Except, later, I understood Ned better—after he was gone. It wasn't just escape, all those mysterious details, that amazing mythical salamander. By telling me the giant salamander could be near where we lived, he was changing the landscape around me. He was changing what we dreaded, and what stifled him, into something exciting and positive and new. Getting rid of the residue of Shot that contaminated everything.

It took me a long time to see it that way. But when I did, years later, I remember I sat down on a bench in a park and wept. From the weight of it and the goodness. The sweetness of it. The pureness.

But I was younger, and Ned must have felt that responsibility. So as Shot got worse and Dad even less present, the fantasy of the salamander that overtook Ned meant leaving me behind for some of it. Daytime expeditions to the usual places were fine. But suddenly one summer, when I'd been looking forward, without school, to more escapes, not fewer . . . a wall came up.

"There are places in the wilderness too dangerous for you," he'd say.

"There are places only someone stronger can get to," he'd say.

I was big for my age but not strong yet. Perhaps that stung. Or I thought he was saying I was clumsy. Perhaps that stung. But not for long. That was the thing about Ned, if he'd ever become evil. He could say just about anything and you'd forgive him.

"There are places." Places I couldn't go without him. It wasn't like the law didn't exist where we lived, but there were gaps.

So we'd have our time, two or three times a week. The well-worn grooves of familiar bogs and ponds and creeks. But then he'd bring me back to the farm and go out again. I remember the narrow space around the side of the barn very well, covered over by trees, intruded on by bushes. Because that's how we'd sneak back onto the property if we thought Shit was around.

"He's going to do what he's going to do," Ned said. "You have to live your life, when he's not, like you mean to."

Even in punishment, caught, I saw a kind of light in Ned's eyes, some lightness to his features that felt like a secret smile. No slumped shoulders. He would look Shot straight in the eye, and, at first, that made Shot worse, but eventually Shot began to look away. As if Ned was showing him something about Shot's future he didn't like much.

Except there was cause and effect. I didn't want to "get shit from Shot" because the more Ned's stare got to Shot, the more he took it out on me. And I had no way to tell Ned that. Not in a way that didn't feel selfish or wrong.

The times Shot would smack me when I was doing chores in the barn. The time he finally figured out my "secret" route and popped out of the bushes in that narrow space coming back from a salamander search and crushed me against the barn wall and punched me in the kidneys and then was off again, manic this time, thankfully. If he'd been morose, he would've spent more time on me. Me, on the ground, staring up at the tree branches, thinking how beautiful it all looked. It was spring. Everything was green. My belly hurt so much I thought something had ripped open inside.

A lot of people have it worse, I always told myself, even when I couldn't stop crying.

...

Ned's most secret expeditions took place when Shot was in town, and Ned used to nudge our father to suggest getting drunk in town to Shot. It didn't take much.

Sometimes, as Ned's adventures seemed to get more

frequent and organized, I wondered if he had actually found a giant salamander. Maybe that's why he took the risk. Maybe that's why he seemed not to mind Shot so much. Even if I wasn't sure that made any sense.

I remember that night, too, because I'll never be able to forget it. Not a day of my life. It's there, peering over my shoulder, and I can't push it away. The only difference is, over time, so many other things peer in at you. The weight shifts. The weight leans on you a little less.

Shot had gone off in spectacular fashion, like a hundred bottle rockets exploding too close, and we were both in our separate rooms vibrating from the aftermath. The way your bones feel the abuse even if your bones aren't broken. So you're both numb and humming, both angry and cold.

I don't remember particulars; they were always so banal. They say a trigger can be anything. Shot's randomness gave me so many triggers, they began to cancel one another out. He had been out of sorts over something about the crops, or some arrangement Father had made with a neighbor, and it just escalated until things were thrown at walls—and then I was.

The usual. But this time I'd seen Ned's lip tremble, and it was getting to him more than normal. Like maybe having been stoic all those other times had used up too much of himself. Why that day, I couldn't ever figure out, though. What else had gone wrong? That he couldn't share.

We'd been punished, as if we'd started it, and sent to our rooms, while Mom and Dad sat at the kitchen table, among the dirty dishes, arguing—but softly, so Shot wouldn't hear. Shot was out on the porch demolishing a rocking chair and randomly taking potshots with his hunting rifle at things in the backyard. The chickens had scattered.

I would've gone in to talk to Ned anyway, but I heard him

moving around with purpose, which alarmed me. So I snuck over and saw he was packing a knapsack.

"What're you doing?" The thought had struck, hard, that maybe he was running away.

"Shhhhh! Nothing."

"That's not nothing."

I felt the gash in my heart again. Without Ned, I wasn't sure I could stand things. I mean, I know now I could, but I was a large, powerful child who thought she was weak and puny.

Ned smiled in the rough light of the lamp by his nightstand.

"Not leaving, if that's what you think. Just an expedition. I've got a good lead. I'll be back by morning. Promise."

It had begun to rain, hard, and Shot had decided to start taking out his anger on random stuff in the barn. We could hear him shouting over the rain.

"The ravines will flood if it keeps up," I said. At the very least they'd be too muddy. "How're you going to see?"

"Saved up. Look." He took a miner's headlamp out of his backpack.

At the time, I thought it was cool in a mysterious expedition way. Brave. Now it just seems sad, pointless. Anyone at all could have seen him coming.

The rain became a squall, hit the windows with a rattle and slap.

"Don't go," I said.

Ned took the measure of me. I remember that. He stopped, took my "Don't go" seriously. Maybe because I hadn't said it before. It wasn't premonition. It was common sense.

"I have to," he said.

Have to? But I thought I knew what he meant from the quaver I'd seen. That feeling inside that if you don't escape, even for a little while, you'll start screaming and you won't stop. That there has to be something better, so you try to get somewhere better. Even if it won't last.

I relented, or gave in, nodded, and said, "Okay, but you'll tell me what you find when you get back? Wake me up. Promise?"

Ned smiled in the way that felt like a hug. "Yeah, I'll tell you." But he never would.

■ ■ ■

When I told someone Ned's story, like my husband, or parts blurted out of me drunk at bars . . . I knew it came out drenched in sentiment, lingered on some rough edges while sanding off others. But it was my story, and it was true. Or one overlay of the truth, depending on the day, the month, or the things that you remember that swim up unbidden or that you try to dredge up, afraid you're going to forget forever. And you become someone else again, and the story changes yet again.

■ ■ ■

The next morning, I woke up to the light, the storm over. I hadn't slept at first, but then had slept like I was dead. I was worried. Ned wasn't in his room. He wasn't in the kitchen. My parents looked at me blankly when I asked if they'd seen him. Shot was dead drunk, asleep somewhere.

Ned wasn't in the barn or the backyard. But when I went down to the creek behind the house, I found him. Lying there, curled up, on the sandy bank.

I remember all the air went out of me and I fell like a sack. I fell, and kept falling. But then I thought maybe he was still alive, and I got up and ran to his body.

He was soaked by the storm, face slack, one hand reaching out. Later, the autopsy would find water in his lungs.

Those blue eyes were open, but dull and staring off into the distance. I couldn't help him. I couldn't do anything. The grief was ripping through me, tearing me into pieces.

But even then, there by the creek, my first thought was Shot. That Shot had killed him.

Which is why, two years later, I murdered Shot.

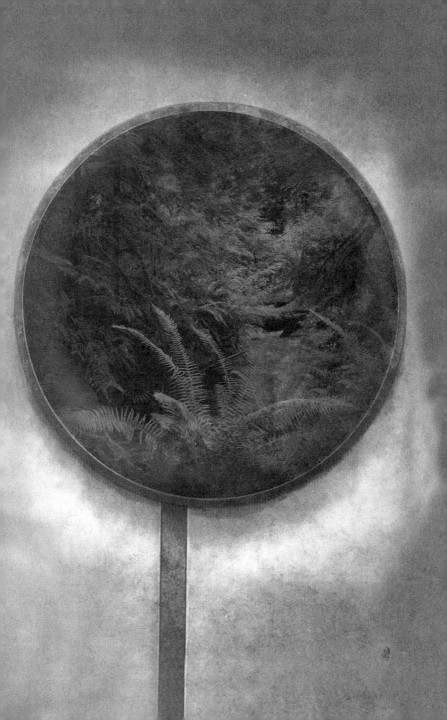

PART 3

SALAMANDER

LIFEBOAT

[68]

A handful of months after I jumped off the balcony of Silvina's apartment, I sat on a stool in a dive bar somewhere remote down the coast, my cane hanging from a hook by my knees. Remote the way your phone doesn't always get reception and places are called towns, but it's mostly a gas station and a convenience store and maybe a kiosk that's the police station. Something you could run over in a pickup truck.

I sat at the bar—a bar, any bar—and drank, knowing I could never return to my home. The wound I couldn't solve with painkillers. My daughter would grow up and forget me. She would actively *try* to forget me. And it would be easy because I'd made it easy. My husband would remarry, move on with his life. He would find someone the exact opposite of me, raise another family. I wouldn't blame him. I wouldn't be able to. I'd be dead by then. Tracked down by Vilcapampa's men or a capricious "Jack" or Langer. Or maybe I'd die before all of that, from the accumulation of injuries.

I sat there, feeling the burn on the back of my neck despite the vodka shots. That throb. The flat smoke aftertaste on my clothes, the soft stale reek of that, and I drank more. They might've taken Hellbender's gun from me, but I'd acquired another easily enough. Concealed carry, no permit. I called it my

"Fusk" because I'd gotten the same type he'd pulled on me. A lifetime ago.

What concerned me most: keeping my hands hidden under the bartop to obscure from the bartender the way I couldn't stop my fingers from moving. A limp folks thought understandable, familiar. They'd seen it before. Grandparents. Veterans of foreign wars. But bartenders, I'd found, took spider fingers as a sign you were unstable or alcoholic . . . and unstable people were trouble. Fears over pandemic and the vagueness of that, of how little was known about its spread, made spider fingers even less attractive.

My fingers were like creatures in search of a piano, but maybe the better lie was that they could never stop trying to work, as if they felt the rest of me would stop functioning otherwise. And, somehow, they were connected to the condition of my left leg. The more my fingers wandered, the more the leg hurt.

I never drink (except I do). I don't like bars (except I do). I just needed to be someone else for a while (except I need to be someone else all the time). Besides, you might overhear something useful in a bar. You might even get to show the bartender an ancient photo of an Argentine woman or a more recent one—a newspaper clipping with a group shot that had "R.S." in it.

Seen this one? How about this one? Nope. No. Never. Mostly I showed Silvina's photo to old people who said they'd never lived anywhere else. Vain hope. But it passed the time.

Alcohol was my only available health care. Mixed with a furtive duck into a clinic, if it was far enough out in the sticks.

Always, every moment, I kept wondering about Silvina, even as I hated her for what she'd let happen to me, or done to me . . . if Silvina would know what to do next. If Silvina would've been better at putting the pieces back together.

Some bars, I've found, people rarely leave you alone for long. Under the squint and crinkle and shadowy rubble of bad lights, a shadow approached me, like a swaying statue, as I downed another shot.

"You look like you—"

I reached out and, swiveling on the stool, pulled him close by his jacket. I punched him hard in the stomach with my other hand, closed in a fist. I felt my knuckles hard and already raw against the flab of his paunch and punched him again. Gasped at the flash of agony running up my leg from putting all my weight on it. Stupid. Forgetful.

Then I released him, as the putrid expulsion of his breath washed over me, and he was rolling there on the floor, along with the barstool he'd taken with him. Entangled with some short mop or other cleaning implement that'd been leaning against the bar. Almost like there was an undertow.

"Why'd you do that, woman?" he whined. "Why?"

Maybe because I was weary of being called "woman." Or weary of being talked to while I drank or because my fingers needed something to distract them. Maybe because I was a mean person or because channeling Shot was, irony, self-preservation in these post-balcony times. Not getting to the gym wasn't great for my mood, either.

I grabbed my cane from the hook, brandished it as I brought my stool to the far corner of the bar, so I could see everyone and everything, including the bathrooms and the front door.

The bartender was a bright owl staring at me motionless. He looked like he'd seen something new after a month of only the usual. I guess he expected me to leave, but the "bar" was hardly a business and at the end of a dirt road in a forest of strange, gnarled trees with a milky-looking bog beyond. I didn't think the place had a license, and I had more than just one gun on me, actually. Along with two knives, one in an ankle sheath and one stuck in my money belt, under my dull-red lumberjack shirt. I'd left most of my weapons back at the houseboat.

I asked for another shot. He poured it, and the man on the floor receded, maybe said something more or maybe he didn't. But I still didn't care, and maybe the three men in the corner playing a clumsy game of cutthroat pool snickered at him or maybe they didn't. Main thing was, they didn't come near me the whole rest of the night.

In the car later, under a contaminated gray-green sky, my back ached, but my shoulders were worse: that brittle shooting stab that, like random veins of lightning, wandered places unexpected and new each time. Sitting was worse than standing for my leg, something wrong with the nerves, like someone had run an iron rod through it, but leg pain I was more familiar with by then.

You never know every part of yourself because you never encounter yourself in all situations. But I'd come closer. I was a wounded beast. A creature that hurt all over. The pain cascaded, reached crescendo, lowered to a murderous hum and shudder, but never left. I could not contain it and had to live within it. I saw through it, worked through it, because I had to, because I thought I still had a purpose.

Maybe I could blame the pain for how I was a different person since the warehouse, since the balcony. Maybe not. But I wanted to kill someone. Anyone who came across my path and looked at me the wrong way.

Back in the old days, they claimed salamanders were born in fire, born to fire. That if you touched one, you, too, would be consumed by flames. But unlike the salamander, you wouldn't survive the encounter. That a poison lived in the conflagration.

I was so much on fire all the time, I should've died.

[69]

Even in pain, even in a kind of limbo, I knew what felt right. I knew I felt right. More *myself*, even if I couldn't define "my self." Why should I be more comfortable in grubby diners or bars in the middle of nowhere? Did it seem more authentic than my life before?

No, it was more that all the things I thought I'd enjoyed . . . I hadn't. Not really. Stripped down, I saw I'd enjoyed almost nothing and, in the end, needed so much less than I'd had. How the idea of "husband" faded, even if the idea of "daughter" didn't. How I couldn't tell if that was due to different kinds of guilt or just a frank admission. I wasn't a dandelion. He wasn't a bear. We just called each other those things in hopes the sentiment was true.

All these gray back roads that called to me, how doubling back and the walk to the houseboat I lived in now weren't chores or a difficulty. The hawk on the wire. The deer staring from a vacant field. The mink staring at me from the side of the road, juxtaposed with dull clay and tall grasses. It wasn't the idea of nature as Silvina saw it. Not the connection with an invisible world. But it meant *something* to me, moving through the wilderness. Maybe because I knew it would've meant something to Ned, too.

The thing that made me chuckle cleaning the Fusk or just staring at the half-burnt salamander: even as dysfunctional as it had been, I'd thought I'd needed some semblance of office camaraderie. I thought I'd needed small talk by the watercooler. The drunken Christmas party with the splayed-out table of miniature, perfectly plated appetizers.

No threat of that now. None of that was real. None of it now felt like it had ever been real.

But the growing sense of betrayal, looming—that was real.

For example, once you looked for a connection between Vilcapampa and Langer, you found it almost right away. Shell companies that colluded on both sides. The way Langer companies gave over to Vilcapampa companies' resources Silvina couldn't find otherwise. Most of these companies weren't the ones Silvina had run, but some were. The way Silvina sold out Contila but let Langer slip away from the authorities. Or someone did.

I bought burner phones like they were breath mints. Tedious work, covering my tracks. Each new connection made me sadder, but also more suspicious. Silvina had needed Langer. Silvina had drawn Langer in. Vilcapampa had said she'd black-mailed him. What did that mean? Vilcapampa had meant it as proof Silvina was corrupt, but how could he be sure? Effective tactic: to accuse your enemy of the crime you had committed. Politicians did it all the time.

I settled on a scenario like a thesis, intending to poke holes in it. What if. What if Silvina got to stay in the U.S. because she gave up Langer's organization to the authorities? Even as she played both sides because Vilcapampa Senior also engaged in wildlife trafficking? Or had at one time. And, during that period, Silvina had a desperate need to acquire or steal wildlife contraband and resell it to fund her own secret project because her family had cut her off.

Which brought me back to a question I couldn't quite answer: Why, exactly, had Langer tried to kill me? Because of the past or because of the future?

[70]

The hardest thing—no, second hardest—I ever did was get up from beneath Silvina's balcony. The agony of it, the painkillers Vilcapampa's men had given me wearing off. The bullet wounds burning eyes that stared out from my body. Every time they blinked, I winced. And they wouldn't stop blinking.

The way I landed, half in the bushes, half on concrete, bruising ribs, destroying my shoulder, some weakness in one ankle. Fractured fingers. I felt like a corpse trying to rise. Like the ground was pulling me down again.

Yet I did rise—and quickly. I ducked or rolled under the awning to the walkway, so they'd have to come down to end me.

Helped that they stood up there for a while trying to get a bead on me. It was dark. I'd bumped my head, and my night vision was for shit. A wash. A blur, like I needed glasses. I tried to remember the area, headed in the direction of a wooded park.

The fall had gotten me free of one restraint, but the other had gotten twisted into the snapped-off plastic arm of the chair and looked like a weird, gangrenous bone dangling from my wrist.

My ankle wasn't right. I kept tripping, feeling something give. I didn't yet know how bad my leg was, or maybe what did the deed was walking on it after. I remember thinking these might be my last moments. Panicked that there was no time, no time left.

A person jogging past ignored me. I remember that, too. The utter banality of it. Was I clueless or was he? Except only one of us was a hulking, shambolic figure awkwardly clutching a dead salamander.

"Drunk," I muttered to ward off evil. "Drunk," I kept muttering when someone appeared on the sidewalk. I didn't look back, kept waiting for a bullet in the back of the brain.

I reached the park. Heard sounds of pursuit, but something else had happened. Sirens rose, but not for me. No, of course not. The police weren't looking for me. Yet. Vilcapampa's men were. But I heard nothing that sounded like they were closing in. Even confused, disoriented, I found that odd. Hillman didn't seem the type to give up like that.

At the back of the park was a shallow, overgrown creek littered with plastic bags and bottles and used needles. A sharp smell like chemicals. I followed it until the onrushing pain caught up and I lost consciousness.

I woke at dawn to a stray cat licking my face. I nudged it away, so thirsty I drank the rancid creek water. I knew I needed medical help. That parts numb felt as bad as the parts I knew were going to kill me. Soon enough, I'd be bruised all over.

Hillman had taken my work phone and wallet, but not the cash in my front pocket. I got a cab to my shed safe house, even if the first three rushed off when they got a good look at me.

I hoped no one knew about the shed, but I had no choice anyway. I almost cried when I saw Shovel Pig. I clutched Shovel Pig to me like a family pet I'd thought I'd never see again. Heavy with all I'd gathered before leaving the house.

I pulled the go-bag out from under the tarp. It had a lot of medical supplies, including painkillers. Once I'd stabilized what I could, I had a bad idea: I tried calling my husband on Bog. No answer. So maybe that meant something had happened to him. Or maybe it meant he'd taken me seriously and wasn't going to answer a number he didn't recognize.

I'd bandaged my ankle. The Langer bullet wounds were through and through. Superficial. But I had a balcony bullet lodged in my shoulder, and ribs that might be broken. Passed out once before the painkillers kicked in. Moving kept me focused. The ways to move that hurt less. Not many.

Everything looked skewed and fuzzy. Kept being lucid and then not. I called the gym and left a long, rambling message for Charlie on the answering machine. I don't know what it would sound like now. Mostly swearing and rambling and paranoid. The kind of thing you'd play for the jury. Charlie never called me back. I know my thought was that Charlie used to train boxers. Used to have a doctor on call. But I don't really know why I did that. Charlie would've said fuck off and he would've been right.

Then I dialed Allie, on a burner phone. When the click came and Allie was listening but not saying anything, I began to babble, and whatever came out was so unconvincing, she hung up right away. The apologies. The pleading. Whatever I said.

That was it. The sum of my connections. I had acquaintances, colleagues, people I performed rituals of friendship with . . . but they weren't friends. Not close friends.

I had no one. Except Silvina, in a perverse way.

I had her journal. I had her account of a trip down the coast.

The go-bag had a lot of cash in it, too, and prepaid credit cards not in my name, which I'd used cash to get. I had the family credit cards. Also, a fake driver's license, name of "Joan Ark." But my passport—that was back at the house. So stupid. No way I was going back to the house for it.

No choice. Or only bad choices. I took another cab to a used-car lot. I bought a clunker with cash. I got on the highway and headed straight for the coast, then took all the little hidden roads and detours. With a bullet in my shoulder and my busted ribs.

I had a list of Vilcapampa subsidiaries operating in the areas I passed through. Gas station chains. Dollar stores. Even plastics factories. A pipeline running out the back of beyond. I had to believe they could see me, in the sense that they might have remote access to on-site surveillance cameras. I would be loyal to local businesses. I always checked where the cameras were anyway. Hit the road in the morning with that in mind.

Fooling myself. I'd studied Silvina's journal closely enough to put together a road map of her West Coast trip so long ago. To guess at places she'd stopped from the natural landmarks she mentioned. Even though once I passed through Crescent City, the details would get murky, my path slower, less sure.

As I performed these rituals, undertook these expeditions, I punished myself with the idea that I had been a diversion for Silvina or part of her sleight of hand. Meant to be roadkill. I spent sleepless nights in agony physical and mental, trying to focus on the positive. But always drawn back to destructive ideas.

I hated Silvina. I loved her. Didn't know whether to blame her or just bad luck. I was in a state of shock and self-loathing I couldn't convey to anyone.

At first, I slept in my car. I had a license, but not really. Everything was forged. A cop might or might not spot the deception. So I drove like a fucking granny. I drove like an ogre in a tiny lima bean of a car. But the coast was glorious when it came into view through the mist. As I put the sea behind me and began to head a little inland, I became sad. But being right on the coast felt too exposed, too obvious. Even the looming brutalist figureheads on the steel-and-stone bridges felt too obvious. Every time I was herded onto one, I felt there was a roadblock on the other side.

The coast saved me, though, while I traveled next to it. The cold. The waves. The isolation. Like home but not like home. I kept thinking I'd gotten out of this place, these kinds of places. How I'd sneak off by myself once I could drive, from the farm and to the coast. Running away from home, except I had nowhere to go. Would sit in a freezing coffee shop watching the surf break against rocks. Then go back. But I had gotten out, no matter how my escape brought me back into proximity with who I had been.

Shovel Pig didn't remember any of this. Shovel Pig must be in shock, too, but for different reasons. That was the kind of spiral of thought I tried to snuff out. Because it was ridiculous. But also because it was dangerous. To imbue the inanimate with feelings. To talk to people in my head who were not there, not physically in front of me. Like my husband. Like my daughter. Like Silvina. Always Silvina.

But as I drove—scared, paranoid—a goal emerged. Not just to hide, but hide with some small purpose. I told myself I'd find the houseboat Silvina had mentioned in her journal, leaping-off point for her expedition into the wilderness of the King Range. Find the houseboat and live there for a time, and then I, too, would plunge into the forest as she had. I would find what she had found there, something she couldn't bring herself to put in the journal but I could sense was there, between the lines.

And if I didn't find the houseboat? Then I'd just plunge into the wilderness beyond and accept whatever came next.

My wounds, somehow, seemed secondary. I'd fix myself only when cause and effect had been broken. I'd fix myself only when I could find a clinic or doctor who wouldn't ask questions.

That took more than a month. My shoulder would never be right again. My leg might never be right again. I would never be right again.

Did I have daydreams, even then, of some return to my former life? Of a way back to normal? No.

But I'd found the houseboat. At least there was that.

[71]

I wasn't alone on the houseboat, though. I wasn't alone anywhere. Not a miracle, the voice that would come spiraling into my head. Not a miracle, the way I let it in. But how do you know what a miracle is anymore? Or what's damnation?

Early on, after the balcony, the messages were either basic or bat shit. They came in over Bog, the phone I'd gotten at the conference. Confused me for just a second, like I was still using my work phone. Then I realized he'd found a way to bug it or use it from our time together at the bar as Jack and Jill.

That far-off magical time that would never return. When I also hadn't been safe.

>>Hello, Jane. Things going well? Or a little . . . sideways?

>>Ever wonder about alkaloids and hallucinogens and hummingbirds? What a high that would be? You're already high, in the mountains, but high, too. Just high and high and hi.

>>Hello, Jane. I started my day with toast and scrambled eggs. I snuck out during curfew to get the eggs. You just have to know the people. Who have eggs.

>>*Did you know that Vilcapampa's actually shoved in a basement somewhere, with a stroke? That was an actor you met. His wife runs everything now.*

>>*Did you see the cruise ships overrun with refugees? They're just drifting out there, getting desperate. Circling the drain. Where can that lead? Talk to me about it.*

>>*You could turn me off anytime, Jane. Yet I know you're receiving this. Why is that? Do you need me for some reason? Or you just have grown accustomed? I know the feeling.*

>>*Ever wonder if this is just a simulation? I do. I wonder every fucking day. Because it sure feels like someone external is turning up the heat. And I don't believe in the devil.*

>>*I can't see where you are. That's clever. I don't even know if you're getting this. But you have to know I'll come for you soon. I've no choice. I know what you plan to do.*

He didn't know because I didn't know. Not really. And I hadn't replied. I just let him "talk." He became a little unraveled when he didn't have someone responding. Or maybe that was an act, too. Psyops, just like the dual purpose of the wig. Throw me off-balance. Keep pushing me forward. Make me believe in his reliable unreliability.

Sometimes I imagined half the texts were sent by an assistant. That's why they didn't stay consistent or on point. But I knew he was a loner. Takes one to know one. Except, unlike me, Hellbender was a loner who needed someone to acknowledge his wit, his brilliance.

Maybe Hellbender was a fed. But it was just a theory. I couldn't know for sure. No evidence, and fewer ways of searching than before. Allie's long-ago, dredged-up secret report could've led me somewhere if only I'd been a hacker. But, also, even with the secret version of the internet available through Bog, I didn't want to leave a trace. There were worse things than a Google search history.

"Reports in the literature of a second species in the genus Plethowen *are apocryphal. Descriptions of this second road newt species are consistent in noting a much larger salamander. Many scientists think this second species is a myth. How could a larger version, a giant version, pass notice when the smaller, more suited for stealth and invisibility, is already dead?"*

Was Hellbender like the giant salamander? Smoke and mirrors? The leftovers from some impulse I couldn't see the beginning of. Except now I knew the salamander was real. Not helping was all the myriad ways pain robbed me of the ability to think. I held on to hauntings. The way Silvina never left me. The way Hellbender would not leave me alone. Except, I didn't have Hellbender's journal. I couldn't suss him out at all. What could I invent out of a single bar encounter? What vital clue I would've noticed if I'd thought it important.

But if he was still texting me, then at least I had distance from him. Maybe that sounds odd. It was almost like I knew where he was if he kept texting. A sense of the enemy. Like his texts were depth charges, but as long as I kept quiet, at the bottom of the sea, holding my breath, I was safe.

The first thing I'd figured out was how to keep the voice in my head without letting it know where I was on the map. The second thing I'd done was change his name in my phone. Didn't want that static confusion, that allusion to a salamander. So, instead: "Hellmouth."

Imagine you miss your husband and daughter but you can't ever see them again or dare to make contact or respond when they make contact. That you know they're alive only if a lone text appears on a phone you shouldn't have kept that hardly ever has its SIM card engaged. Or because there's nothing in the newspaper about them being found dead.

Imagine you believe this charade of being a detective has

a purpose, a point, and it's not just about making sure you still have some connection to the world.

Imagine you still possess a half-burnt salamander you hope will give up its secrets.

Imagine the deep forest is right there, and you wonder why you can smell salt spray at all. But you know why the salt spray always brings you back to a burning warehouse.

[72]

The morning after I hit the man in the bar, I crawled from under the blankets to the bathroom and took a hot shower. I was used to the slight lurch of the houseboat under my bulk. Mornings were better for the pain, as if it had to wake up, too. Or was disguised by the regular aches of middle age. Or maybe the chill froze the pain.

The houseboat lay on the bank of a river a hundred miles north of the King Range. With the trees smothering everything, and islands of gray-green moss and lichen smothering the trees. Even in the cold. Remote, in how the overload of texture muffles sound and changes where it comes from. How even the trickling tease and sometimes surge of the river feels like a dream or memory of sound.

Lashed to the sunken, moss-covered riverbank, the houseboat lay in mud next to an eddy away from the main force of the river, which gathered momentum farther south. Just beyond, it bifurcated and, after some slick rocks, took parallel paths to the same destination. Beaver dam just around the bend of one.

Out the window, I could see my landlord's "houseboat,"— more of a jacked-up mobile home—jammed against the opposite bank and up on rocks. A perilous pontoon bridge between me and him. I'd measured it. Only thirty feet, the river narrowing here, shallow and full of sediment. You might not drown, but you could get trapped in the mud. I didn't trust him to get me out.

Silvina's houseboat deserved only unglamorous descriptions, unlike my vision in advance. Derelict, prefab. Down to the wooden frame and the small windows with the off-white, frilly curtains. A galley kitchen. A living room and separate bedroom area, but not much else except a closet or two. I had to ignore the dull mold smell, which I knew would be like an alarm bell in the summer. The walkways looked out over the silt-choked river, and maybe someone else would've needed to sit in the broken-down chair outside to avoid going stir-crazy. But I liked dark, quiet places.

I'd "rented" it from an angry white guy with a mud-spattered pickup truck he drove somewhere late at night. He lived in the almost mirror image across the bridge. I don't think he owned Silvina's houseboat, but why argue since the money he was asking for was so paltry. Didn't know if he was a militia member or made illegal drugs or was just escaping something. *"Are you Jewish?" "What the fuck do you care?" "All right, then."* The wary side-eye of aliens from different solar systems. Bound by mistrust.

Mostly, though, I thought he was the standard bullshit libertarian, and once, while he was out, I'd made sure to put a little surprise under his pathetic stub of river deck. Just as insurance. Also made sure he got a good look at the arsenal I took out of the trunk of my car when I moved in.

I dressed like usual: overlarge plaid shirt, jeans. My only other choices were my hiking pants and shirt or a white blouse and dress slacks. I liked to look more local than that, saved the blouse for going into banks or places more urban. It looked like a sail on me. Usually, I wore a black baseball cap. Which I guess was like putting a baseball cap on a bear.

Seven miles through a maze of dirt roads to the houseboat. No one could follow me without being seen. Still, I doubled back, I took precautions. I often left the car a mile from the houseboat, hidden under branches in deep undergrowth, and walked the rest of the way.

That morning, after coffee, I went to meet my client at a breakfast joint. What would Silvina think if she could see me now? An unanswerable question.

But this was my life. For a little while, at least.

[73]

Nora lived three towns over, which was the kind of distance I had learned to prefer. A forty-year-old office manager, a redhead with faded freckles who worried her husband was cheating on her. This was my sixth case, sixth different town. Five had been about infidelity, the last about an intruder that turned out to be a raccoon. I didn't charge for that one. But I should've.

I never took any serious cases, advertised my services in the local penny-pincher classifieds, whichever area I'd decided to focus on for a while. I had a fake name, fake driver's license, and a sharp-looking business card with a laid-back handle: "Plain Jane Investigations." But my rates were so low, people didn't even care about my ID. I didn't list the name of my business in the ads. I was cautious; even Shovel Pig rarely left the houseboat. But, then, Shovel Pig contained the sum total of my old life. Practically a holy reliquary.

"He's always late to everything. Couple times, he's been at the office overnight. Won't answer his phone."

She was wearing a more thread-worn version of the blouse I'd left in the houseboat. Or the curtains in the houseboat. She smelled of bandages, blood, and vinegar. Or I did.

"Anywhere you want me to start?" I asked. It was better if I didn't have to do a lot of work.

But Nora was somewhere else.

"We've got two small children," she said, like she had to convince me to take the case. Or like that would help me solve the case. Two small children had never solved a case. The two small children would almost certainly like to be left the fuck out of this.

"I'm sure it's nothing." Something I said a lot. "But best to be certain, in my experience." Which wasn't much. "Because otherwise this can seriously affect your life . . . Does he have an assistant?"

That broke the spell.

"Yes. Someone he's training at the car dealership. A man. Jim."

Which clearly ruled out the assistant, to her way of thinking. I made a note to check out Jim. If I had to. If it got that far.

"Is he a regular at any bars or restaurants?"

She gave me a short list, which also gave me a list of places locals went. Useful because I didn't know this town, and Silvina had been here long ago.

The bar from last night was not on her list. A little out of range, or too rough for a used-car salesman.

"He has a poker night with Ed on Fridays. It's at Turtle's."

Tomorrow was Friday. I knew Turtle Fred's. A weird regional chain, with franchises always built next to a pond. Stormwater. Wastewater. Natural. Didn't matter, it seemed. Served wings. I hadn't eaten there because it had several health citations, and the folks hanging out in the parking lot tended to be conducting business.

"Who's Ed?"

"A high school buddy. They played baseball together. Most of his friends are Ed's friends."

The breakfast came: poached eggs on toast for her, a full breakfast of scrambled eggs, hash browns, corned beef hash, sausage, and oatmeal for me.

While we ate, mostly in silence, I marveled at how the world worked today.

Here a woman could worry about her husband cheating on her while just two hundred miles inland there was a mass exodus of disaster refugees headed north to a Canada that might not take them in. A "sanctuary" where aquifers and other water sources were drying up. In the Midwest, privatized security forces were brawling with protesters in the streets of small towns. Disease outbreaks had led to mass slaughter of affected livestock. While stocks remained bullish about the future even as the window for reversing climate change had shrunk to an unreachable dot.

What would Silvina think if she could see me now, in light of all that? An unanswerable question.

The grease on my breakfast plate brought a singe of warehouse to my nostrils. The snout of a badger with only one glass eye, shoved up against my face. On fire. The stench.

To cover my distress, I shoveled the last of my eggs and hash browns into my face. Eat the smell, eat the memory. Didn't quite work.

"You might start by watching his office at the car dealership. It's a separate building. He's supposed to come home for lunch but hasn't been."

"Sounds like a good lead," I said, cheery. "That's where I'll start. Then Turtle's tomorrow." A lie. Turtle's today, to scope it out.

I'd learned clients didn't like my smile, but "amiable" and "suggestible" were traits I could at least play-pretend.

"Oh, yes—so how long did you say you've been doing this?" she asked, in a way that made me feel like she'd forgotten the first line in a script.

Three months?

"Six years."

Nora smiled, and I felt a sense of responsibility. But, then, I liked solving these cases. I wanted to solve them. At least it meant I'd solved something.

"Is that enough to go on? Especially his office? That's important."

"Yes. But, if possible, I need his Social Security number, driver's license number—to check if he has any secret credit cards. Things like that."

She blanched, then nodded. "Sure."

By the date I was supposed to report back to her, I might have taken a case somewhere else, never come back to this town. If all went well, I would've performed some subtle surgery on her husband's credit cards. Not enough for someone sleeping around to bother reporting. Along with letting the man know someone knew his secret. That would count for some sort of revenge.

Strange, how it felt like Nora needed the structure of hiring a detective to do what she might have done herself. Strange, how I needed the structure of a client. But those were strange times all the way around.

[74]

Some days I had the self-important or selfish or totally appropriate thought that I had broken something with my fall. That all over the world people were jumping off balconies and breaking the planet. But the truth was what Silvina had seen: we were already ghosts. We just kept haunting each other for no reason. Even as we kept awaiting the mortal blow. But there would be no mortal blow, just endless depths.

Yet there I was . . . on the houseboat Silvina had used so many years ago, back when it hadn't been a rotting shithole.

A useless task, I'd found. A floating derelict, not even a reliquary. No note to me stuck down the side of the molding plastic cushions on the weird, low yellow couch. No secret compartment under the floorboards. No remnant of any kind.

All I found was a creased map of Unitopia on the coffee table. Too jaded to think it meant anything. To hope that Silvina's hands had actually touched it. I wondered if she had ever gone back, what she would've thought of the overgrown, half-abandoned version? How ironic if the kind of place Silvina had imagined could only begin to truly exist once the construct called "Unitopia" became derelict.

Obscuring her presence further: all the others who had visited the houseboat since she'd left. This gave me evidence of Silvina's cult, but that was no kind of evidence at all. First of all, it was ancient. No one had been there for a year at least. A little, spiderwebbed shrine with candles and letters. People who had lost touch with her but knew the houseboat story. People cast out from her inner circle until there had been no circle, nor even a parallel line. The curled-up edges of handwritten pages a rushed, breathless tribute to Silvina's waning soft power. The pathetic fallacy of a plate of brownies left for Silvina, as if she were Santa Claus. Moldy, and ossified into oblivion, recognizable only through forensic investigation.

I'd been puzzled by the pink sticky remains of some soft insulation applied to the bedroom walls. Only to realize Silvina had put up crude soundproofing and her devotees had pulled off most of it as mementos.

So I had only Silvina's disciples, nameless, and their bleating regard for her, and nothing at all of her. Even so, grudging respect. Among the things I didn't get to say to Ronnie before she got away: that I understood why she had followed Silvina. That I didn't want Silvina to be a fake, either.

Her absence aboard the houseboat rang loud in my ears, made me realize once again how I couldn't imagine Silvina as a person, her life day to day. What did that look like? I didn't know what clothes she'd liked to wear. What she liked to eat. A thousand details. I had her as thesis and theorem mostly, as a raw emotion like passion. Almost operatic, not surgical or quiet and mundane. Was that because of the journal or . . . ?

But that wasn't all that was missing from the journal. No mention of enemies except in the vague sense, not the personal. Which led me to the unsettling question: why do you render something invisible? Maybe you do it so it has no power over you. Or, perversely, maybe you do that to protect it.

Only one other kind of remnant: when some stirring of wind rocked the houseboat, I was back in my fever dream, sunk beneath Unitopia, with no way to get to the surface. With Silvina's voice in my ear from that long-ago video. *"If we could only see the world, really see the world, how radically we would change how we treat it. How different we would become."*

I found the dream relaxing. I could sink into the bed and welcome it, let it come flooding in. My pain didn't follow me there.

Nothing could find me there, down beneath the reeds, in the deep water.

[75]

The day I met with Nora was the day I learned there was a missing person report on me back home. That was also the day, as I left the breakfast place, that I thought I saw Hillman drive past in a black SUV with out-of-state plates. I almost missed him, distracted by that weird emerald-gray sparkle in the sky that was our new normal.

I was too stunned to get the license number. Backed up against the outside of the restaurant door, to the anger of the old man trying to get out. But the driver was staring in the other direction, and I couldn't be sure. I'd been paranoid before, wrong before. Too old to be Hillman, I told myself. Too haggard.

For five months, I'd noticed no signs of pursuit, and no one had come for me in the night. Yet I knew they had to be looking for me. I knew they did. For one thing, I had their salamander. Vilcapampa would be paranoid about that, as if I could conjure some magic out of the charred body. That I might find a clue they'd missed.

Or maybe they just thought I'd get so desperate, I'd go to the police. Or maybe I was dead wrong and they didn't think about me at all. That was the scenario that made me laugh sometimes. Me and all my precautions.

As I released the old man, cursing me, out onto the street and walked fast to my car, I pondered that all over again. It'd been nothing. Couldn't have been anything.

But as I made my way back to the houseboat, I knew it wasn't nothing. Because my pain levels had shot way up. Part of my life: managing the pain. Managing my expectations. I kept myself distracted with useless searches of key words. "Friends of Silvina," "Unitopia," "warehouse fire." The fire hadn't rated an article, just a police report item about arson and contraband, no one hurt. Didn't believe it. I just figured Hillman had moved the body, or bodies. Alex, though, showed up in two paragraphs about "CEO of security firm mugged in alley." That would be good for business, but mostly I felt relief he wasn't dead. What he would do next felt distant, unimportant. I couldn't see him going to the police. I couldn't see him doing anything other than damage control for the company. For the obvious reasons.

Another good way to distract myself, but pretend I was making progress: immerse myself in the obscure slow-burn hell of chat room conspiracy theories about Silvina. In tucked-away corners. Meaningless shit that led nowhere but passed the time. Unitopia came up on messageboards, sometimes perverted to eco-fascist ends. Sometimes held up as some lost holy grail, with myths and stories surrounding it I knew were bullshit.

"Off the grid, remote—that's how you do it. That's how you start to build a new society. You become self-sufficient. You have your own money. Your own security."

But there was nowhere to escape to. Silvina knew that.

"The past was pure. Prior generations had a good work ethic. They respected the land. They knew how to take care of it."

Yes. The good old days of slavery and peasants and indigenous people slaughtered. Silvina would have hated that, too.

But none of this, damaging as it was, worked this time. Maybe because the salamander stared sightless at me and I felt that gaze, more than before I'd seen the almost-Hillman. The mythic giant version of the road newt that was supposed to just be a story campers told themselves around the fire. I'd already burned through all the intel on the salamander I could find. A dead end. But, also, I couldn't bear being all-in on that attachment, too. In a strange way, I was loyal to the hummingbird. I'd invested so much emotionally, and where had it left me? And every time I looked at the salamander, I saw Ned. I saw the warehouse, the fire. I saw Hillman's face as he roughed me up.

I had been brought into mysteries previously unknown to me through contact with a dead woman. I continued because I had lost everything, and the only way I could make sense of life was to investigate the mysteries of others. But beneath every moment of this new existence beat the pulse of the old, and in every detail of the cases I took on I looked for the outline of the intent of Silvina—hoped and needed to see it. Longed to find something beyond the mundane that might plunge me back into that world.

But no sign appeared, nothing was revealed to me, and I feared it would not happen, that I would become lost in this purgatory, or, worse, become comfortable within it.

At some point, I turned off the pathetic, entombed space heater embedded in the wall and let the room freeze. It made my bones ache, but it numbed the rest. Along with a couple shots of bourbon. The go-bag money would be good for another couple of years if I made it stretch, along with what I'd gotten early on from maxed-out credit cards. Then what?

Increasing desperation made me go over Silvina's journal again, like I always did when I began to panic, only to find nothing new. Just iterations of the same. Was it smoke in search of a fire or was it something that would change the world? I didn't know anymore.

"I want to abandon words for action. I want to blow up a dam. I want the world without us in it, but to be invisible eyes and ears and breath gliding over that world. To demolish all of it. But not even that—to be rid of this illusion of consciousness, to be a tree or bush or algae on the surface of a pond. Not even a fish's quick nip of a water glider. Not even that level of intent, but some other intent altogether. And by the time you read this, I will be, my body will be . . . in the ground, eaten by beetles, eaten by maggots, distributed in a hundred ways, laid low and made mighty . . . while you remain behind and have to deal with all of this. I'm sorry for that, but it had to be."

And:

"Democracy is not enough because it is never really Democracy. The -ism that will fix this has not been written down because it exists in what remains of the world beyond us and we cannot read that language. So we are left with flawed ways of thinking, mechanical ways, that work against the very organic nature of our brains. We have built so many toxic constructs, we cannot see through the latticework. We have built so many mirrors, there are no windows to shatter. But still we must try."

Furtown, like the poison to the antidote, lingered because Shovel Pig was so big, I'd shoved the book in there like it belonged. Unlike my passport.

"We are flattered when the mixtures of your advanced chemistry dye us in every shade of nature's picturesque rainbow, thereby harmonizing with the color schemes of the apparel

of milady. We are convinced that these operations must be com-
pleted if we are to be your colorful fur gems of trading. So be it,
Mr. Fur Man!"

I was happy the author was dead (1985, stroke), even happier it was his only book. I wondered sometimes where Fusk
had found it, whether Fusk was even alive or had been crushed
underfoot by greater powers.

In my weaker moments, when I felt like I'd made no
progress—and I was never making any progress—I almost
called Fusk. One day I would, when I had the perfect question. But that question eluded me.

I kept the half-burnt salamander on the floor beside my
nightstand, too. It was the first thing I set out in each new motel room, before I'd had the anchor of the houseboat. No numbers behind the eyes. Nothing hidden inside it.

But I'd discovered the type almost immediately due to the
two yellow stripes. "Road newt," the common name. *Plethowen
omena.* Family: *Caudate.* Genus: *Plethowen.* Species: *omena.*
Extinct. Formerly found in mature forests of the Pacific Northwest. Only thirteen to fifteen centimeters in length. A fragile
membrane covering the tail. An expandable tongue to probe for
prey along the forest floor.

But there was a complication. The obvious.

The one I had was a giant subspecies, never before recorded.
By anyone.

Had Silvina really discovered one in the King Range? Perhaps Fusk had fudged the truth and she'd bought the taxidermy. Perhaps she had found it in a shop like Fusk's: dusty and
worn. A curiosity no one else had known the significance of.
Perhaps it was a fake.

Burnt, mangled, it could not argue for its own reality.

I guess I went a little off then. Maybe it was the pain. The salamander made me think of Fusk, and looking at *Furtown* again,

I devolved into a paranoid loop. The alcohol didn't help. Nor the isolation.

Why did Fusk switch copies of Furtown *on me?*

He could've charged me five hundred dollars for the thirty-dollar copy. But he'd switched them. Then I was cursing myself, throwing things. A cup. A plate. A knife, which surprised me by embedding itself in the wall. Realized I was screaming.

Shut up. Put my hands over my mouth. Like I was two different people. But, in reality, I was a lot of different people, like everybody. And a few of them were really fucked up.

I spent a good long, silent time tearing up *Furtown* looking for something hidden in it. I removed the clear plastic protective cover, held it to the light looking for etch marks on it. Microfiche. Anything. Nothing.

I tore the hardcover boards off like the stiff wings of a bird, pried up the endpapers. Nothing. Then took a pocketknife to the spine, cut the cloth binding. A good spot to hide a piece of paper with a message. Nothing. No page where I'd missed a soft pencil mark or circled letters.

Until finally the whole flayed copy lay in ruins on the floor. Nothing. Not a goddamn thing.

Fusk was just fucking with me. I was fucking with myself. The only reason he hadn't made me pay five hundred bucks for a thirty-dollar edition was a kind of rough honesty. By his standards.

I should've put *Furtown* back together best I could. Until it looked like a bad attempt at taxidermy. Or the state of my mind.

Instead, I just stabbed the knife through the broken boards and affixed it to the floor. Left it there.

An evil book. An evil mood.

I needed to remember not to do anything this crazy again. So there the book would stay as long as I lived in the houseboat.

I didn't know anymore if Silvina was a false beacon. The

kind that wrecked you on the rocks. But she shone so darkly in my imagination. The only light I had to guide me.

[76]

Even after I turned the space heater back on, the cold was like a slap in the face as I came to my senses. Warming my hands while my ass froze. The cold I couldn't shake helped me think. Made me concentrate, restless, on where I put my feet, how to position the cane, so I wouldn't slip.

I alternated shivering on the walkway, staring out at a sullen brown-gray river marsh of dead reeds, and sitting propped up against the headboard of the bed, staring down the length of the floating mobile home at the kitchen. Trying to ignore the dead, pinned *Furtown*. Pondering as I drank a beer from the mini fridge. The pillow at that angle helped the shoulder. The loud pain had muted itself a little, by some alchemy.

I still hadn't responded to a single text from Jack. I'd let him stew in the silence. I'd let him wax ever less and more eloquent, unsure I would ever respond.

But sighting that almost-Hillman made me feel even more alone. I took the phone out and I texted Hellmouth. The reply was immediate, like he'd been waiting to pounce. I felt like that needed to be punished.

>>*Jill!*

Me: *No.*

>>*No?*

Me: *You're talking to Silvina. I'm Silvina.*

>>*Very funny.*

Me: *I killed "Jill." She was getting too close. Now I'm coming for you.*

>>*Stop.*

Had I caused genuine distress?

Me: *I might let you live if you tell me why.*

>>*Silvina is dead.*

Me: *Then you have nothing to worry about. But tell me why anyway.*

>>*OK, will play along. Why what?*

Me: *Why did you decide to stalk Jill? Didn't you know that could be dangerous?*

>>*Because it killed two birds with one stone. To use a cliché.*

Me: *I'm a porch light.*

>>*OK. You're a porch light.*

Me: *Moths. You're after the moths.*

>>*If that were true, any bulb would do.*

Me: *So why me?*

No answer. For a very long time. So I went in another direction.

Me: *Interesting fact. I'm right outside your door. Waiting. Me, Silvina.*

>>*Nice try. I'm in a car. Outside your place. Me, Langer.*

Me: *Nice try. I doubt Langer knows how to spell this good. And I'm in the penthouse suite of this luxury hotel in Singapore, with a guard at the door.*

>>*Seventh floor, right?*

Now it was my turn to deflect.

Me: *How do I find and kill Langer?*

>>*Not fond of him?*

Me: *Neither are you.*

>>*But I don't like other people doing my work for me.*

Me: *That's a big fat lie.*

>>*That hurts.*

Me: *Doubt it.*

>>*I don't have a good location on Langer. Probably because I don't have a good location on you.*

Me: *Nice try. How can you even text this phone? How did you do that? In the bar? Some sleight of hand?*

>>*No, through your Jill twin. But she only sold you out*

partway. I was supposed to be able to track you, too, not just text you.

So it hadn't been my efforts. Just my conference friend feeling guilty and me ditching my work phone. How Hellmouth must have relished my use of that name in the bar.

>>*How about this? You should tell me where you are, because Langer's going to find you eventually.*

Me: *Not sure any of that is true.*

>>*I know one thing that's true.*

Me: *What's that?*

>>*I think you'd like to be Silvina.*

Me: *Dead?*

>>*A martyr. A dangerous martyr who lost perspective.*

Me: *You don't know me.*

But I knew that wasn't true either, just from his choice of "Hellbender."

>>*I know you came up to find my room at that conference. I know that.*

Somehow, that's what got to me. The most insignificant thing. The way he kept pushing that at me.

Me: *Other than a really shitty pickup artist, who are you?*

No response. One last salvo across the bow a couple minutes later. I was in a houseboat, after all.

Me: *I'm not sure why you decided to write your diary as texts to me the past four months. It's kind of pathetic. Don't you have any friends? A therapist?*

I waited.

Nothing.

Tossed the phone onto the bed next to me, took out an area map. Even faux, Hillman had me thinking about the next leg.

I don't know what had been holding me back. What better form of oblivion than to be lost in a virgin wilderness without people?

Mythic salamanders. Mythic me. I'd play detective in creeks

and in rivers, look under rocks like back in the day. Forget anything that came after.

Except I hadn't been able to ask Hellmouth the deadly question. The question I didn't want to know the answer to.

What was the extent of the connection between Langer and Silvina?

[77]

Me and Shovel Pig and Bog and Road Newt needed to leave the houseboat behind. Another bleary morning, that was my first thought. Almost-Hillman seemed like a premonition. But I spent that day pretending to be a private eye. I went to the husband's favorite places just as they opened for lunch, before they got busy. I asked around, in all the innocent ways I'd learned. I talked to waitstaff who were afraid of me or wary of me or amused by me. I went through the motions of showing a photo of Silvina. Langer. I never mentioned names. I tried to ask people, who I felt, by some intuition, had lived in the town a long time.

I built up a portrait of the husband as a good guy, a humble guy. A guy who was a little boring. Who people liked because he was a little boring. There are worse things than being a little boring. Although not many.

Where I could, I walked, despite the pain. The cold was good. Being wrapped in a greatcoat was good. The pale haze of the winter sky, the enrapturing mountains and forests peering down—all good, all so normal.

I usually stopped talking to people when I felt the compulsion to say "I've got a giant salamander in my room no one's ever seen before."

I usually stopped talking when I felt the need to start sharing anything. It happened. I may have come to realize I was a loner posing as someone normal. But I still needed to connect to people. Share with them, out of politeness. And I hadn't made enough fictions about the private eye I was pretending to be. My background was paper thin so I wouldn't slip up. Because it changed so often.

The doctor who had taken the bullet out of my shoulder in the back of his not-antiseptic van had said, "You're lucky it jammed up against the muscle. You're lucky it wasn't higher caliber. You're lucky you found me when you did."

But was I?

One thing I liked to do in a case like this is talk, under some pretense, to the mark. My car was so close to being junk in a scrapyard, I clearly needed a new one. Why not visit the husband at his job? I liked the comforting risk in that. I'd resisted only because Nora had been so insistent.

It made it feel like a bad lead. Too familiar.

Hellmouth texted me again while I ate a lousy chicken sandwich in the parking lot of Turtle Fred's. It should've been comfort food, but the grease smelled like the skin I'd covered myself in against the flames. The crackle and snap of the pockets of fat.

I forced most of it down, tossed the rest out of the window, phone beeping.

>>*Good afternoon, Jill. Want to meet up?*

Me: *No. I'm booked. But I have a question.*

>>*I probably don't have an answer.*

Me: *Langer and Vilcapampa: how did that work? Before it went sour?*

The evidence circumstantial, perhaps coincidental, but . . .

>>*The usual way. Part of it worked. They both saw themselves as humanitarians. As people who understand the way the world worked.*

Me: *Deluded.*

>>*You don't understand Langer. He began to see himself as an anarchist. Someone changing the world order.*

Me: *By killing animals?*

>>*Just the means. One set of means. Allowed him access to a forbidden world, rogue scientists, rogue players. The ones he thought would actually make a difference.*

Me: *Vilcapampa?*

>>*Vilcapampa made his early money off drugs and smuggling live animals for the exotics trade. Never totally got free of that, really.*

Me: *Another reason to be vague about the past.*

>>*And Langer got Vilcapampa illegal big game hunts. That sort of thing. Arranged it.*

Me: *A real humanitarian.*

>>*Like the devil is a humanitarian.*

Me: *And where do you fall in that spectrum?*

>> *And it was a while before Vilcapampa's people realized they were in too deep with Langer. With Contila.*

In that lack of answer about the Devil, I knew I should see the answer. It was right there, staring from the darkness, but I just couldn't see it. Decided to pivot.

Me: *Agency?*

>>*Pardon?*

Me: *You decide.*

>>*Clever. Langer had agency for a time, a clear agenda. A kind of Robin Hood. Help the poor, hurt the government, corporations.*

Me: *And who do you work for? Vilcapampa?*

I knew he didn't. Just wanted a reaction.

>>*I forget. It escapes me.*

Me: *And Langer and Silvina?*

>>*It worked the usual way. All the parts fit just fine.*

It took me a moment to process that. To understand Hell-mouth meant Silvina and Langer had slept together. I began to type my surprise, thought better of it. Started over.

Me: *And Silvina was drawn to, what, his sexy anarcho-sociopath qualities?*

>>*More that love-hate thing.*

Me: Physical, then.

>>*Very. You should see the surveillance photos.*

Me: Show me.

>>*Voyeur! Kinky. But I don't have them anymore. Just trust me.*

Considered that a moment. Didn't trust it. In what capacity would he have been privy to the intel? Felt, again, like a fed thing. Or Hellmouth had had a mole.

Me: She thought she'd turn him. Convince him. Use the Robin Hood impulse to pry him wide open.

>>*Why do you care? It must bother you. Why does it bother you, Jilly?*

Me: Don't call me that . . . Then they split up.

>>*Obviously. Silvina dumped him.*

Me: Would you have slept with me?

>>*Field work. Magic. Who do *you* work for?*

So that made *him* uncomfortable. Good.

Me: No one.

>>*Are you sure?*

Me: What do you want?

>>*Want or need?*

Me: What is your purpose?

>>*What. Is. Robot's. Purpose.*

Me: Yes.

>>

Me: Well?

>>*Purpose is overrated. Along with mission statements. You know Larry died in the hospital, right? Allie's gone missing.*

Me: Was that you?

>>*No, that was us. Working together.*

Me: Fuck you.

>>*I thought we already covered that. Oh—and Alex shuttered your company. You must have seen that.*

I put the phone down. Hellmouth was full of unpleasant

revelations. Silvina. Allie. The company going under didn't surprise me. I didn't care, either. I *did* care whether Allie had been hurt.

I wanted to throw up. I couldn't. Wanted a cigarette. No, I didn't. Thankfully, I never allowed the bottles of booze to follow me into the car.

I could smell the sweet, subtle odor of tenrec following me from the warehouse. Curling around me, as physical as wire against the throat. I'd had to look that one up. Not knowing what a tenrec was had haunted me. But knowing hadn't helped.

Part of me wanted to tell Hellmouth where I was and just get it over with. Whatever he wanted, whatever he was after.

Unless what suited Hellmouth best was me in limbo. In which case it didn't matter.

[78]

Sometimes I feel as if we live in hell and don't even realize it. The lacerations are endless. The lies we accept, the rituals we perform. All these useless acts.

All these worthless cases I thought were worth taking on. While the world burned. While Vilcapampa was taking god-knows-what measures—and not just against me, but, I imagined, against the remnants of Silvina's network. If "Friends of" could be considered a network and if that network still had a purpose. While Hellmouth searched like some infernal floating eye. I might've put Ronnie in danger just by going to Unitopia. Everything I turned my attention to turned to shit.

Small beer. Small potatoes. Small towns. Where would these cases have gone without me? These needs and wants, these paranoid fears that half the time were actually something. But usually not worth the victim knowing the truth. What I really owed them was to put the truth in the widest possible context. To spread Silvina's gospel, to overturn the comfort of the everyday with the knowledge of what would come tomorrow.

No matter who Silvina had been in bed with, literally and figuratively. No matter what Silvina had meant to do, no matter whether I agreed with it or not, I knew she was right about the state of the world. So maybe I was hiding in more than one way. Maybe I was hiding from the future.

The ethics of surveillance. The ethics of spying. Well, I'd thrown that all out the window with my small-beer cases. Everything existed in a tactical state of gray. You couldn't untangle the passion from the logic, the underlying philosophy from the technology.

Fuck it. I had a job to do.

■ ■ ■

I arrived late in the day. The car dealership slumped across a lot on the edge of town, the kind of generic place with streamers and banners that fades into the background so easily. The streetlamps here were a sickly yellow that leaked light in strange patches. The competing green-gray of sky sparked against the steel of flagpoles and chrome of car hoods. I already knew the business wasn't doing well—the financials were terrible.

The office Nora had mentioned was a kind of island: a shed on the west end of the property that looked like the kind of thing that'd get blown up in a TV comedy skit. With a stand of tall conifers to the right, under which loitered suspect-looking cars that no amount of fresh paint could stop from looking decrepit. Spilling out to the east, the rest of the cars seemed disjointed, unconnected. More like the failed exodus in an apocalyptic movie. A large wooden sign at the entrance proclaimed "Ed's Bargain Deals & Extravagant Savings." The paint had faded so much, I hardly noticed it.

I'd spent too much time figuring out where the threat might come from to feel comfortable with this setup.

I parked at the Dollar Store that abutted the dealership. This particular one wasn't owned by Vilcapampa Corp, and the security camera faced toward the front door. I walked to the corner of the building, the stuccoed concrete a dull egg yellow. Stood there for a moment, checking the place out with my small scope. Any walk up to the shed would provide a clear line of sight for anyone watching for me.

After a second, three men emerged from the shed-shack-office. One was Nora's husband. The other two registered as employees. One of them must be his trainee. The other one might be Ed. Nora hadn't told me Ed owned the dealership, but no matter: it was a three-in-one deal.

I took a deep breath, like I was about to jump off a balcony. Walked around the corner, heavy on the cane, started across the gravel parking lot, husband straight ahead, stand of trees to the right, reassuring Dollar Store wall still to my left. I remember thinking it'd be some small challenge to meet all three and then tail the husband without them remembering me buying a car off them. I liked that.

I remember being puzzled in that split second. That infinitesimal moment when the gravel was kicking up dust, like something was underneath it. The gravel jumping. Staring at it like it was inexplicable, or even supernatural.

Until I realized. A silencer.

Bullets.

It was bullets.

A figure had risen from among the cars and conifers. Indistinct, like a phantom. Hillman? I dropped like a sack of potatoes, cane clattering to the side, pulled out my sidearm, returned fire. Saw the figure hesitate, hunch down.

That small motion. That tell. But it was enough. The triad by the office had seen the shooter, but not me. As I watched in surprise, all three drew concealed handguns and started firing back. My jaw dropped. I forgot for a second to seek cover. Like this was something that happened too often. Another fucking day at the office. Another normal afternoon of firing into the tree line. The rattle-ricochet of bullets off car metal. The splat-split of windshields cracking.

The figure in the conifers fell over, got up, returned fire. Couldn't tell if they'd really been hit. Or just been caught off-balance.

I took that as my cue to get to my feet, grab my cane, and run back to the Dollar Store. No matter the agony of that. Slammed up against the corner, I dared a peek back out.

The gun battle continued. Percussive insanity. The figure in the conifers in retreat. I heard a car's engine, the vehicle hidden by the trees. The figure running. The triad content to just feed the little forest bullets, but not pursuing. Framed in a strange light that lit the trunks of the trees golden green and cowled the canopy in shadow. As small ink silhouettes labored murderous below.

By the time the shooter had escaped and the triad had stopped shooting, I was in my car and driving away. Who the fuck started firing instead of hightailing it for the shed?

Only then did I feel the nick. Lucky. A bullet had grazed my left calf. Maybe in another time, another world, that would've felt traumatic.

But now it was just a distraction from all the rest.

I didn't have to worry about Nora's husband anymore, and neither did she. The last thing I'd seen was Nora's husband's head bursting open.

The parting shot. The last retort.

That would bring down attention. Of all kinds.

That was my lasting memory of my birthday. I'd almost forgotten. There was no cake. There was no celebration. No one cared, not even me.

I guess my only present was not dying.

79

Silvina had no advice in her journal for the aftermath of gun battles. But I couldn't find it in me to be shocked or surprised or anything other than numb.

I drove around aimless, just trying to put some distance between me and the dealership as I heard the wail of sirens. What should my next move be? I entered a maze of older neighborhoods, drove slow, kept moving. Doors locked. Windows up.

Nora had set a trap for me. Someone had paid her to set me up. And her husband clearly hadn't been in on it. So maybe she already knew her husband was cheating on her and figured this might solve that, too, permanently? Or maybe this moment Nora was wailing like the sirens.

A whiff of something sharp and bitter from outside. The pangolin's scales against my arm, the bristly skin between the plates, as we all burned. I put the air on recycle to get rid of it. A kind of magic. But it would remain there, in my head.

I had seen Hillman. It was all I had. The shooter had to be Hillman or one of his men. Or connected to him. I could drive back to the houseboat, gather my stuff, and get out. Like I planned to do anyway. The shooter didn't know where my home base was or they'd have ambushed me there.

Manic, hyped up, awake again. Didn't suit to run. That'd be setting up the same situation again. Next time, it'd be my head exploding in a parking lot somewhere.

No, not interested in running. Not yet. Not again.

I headed for the strip of town on the outskirts, with its row of shitty motels and gas stations. I remembered Hillman's car. If I didn't see it, I'd return to the houseboat.

Dusk, with the low sun fuzzed with mist and the gas station lights muffled. The whole coast felt too gloomy. It'd be easy to miss the car. What if Hillman parked around back? What if Hillman had left town?

Nothing at Snow White's Motel, whatever that was, and nothing at the Marquis or the El Dorado or Mickey's Irish Inn.

I had the heat on, and gloves on, too, as the temperature had plummeted like a duck shot out of the sky. Sleet, and the wipers on. But, then, out of all that nothing, I found it.

Hillman's car. In a spot under a good, bright streetlamp. Sitting there innocuous in front of Room 112 of the Black Bear Motel.

I parked three spots over. Thought better of it, hesitated, then pulled out my gun, safety off, and got out, leaving my car door ajar to avoid making more noise. The ice machine in front of 114 growled and complained, which helped. As did the logging trucks rumbling past.

The garish pink of the motel doors made them seem to pulse against the mist like they were breathing. I stood there in front of 112, deciding whether to knock or not. Not even passkey technology. I could see where the frame was rotting and how the space between door and frame was too wide, the lock silhouetted within not quite fitting.

This would have to be quick.

One bad shoulder. Bleeding in a new place from that mosquito-bite bullet. Leg suspect.

Well, use the one good shoulder.

I smashed the door down on my first try. I wasn't even breathing hard.

A person sat inside the freezing room. Hillman, leg still in a brace from the damage I'd dealt him. Slouched, haphazard, in a crappy chair beside the even crappier coffee table. Older, wearier-looking.

A bullet hole through the back of his skull.

80

I had decided, on the frantic trip down the coast, in agony, in a kind of despair, that I would not be taken alive. I can't say why the thought came to me. *I won't be taken alive.* This idea that I would be trapped, captured. That I would need to make that choice.

So I did have a small arsenal, including two thousand rounds of ammunition. Police-issue Glocks. AK-15s. Some of it from a gun show with lax standards and some from individuals I wouldn't categorize as chatty. Among other things. If I could've found someone in the back country who had a rocket launcher for sale, I would've been tempted. I didn't like guns, because Shot had taught me how to shoot. But I knew them. Didn't fetishize them, but I didn't mind using them.

When it came time to kill Shot, I thought about using a gun. Accident. Or maybe something more imaginative. Something that didn't include his name. But I didn't like that any more than drowning, which felt too on point, too clearly like an act of revenge. Beyond that, I didn't put too much thought into it. I believed at the time that the less thought, the less evidence there would be. The less evidence written on my face. Hidden in my body. That I could answer any questions from the police more honestly. Is that true? I don't know.

Some people get more kindly as they shed memories. Not Shot. It seemed to hone and focus the worst of him while leaving fewer landmarks for him to find his way home. So his rages lasted longer and had even less point. So his abuse became harder to predict and thus to endure. I want to say Ned's murder accelerated his condition, but that may just be me telling a story. Me wanting the story to match up in some symbolic way. Or just me wanting Ned's death to have made an impact.

In the end, I confronted Shot, drunk, on the path beside the barn, because it was out of sight and because I didn't feel I had a choice in the moment. But he saw my intent and ran into the barn looking for a weapon. But I'd removed the hoe, the pitchfork, anything he might have used. So Shot climbed the ladder, and in the end, I pushed him off the roof and he cracked his skull wide open. Before he had much of a chance to cry for help.

A surge of emotion erupted from me in the act. I had thought it might be dispassionate, but it was too physical for that, too personal. Using what I'd learned as a wrestler. But also because, in those final moments, I saw all of Shot. I saw the truth of him laid bare. That there wasn't much difference between who he'd been before the sickness and after. And that there was enough of him left to know what was happening to him.

Which I was grateful for, that mercy. Because I would not have wanted to kill a stranger.

[81]

Hillman's wound looked fresh, but the blood on the floor had begun to dry. The police could pull up any second. No time for anything other than looting the room, looting Hillman. I can't say I was sentimental or respectful.

No suitcase. Just toiletries in the bathroom. I put my gloves back on and awkwardly searched his body. Nothing except a pack of gum in his shirt pocket. His wallet lay on the floor in a spackle of blood, next to a riffled-through backpack. I took both, wiped down the doorknob, and got the hell out.

The car engine barely turned over and then kind of sputtered to life. The car dealership was a no-go, but I doubted I could make it back to the houseboat. And I didn't know how to hot-wire a car.

So I took a chance. Although, by then, what was taking a chance versus taking an opportunity? Another few months like this and it wouldn't even seem like a risk. It'd just be another thing I'd done.

...

I pulled up outside Nora's workplace. She was the office manager for a life insurance company. I could've waited there, in the corner of the parking lot, half hidden by a huge green truck covered in mud. Maybe she would've come out before the end of business. Maybe not.

I cut the engine. That car wasn't ever going to start again. I got out, stood on the curb of the pathetic gray-beige strip mall that stank of some cheery pesticide. A few wary red-winged blackbirds on migration sipped from a puddle of water by the road.

Text Nora? No, I didn't think so. No guarantee she wouldn't alert whoever had set me up at the dealership. But the bank kiosk next door had a fire alarm, so I went and pulled that instead.

There came that weird hesitation built into the rituals of emergency. That moment of indecision when people just sit or stand, wondering, "Is this real?" Is it real? When no reassurance came, employees began to spill out the front doors into the parking lot.

Even a rote emergency takes away the ability to notice other details. I lurked behind a concrete column surrounded by potted plants until I saw the familiar blouse, the large glasses, the awkward stride. Then I came out, smiling like an old friend, my arm quick around her shoulders to guide her to the side, amid some polite blather of conversation. So great to see you. In the middle of this wonderful fire drill. Imagine bumping into you here.

I had her around the corner, behind the column before

Nora had a chance to react, to resist. Before anyone else could really notice.

I could tell from the fact she was even there that she didn't know her husband was dead. Didn't yet register I was dangerous.

"Don't shout, don't scream, don't do anything but smile and nod. I have a gun. Pointed at you."

At least Nora didn't insult me by pretending.

"What do you want?"

A hardness to her features that made me think she'd have been perfectly capable of taking care of a cheating husband herself.

I smiled. "I want your keys to your car and also your car. Which you will not report to the police as stolen."

"I can't just—"

"Shut up. Give me the keys."

"I left the keys in my office."

"No, you didn't. No one does that."

A glare, but also a tiny wobble. A tremble to the lips.

"Or, we can go to the police and I can tell them how you tried to get me killed. Whoever paid you to approach me."

She tried to take a step back, but I had my hand clamped to her shoulder. She registered, then, that blood on my gloves had smudged onto her blouse.

"Tell them you had a nosebleed."

Panic leaked into her features. I imagined I'd looked that way, early on. She scrabbled in her purse for the keys, handed them over. I didn't think so pale a person could get whiter, but she did.

"I didn't—"

"Is this the man who hired you?" I held out a photo of Langer.

"We've got a mortgage. And two kids."

The two kids again . . .

"Are you trying to say being dead would be a blessing?"

"No, I . . ." Shock. Definitely not professional, but I hadn't thought she was.

"Do you know this man?"

"No. It was over the phone. Cash in the mailbox. I never saw anyone. He said it was a prank."

A prank? That sounded more like Hellmouth than Langer. But what did I know.

"If he contacts you again, don't answer. Leave town for a while. Get a ride from somewhere other than the dealership. Maybe a relative."

The realization of what I was saying blossomed across her face.

"And my husband?"

"No more poker nights," I said.

But no reply had been necessary. She could tell as soon as she asked.

I took the hand off her shoulder. She sagged. I let her slide to the curb. To come to rest there.

"Point out your car."

She began to cry, quietly. Not that tough after all. I didn't have time to care.

All I cared is that she pointed to the right car.

An old Subaru wagon. Stick shift. Dependable.

An old beat-up blessing.

[82]

By the time I made it back to the houseboat, the weather had turned yet again. Humid. Sticky. Snow and sleet transformed to a driving rain. Not the usual dull drizzle. Less and less of the gentle kind.

I took off my coat. The temperature had risen twenty degrees. I could smell something acrid as I got out, like the place had always been polluted but only recently decided to announce it. The river had gone from turgid and ice-bound to a semi-rapid torrent. The pontoon bridge flailed and buckled. My neighbor peered out a window to take a look at who had pulled up, then curtly drew the curtains.

I would leave in the middle of the night or early morning. Lose myself in the King Range where no one could ever find me. I would be free . . . of everything and everyone. I wouldn't pretend to be a detective anymore. I would abandon this deranged idea of picking up Silvina's trail, of unraveling her mystery. I would keep the salamander only as a reminder of what might have been.

But before I began to pack, I had to at least look at Hillman's stuff. To protect myself. There was no way that the same person who had shot at me hadn't also murdered Hillman. Which begged the question: had Hillman been following them or searching for me?

It wasn't much like going through Shovel Pig. More like going through Shovel Pig after someone had already ransacked Shovel Pig. The most conspicuous things in the backpack were a Bible and a Rand-McNally spiral-bound, grid-by-grid atlas of the West Coast. If he'd been looking for me, Hillman had been both praying for miracles and systematic.

The Bible didn't have a secret compartment—my first, amateur, thought.

Other than those items, I found more chewing gum, an expired bottle of prescription pain medication, paper clips, an empty water bottle, and lint. What else had been in there?

The rain became more urgent outside. Smashed against the tin roof. Good thing I was already in a boat.

I turned to the wallet. Hard to tell what was missing because of what remained. Hillman's killer had decided two hundred dollars of spending money wasn't worth taking. No credit cards. A car insurance card, with what looked like a number code written on it, like the way someone stupidly remembers their PIN: 381 552.

Plus a driver's license. As ever, his photo made him look like an incompetent mass murderer. But much younger. I'd almost forgotten his name wasn't "Hillman."

But I didn't expect it to be Roger Simpson, either. Alarm bells all over.

Ronnie Simpson.

Roger and Ronnie.

Imagine that. One employed by Silvina, the other by Vilca-pampa Senior. Too much of a coincidence.

I took a closer look at everything.

Why a Bible? I wouldn't have thought of Hillman—Roger—as a religious man. At least, he'd exhibited few religious tendencies while I was in his care.

I looked at the numbers on the car insurance card again. It couldn't be that easy, could it?

It wasn't. I turned to page 381 of the Bible. Nothing. Examined the page with my flashlight. Still nothing. But holding that thin sheet to the light revealed a mark of some kind on the other side. Even a light pencil stroke left an impression.

I turned the page. And there it was. A number of verse underlined. The numbers 1 and 7.

I felt a sudden lurching dislocation. Quickly, I turned not to page 552 but page 553. Two more numbers underlined: 5 and 2.

1752.

Could it be a historical date? Safe combination? No.

5712.

I don't remember dropping the Bible, just the slap-thud as it hit the wooden floor.

5712 Orchard Road.

Like a bomb had gone off.

The place I'd lived for so long. The family farm.

I looked over at the eyeless salamander on the kitchen counter, as if it could help me.

17 52.

The only explanation I could think of: when Hillman had

found the salamander and pried out its eyes, he'd found the address of the place I'd left behind so long ago. He'd known it was important. He just didn't know what it meant. Didn't know it was about my past. But knew enough to hide it. For Ronnie's sake?

I tried to imagine their conversations as their paths took them farther and farther apart: Ronnie working for Silvina, Roger the heavy for Vilcapampa. Had they been talking the whole time? How had this looked at family reunions? Arguments? Or had they worked out a truce? Closer, yet no closer. Silvina's secret like stolen Nazi gold: everyone was after it.

It struck me that maybe "Roger" had been playing both sides. Had Vilcapampa sent him down the coast to kill me or had he come on his own mission, spurred on by Ronnie?

There was nothing in the Hillman-Jane interrogation that I could recall that knocked loose an answer. He had probably just come to kill me, no matter what he owed his sister.

I couldn't lose myself in the wilderness. Because Silvina didn't want that. So I couldn't want that.

Silvina wanted me to go home.

A place I hadn't been in more than twenty years.

...

The next hour felt like panic because it was panic. A threat gathering amorphous, and I didn't quite know from where. I just knew I was *late*. Struck me in my gut, irrational. I was *late*. Silvina would've expected me to receive this information much earlier, not five months later. Instead, Hillman had hijacked it. And where was Ronnie? Close by or not a part of this?

I packed the way someone does when they don't care: dumping clothes and toiletries and any old random thing in my suitcase. Just shoving it all in and making it fit. Followed by an inventory of weapons, ammo, food, water, emergency supplies. Gathering what made sense to gather by the door. I could leave right away. Drive through the night. Be at the farm by midmorning or noon. I was manic by then, suffused, ecstatic, talking to myself. Perhaps in my frantic daydreams, too, I dared to imagine that this was the end of the nightmare. I would have the answers. Clever of Silvina to put them somewhere familiar to me. Considerate, not considerate.

In some other world, I do none of these things.

In some other world, I analyze the odds like I was taught to do. Calmly, with a coldness born of distance. That person turns their back on Hillman's revelations. That person goes off into the wilderness anyway, knowing it's the best move for their survival. Their sanity.

But I was stuck in this world.

[83]

If I could, I would've rigged this confession with traps and protocols. Things you have to get through to get through, if you know what I mean. Hack your way through a jungle on your way to Quito. Make it so you can't see everything. Until it's almost too late.

Are you here now? Can I count on you being here? That you made it through. That someone made it through.

Or will I always just be writing this to myself?

[84]

At some point, the rain lessening, the temperature plunging yet again, I picked up Hillman's atlas. It was more detailed than my fold-out map, and I'd decided against any online searches for the best route. Any online activity, even from a phone I considered secure.

I flipped through to the right quadrant. Which is when I

noticed the torn-out pages, by the ragged paper shreds left behind in the spiral binding. I checked the pages to either side, looked at the table of contents.

The missing page showed the river. Somewhere in the middle of that torn-out page lay my houseboat. I was willing to bet Hillman had marked the spot.

I just stared at the rip. Tried to control my traitor hands.

It didn't have to mean anything. There were a lot of reasons it could've meant nothing. So few.

I could see my landlord through the front window. He'd emerged onto his deck in his familiar lumberjack jacket/shirt combination.

The need to talk to him came at me sharp, insistent, even if just to reassure me he hadn't seen anyone on the property. That all I had to worry about was him.

So I stepped out onto my deck and waved to him.

But it wasn't my neighbor.

It was Langer.

[85]

Did Langer expect me to step out at that moment? No, his automatic rifle was pointed down. Apparently, he didn't trust a handgun with a silencer would be enough.

At least he knew enough not to raise the rifle. Not with my hand in my jacket pocket.

We could see each other clear in the faded light, with the river slowing again but loud. It would take a miracle to hear each other unless we shouted. So we shouted. To the water and the birds and to each other. Two absurd, deranged apes hooting and posturing. Infusing even small, unimportant words with violence.

"Slowly take your hand out of your pocket and lie down on the deck," he shouted.

"No!" I shouted.

"No? What've you got in your pocket?" he shouted.

"We'll talk like this and then you'll leave," I shouted.

"How do you know I want to talk?" he shouted.

"How do you think?"

I saw him consider that a moment. Run-down, shadow embellishing his cheekbones.

"All right. I'll play along for now."

Then it was like he didn't know what to ask me. Before something clicked. A flushed quality to his face, as if he'd taken drugs.

"You're not easy to kill."

"You almost did."

"Yeah, well, it's something I'm good at."

"I have no quarrel with the truth of that."

Langer smiled. "What are you? Out of an old book?"

"Some days."

"Rope-a-dope, huh? Well, I'm no dope."

A fire ate at Langer from long before the warehouse. A kind of disease had taken him, but he was still alive and walking among us. That's what I decided the longer we shouted at each other.

I was still figuring out what to reply when he shouted across the void again.

"Why did she *give* you things?" *Instead of giving them to me.* Genuine. A genuine hurt behind it. "Why'd she take the time? Why'd she bother with *you*?"

I hated Langer on principle. But I also hated him for presuming to make me small in Silvina's estimation. Even as I tried to do the same to him. How had she ever loved *this*?

"What about you? What did you give Silvina? Biotoxins? People who wouldn't think twice about—"

"Shut the fuck up! You don't know! You have *no idea*."

Then he began to kind of argue with himself. And that's

how I knew he'd been having a lot of conversations with me in his head. And this *other* Jane didn't understand . . . anything.

"The truth is, the only way we save ourselves is to get to the end faster. Silvina knew that. Somewhere, what she set in motion knows that. And no one—no one!—has the right to stop that."

"I don't believe that. I don't think Silvina believed in that." Didn't know that's how I deep down felt until I said it.

Langer considered that, nodded, came back at me from another direction.

"You got a voice in your head, too? One you can't shake?"

"No."

"Liar."

"Sometimes."

"He calls you 'Lucky Jill,' you know."

Unexpected/expected, but I was too busy watching his hands to give him the satisfaction of reacting.

"Who? What's his name? His real name?"

"The madman who wants to destroy Silvina." So, no real name forthcoming.

"She's dead. Somebody already destroyed her."

He considered that in a way I found unsettling. Like Silvina was a giant stone statue in the wilderness.

Then he said, "He's killed almost everyone I know. Or ever cared about. Destroyed it all. Even the things we created."

We created. I chewed on that. "Maybe everyone you ever knew was a fucking asshole."

The gun fluttered briefly upward, then pointed down again. He couldn't know what was in my pocket. The hard, cool shape that gave me confidence.

"You want Silvina to succeed," he said. "So why couldn't you just step away, go away, leave it alone? I only need you dead because *you won't stop.*"

"Is that what 'Jack' says? That I want Silvina to succeed?"

He laughed, bitter. "He's a ghost of the old world. Doesn't understand the new world. The one that's coming."

"Who does he work for?"

"Doesn't matter. Works for himself now, and he wants every part of Silvina gone."

Did Jack want that? Or did Jack just want to mess with Langer's head? And how had he gotten into Langer's head so thoroughly?

"Maybe he just hates you, Langer. Maybe he thought Silvina had already killed some people."

"A lot of people need killing. Ask him—ask him about what he did to us. That week on the beach. Have him tell you about that."

The way his face crumpled at his own words, I knew he meant him and Silvina, not what Hellmouth had done to his men.

"What week on the beach?" The most ludicrous, sentimental thing. But it still tore at him.

"We were going to change the world. But he broke his word."

The way Langer said it made me jealous in some formless way. Langer radiating such emotion about Silvina and Hellmouth. Like in trying to glean Silvina from Hellmouth I was opening myself up to more disappointment.

"So why go after Roger Simpson and not Jack? Kind of a failure, isn't it?" Wanting to drive in a knife.

"Vilcapampa's evil. Jack's a phantom. No one knows how to get to him." All in good time.

"That's not an answer."

"You'd have liked to talk to Roger again, wouldn't you? Good old Roger. Family protector. Him, Ronnie—that'd be rich. What they might tell you."

It struck me Langer had gone rogue, too. It struck me that he was supremely unreliable. That it didn't really matter what I said to him or he said to me.

Apparently, Langer'd had the same thought, because he raised the rifle. A tough shot in the rain, but he might catch me in the spray.

"Anyway, it ends here. Take your hand out of your pocket. Put the gun down."

"It's not a gun," I whispered. "It's a message from Silvina."

I saw the look on his face as I pushed the button on the device. Saw him understand I didn't much like my neighbor. And I realized he could read lips.

He was already diving into the river as the deck exploded around him. He was already being carried downriver, surrounded by hot embers and burning shards of wood. I saw his head bob to the surface, go under, as he tried to right himself. But the river was too swift. He went under again.

By the time he washed up somewhere, alive or dead, I'd be long gone.

THE FARM

What folly, by a different name. The blaze. The way I saw it entire because I had created it. How it enclosed the world. No light upon the water not forced there. No sound not inflicted. No heat. Oh, the heat. The light. Everything Silvina hated. I was sure of that. The way the edges of the water winced away from the aftershocks. The way holes appeared symptomatic, like reverse miracles, in the tree trunks lining the riverbank.

A haze to the sky that took over, that overtook me. What better way to give away my location to the world? I'd never thought it would work. But the instructions online had been simple and clear.

I loaded up the car with my supplies. By then it was dusk, and the neighbor's place was a smoldering, damp wreck. It didn't take much imagination to realize my neighbor's blackened body lay somewhere in the wreckage. Langer would've had to strangle him to make him quiet. Which told me more about what he, or his ghost, was capable of. And what I was capable of. Maybe even capable of whatever Silvina might want from me. I had plenty of explosives left.

I felt more at peace than in a long time. So much I didn't know, and the stress of my destination, but at least I knew where to go. No doubt about that.

Idly, without much interest: wondered whether my father was still alive. I assumed not, but I hadn't bothered to check, the past twenty years.

When I'd finished packing, I drove fifty feet down the driveway, stopped, got out to take one last look at my sanctuary. The place where I'd hidden from the world. The place I'd tried to use to cast off my destiny.

I'd left Silvina's journal on the kitchen table and *Furtown* stabbed to the floor. I didn't need them anymore, for different reasons.

I pushed another button and blew the place to hell.

[87]

Things I could never know. The list kept adding up, as I drove down dirt roads, down roads with no names, heavily rutted. As I let Nora's car take punishment normally meted out to pickup trucks. The rain wouldn't stop, and turned to sleet or snow as bands of cold and warmer air battled. I had protein bars and bottled water. I could go to the bathroom roadside; I wasn't shy. Anymore. Stopped for gas and directions, and that was all. Cut the engine, along a grassy embankment, a graffiti-lined concrete berm, along a deep forest road, when I was tired and couldn't keep my eyes open.

The air often smelled electric, almost chemical, and maybe the green-gray would never go away. Maybe we wouldn't even notice it, after a while. Maybe we wouldn't remember it had been different, until the next thing that happened to us. Until it killed us.

Something fundamental had shifted in the world. Or maybe just in my perception of it. I had to keep the radio on to stay awake, but only to music, because the news seemed like fiction. Sermons and apocalyptic threats from talk shows were no better than news. The thought that maybe even Vilcapampa

Senior, from some golden mansion, might one day hide in fear from the future.

As water lashed the car windows, as the wipers struggled to keep up, as more than once I went slow and almost floated off half-flooded bridges, I tried to make sense in my head of what I did know.

Fusk loomed like some sort of original sin. The fact that Ronnie had commissioned the taxidermy. Ronnie and Hillman (I balked at Roger) as siblings, divided in their intent and purpose. That Langer, existing for me in a purgatory, dead alive, had such a fixation on Silvina, after their affair. That he had felt risking the remnants of Contila and killing people meant he was protecting her. He didn't need answers. He had them already. All of them lost in a maze, or web, of Silvina's making, or just in the idea of a cause greater than themselves.

A moment, I was convinced. There had been a moment when Langer, Hellmouth, and Silvina had been aligned in a very personal way. Not just one run by the other. Not just one sleeping with the other. Maybe it had been on a Miami beach somewhere, summoned by Hellmouth. Or in Argentina. But it had been the kind of experience that made you bond. Or made you think you were part of something greater. I couldn't see the anger and the passion in him now as just betrayal. I couldn't imagine Silvina with him without seeing some sort of understanding with Hellmouth. And then it was gone and they fell out of each other's orbits and yet they remained . . . entangled. Couldn't quite ever become unstuck again.

What I couldn't tell for certain was Hellmouth's position within that maze. Or did he exist outside of it entire somehow? The magician. The fool. Who had miscalculated in this sense: that Langer's entanglement, his engagement, was absolute. That Langer could have been *emotionally hurt* by Hellmouth's betrayal. Wide and deep yet claustrophobic and small.

All of them had been involved, in some sense, in wildlife trafficking, even Silvina. Vilcapampa Senior lured back into that or jumping in headfirst? Langer had said it plain, that Contila hardly existed anymore. Almost as if Contila had always been part ghost, and not because of Hellmouth's localized predations.

What was Hellmouth protecting or obscuring? What did he want? Or did he want nothing, but, like some windup automaton on a track, kept completing the same loop?

Feverish with these thoughts. Going back and forth, round and round, until I realized if I didn't set it aside, I would descend into a kind of mania.

I almost ran into a herd of elk around a corner, with a steep rock cliff to my left and old-growth redwoods to my right. Came to a gasping, skidding halt on the gravelly emergency lane. I'd been navigating a series of extreme switchbacks, taking a shortcut through mountains. The elk stared placid and yet unyielding at me. They had no panic or indecision to them. In that strange light, that moment of encountering life that didn't care about my journey, their large, calm eyes seemed like those of all-knowing deities.

I took it as a sign. I called Hellmouth/Jack. Sick of texts. Sick of foreplay.

Hellmouth Jack's voice was as I remembered from the bar. Sexy. Voice of the Devil.

"Nice to hear your voice, Jill," he said.

"Not nice to hear yours." But it was. Why should I be so comfortable with it?

"I understand your complaint."

"I think I killed Langer," I said.

"Think?"

"I tried to blow him up."

Hellmouth Jack guffawed at that. A kind of admiring laugh. Like he admired the audacity.

"Hard to kill, as I've said."

"What am I not seeing about him?" I asked. "What haven't you told me?"

"Just continue on your course. Just keep on keeping on."

"That's not an answer."

"Just don't be surprised if he's not dead."

That wasn't an answer, either.

"Who do you work for?"

"At this point, I think I'm doing the lord's work. Don't you feel you're doing the lord's work?"

"Rebel angels," I said.

"No one gets to decide who god is anymore. I think we both know that by now."

Was that true? Silvina was dead and still playing God.

"What do you think Silvina was up to?"

A pause, but he answered. "Something radical. Barely controllable. The things you don't know, about the people Langer helped her meet. You know when they say someone grew human brains inside some fucked-up animal because they don't have the ethics god gave a pig? That kind of person. People who think that's exciting."

"Roger Simpson is dead," I said, hoping for a reaction, but it just felt like anticlimax. Deflection.

"Is that a fact." Flat. Too flat. Some equation changing.

"Do you want to know who killed him?"

"He didn't die tripping on a banana peel?"

"I guess you don't want to know," I said, and cut the connection. A mistake. Calling him. Stupid.

But after I hung up and continued on, I was calmer. Colder. Another hour and I'd be back at the farm.

Silvina had known my address. My rational mind said that was just dedicated research. My irrational mind wanted to feast on something more than that.

What would I find? Hellmouth on the stoop? Or just a disembodied series of stairs into nothing and nowhere, each step composed of the latest numbers.

Years from now, I could imagine myself still following the ever-staler bread crumbs, convinced that just one more clue would bring me the solution.

[88]

It wasn't all terrible on the farm. Just most of the time. Even something like my mother's mania could be funny, joyous, uplifting. It could draw my father out of his shell, place a light in his eyes as surely as Shot could put dull nickels over those same eyes. She liked to dance when manic and would put on her grandmother's ancient white lace dress and hand silly notes to us. Little stories about the animals around the farm. The adventures of cows or chickens or raccoons. She memorized them so she could tell them to us even after she'd handed them out.

This cheerfulness made us happier because good humor soured Shot, but also drove him away. He wanted no part of it. While our mother wore those clothes, he could put up no meaningful or just plain mean protest.

"Oh, c'mon," she'd say as he got up to leave. "C'mon, dance with me."

But he'd scowl and spit and leave and as soon as he was gone, she'd sit down heavily on the floor and giggle. A sound as infectious as hysterical.

Sometimes she'd get up again. Sometimes she couldn't stop. One time she looked right at me, a troubled expression on her face, and asked, "What is happening to me?" As if some outside force possessed her. Perhaps it did.

No point asking our father. He would just become empty again. Of opinions. Of an inner life.

In the end, laughter led to tears, and we knew the signs. We always made sure to be absent by then. Because we couldn't fix that, either. The stories turned morose and sullen. The talking animals murderous. The moral obscure.

And also in the end, just like my mother, I had no idea what had been going on back at the farm. I just knew she wasn't there anymore.

But as I drove, I thought of her funny stories. I tried to conjure her up whole and like a mother should be. Like a shield against what I knew I was going to find back on the farm.

Hold on to that. Discard the rest. Even though it didn't really work that way.

[89]

"Family exists to betray" Silvina had written in her journal. *"Family doesn't know another way."*

Still raining when I reached the little side road in the valley leading to the farm. Sometime in the past twenty years it had been paved. I didn't like that. Didn't like the erasure of memory. I'd already wound down through change, from the heights. Ghastly, modernist cubes, almost all glass. Trying to pretend they were part of the landscape.

Large lots. Rich people's summer homes. They'd been rare, back in the day. Now the entire ridgeline looked like a tech bro campus. If oddly still. Silent. I could already tell they'd cut off the creek water to put in wastewater ponds and other "improvements." All that was left was a beautiful waterfall down a rock face that dribbled off into nothing.

My sense of being remote faded. The farm was in commute territory. I felt defeated. But maybe it was just because I'd driven for twelve hours.

The next surprise: the family name still on the mailbox. Where the side road split off from the paved main road. Except the side road, too, had been paved, and a low white wooden fence ran alongside. Cheery.

I drove slow, and not because of the rain. A mounting dread. Landmark after landmark came into view. The weird weathervane stuck in the ground, now rich with green lichen. The huge rock formation jutting out of nowhere that we'd imaginatively called "Comet." But new things, too. A meadow where I could've sworn there had been woods. A new forest that looked like a tree farm where my father had once planted crops. The whole time the sense of the rich looking down on us, because if I craned my neck, I could see the LED lights from glass boxes on stilts. A kind of odd, alien judgment.

The greens were so various, so fresh, though. Seen through the rain-smudged window. Reduced to textures. I put the window down a crack and let in the same clean smell I remembered. That unique dead leaves, new growth smell.

By the time I pulled up in the driveway and parked next to the house, I was both restored and hollowed out. But the house defeated me all over again. Everything had a sheen and sense of being well maintained that felt off.

The barn freshly painted a deep red with white stripes. The house a dull yet feisty blue, also with white trim. The roof gray and in perfect condition, except for leaves and small branches from the storm. A few chickens pecked in the gravel and weeds, enjoying the rain. Off to the side, past the oak tree, an enormous white tent had been set up. For what purpose, I couldn't guess.

I got out, holding my cane, but not bothering with the extra struggle of an umbrella. The people who lived here hadn't been downtrodden, surely. It felt like an exhibit or a model home. Made me doubt my memories. A stranger who came upon this place wouldn't guess a madwoman had lived here, an abusive grandfather.

A cheery light shone butter yellow from the kitchen. The door had a piece of driftwood nailed to it with the words "Peace in the Lord's Home" painted on.

It felt so unreal, I wondered if I'd died, jumping off the balcony, and all the rest was purgatory or hell. That would explain a lot.

I knocked anyway, sure a stranger would answer. Leaning on the cane. Trying to compose a smile that wasn't a wince.

The door swung open and Shot stood there.

I stepped back sudden, lost my footing even with the cane, went sprawling on my back, one hand out, fallen to the wet gravel.

Shot had been smiling, but now he looked concerned, said my name, came out to help me up. And I let him, because it was my father, not Shot. He had just grown into, or shrunk into, Shot with age. Couldn't figure out which. My father wore one of those same wool plaid shirts Shot favored. His beard grown long and wispy-white like Shot's. As if my father had made a kind of disguise out of his own father.

But the eyes were different. The hard glint, the cold, black reflection, wasn't there.

Imagine you expect the House of Usher.

Imagine you've steeled yourself for rot and decay and dysfunction.

Imagine you brace your will against that door opening. And when it's all different. When it's different, it's like the weight you were fighting against dissolves into mist and you fall because there's nothing left to lean against. And you wonder about all the other things that prop you up.

Silvina, is that part of what you wanted me to know?

[90]

Inside, they sat me down at the kitchen table. I could feel every one of my injuries screaming at me. I'd put too much strain on my body. Thought my strength made me invincible. Now I would pay, and keep paying.

The kitchen table was different. A remodeled kitchen.

"Bright and cheery," like one of my husband's real estate listings. "With a chipper blue backsplash and stainless steel stovetop, along with light rosewood cabinets." The smell of lemons too antiseptic to be real.

I preferred to look at the kitchen than at the bird-like woman who brought me coffee and a day-old chocolate donut "from the co-op." "Bird-like" meant "alarmingly tall and stork-like." Not an unfriendly bird, but wary. How could I blame her, even as I blamed her fiercely. A giant lump of black sheep daughter, sodden, had come unbidden through the door. A burgeoning arsenal hidden in her car, trailing a wake of carnage. On a quest that could not be explained with ease or confidence.

She was my father's wife. "Lorraine," let's call her, after a pinch-lipped Lutheran I once knew. I guessed the Bible quote was hers. Lorraine and Lawrence, as if meant to be. Or some other consonance. Did I begrudge my father a new wife? Or was it more that I begrudged him some form of success, as it had clearly come to him after so much failure.

How could this place coexist with a burning houseboat? With a gunfight in a car lot? With a warehouse full of death? But the trick of the world was to contain all things.

Lorraine had picked up my cane and restored it to me. Lorraine had brought in Shovel Pig and my little bag full of fresh clothes. The guns were all in a locked box. While I just sat there, on a different trajectory, like an injured space alien crashed to Earth.

I couldn't quite look Lorraine in the eye, just as my father could not look at me.

"How long?" I asked.

My father looked confused, so Lorraine answered, showing me the wedding ring. "Five years. We met at a church dance."

The Church of Bewildered, Lonely Failures?

"That's nice," I said. A sense that they'd been together much longer than five years.

How could I find fault? I did then, but, now that the hurt has passed, how could I blame my father for being successful, for having a new wife? He had lived with an abusive father and had had an absent wife for a companion.

"We rent out the three cabins on the property," Lorraine said. "We also sell wild honey and candles and soap. People come for riding lessons sometimes. Your father has done a good job of diversifying."

Diversifying.

"That's wonderful," I said.

So it went. Fifteen minutes later, a torrent of heavy rain like bullets on the roof woke me up. I realized I was being lulled. Into small talk, into normalcy. Mostly by Lorraine. And I couldn't afford that. It was too much like being back in my house with my family. Everything I'd put aside. I didn't have the armor for that. I would lose my mind staying here too long, in this alternate reality. This false place.

"I need to talk to Dad," I said, interrupting Lorraine on the subject of jam.

Lorraine gave Lawrence a protective look and then a look toward me that was open to interpretation. A welcome with an end date and a warning both.

"I have chores and a phone call." She went past the kitchen into the back. Maybe even into what used to be my room.

But my father was not a talker.

"A long time," he said. "Such a long time. Too long."

I had not come to my mother's funeral. I had not written or called. I had two early letters from him I'd never opened and then I'd changed addresses, left no forwarding information. Thought that was the only way. A rage that you never lose.

After another awkward pause, a nod, a vague exchange of what might be called "catching up," I could only feel relief. No way to reconcile. No way to find within my father the things I had needed from him—because they had never been there. Not withheld. Never present.

Kinder to us both to consider him an eyewitness and move on. Safer.

I pulled out a slightly damp photo of Silvina.

"Do you know her?"

"Yes. Of course." No doubt. No hesitation.

I sat back in my seat, chest tight. "Of course?"

He still wouldn't look at me. "She lived up on the ridge for a time when you and Ned were teenagers."

"What?"

"Yes—in that new development. New back then. They kept to themselves. Never came down to the farm."

I don't think I had a single thought in my mind for a second, or five seconds. I wasn't numb. I was nothing.

"How did you know her?" My voice felt distant, thready. My mouth was dry. Was it the physical toll or the mental? I couldn't keep taking shocks to the system. Yet I did.

"Her family hired Ned. He did . . . odd jobs . . . for them."

"I don't remember any of this. This isn't true. It's not true."

He shrugged, gave me a thin smile. And I realized.

"You hid this from me. You hid it." Worse, Ned had hid it. All those expeditions to places that weren't safe for me.

"It was illegal, what Ned was doing. We needed the money. I didn't tell anyone. Your mother didn't know. Grandpa didn't know. I wished I didn't know."

"What kinds of things?"

"Poaching. Courier for . . . what they were growing the other side of the ridge."

I tried to absorb that.

"And I never knew any of this." Searching my memory for any hint, any clue, other than Ned's disappearances.

"Ned specialized in salamanders."

"What?"

"A big demand in China for salamanders. Other places, too."

I couldn't breathe. I couldn't breathe.

"Ned would never do that." Silvina would never do that.

Langer and Vilcapampa, though. In business together. They would do that.

My father shrugged. "It was a long time ago. You idolized your brother. What would I have told you? It just would have hurt you. Shot was already hurting you."

"While you did *nothing*!"

I shouted it.

Lorraine came back into the room.

"Get out of here," I said, murder in my voice.

Instead, she retreated to the doorway.

"Don't talk to her that way," my father said. It was the most aggressive sentence I'd heard from him. He'd half risen from his chair. Now he looked at me and I couldn't take it.

"Ned wouldn't do that," I whispered.

"You just didn't want to know," he said. "You were always so smart. But you didn't want to know. So you didn't. You forget all the things that happened. I felt at times like you made your grandpa too important. I loved Ned, but he was manipulative. He was petty. He knew he was handsome and he used it. He wasn't an angel. Not even toward you. You just don't want to remember."

"Not true."

He hesitated. I recognized the look on his face. Pity. The same look I'd given him so many times.

Then he said, "Your brother made fun of you behind your back. He made jokes about you."

Silence. I just shut down for a time. Staring out across the kitchen. I wish there had been something out the window to distract me. There was nothing.

Why had I wanted the farm to be in ruins? Why had I wanted my father to be dead or some pathetic, lonely hoarder, no more lucid than my mother? It struck me that only after our whole family was gone had my father been able to be happy.

"That's a lie," I said. "If Ned didn't tell me, it was to protect me." Already constructing a reality of a noble Ned, making money for the family. Necessary, but not liking it.

My father sighed. Lawrence sighed. It was like he'd not breathed for so long that it came out all at once in this prolonged sigh of disappointment, of loss, of whatever the things were he felt that I couldn't feel, or couldn't recognize, coming from him.

"To protect himself. You don't realize how angry you were back then, how violent. Toward your mother. Toward me."

"I wasn't," I said, but even as I replied I knew it was true. Could see it now. Could remember it. Not like I'd repressed it, but like I'd told a different story for so long, it had eclipsed the truth.

Lorraine remained frozen in the doorway. Who knows what I would've done then, if not for what my father said next. A shouting match. Smashing things. Making my mother cry. Raging through the barn, destroying tools, smashing shelves.

"She came here," my father said. "She left something for you."

I didn't need to be told who "she" was. The truth of it. The yearning. *She* had left something for me.

"What did she leave? When did she leave it?"

"About eight months ago." A month before her death.

He placed an envelope on the kitchen table between us. So, he'd been prepared. He'd known I would be coming at some point. He'd kept the envelope close. Or had it been there the whole time, collecting dust in a kitchen drawer? An afterthought.

I knew I was looking at it like it was radioactive. Wanted to open it. Didn't want to open it.

"She said you'd understand. She said it was important to her that you knew."

No point in asking why he hadn't called. I'd cut him off. Disowned him. But he could have found me. He could've reached out.

"I don't understand. I don't understand how you could keep

all of this from me for so long. I don't understand why you keep lying about Ned." I felt like a child. I was a child. I could blow things up but I couldn't put things back together.

"You were twelve pounds six ounces at birth," my father said. "I saw you in the hospital and you were the biggest baby there. Like a giant. Mother said you'd be trouble. I said I didn't care. But both Ned and you were trouble."

"Don't say his name again!" I screamed. It felt like blasphemy. I could feel my self coming apart at the seams.

"I know you killed my father," he said, flat tone. Unforgiving. "You killed him. For nothing."

For nothing. For something. He had known. Of course he had known.

That was enough, I guess. Lorraine had heard enough.

She swept in, gave me the focused murderer's look a heron gives a frog or snake. She was almost as tall as me. Her hands had nails like claws.

"Enough! Enough now. Quite. Enough. Your father's a sick man and needs rest."

Like something rehearsed. In case the black sheep ever came home and baa'd too loud.

"I don't think this concerns you," I said, with as much control as I could muster.

"Lawrence, go lie down a bit," she said, ignoring me.

He stood and with a wincing look that admitted no apology he walked off into the rooms beyond the kitchen.

That would be my last sight of him, ever. Stooped shoulders. Walking slowly away from me. Framed by the hallway and then turning into shadow. Just as I remembered him, finally, from childhood.

Lorraine sat down in his seat.

"There are a lot of people coming here soon," she said pointedly, nodding toward the tent outside. "Good people. Godly people. Why not join us in prayer before you leave? It might give you some comfort."

Comfort? She had done nothing to me, but I wanted to punch her.

"End-of-the-world stuff? No thanks." I'd no patience for evangelicals.

"I can tell what you think," she said briskly. "But we're not like that. We want to save the planet from Man's ruination."

Two cars had pulled up outside, with the sound of more approaching. For the revival. For the worship of Mother Earth or whatever they thought would make a difference but didn't.

"No thanks. I'm good."

"Then I'll ask you to leave for your next appointment."

"Not until I talk to my father again and ask him—"

"No," she interrupted, and I realized her hands were under the table. "No, I think not. We're not stupid around here. We know what it's getting like out there. I've got five strong, armed men outside. All it takes is a shout from me. And there's a shotgun strapped to the underside of this table. You will leave now. And you will not come back."

I stared into her gray, cold eyes. I'd been wrong. This place wasn't a different reality. It was the same place. And I had to admire her. I had to admit that, in some ways, I might've preferred her as a mother.

"I could call the police when I leave," I said. "Threatening me."

"You won't. We already know you won't."

"I could walk right back through that door to my father and you wouldn't shoot."

"We already agreed I would."

Nothing about her aspect made me think she was lying. But it didn't matter. The intent was enough to hurt me.

I raised my hands in surrender. I rose slow, relying on the cane, walked slow to the door.

Before I could close the door behind me, Lorraine said, "You remember that cabin halfway up the ravine?"

"Yeah."

"Someone's waiting for you there. Been there a month.

When you see them, you can tell them time's up. They need to leave by the end of the day. I don't want to see them again. You, either."

I looked back at her in confusion. The shotgun was above the table, all messy with duct tape, and she was looking down the barrel at me. I hadn't even registered the sound of her wrenching it loose.

"Who is it?"

"Trust me," she said. "You want to see him."

Hellmouth Jack? Langer? The possibilities seemed limited.

"Trust me: I probably don't."

I left with Silvina's letter shoved in my pocket, like it was meaningless. Not that it was the most important thing. Disappoint, horrify, or mean nothing.

Even as I was cast out.

I read Silvina's letter in my car, in the driveway. People were emerging from cars all around me. Dressed normal, like normal country folk dressing up for an event. Walking to the big white tent. Ready for whatever Lorraine was going to tell them. Because I knew Lorraine must be a preacher. Somehow, it just made sense.

Wanted the words out of me. Wanted them cast out cast out cast out. Kept breathing them in anyway, like a contamination you couldn't avoid. No mask would keep it out.

Aware but not aware of Lorraine's bodyguards glaring at me from the tents. I could smell each and every burning animal skin from the warehouse. I could smell them all as I read. I read and reread until the words made no sense. Didn't want them to make sense. Immolation. That's what it felt like. Like I was burning. Burning up all over again.

The photo Silvina had enclosed fell out onto my lap. The tattered, folded-over photo. For the longest time, I couldn't bring myself to pick it up, to see what it was. Who was in it.

Then I drove to the cabin.

91

Lorraine had been sharp, certain, so I borrowed that to survive. Even though I felt like I was drowning. Get through the next bit. Charge up one more hill first. Like something mechanical, just an extension of the car. With a head full of nails Silvina had put there.

I went back to the fork that led up the ravine slope in a series of sharp, steep switchbacks. The slope had, since I had last seen it, suffered a storm or disease or clear-cutting. Every time I came out of a bend, I saw the same spill of earth and broken cedars. A snarl and mess of rotting wood and then the clear gray-green light at the top, like a tunnel that was a telescope. I felt so small.

A crack in the car window to feel the cutting cold, the bitter cold. It had stopped raining. Maybe in an hour it would be balmy again. You could lose your mind just trying to predict the weather.

The lies I told myself. That I'd sneak back to the farm later, creep into their bedroom, wake my father. That we'd go outside to the porch and finish our conversation. That, freshly woken, in confusion, he'd finally give tongue to his inner self, in the face of Silvina's letter. To some well of emotions. That we'd laugh together and cry together and forgive ourselves.

But I already knew he had an inner life. Lorraine told me that in everything she said and did.

He just would not share it with me.

* * *

The cabin had a wan yellow light on outside, fuzzy through the green dimness. An unfamiliar car. Not an obvious rental. I put my money on Hellmouth. I just didn't think waterlogged, river-bound Langer had been here a month, driven down to kill me, then somehow made it back up. Unless Lorraine was mistaken and the place was vacant.

I parked in the shadows of trees a hundred feet downslope. I'd cut the headlights well before that. I opened and closed the door with the slightest of clicks. I hobble-crept up that steep slope of a driveway to that too-familiar place. Knew exactly which floorboard on the porch not to step on, to muffle my tread. My Fusk gun in my hand. I was in a mood to shoot first, ask questions after. But, in a pinch, I'd beat Hellmouth Jack to death with my cane.

I peered in the window from the side. A large man sat there looking at his computer, his back to me. But unmistakable. Bigger shock than Hellmouth Jack or Langer. Emissary from the lost world.

Inhaled, exhaled deeply. Bracing myself, I knocked on the door.

A moment's hesitation. Good. He was seeing who it was first. Not as open and trusting as he'd been a few months ago.

The door opened.

My husband stood there. I was shocked. He'd put on maybe thirty pounds, yet his face was hollowed out. Hair long and disheveled. Streaks of gray I didn't remember. A darkness around his eyes like bruises from punches. I smelled Vicks and cigarettes. He'd never smoked before. Absurd, sick idea that Hellmouth Jack had gotten him addicted.

"Hello, 'Jill,'" he said, unsmiling.

Imagine you've seen your father for the first time in twenty years.

Imagine that in your pocket you've got a letter full of revelations, from a dead woman.

Imagine you're beyond surprise and shock and you just expect that you will live in this condition forever.

92

Inside, we sat at the long, family-style table into which Ned and I had carved crude figures of animals. The cabin felt small, cramped, claustrophobic, the rudimentary kitchenette in disrepair. Nothing like how I remembered it, our sometimes sanctuary. The stolen moments of freedom, careful never to linger long. If Shot had found us in there, he would have prowled that place continual.

"I know who sent you here," I said. "Why'd you listen to him? He was the one standing in the woods outside our house."

I couldn't get over the altered architecture of my husband's face. How he drew in light and destroyed it. How *still* he was. How devoid of good humor.

"You look like you've been in a war," he said. "Like you actually fought in a battle."

"I know what I look like," I snapped at him. By what right?

He took that, held it a moment, looked about to snap back. Stopped himself. But the flood came pouring out anyway.

"I didn't have a choice in who to trust. You gave me no choice. I didn't hear from you once. You didn't try to send a message. You didn't answer your texts. You—"

Hurtful. False. Coming from the wrong place. Yet he was also right.

"I couldn't. It was too dangerous. *This* is too dangerous."

I was vibrating, my hands fit to thrash if I didn't steeple them. Like there was energy waiting to pour out.

But my husband didn't hear me any more than I heard him.

"Allie from your work even contacted me, but you didn't."

"Allie? How did she find you?" Another breach.

"I don't have your experience hiding. She couldn't find you. But she could find me."

"What did she want?" Wild thought. Allie had been working

for Hellmouth Jack or Langer. Faked concern for Larry. Been a plant all along.

"She'd been badly beaten up and thought maybe—just maybe—if she could find you, you could help her. But I couldn't help her. Because I don't know what's going on and I couldn't find you."

"I couldn't," I said, helpless.

"She got beat up because she wouldn't tell them where you were. Because she couldn't."

There it was. All those centuries ago when I'd asked her to research Silvina. There was the damage coming back across the divide at me. When it didn't even register with me. When I didn't have it in me to care, except in a distant, disconnected way.

"What did you tell her, about me?"

"I told her you would be no help, because I knew you would be no help. I told her to stay far away from you. . . . And then— hey, presto!—this smiling lunatic appears at the safe house we're staying at, scares the living shit out of me. Says his name is Jack, that he knows where you are. Or, where you'll be. That he's sure of it. And he gives me the address of your family's farm. A whole farm! Which you've barely ever talked about. And there's a new thing I learned about my wife, too. That her father *isn't* dead. That—"

"Why did you come here if you hate me so much?"

Cutting through the recriminations because they struck me as so meaningless now. No future could contain them or make anything better.

He recoiled, leaning back against the chair. Looked like I'd slapped him.

"You broke everything. You cheated on me. You lied to me. Then when I've gotten over *that*, you lie again and you disappear after a frightening phone call that destroyed our lives. You met some guy at a convention named Jack, who works for the government, and gave him a fake name. A Jack who said this was my last best chance to see you and I should take it. I don't even hate you. I just don't fucking care about you anymore."

The smell of hides ablaze as I rolled to avoid them. So tattered and old I couldn't tell what they'd been. Stench of burnt hair.

"Why are you here, then?" Said flat, so maybe he'd just tell me.

He looked down at his hands.

"Closure . . . and I need money."

"Seriously?"

Mistake. Now the anger really spilled out.

"You maxed out all our cards! You took what was in the joint bank account. Our savings. I wake up one morning, a week after you disappeared, and it's all gone."

"I needed it." I still needed it.

"Meanwhile, I'm paying all the bills, the mortgage, everything else."

"You have your real estate business."

I said it, but I couldn't look at him.

"You mean commissions on sales that don't fucking exist? I have no incoming revenue. No one's buying houses in this market. The world's going to shit. I have no access to money other than the pittance you left in the accounts and loans from my family."

My husband never swore.

"I have a bag of money in the car," I said. "You can have most of it."

He wheeled out of the chair so fast and hard, it fell over. Went over to the window, as if afraid if he got close, he'd strike me.

"As if that solves it," he said.

"You said you needed money."

That look from him again. Couldn't bear it. Couldn't be that person, but kept being that person. Couldn't look him in the eye.

The table had a history. It would've meant something to find a salamander carved into that table, a hummingbird. But Ned and I had mostly drawn creatures that didn't exist, like bats with human heads or cats with wings. Still could faintly see a crude sailing ship like an ark, full of all manner of imaginary beasts. I'd forgotten that. A mythos of discover and escape. Created together in such a way that I couldn't recall who had done what.

"You haven't even asked about our daughter," he said.

Rambunctious, curious, mercurial child. No, I had not.

"She's not here. That means she's somewhere safe."

He would not have left her unsafe. If I knew anything about my husband the bear, I knew that.

"She is," he admitted.

"Where?"

"I'm not going to tell you."

Good.

"Do you have a photo?"

"No."

A lie, but I had no right.

"Don't you know what this is all about? Why I've done this?" Why this has been done to me.

His look was pitying, like my father's. He'd made up his mind about something and he didn't understand what I meant. But that was okay. I could let him go. I really could, because I already had.

I took in the contours of his face. Really looked at him, past the weariness and wariness. Fix him someplace in memory that meant something real, before he faded. Before I never saw him again. We had an urgency once. We did. We had a rhythm and a secret language. I could half remember it, even in that moment.

Don't you know? I wanted to say to him. *Don't you know that I don't worry about our daughter? I worry about you.*

After a while, he stood, looming over me.

"Let's just go get that money."

I watched him drive away from the old family cabin he'd never known about a month ago.

Didn't my husband know I thought my daughter was better off with him? That I wouldn't see a photo of her now and demand to know where he'd hidden her? That I knew how devastating it might be for her to see me like this? Broken down. A different person. In thrall to an idea, a person.

But I'd taken one risk. I'd left an anonymous message in the inbox of her account for an online game she'd outgrown. An account I'd set up. Maybe someday she would remember to check it. Become nostalgic to play the game. See the message. Know that I had reached out. Or maybe not. But it made me feel better to know she might see it.

"I'm okay and I love you. I'm sorry I'm sorry I'm sorry . . ." Don't look for me. Don't remember me if it hurts. Don't be like me. Don't don't don't

The old, dead things Ned and I had carved, the roughness, to recall what had been good then.

I didn't want to be alone. Didn't trust myself alone. I called Jack. No one else was left.

"You set my husband on me."

"I wouldn't put it like that. But now I'm certain I know where you are."

"To set me up?"

"You didn't call me for this."

Pathetic comfort of a familiar voice in my head, someone who claimed to understand me.

"Do you want to know what Silvina was up to?"

"Yes."

"Meet me at my house. The place where you used to be a creeper in the woods."

"When?"

"Just be there."

Didn't give a fuck if he had to wait a long time. Like, forever. But maybe it would keep him close but not too close.

Me, I was going back to the storage unit.

Knowing I was a murderer without real cause or claim.

Shot hadn't killed Ned.

[93]

The letter had no signature. It was addressed to no one. It was in Silvina's handwriting.

> I have thought about this moment for many years. How to say it. How to express it. What might be meaningful. I know that your life has hinged on that moment. I know that you took action based on that moment. And I remained silent. Because I was forced to, but also because I had to.

> I knew him, but not what he did for the family. I talked to him several times. From the house up on the hill. I thought that Roger employed him to help with the gardening. I didn't know at first what my family did in those parts. I didn't know we used local boys as couriers and suppliers.

> It's my fault. I liked him. I let him come into the house. I fed him lunch sometimes. He seemed so sad, and he was beautiful and so smart. He felt safe to talk to because he wasn't family or one of my father's friends. But, once, he came to the house when I wasn't there, let himself in, and saw something he shouldn't have seen, in a place he shouldn't have been. My father was even less merciful when younger.

> I was away on vacation. I hadn't told him because I didn't think it mattered. My father didn't let me go back, after.

I was kept under what you might call "house arrest." My father feared I would find some way to go to the police. But even then I was already working on my plan. I couldn't involve the police. I couldn't do anything.

I didn't know you would kill your grandfather. I didn't even know you existed until you killed your grandfather.

I broke with my father over this, and many other things. I held on to the guilt. I used it.

Roger Simpson murdered your brother and made it look like drowning. I'm sorry.

I don't know if you'll read this. I don't know if you'll make it this far. But I needed you to make the journey to feel it, to understand it.

Maybe you ignored the gifts I gave you. Maybe you never understood why I chose them. Maybe that's why you never read this letter.

Nothing can ever change what happened. But you can judge me and find me guilty. I'm at peace with that. Who better to judge me than the sister of the person my family murdered.

We try so hard to escape. But we cannot escape the world. That is the point.

Salamander . .   . .   . . _Hummingbird_

A photograph, along with the letter. Folded, as if it had been in a wallet for a long time. I knew it was the original. Maybe the only one. Browning from the years. Silvina and Ned standing in front of her family's house up on the ridge. Silvina is smiling, but Ned's look is ambivalent, complicated, half in shadow. I can't read it. People I didn't know stood to either side. Employees? Gardeners? More people Ned had known, at least in passing, that I hadn't known at all.

"The fools on the hill," I recalled, or thought I recalled, Ned saying once. "The fools on the hill." But said with a kind of envy that was regret. Like he really meant the fools on the farm. The only time I remember him saying anything about them.

I liked him. I let him into the house.

Did I hate Silvina? No, I didn't hate her. Did I hate Roger? Yes, but he was dead. Langer had delivered my revenge for me.

He seemed so sad, and he was beautiful and so smart.

You could say anything in a letter. Tell the truth. Tell lies. Half-truths. Create whole lives for people that weren't real. Harder to do that with a photograph, if easier every day. I knew doctored photographs, had analyzed so many of them at the day job. This one was real.

A bitter vindication. That I wasn't random. That I wasn't just bait or distraction. That maybe that was also true, but there had been a connection between me and Silvina. That I had known her, in a sense. If only through Ned.

I didn't feel remorse about Shot. Not really. In time, Shot would've killed one of us, made me into him even more than he had. I felt regret, but that was different. No one was ever going to save us but me.

What else did I *feel*? I don't want to tell you. You might not understand. The dominant thing I felt.

What I felt was relief.

While all the world was in motion, colliding, nonsensical.

Imagine what it feels like to have an answer. To come to rest.

Because I knew what she wanted me to do.

Go back to the beginning.

94

The giant salamander felt through its skin even though it didn't want to. The giant salamander kept receiving the world even if it didn't want to. Even if the world poisoned it. How if the world was right, the salamander was healthy. If the world was wrong, the salamander was sick. If the world was wrong, Silvina was sick. I was sick, but not because the world was wrong.

Salamanders live in two worlds: the terrestrial and the aquatic. Humans can't do that. Humans find themselves caught between, having to choose. Salamanders don't have to choose. Part of both. Leaf litter and the banks of forest streams, in vernal pools, swamps. Foraging by night, capturing prey hiding in crevices.

To minimize danger, salamanders hide in rotting logs and under rocks. The stone foundations of old houses, like memories. If seen, the two wide yellow stripes of the road newt warn off predators. The yellow is produced by chromophores bound to proteins in the skin. These visual pigments pulse light at a specific wavelength visible at night. The pigments are toxic. The yellow lines are poison. When attacked, the salamander expands its spine and its ribs pierce open the poison cells into the skin, releasing venom in a powerful sting.

The attacker is injured, but so is the salamander. It must repair the skin to avoid infection. It must hurt itself to defend itself. So it knows its enemy by the self-inflicted damage. Knows, on some level, the state of the world.

When the moon is right, the road newts creep in great numbers to their natal forest ponds. Always the same pond, returning to the place where they were born. They know. They just know. That home may be changed beyond recognition. It may no longer be a safe place, or never was a safe place. But the newt has no choice but to return.

In the water, they lay eggs, and when the eggs hatch, the immature salamanders breathe through gills. Years are spent in this miniature stage, to prepare for their transition to the harsh terrestrial world. They must have every advantage to survive in their mature form. The hazards until they, too, return to the pond of their birth are many and unpredictable. Many never make it back.

Through metamorphosis, *P. omena* learns to live on land. Adapts to a place so different from what it knew. Glands develop that enable direct oxygen diffusion without investment in lungs. The skin infused with capillaries creates a respiratory service for survival. It also easily transmits pollutants from the environment into the delicate interior.

"*To be porous. To see colors no human can see. To receive what we cannot receive. To be receptor. To be transmitter.*" Part of Silvina's journal I'd almost forgotten.

The intimacy that salamanders have with their environment forces them to be sentinels of environmental change. Environmental degradation of air and water from pollution that dumps chemicals will distort and damage the pores of the salamander's skin. Extinction of *P. omena* is attributed to habitat degradation. Extinction of *H. sapiens* is attributed to destroying its own habitat.

There are no vernal ponds these days to which the road newts return. Those thousands upon thousands of years of return are gone. They are gone forever.

By the time I found the little windy road up to the storage palace, it was dusk.

An urgency possessed me. I had to make up for lost time. Silvina's salamander had reached me late, which meant the letter had reached me late, too. Now the timing was off. Now my timing was off.

If I was right about any of it.

If this wasn't just another game or test.

95

The road ended with the storage palace. Lights remained on, but the front door had been wedged open and the green plastic carpet shoved to the side for some reason. A squirrel darted out of the doorway and ran, panic-stricken, for the trees.

No cars. No sign of anyone following me. So I went inside. Accompanied by my cane and an automatic rifle. I didn't trust the Fusk gun for this one.

The lights were on, but no one was on duty. Why would they be? The little door to allow access to the kiosk and counter lay ajar. I found the key to number 7 hanging on a hook. Everything was neat behind the counter, nothing out of place.

The storage unit wasn't my first guess about Silvina's project. How could something so small contain something that must be so large? But I wanted to rule it out. Back to the beginning. *Salamander back to hummingbird.* What if something new lurked in the storage unit?

But it was empty. But it didn't matter.

Even the chair was gone. Same moldy panel of wall. Same flickering light. Same emptiness.

Came back out careful, watchful, sure I'd be ambushed at the doorway. Still no one. But night had overtaken the trees in that brief moment. The road gleamed with moonlight, mixed with shadow. A thick insect sound bursting forth, waning, bursting forth.

On a moonless night, I might have waited. But I had that urgency that Silvina needed me, that I was late. Or, that I needed to stop her. Or, that it wasn't clear to me. I wasn't an ideal receiver. Just that I needed to find her . . . or the next message (terrible thought) as quickly as possible.

My best guess, given the scope of the project, the funds put into it, was that whatever her secret was . . . she had hidden it behind the barbed-wire fence that sequestered the abandoned mining project. That up on the ruined mountaintop, she had built something or made something. Made it her headquarters. That the mining operation itself had been cover for another project altogether. What else could it mean?

It had struck me in the car that it could mean Silvina was deranged, delusional. That I might be delusional, deranged. That Langer chased ghosts. That whatever Hellmouth Jack wanted didn't exist, either. Scattering cigarette butts. Dressing up in a clown wig. For nothing.

I left Shovel Pig in the trunk. Put on a backpack with food and supplies. Took the Fusk gun and my automatic rifle. Hid the rest of the arsenal under some leaves and branches to the side of the parking lot.

Then, cursing, I opened the trunk again and took Shovel Pig with me. Stupid, superstitious, but it felt wrong to leave her behind. It just took time to empty her of what I didn't need. All over the backseat of the car.

The fence a little ways up from the storage unit was a beast. I'd brought bolt cutters, but some animal had dug underneath a section and it was easier to put on gloves and just dig it out more. Even so, I scraped up my back, almost torqued my bad knee. Great start, but I felt jaunty. Doing something physical. Far away from the farm.

I started haltingly up the incline. It took a while to get used to the cane with the ground wet, sometimes muddy. Along not so much a path as a rut from rainwater flowing downslope. Bending at the knees like I was on a boat helped.

I had a map I'd hastily drawn from an online source showing Vilcapampa's mountainside holdings. Predictable, that search engine maps of the area were blurred out and a decade out of date. But some of the topographical detail would help.

It felt possible no one but Silvina and lost hikers had been up here in decades. I was looking for a building or a bunker or anything that suggested human activity. The land had been placed in an environmental easement, ironically enough, and in theory nothing had been built on it since the mining excavation.

Just a half hour in, visibility changed. Fog came in and the moon tore at the edges of that, made the shadows more prominent, light rationed out. Patches of glistening reflections off the water onto leaves and branches, latticework that confused more than helped. I tried to just look down at the rough trail.

Surprisingly soon the grass, leaves, and rutted ground turned into black, glistening gravel shot through with dying weeds. Not a road, but a kind of ruined excavation. A suggestion of prior rockfalls from above.

The gravel widened, and I realized the trees below had grown high enough to hide the scar from below. Almost everything up here, except at the very highest elevations, was hidden from any angle below, especially since the gravel traced a wide path to the left to take advantage of a shallower slope.

Animals had reclaimed the mountain long ago, despite the rips and scars. I could hear things moving through the tree cover to the sides and on the slope below me. Silhouette of a scenting raccoon. Bumbling path of a skunk.

I had thought of the cane as a walking stick, but with this slant, the exertion was intense. Already, I was breathing heavily, and all the old, familiar pains had returned. My lungs felt compressed and weak. I couldn't always keep my footing on the gravel. Perhaps someone more graceful could have.

After a while, I realized I had lost all sense of where I was, except for the fact I was continuing upward.

Rain began again, soaking me. My legs ached from the sand-like exertion of walking on the gravel. This was a trek for a younger, fitter me. But this body was all I had. Swift, abandoned thought of turning back, waiting until morning. The fog was so thick that I couldn't be sure of finding my way. Of not pitching forward down the slope and breaking my neck.

Through the fog, distant, there came in time an echo across

the gravel. Dismissed it as weird acoustics. The sound of a huge monster—me—dragging itself across the gravel, ever higher. But when I stopped to rest, I still heard it. Coming closer.

I picked up my pace, at the risk of giving away my location with more noise. But whatever or whoever it was kept pace. Nothing good could come of this trajectory.

When the fog lifted a little, ten minutes later, I could see a copse of trees ahead on my right. Stubborn defense against the gravel. Unwilling to capitulate. I reached it and hid behind a clutter of dead fallen trees. Anyone coming up the slope would guess I had hidden there. But it gave me a clear line of sight to send a bullet or two their way.

I waited for someone to appear. Instead, the treacherous fog came back, rolling in from farther up the slope. Now I was lost in a welter of trees, unable to see anything downslope.

A flat, thick sound. A bullet zipped past my neck and I hit the ground. Undid the safety on the automatic rifle, strafed the slope.

Nothing. No sound. I'd missed, too.

Weird panic. What if whoever it was didn't know it was me.

"Identify yourself!" I shouted—and rolled well to the side, to the shelter of a huge fallen tree trunk. The earth between roots smelled like bitter medicine.

A spray of bullets, but far off to the left. The fog was doing strange things to the acoustics. Okay, so no mistake. They meant to shoot at me.

I stood up behind the tree trunk, shielded by its ten-foot circumference of unearthed roots.

Listened intent. Crack of a branch to downslope, to my left.

It sounded so close, I emptied the clip in that direction. The bullets sizzled through the trees, into the trees. I heard a gasp, a scream. A man's voice, I thought.

I stood there a second. Listening again. Didn't want to give up my position behind the tree trunk.

Silence.

Then a furious fire from my right, through the fog, bullets snapping into the roots, into the trunk, as I slid to the ground, unhurt. Another year of wood rot and one of those bullets would have reached me.

My other clip was in my knapsack. And my knapsack was back where I'd been.

I pulled out the Fusk revolver. Hesitated. Too late. It felt too late to fire back. Didn't think they'd be in the same place.

I was staring in the middle distance when a shape loomed up from the side, not ten feet away. Staring in the other direction. But I couldn't help a gasp. The figure turned, shot, hit my arm. I screamed, dropped the gun as I fell.

He shot again, but I was already rolling as I fell, throwing the cane at him, so he flinched and had to duck. By then, I had closed the distance. I smashed into his midriff, swatted his gun from his hand, still burning up from the bullet lodged in me.

I don't think he expected me to do that. I don't think he expected I would come toward him.

Langer.

It was brief and brutal. Langer had no experience with close-in combat. I used my weight to crush him beneath me. He bucked, tried to get away, punched me in the face. I punched him back. We said nothing, made no threats or pleas. What would we have said? There was only the moonlight, the shadows, the vapor rising off our bodies, our thick, rapid breathing. Langer tried to punch me in the kidney. Didn't care. He brought his legs in and kicked me in the belly. I guess he thought soft meant soft.

But as he did, as Langer thought I would crumple and he would pick up his gun and end me, I hugged his shoulders, brought his torso close. Changed levels as he reacted. Twisted his legs to one side as my weight landed there, off his torso. Langer fell back, with a surprised, squeaky sound, something having popped in him or me. I wanted him to be gone from this Earth. I wanted him to be out of my fucking way. More than anything I'd wanted in a long time.

We thrashed from forest onto gravel, frenzied. Langer tried to dislodge me from around his waist, beat at my back, and it was just like a gentle tap, tap, tap to me. Tried to gouge out my eyes, but I moved my head and bit deep into his thumb. Brought his other hand to his side to pull out a knife and with his bitten hand punched me on the top of the head.

While I tried only one thing. I braced myself and half rose with Langer in my grasp, and as he flailed, I brought him down on his side with such an impact the air left his lungs. Went for a choke hold from behind. Held Langer tight, his back against me, his throat pulsing, trying to shout but gasping instead. My legs were wrapped tight around his legs, to keep him motionless. I hoped my bad leg would hold. Langer began to concentrate on breathing, trying to pull my arm away.

I thought I had him. I had him.

But he managed to reach his arm around and get to the knife and stab me in the bad shoulder just as the bad leg gave way. I could feel my choke hold shift. Another second and I'd lose that position. Langer would be on top of me or straddling my side. Stabbing and stabbing until I was dead.

I bought some time clubbing him with Bog. Opened a cut on his head before he managed to smash it from my grip. My treacherous fingers.

But there was the slope. Literal last ditch. The leverage of one good leg. I used my weight to roll and let gravity do the rest, keeping the choke hold, loosened, as we rolled and rolled back down the gravel slope, bruised and torn by the sharp black pebbles and our own momentum. Dizzy with it.

Knife gone flying. I saw it kick back up slope. A glittering glint lost in the haze.

Langer shouting now. Incoherent, bucking, trying to get free, even as the slope pummeled us.

The difference between us: I didn't give a fuck what came next so long as I kept my weight on him, kept my arm around his neck.

There came a crack and smack that knocked me half unconscious and I lost my grip on Langer. He'd landed up against another dead tree, me facing him. Washed up on this strange shore of moss in the moonlight. I could smell only the fresh, rich smell of the cedar trees. Blood in my mouth. Felt like a brick had been thrown through the back of my skull.

I heard a weird sound. Langer.

"Don't destroy it," Langer was mumbling through the gash in his mouth. "Don't destroy it."

I lay there too tired to reply or to move. Drifting in and out of consciousness. Getting colder and numb, but not caring. In the end, it was too much. I had limits. I wanted an end, but I couldn't get to my feet to get to the end. Something essential to standing knocked out of me.

The stars above blurred, came back into focus, moved in odd acrobatic orbits. Thought I saw the knife still spinning, falling toward me. The thick black hilt. The silver, shining blade.

I struggled to my knees, stared at Langer. He gave me a weak smile. He was delirious. His eyes weren't right. Or his expression wasn't right.

"I loved her," he said. "I loved her. I love her."

I wanted to tell him that was pathetic. That he was delusional. I meant to tell him that when I should've said "I know." Because what was he in that moment but stripped down to the truth?

But we didn't have time left to talk, anyway.

Langer's head split open. The blood spatter slapped against my boots, my pants. Whatever was left hung down lopsided. So that's what happens next I remember thinking. A bullet in the brain. A bullet to the brain. The recoil from the gun burned in my ears. Made me fall to the side. I winced, waiting for me next.

But my time didn't come.

Above me, Hellmouth Jack loomed up out of the shadows, looking just as he had in the bar centuries ago in New York. A peculiar anticipation on his face. Something akin to excitement. Or greed.

He had a Glock trained on me.

"No slacking, slacker," he said. "Time to rise and shine. Jack and Jill have to go—up a hill."

[96]

We waited until early morning. The fog had turned to drizzle. The bullet had just grazed my arm. I didn't even bother to stop the bleeding. My shirt would stanch it in time. My head felt better. A dull ache. A dull ache, too, that I was a prisoner.

"He always talked too much," Hellmouth Jack said. But I didn't much care that he'd ended the man who'd tried to kill me.

"How did you find me?" I asked.

He was squatting on a tree stump a good ten feet away. Wary. The way I'd brought Langer low wouldn't happen to him. Smoking a cigarette, Glock in the other hand, vaguely trained in my direction. Not as bad as my husband, but in the new light he didn't look great. Either he'd been dyeing his hair before or the gray had just begun to come out around the temples. Subject to current events. Smelled the alcohol on him even from the ten feet. Rum, not whisky.

Langer's remains lay among meadow grasses thirty feet farther down the slope. Neither of us had suggested burial.

"Called in a last favor with Homeland Security. I knew you weren't going *home* home. Drone triangulation on your car when you parked at the cabin to talk to your beloved husband."

A trap, then, and I'd walked into and through it, and here we were.

"Homeland Security still exists?"

"Not by that name. Just their drones. Do you know how many secret drones lacerate the sky these days? They'll outlast us all. Form their own civilization."

"Thanks for saving me," I said.

He smiled at that at least, even if grim-faced. His voice had such a flat certainty to it. A clipped certainty. So unlike the flirt at the bar or even him over the phone.

"You did me a favor, bringing all the bad actors out of the woodwork so I could get at them. But, in the end, it didn't much matter to me who took care of who. So why get involved."

"What if I'd swallowed the key?"

"The key? Oh—the clues? Good idea to bug both the cabin and the house, as it turns out. Once I knew the letter existed, I got the gist from your lovely stepmother. Just recently."

Flare of anger.

"She's not my stepmother. Did you kill her, too?"

"My, the things we worry about at the end of history. No. I didn't have to—she was happy to tell me."

To be expected. I felt more betrayed by Hellmouth Jack. That didn't make sense, meant I'd relaxed too much into the banter of our conversations.

"I've always been more discreet than Langer anyway," he added.

"Langer was the last one, wasn't he?"

"Last what? Lone ranger? Anger management counselor? Inept courier?"

"Last member of Contila. Of any note."

"True. Contila membership has become very elite in recent months. But there's one left."

"Who?"

"Silvina, of course. And she—or her 'child,' her pet project— is up here somewhere, isn't she?"

I said nothing.

"Surely you, too, have looked askance at that hit-and-run report. Surely you, too, would like someone to find her ashes in the ocean and run a DNA test?"

I said nothing. Didn't want to help him. Didn't want to be complicit that way. I felt his gaze would warp the discovery. Irrational, but I'd just found where Silvina had existed in my life, the compass point. I wanted that kept pure.

"We could do this 'the hard way,' as they say. But I like you, Jill. I like especially how tough you are. Maybe I did shield you a bit, but you took chances. You made your own luck. And you have been a tremendous help to me. It's not hard to guess now, anyhow: Silvina used the cover of the mining operation to complete her project up here. And we're going to find it—the rebel angels."

"This is what you were after all along," I said. "Just chance it's me, not Langer."

"Three birds with one stone is better than one, better than two. Whatever Silvina planned, neither you nor Langer should be the ones to decide what to do with it."

"'It.'"

"A biological weapon, of course."

But that could mean so many things. Weapon. Biological. It could mean a living mask that helped you breathe or it could mean a poison that wiped out a million people.

"What will you do with it?"

"Inform the agency. Contain it. Dismantle it."

But his expression had a hunger to it that told me he was lying. If Hellmouth Jack still worked for an agency, the place would have been crawling with agents and military. Which meant he had nothing behind him. No one backing him up. Which meant he planned to use this moment for himself.

As the light got brighter and you could almost sense the sun, I could see the rumpled contours of his tattered gray suit. The left sleeve of the jacket had a tear. A fresh cut along the side of his face. His fancy shoes were caked in drying mud. A line of blood had dried on his white dress shirt.

"How many people have you killed?" I asked.

"Enough. Langer did some of it, at my urging, before he got wise. But I ran over Larry—botched that. I killed quite a few of Vilcapampa's people. Never cared for Vilcapampa. I would've killed Allie if I'd had to, but, in the end, it was clear you hadn't told her anything."

"But you left my husband alone."

He laughed. "Jill, it was clear you never confided in him. About much of anything. Now, get up. We're going to find Silvina's secret, you and me together. I owe you that much."

I think he meant to murder me, in the end. After we'd found the promised land. I do believe that.

Starving, dehydrated, I got to my feet. Rough canvas with nothing much inside. I stumbled, caught my balance. Hellmouth Jack let me get my water out of my pack.

I threw the empty bottle at him and he ducked.

A big grin then.

"Don't you want to know my real name?" he asked. As if it had been on his mind.

As if he'd seen this encounter in his daydreams a hundred times before.

I said nothing.

It didn't matter. It didn't matter now.

[97]

We searched for three days. All along the gravel slope, the plateaus above that greeted us like strange moonscapes. We labored at our task with at first the serious formality of captive and captor. Then, as we found nothing, more like coequals. Because I had begun to become frantic, too. The site of the main mining excavation had been filled in. A brief elation at the discovery of a kind of silo dissolved when it became clear it was empty. Some sort of nascent septic system.

By the second day, I knew in my gut that we wouldn't find it. If it had ever been there. Jack was surly, snapped often, smoked more. Urged me on as if I was the problem. As if he would have found it if I hadn't been there. As if I put out some invisible field or aura obscuring the truth. When he accused me of knowing more than I'd told him, I shrugged. And he could see in the resignation that I had given up.

The weather got worse. We shared Jack's tent on the wet gravel, me tied up, hands in front. He had a couple bottles of rum. He offered me a cup. I took it. I didn't know rum from Adam, but it tasted good.

The lantern made his face crooked, febrile. Took away the redness. I could almost imagine he was the attractive man from the bar.

"Senseless anyway. I should've known better. How big a hole can you put in the world to kill it dead? You can't. Whatever Silvina wanted to do—virus, bomb, whatever. It's already done. We did it to ourselves. We're always doing it to ourselves. And first rule of dealing with wildlife traffickers: they do not give a fuck about anything. Except money. Except Langer. Who thought he had a soul. What love does to you. What love deforms."

"Sociopaths have souls?"

"Don't be cute," he said. "Shut up and drink your rum . . ."

Don't be cute.

Langer, being interrogated by someone at a federal agency. The pages Allie had given me of the transcript. Mr. Redacted had used that wording, more than once. "Don't be cute, Langer."

"You ran Langer," I said. "But why? What *was* Contila?"

"Eh? Says who. Who says I ran Langer?"

I ignored that.

"Agency-wide or just you solo?"

Hellmouth Jack gave me a look of respect that made me shudder inside.

"Jilly! You *are* a detective. Sort of. Okay, let's do this. If you can answer this riddle. Tell me: what's bigger than a breadbox and smaller than a breadbox?"

"So not agency-wide, but not just you."

He looked at me sideways like a crow. "You're not supposed to solve that riddle."

"Maybe I just understand you."

He'd picked up his gun, like I'd insulted him. No one was supposed to understand the great Hellmouth. Then he put it down, took a swig of rum.

"Langer worked with Vilcapampa on all sorts of import-export ventures. Through Contila. I was ambitious, wanted to make my mark. I thought, 'Why create some fake company? Why not just use Contila?' So we did. We got dirt on the CFO and took it over and tried to embroil Vilcapampa in shadier and shadier shit, some of which involved wildlife trafficking. Wasn't like they hadn't done it before."

"A sting."

Flash of anger. "More elaborate than a sting. Less contrived. Would've had political consequences. I would have had quite the career."

"Silvina met Langer because you were going after Vilcapampa Senior."

"More that I thought Silvina could give up Vilcapampa Senior. But by the time I knew Senior kept her at arm's length . . . it was too late. She'd forged her own alliances, used Contila her own way, and blew everything up. Figuratively. I had to clean house."

"What happened on the beach, before that? That week on the beach. Langer was hurt by you. Damaged."

The smirk to avoid anything real. "Oh, we had a fun time that week. Maybe by the end, they thought they were going to change the world. Maybe they thought we were fast friends. But it's not my fault I'm a good actor."

"Better for Langer if he hadn't truly been an idealist." In his way.

Silver tongue. The smooth exchange. Made them laugh, maybe. Some kin to grudging respect. The things they said to each other. Langer against the system. Silvina convinced she could strike a blow against her family. Hellmouth the one who could make it happen, as if his presence made it easier for Silvina to be with Langer. Or see Langer's point of view. Like I was trying to glean Silvina from Langer, from Hellmouth.

"And sometime later Silvina needed money and went to Langer."

Hellmouth Jack leered. "Awkward conversation, right? Since their fling had fizzled out. I was still running Langer in the ruins of Contila and covering up what I could because by then what was left of Contila was, ironically, a real criminal enterprise—the networks and all the rest. Exactly what we'd tried to stop. And, then, in time, I lost control of Langer, too."

I could imagine why. A cascading series of failures had sidelined Hellmouth. And the interest and energy went elsewhere. Maybe Vilcapampa Enterprises had even found a way to nudge that along.

"What about the warehouse?"

"A Frankenstein monster. A nightmare. Mostly stuff we planned to sell through Contila and Langer to get to the big players, like Vilcapampa. Wound up under Vilcapampa control. It wasn't Silvina's. But they didn't know what to do with it. She just knew about it, and then when she needed money, she and Ronnie disappeared it in that clever way of moving it from one abandoned Vilcapampa property to another. Thought they could use it. But it was just another albatross."

"How did Silvina get hold of the salamander?"

"I don't know." Irritated. Just like that his mood shifted. The salamander bothered him.

"Take a guess?" I prodded.

But Hellmouth Jack wasn't interested in answering any more questions. He drank more rum, stared out toward the horizon.

"Nothing like fresh mountain air! Invigorating." He turned to look at me, much as a crow would a mouse. "So, what would you have done if you found it. Silvina's secret? If you were up here alone?"

"I have explosives in the car." I'd booby-trapped the trunk. Maybe Hellmouth Jack would find out the hard way.

His face lit up, eyebrows raised. "A bomb to destroy a bomb. Smart."

"It might make more sense than you know."

Hellmouth Jack considered me with a kind of regret. "We would've made a good team."

"You mean we're not a good team now?"

"When I find it. When we find it . . ." But he trailed off, and he looked lost, confused. Lost some vital thread.

If only his head had dipped lower. If only he had fallen into drunk sleep.

But instead he went into a rage and took my bottle of rum away and stormed out into the rain.

I heard him arguing with himself. I heard the voice of a man who had only the vestiges of a plan left. And that was fraying.

The way the world does that to you.

[98]

At the end of the third day, Jack sat down heavily on the gravel. We were both utterly exhausted. My leg and shoulder burned and ached, and in all ways I wanted the weight of my self lifted from me. The sky above, as I collapsed, had a blue-tinged gray that mocked with that hint of normal. Soon enough, the hail. Soon enough, snow and sleet. It stiffened you. It brought you to a stop. Hands abraded from scrabbling in rubble. Chasing ghosts.

Hellmouth Jack began to weep. Hunched over, knees drawn up, he wept. Uncontrollably. Like a child. Like a breakdown. Like nothing I'd ever seen or wanted to see since leaving home.

"Total fucking waste of time. All of it. Total fucking waste of time."

"Maybe not. What if you just like to kill people?" Because it had worked so well last time. So he'd stop fucking crying. It got his attention.

"Fuck you."

"What if you just like playing games? Like some kind of child."

"Silvina played games, not me," Hellmouth Jack said. "Silvina was twisted in so many ways."

His tone had gone flat, his face emotionless. How quickly it happened should have frightened me.

"At least she had a reason," I said.

"You mean a 'greater good'?" Lip all twisted up with contempt. "I'm a greater good. *I'm* a greater good. Me."

I began to laugh. Laughed like it was the happiest day of my life.

Maybe because Hellmouth Jack was pathetic. Maybe because it was over. I was free, in a way. I had lost everything. Bet it all on nothing. I had nothing. But that was okay.

He didn't like my laugh. He beat me for it. He beat me hard and said not a word while doing it. But I kept laughing. I'd been through it all before with Shot. What did I care from beatings.

As he beat me senseless, at least one of us had begun to understand that history would wash over us indiscriminate, like the gray-green, the green-gray dawns and dusks. That so little would matter. That my laughter was, unknown to me, for the future.

In the early morning, I regained consciousness. Hellmouth Jack was gone from the mountainside, as if he had never existed. The rope on my wrists magically gone, too. As if I'd made him up to goad me forward.

Except he'd left me a pack of cigarettes. For which I was thankful, in the end. Sitting there waiting for the rain. Waiting for the next thing.

I never saw him again.

[99]

I wrote letters back to my mother for a few years. This was before I had the job as a security analyst. My college years were hit or miss academically. I drank a lot and thought it didn't matter because I'd built up so much muscle mass. If I'm honest, I dropped out of bodybuilding competitions later because I wasn't disciplined enough. As much as anything else.

The dread of those envelopes from her. How they smelled of her hand lotion. A soft, gentle lilac. While the contents were a kind of violence. I'd be in the dorm, on my bed, just staring at the latest one, while my roommate chattered on about how much she hated classes. But I'd always open the letter. Receive whatever lurked there. Whatever beast. Along with news of Ned.

Such detailed storytelling: that I was a cocaine addict in a specific neighborhood or a failure as a fisherman or had jumped off a cliff on an island she'd always wanted to visit. Kidnapped or murdered or worked as a custodian in a shopping mall. Lived at home, on the streets, in a halfway home, in the basement we didn't have.

Most of the time, I was older in these scenarios. Sometimes as old as Mom. Sometimes I had the same symptoms she did and was ancient. It frayed my nerves. But I had to read them to find Ned again and to push back, to provide the antidote particular to her delusion. It helped me sleep.

When I replied, I made up my own stories. About how I had straight A's. Or, for a while, about how I knew I wanted to become a doctor, because Mom thought doctors were highest in the hierarchy of life. Then I began to roam into the future.

Sent her letters about my life as a doctor. The illnesses I cured. The day-to-day of the practice. Or maybe I wasn't a doctor, but a lawyer. Sometimes I played the stock market. Professional gambler. Professional bodybuilder.

In one letter, I was old and gray and I had grandchildren. Many, many grandchildren. And I was writing to my mother after her death, to thank her for raising me right. For always supporting me. For having my back. For knowing what was good for me. For not inflicting harm.

I never sent that one. I wish I had. Don't know if she got even one of my letters. Or if she'd have read them if she did.

As I fled the mountain, I thought about our wounded correspondence. Wondered what my mother might have thought of my letters. If she would have understood why she should be proud, no matter what was true. And I wished, in such a desperate way, that she was there to tell me what to do next.

A moment of weakness. But I was weak. I am weak.

Unitopia

PART 4

HUMMINGBIRD SALAMANDER

Hard to describe what those next years felt like to live through. Except as a hollowing out, a loss beyond repair . . . even as it kept begging to be repaired. While the promise of what had been so very close haunted me. In so many ways.

"So much in motion, such energy, it disguised the decay of things, the incremental rot. How much was hollowed out."

Impossible to tell how fast society was collapsing because history had been riddled through with disinformation, and reality was composed of half-fictions and full-on paranoid conspiracy theories. You couldn't figure out if collapse was a cliff or a gentle slope because all the mental constructs obscured it. Multinationals kept their monopolies, shed jobs or even their identities, but most did not go under. Governments became more autocratic, on average.

Here was fine, *there* was a disaster. But *here* was just a different kind of disaster. A thick mist drenched in the smoke of flares that kept curling back on us. Why fight a mist if all that lay ahead was more of the same?

Those of us who survived the pandemic, and all the rest, passed through so many different worlds. Like time travelers. Some of us lived in the past. Some in the present, some in an unknowable future. If you lived in the past, you disbelieved the conflagration reflected in the eyes of those already looking back at you. You mistook the pity and anger, how they despised you. How, rightly, they despised you.

So we stitched our way through what remained of life. The wounds deeper. The disconnect higher.

The shock that shattered our bones yet left us standing.

[101]

But the world didn't really end. I'll give it that. One year passed. Then two. Then three, four. My husband died in the pandemic, one of the pandemics, at the lake house in which he'd sought refuge. Not an easy thing to absorb or put aside. But I had to.

Things found out in the wrong order. At a remove, so my grief was late, distant from the event. The way information became intermittent due to circumstance or location. How this became the disconnect.

My father and Lorraine passed away under circumstances the police could never unravel, amid a torrent of religious ecstasy and violence. Random or a disciple? It didn't matter. The family farm became what I'd always thought it had been: ramshackle, falling apart at the edges from neglect. Empty. Hard to give my father a final eulogy when, for me, he'd been dead so long and only briefly resurrected.

I clung to the thought that maybe I would see my daughter one day and we would grieve together, even if she had gone to stay with a distant relative in a gated community in Canada. But the truth was: I would never see her again. I did not, even when I had Wi-Fi, check the obscure game inbox where I'd left my message for her. I couldn't bear to see no reply. And if there had been a reply, how terrible. How unthinkable. What else could I say to her? What could I be to her now?

Even coming off the mountain in bad shape, I'd seen the course of things. The lines at gas stations. The closures of businesses. The empty shelves in grocery stores. Wandering aimless was a good way to get a reading. To analyze incoming evidence—and the evidence all pointed to a kind of reckoning. In that sense, Silvina hadn't been wrong.

Fires, floods, disease, nuclear contamination, foreign wars, civil unrest, police brutality, drought, massive electrical outages, famine. Always somewhere else. Until the garbage piled up and the buses stopped running and security forces patrolled streets instead of cops. Some places, militias conducted roadblocks, and no one tried to stop them. Military tribunals popping up. A federal government in crisis. Cell towers destroyed by conspiracy theorists. At the very least, we had become a failed state. Was the world a failed state, too?

Somehow, in the midst of this, I sorted myself out. Lied to myself that I had to find a purpose for my daughter, for whatever in Silvina had been good. All the things she'd striven for, even if, in the end, she couldn't outstrip delusion or hypocrisy any more than the rest of us.

I decided to remain true to Silvina's journey and explore the King Range. Turned most of my remaining cash into goods to barter with. Acquired a military armored jeep, painted civilian colors, from a semi-willing seller. I stashed gold coins near the burnt-out houseboat. Doubted anyone would ever live there again. I had barely lived there.

Armed with detailed physical maps, I undertook my expedition. As if I had always meant to. As if I wasn't afraid of Vilcapampa or a new eruption of Hellmouth Jack. Weapons, provisions, the ever-shabbier Shovel Pig by my side along with Fusk. Good old Fusk. Bog, though, was less and less useful.

I hid the jeep on the edge of old-growth redwoods at the northwest of the King Range, under a tarp and underbrush. Near a stream at the bottom of a steep ravine, I buried Silvina's miraculous salamander. It might've been dead, blind, and burnt, but the longer I had it the more dignity it had accrued.

It felt right to bury the road newt near its likely home turf. I did not mark the grave. That would have been a human thing and I knew Silvina would not have approved. Besides, the salamander would always burn true and clear in my mind.

How had Silvina found it? How had it died? Under what conditions? I would never know the answer, but the beast itself restored something mythic to the King Range, even if it was the only one.

By sign and symbol, by having once existed, the salamander gave me a kind of hope.

[102]

For a handful of years, I lost myself in the King Range, living off the land most of the time, often poorly. An eye out for a huge salamander in a quiet pool. An extinct hummingbird up in the trees. Found neither, but instead waded through unpolluted creeks, encountered black bears, mountain lions, elk, muskrats, and skunks. So many birds of every description.

The birds still migrated north, and south, despite the changes to climate and the disintegrating political situation. Uncertain, dangerous times. I felt for them and their journey. Did not take them for granted. They had not heard the news about the human world that so impacted theirs. They had no choice but to keep on living, keep on flying to sanctuaries that might no longer exist. But, also, the resistance in that. Some might survive. Some might adapt. Keep adapting.

By chance, I had removed myself at a critical time from confusion of the world. Because I could. Because I was burnt out, a walking corpse. Because I did not want to end myself but had to end something.

Even if I kept expecting to die in the wilderness. Even if the wilderness kept surprising me. Or I surprised myself. How was it that I became so attuned to and at peace with the change of seasons, even so corrupted? How did I become so content with silence?

In time, I got better. On some level, I thrived. My leg healed enough that I didn't need the cane except when the barometer dropped and my joints ached. My shoulder popped and crackled, and cold days around a too-small campfire made it cry out. But mostly I felt well, almost good. Even if I could never really escape the burning warehouse, or the deep water beneath Unitopia.

Live in the moment. Funny how if that had been a saying carved into Lorraine's front door I would've sneered at it. But there was such blessed relief, among all the regrets, to put Shot aside, my mother and father aside. They didn't live within me as they had before. Ned had faded, too, as if he was a problem I'd solved or decided was unsolvable. He was still there, but I'd kept him in my thoughts for so long that I was exhausted by him. No matter who he'd been.

Memories of the outside world came to me more as glimpses of people I'd never really known. The man who drove me to the storage palace. The woman behind the counter at the storage palace who wanted my ID. The barista who handed me Silvina's note. But Charlie at the gym most of all. The one I'd seen so often but only ever really exchanged pleasantries with. Perhaps I puzzled over them because they might be alive. Or because they'd existed on the fringes of a mystery so central to my life.

I came across people rarely, I had struck out so far into the roadless interior. Often, I kept to high elevations, coming down to the same streams as the bears and deer. I learned to travel during moonlit nights and sleep during the day. People unsettled me. Gruff or polite, friendly or wary—didn't matter to me. Had nothing to say to them—sometimes drew my gun as a precaution. Didn't want to meet their gaze, know their stories. Just waved them on, or stood aside on the trail, amid moss lumps and thick stands of giant ferns, waiting for them to leave.

Still a paranoia about Vilcapampa, some lingering doubts that Langer's death had closed that account. But mostly Vilcapampa. Because even in the midst of crisis, when I came to places where my phone worked, I could tell that the Vilcapampa companies soldiered on. It might be short-term, but in the moment, they had converted over to making vaccines, to making masks, to providing essentials like bottled water. Even fossil fuel extraction, even this late in the game.

The sting of guilt came less often, unexpected but sharp. Washing my shirt in the stream, wringing it dry, and, in the twisting, the twisting free of anguish at having lost so much in return for so little. All the usual, useless things. Because I couldn't shake Silvina's letter. No matter how I tried. Kept the photo, though I felt I was better off without it. Felt that Silvina had broken a contract with me. Even with the relief that there was no "ground zero" event with her fingerprints on it. As if Unitopia had been the actual pinnacle of what she could accomplish.

I told myself that sometimes powerful forces pass through your life that speak to you but, in the end, keep their own counsel. That they wash over you like an extreme weather event, then are gone.

No analysis can fill in the rest.

[103]

In the spring of the fifth year, things changed for me. The winter was harsher, or felt harsher. A near disaster slipping on some rocks and falling twenty feet down a steep slope made me less sure of my existence in the King Range. The way my body felt for weeks after. How I moved in more tentative ways and how that affected my judgment. In short, I felt old.

Even as more people were coming into the area, and federal officers had begun a standoff with a nearby Native American reservation over water rights and sovereignty. Twice I also stumbled across what I believed were right-wing militias on training exercises. Came back to my camp one night to find it ransacked, although I'd hidden anything valuable before I'd left.

I could survive among these new intrusions, but the mental strain became intense. How I blocked the outer world from my thoughts, only for it to intrude. Each time more alien, more different than memory.

By then I had no evidence Vilcapampa cared about me anymore. No evidence that the police sought me. Where I'd buried Langer, no one would ever find him. I began to think about the old house. That was what really began to draw me back at first. A fixation on what it was like now. It might be in foreclosure, but it might not. My husband had kept up the mortgage and property tax as long as he could. I might have a little while before it was no longer mine. Or, at least, it might be derelict.

If I could visit just once, bust in a window, I could take more things for barter. Maybe even have a yard sale, if the neighborhood was safe. If no one had already broken in.

Maybe, though, I just yearned for something other than what I had. Which was nothing. Maybe I believed a purpose waited for me out there. Or some thread I'd lost would come back to me. Because with the way the world kept cracking open I recognized something delusional in words like "yard sale" or "mortgage." As if, soon, some words would be extinct.

But I couldn't shake the memory of the photos of my daughter over the fireplace. Which might still be hung with dusty stockings. In all my repurposing of Shovel Pig, I'd lost my only photos of her. I had begun to find it hard to see her face.

[104]

But I didn't make it to the house. The jeep ran fine. The world did not. Even stopped short, I would have to become fluent in new languages, discard old ones. Languages of the dead and languages of the new. Curfews and lockdowns took unusual new forms. The National Guard had been called out to deal with an unspecified disaster. There was gridlock and confusion surrounding the city, early that summer. There was, too, old friend, the intensifying green-gray tint to the sky, tinged with gold from the distant glow of uncontrollable fires from a natural gas explosion. Or so they said. A general advisory to use a mask, to avoid breathing unfiltered air. With little explanation.

Even as the rain kept coming. Ever-present and meaningless, like thought.

"Landscape isn't fragile. It's what we impose upon it that's fragile. We must be ruthless about the foreground. We must trust the backdrop. Do you know how to do that? Can we trust in that?"

Funny how even then, as systems failed, flickered out, institutions revealed as paper thin, that so many couldn't bring themselves to believe in anything. That it helped if you didn't. Better to observe the rituals, use the catchphrases. Share your concern.

Express enthusiasm for reliquaries that some still held a mirror to, claiming to see breath form.

On a little-known stretch of state road about a hundred miles from the city, I came to a barricade with slogans on banners that canceled one another out. Didn't hesitate. Gunned the engine and smashed through the wooden fencing, firing from the open window for maximum discouragement. Some people believe in nothing.

Some people just want to kill other people, because they can. Maybe it was a joke or some form of performance art, but I didn't have the temperament to stop and find out.

I stopped for a deer a mile later, my pulse humming bad in my ears. Too irregular. Almost abandoned the jeep and followed the deer's silhouette into deep forest.

Continued on. But I knew I wouldn't make it to the city.

So I tried to find a different homecoming.

Noon of a day pretending to be ordinary, the rain a memory that would return transformed, as memory does. A moment like all the other forgotten moments in history. Silvina, did you know I'd keep returning? Did you count on me, relentless to the end? I can't see how.

The storage palace had three burnt-out husks of cars, tireless, in front. Not a soul in evidence, living or otherwise. Grass grew thick and tangled at the margins. Smell of tar and chemicals from no visible source.

The front door had been smashed off its hinges, and the outer walls grafittied with tags in green, orange, and white. It was like the rest of the country, no better, no worse.

The electricity had gone out, so I took my flashlight with me along with trusty Fusk and Shovel Pig. The cane more out of habit than necessity. Entered that hollowed-out place to the forensic evidence of earlier looting. Any junk had been dropped in the antechamber, a spree of plastic garbage and twisted bicycle wheels, broken glass and torn kiddie pools. Corridors had much the same debris, storage unit doors forced open, a few no doubt more politely opened with keys. The security counter had a firebombed quality to it, stripped of anything valuable, including copper.

Nothing much surprised me, the farther I went. More burn marks. Even the remains of a campfire with logs. Everything covered in a stillness so utter that my footsteps sounded like sacrilege. The amplified skitter of a mouse or rat in the shadows conjured up monsters.

I barely remembered the way in that transformed landscape. Pathetic enough. Nostalgic enough.

Storage Unit 7.

The door was closed, but unlocked, swung open easily.

I stared a moment, began to laugh. Unit 7 was empty as ever. Lit by the flickering fluorescent light above.

Out of habit, or established ritual, I searched the shadowy corners one more time. Tested the walls for hollow sounds. Tapped discolored parts of the floor with my boots. Nothing. Just the sound of dripping water from down the hall.

The outer areas were warm, but Unit 7 felt cool. I lingered a moment, wrestling with whether I should walk up the mountain for old times' sake or head back, defeated, to the King Range.

The mountain, I decided. Once I left, how could I be sure I would ever be able to return?

I came out into the murk of corridor. Then stopped. Something nagged at me. A ringing in my ears. Some detail I'd missed. When I realized what it was, I felt faint, remote from my body.

I looked back into Unit 7.

The ceiling light flickered at me. Taunted me. Told me I was stupid.

The entire complex was dark. No electricity. Not a single exception. Except for this one light.

I just stared at it, dumbfounded. Could it be that simple? Had it been that simple the whole time?

I became frantic, manic. Then frustrated as it took almost half an hour to find a sturdy stepladder amid the wreckage of that warren. Clung awkward to it, finding it difficult to breathe, as I pulled delicately at the light casing.

Nothing out of the ordinary. Just the usual. The world fucking with me again. In frustration, I gave it a swat. Still nothing, but now I saw a tiny button up against the frame on the right side. Cursed trying to get my sausage finger in position to push it.

But finally I succeeded—and the casing swung open on a hinge, knocking me on the head. I almost fell off the stepladder, cursing, looked up.

Behind the casing: a blue glow cocooning a sophisticated pass code keypad.

Always here. Never on top of the mountain. Always *here*.

I didn't want to exhale. Didn't want to make a single sound, as if it might all disappear in an unwary instant. Crept back up on the stepladder, examined the keypad more closely.

An eight-digit code.

Could the ghosts of a hummingbird, a salamander solve this puzzle? Game-playing Silvina, but most games had a reason. A way to win. An endpoint.

It felt almost as if it was a matter of faith as much as numbers. What if nothing happened? What if I was wrong about what those numbers were and the system locked me out? Panic then, as I couldn't remember the address of Silvina's apartment. Before it came back to me.

I entered the numbers, in their random original order, from behind the eyes.

Nothing, for a horrifying moment. That stretched and stretched.

The blue light turned green. A rumble and crack from the left corner of the far wall. The left panel of stone—waterstained, moldy—pulled inward and slid to the side. Revealing a rough-hewn, square tunnel lit by soft blue emergency lights that lined old-fashioned stone stairs.

A slow ascent into an unknowable darkness. A secret world under the mountain.

No time to absorb this miracle, this ultimate message from Silvina. No time at all.

Because a body was sprawled on the stairs at the edge of the light above me.

[106]

Ronnie Simpson, Unitopia's last guardian, lay across the steps as if she'd had a heart attack. One arm pinned beneath her. Legs entangled, the left at a right angle at the knee.

The laces of the boot had come loose. The back of her head was soaked in blackness. Her face, half turned toward me, had a pinched, mummified quality. She had no eyes, no soft tissue, all the flesh pulled tight. Even under generic gray army fatigues. The way the fabric drew in because there was so little underneath.

I was struck by the way Ronnie's mouth gaped open. The way the lines of that sunken face radiated out from a soundless and surprising ecstasy. A pale green powder on the dry lips contained evidence of vomit, in how it continued down the chin. Yet she had died in the throes of an overwhelming joy. That unnerved me more than agony.

Poison? Taken internally or carried by the air? If in the air, I was already compromised. Contaminated. Dead.

I felt fine. No different than when I had entered the tunnel. But I distrusted her condition. Something about the way salamanders received damage, through their skin. Rates of decay. I tried to do the math. Dead yesterday or dead five years ago while Hellmouth Jack and I wasted time on top of the mountain? Some date uncertain in-between. But nothing about the contrast in mummification and freshness made sense no matter the timing.

Didn't much like the idea of walking around the body and ignoring it. Put on latex gloves from Shovel Pig, did a search as fast as I could without missing something. Nothing much in her pockets besides ID. No weapons.

So light. Her body was so light, like a canvas frame. Tiny veins had ruptured all over her hands and arms. The smell I couldn't place. As if dust motes had sparked and burned while afloat. So the air around her had a char of pinpricks. A whispering, charred scent. Couldn't describe it any other way.

A shadow of my original fears swallowed me. Biological weapons. Ronnie following Silvina into something she didn't understand, any more than I understood it.

Well, I would know soon enough if I was sick.

I found the hummingbird pinned under her. As if it'd come loose from a pocket or Ronnie had been holding it when she succumbed and fell. Twisted wire. One tiny wing bent. But still glossy black. Stirring a fatal sense of beauty. Old friend. Comrade come back to me.

I saw now that the darkness of the steps beneath Ronnie meant she'd bled out, though I could find no wound. I knelt in her dried blood and took the hummingbird away from her. I could not leave it behind.

That Ronnie had gotten the hummingbird from her brother seemed certain. Whether Ronnie had come here because she remained part of Silvina's inner circle seemed less certain. Thought of "Hillman" and his bible of numbers. Of how it didn't matter which Vilcapampa they'd served. Both had wound up dead.

I stood there on the steps, stooped, overcome by so many emotions. It was hard not to cry over something.

But then I took a step forward, and another. Heavy steps, as if the hummingbird weighed me down. Or something did. My boots thick, awkward, made of solid metal.

Each step upward was easier than the last.

At the top of the stairs, an hour of climbing later, I came to new concrete steps and a portal of a door. Framed in a circle of stainless steel, the oval of the door shuttered like a closed storefront. A button next to it. No pass code here. But the button was thumb shaped, interactive.

That gave me pause. If I wasn't the right person, would I suffer Ronnie's fate?

I pushed the button anyway. The door slid up revealing a red-lit antechamber. Stepped inside and the door shut again. A light mist hissed out of holes in the walls. Moment of panic. Drugged, poisoned. Found out. Didn't belong here. Had never belonged here.

But the mist had a pleasant scent and I realized I was being decontaminated. Run through some protocol.

Why did I have to be clean to get to the other side, but Ronnie had come back out contaminated?

After it was over, the portal opposite slid open, a large, dim-lit space beyond.

I hesitated once more. I'd been given so many last chances to turn away that I hadn't recognized. Now was being given another one. To heed the warning that was Ronnie's corpse. To recognize the limits of what I had left to give. No normal life waited outside. But life of a kind waited. I could try a different part of the King Range wilderness. I could become expert at avoiding militias. Sleep by day, wander by night. Pipe dream. Faint home.

One thing I knew: if I crossed that threshold, I wouldn't be going back there. Felt it in my bones.

So I bent and leaned through the door into another world.

[107]

You could say Silvina had built a bunker out of a cavern. Or a command-and-control center out of the top of a mountain. You could call it many things. You might be looking at it right now. You might know more about it than me. It would've taken years. Secrecy. Patience. So many millions. Piece by piece. Using different experts and contracts so no one knew the full extent of it. Toward the end, she must have trusted only "Friends of." I had a vision of servants entombed with their ruler.

I had come out into a nondescript, rectangular space shoved up against the side of the mountain. Framed by rough-hewn stone walls and a steel-beam-reinforced ceiling studded with the dimmest possible blue lights. Every surface seemed chosen to reject mold and decay. A sterile quality I didn't like but that was purposeful.

Not much of it registered as important. Just unfinished or hurried. You could see the outline for an elaborate kitchen and island on the far side of the room, with the mountain rock jutting out uneven above another concrete wall. But it had never been built. Instead there was just a sad-looking kitchenette with a cheap mini fridge. One huge doorway, opposite me, led to an area stacked with bunk beds, none of them used. A small medical clinic. A space clearly meant for exercise. Spartan, with mats and little else.

That Silvina had run out of money became obvious the more I explored. That she had spent it only on the most important things.

As I remembered Unitopia, I understood the space better. The disconnect was the scale. The scale was off. And the function. Not an island. A bunker. A cavern, with most of the same layout as Unitopia. Just that the "domes" were rough, limited by the conditions. Strange how that altered so much, how what should be familiar became so unfamiliar.

A smell of age and mustiness that came not from what Silvina had built but what surrounded it. The feeling of a cathedral, thick with history. Unitopia had that, too, but I recognized it here because it felt less human.

A door led to a cramped room with a few monitors against a far wall and more chairs and tables. A desk. A logbook with terse scribbled entries. The sense that Silvina at one time had meant to have a staff here, under the mountain.

The monitors alternated showing different views from the mountainside. Some reflected the long view of private satellites and drones. But some, from their vantage, were disguised as bits of the very gravel across which Hellmouth Jack and I had frantically searched five years before.

The ghost of my other life found that clever, even roughly elegant. That the ground had been alive with surveillance. That we had been shoveling cameras, not just stones.

The main dome, past all these unimportant adornments, lay

beyond these impermanent monuments. Of this odd version of Unitopia. If the blueprint was true, nothing else remained that I had not seen, and all the rest was empty, and bleak.

I don't think I hesitated. My steps were as steady as before. I leaned no more heavily on my cane. It was all laid out as perfectly as if a dream and there could be no tension, no suspense, because in a dream you were carried along without a choice.

In the dome, there was a great and terrible window at the far end through which, even from the entrance, I could tell things were moving. So I resisted the window, because it wanted all my attention. Instead, I tried to take in the place entire.

In that dome, too, was a kind of medical station, and more monitors—larger ones—along the left side. On the right side, built-in shelves housed books, but also technical equipment. Any odds and ends. Perhaps personal effects. A sliding ladder had been attached. The bookshelves weren't painted. The raw wood and shoddy construction told me there'd been no time or no money to paint.

The silence here was profound. A kind of holy quality. The budget for soundproofing must have been unlimited. The soft blue light in that space soothed and suffused in such an unearthly yet pleasant way. The smell of stone rich with water. I could see in the near distance, where the stone lay exposed, the water glistening. Moss glistening. More cave than construction.

The muffling of so much, the vastness of the space and how that made so small what had been placed in it, made me not see everything at first.

But as I walked slowly forward, as my eyes adjusted to the scale . . . I came across a second body.

Slumped in a chair, in front of the medical station. Even at a distance, I could tell it had been there longer than Ronnie on the stairs.

I hesitated. Came closer. Lingered on details to avoid the larger question.

Clothed in a green jumpsuit, her dark hair tied back in a ponytail. Her eyes were black, open, blood vessels exploded. Her hands gripped the chair like claws. There was to her aspect a kind of convulsion of purpose. A motion interrupted that encoded motion into the stillness.

Oh, Silvina, even so long dead, you had the aspect of someone who might return to life.

I approached her as if she were delicate and made of something breakable, that she would shatter at the slightest touch. But she'd never been fragile.

"To be a weakness that is a strength. To let the world breathe into you and out of you. To find a path through."

Had no place to put this revelation. So casual, in its way. So terrible and casual. This dead body in an office chair, in a cavern with monitors. Under a mountain.

I tried to be coldhearted. To focus on the details. To make some sense of the incomprehensible.

But a horror had come over me, the more I examined the body. Never touching it, but circling it. A drowning, buried feeling crawling over my skin.

A sound left my mouth that was a keening. A sound I bit my tongue to stop. If it went on much longer, it would never end.

The terrible thought. The unthinkable.

That as Hellmouth Jack and I searched and searched and searched for this place atop the mountain . . . that Silvina had been down here, watching us. Observing us through the pebbles at our feet.

That she had still been in the world then. That if only I had been smarter, more savvy, more observant, I would have come up those steps into her secret place to find her alive.

That if I had been alone, not chained to a sociopath, she would have revealed herself to me.

Physically ill at the thought. So ill, I bent over and would have retched, but suppressed the impulse. Blasphemous. To do it in that space. I took a breath instead. Another. Stood up straight and let the cavern air, withered but pure, fill my lungs. Felt better. Felt clear. Did not want to be empty.

When I really *looked* at Silvina's face. When I looked clear and unflinching. It wasn't ecstasy I found there. Not like Ronnie. No, not ecstasy and not terror, either. More a sense of . . . completion.

Of coming to rest. Finally.

I was conditioned to look for clues from Silvina. To look for messages. It took long moments before I realized she had left no message. That the letter was the last of it. That her body was the last of it.

A huge, black three-ring binder sat on a desk nearby. Inside, a two-thousand-page manuscript in Spanish. Titled "Unitopia." My college Spanish was rusty, but even a glance, a skim, told me that this was her real manifesto. Not the one meant for me and people like me. Not the middle-class, watered-down version. In English. But the unadulterated vision. It would be harsh, uncompromising. It would not budge on how the physical laws of the universe worked. Of how the laws of cause and effect worked. It would not try to give false hope, but give the hope of a real way forward. No matter how uncomfortable.

I wept, reading what I could of it. I wept because I knew that she had not believed anyone would implement her ideas. That was why it existed here and not out in the world. Delusional. Naïve. Unworkable. Dangerous. That is what the enemy called the necessities for survival. For flourishing.

So she'd left it here and found another way.

And it had killed her. Hadn't worked.

Clear to me there, in that moment.

In front of her like an altar, that odd medical station, which had three tubes for syringes held within a clear polymer container, radiated the cool hum of climate-control. Two were missing. One of the two lay cracked on the floor beneath Silvina's dangling hand. It took no imagination to guess that Ronnie had taken the second.

Whatever it was, Silvina had thought it would change the world. Each was a different "approach," according to the documentation. Each promised radical transformation. Each promised contamination until you would see the world so differently. And as you walked out into the world, what had captured you would capture others and they, too, would be transformed. "We must change to see the world change."

Or was it transform the world? Would the recipient change the world? The science in front of me, the documentation, was not meant for a layperson. A change to the genetic code? Or changes. Radical changes. Not to become superhuman or erase difference or erase anything. References to the salamander's unique defensive toxin, and the alkaloids in the flowers preferred by the hummingbird, which could be hallucinogenic to humans. Some evidence of a quest to harness their power without the toxicity. Chemical biomimicry.

Could it mean a kind of healing? A kind of healing, an ebb and flow. A restoration of the health of the world? Is that what the diagrams meant? Incoming and outgoing. A contamination that meant the ecstatic.

I was irradiated by my belief. Riddled through. But was I ready to follow?

One last magic potion.

One last chance. One last terrible, awful choice.

I spent some time frozen, arguing with my own thoughts.

Derangement or genius? Was it even possible? If I was right, to create not a deadly pandemic or a biological bomb but a new, true seeing? Let the world in through your pores like a salamander, see all the colors of the flowers only a hummingbird could see.

Yet both Ronnie and Silvina were dead. Not ascended, not "repaired." Dead. Sick, sick, stupid thought. Maybe they had been the wrong hosts drawn to imperfect serums. Maybe they hadn't, in the end, been strong in the way I was strong. Could that be why I had been chosen? If I had truly been chosen. By fate, if not really by Silvina.

What if one last syringe was just chance?

What if Silvina was just delusional?

I left the question, along with Silvina's body, for a time, because I trusted there was something more to find. Because I needed to sit with that question for a time.

Because I needed to look through the enormous round window.

[108]

An ark existed there beneath the earth. Or a kind of ark.

I would have been the first to look upon that miracle except for Silvina, except for Ronnie. Because she would have had to create it with only the most trusted, loyal friends. Because double-blinds were necessary to prevent any one person from knowing what it meant. Because it would have taken decades from first thought to last. Because when she started no one had ever built an ecosystem this way.

What I saw, when I came close to the window, was a scene lit by an artificial sun. The glass so thick and rimed with green, it was like looking into the past.

But it was actually the future.

A creek surrounded by understory trees and bushes, framed by ferns. Birds stitching through the undergrowth. A squirrel drinking from the creek. Fish visible in the creek, fins cutting the surface. Clean, pure water. Butterflies and bees. Lizards and, yes, according to the species list on the wall, hummingbirds and salamanders. Just in glimpses. In blinks.

It was painfully like the creek near the farm. Painfully like the places I had explored as a child. The mud and flux of it. The smooth, flat creek stones. The moss. A dream of what I'd been.

Mundane. Extraordinary. It could be any half-unspoiled habitat. But artificially created, it became a work of extraordinary imagination. The detail that had gone into it. The sheer ambition.

Collected over time. Relocated. A simplification of habitat. A simplification of species. Calculating what could be sustained and what could be maintained. And, on the wall opposite, safe in what I saw now had the detail of honeycomb, samples of all that could not. A fortune had been thrown at this, and a fortune more required.

The DNA for revival.

It would last at least a century on its own, Silvina believed, from the documentation I could find. It would be there if the world destroyed itself, to help. Preserve, change, and save.

On the raised platform, also, a complex control panel, automated. Fail-safes, and fail-safes for the fail-safes. Heat, cold, light, water levels, food dispensed where necessary. I could hear the sweet, soft hum of generators buried in the earth. Muffled, like every other sound.

Her dead body across the room. This towering above her. A kind of balance to that. A kind of hedging of bets. If *this* doesn't work, there would be the ark. If one solution didn't fit, wasn't ready, then . . .

Dying for an elixir that might transform the world. Sacrificing your entire life for an underground creek beneath a midnight sun that you, by pure will, sheer strength of mind, had wrenched into a self-sustaining pattern . . . of whatever duration.

And still I didn't know if it was hubris, if it was folly. Would the ark begin to die now that Silvina was dead? Was it dying now? Would it soon be as lifeless as Ronnie on the stairs, the hummingbird in my pocket? And how much did the world need to change or did it just need to be rid of us?

The rheum of green around the portal window. The sense of algae encroaching. In a hundred years, if this survived, would it be something strange and different and mutated? The roof set to open and the air that came in kill what had waited so patiently within for renewal.

I thought about what world waited for me out there. What was left. Knew maintenance of what I had found was beyond me. Knew that had not been Silvina's purpose for me. If there was purpose.

In the slow sinkage of that, the recognitions, I began to know what to do.

If not for the ark, I would have made a different choice.

The end of the text I'd seen in the Unitopia visitor center, so long ago, read:

> But once you got used to this new perspective, you'd look at the ground and it'd open up its layers, past topsoil and earthworms, down into the deeper epidermis, until you're overcoming a sense of vertigo, because even though you're standing *right there*, not falling at all, below you everything is revealing itself to you superfast. And maybe then, while still staring at the ground, even more would open up to you and you'd regress to the same spot five years, ten years, fifty years, two hundred years ago . . . until, when you look up again, there's no street at all and you're in the middle of a forest, and there are more birds and animals than you could ever imagine because you've never *seen* that many in one place. You've never even seen this many old-growth trees before. You've never known that the world was once like this, except in the abstract.

You're, in fact, standing on an alien planet. And once you got used to that, maybe then . . . only then . . . you'd be able to reach a level in which you inhabit the consciousness of an animal—something less advanced, at first, like a tortoise or squirrel, and then work your way up to something "fairly" intelligent, like a wild boar or a raccoon.

And once you'd worked your way "up" to human, or sideways to human, or down to human . . . whatever that looks like . . . then and only then would you be allowed to look to the future, to think of a time beyond, only then would you know enough because you'd feel it in your skin, and in your flesh . . .

I don't know if that is the change Silvina sought. It feels like just one part of something bigger. Just to see the world better, to be vulnerable to it, is not enough. No one thing can be enough. The ark told me that. The three formulas told me that.

To take the chance is to believe in death as well as life. To believe that, even with the odds against you, you should jump off the balcony. To trust you'll get through it. Somehow.

I've lost everyone I've ever loved or cared about. In the end, I didn't think I could bear to find Silvina again . . . and lose her. Not really.

• • •

After I have finished this account, I will leave a hard copy next to Silvina's treatise. I will also use the laptop to allow for dissemination on a rather long delay. Allow the hundred years Silvina wished for. Let my words become visible just as the roof of the ark splits open and brings in the real sun for the first time and all that is down here in the dark and secret is made plain.

It will all be there waiting for you.

It doesn't matter if Silvina never really thought I would

make it this far. If I'm just a fail-safe to a fail-safe, an afterthought to her memory of Ned.

The things you think in what might be your last moments. How you've had a lifetime of unhappiness and yet happiness, too, but never recognized it. How you might be searching for salamanders with your brother in one moment of your life or listening to your daughter talk about her day . . . and at the end of your life wind up in a secret cavern at the beckoning of someone you never met, deciding whether or not to take a chance on dying.

I am going to take the third syringe with me. Close the secret wall. Take a hammer or a baseball bat to the control panel, disguise the fact it was ever there.

I will sit on the hill outside the storage palace among the trees, me and the hummingbird and Shovel Pig and all the ghosts of this place. Inject myself and lie back and watch the clouds go by. The magic elixir. Worth the price, to change the world, because I've seen this world and it needs to change. Even with the terrible ache as I type this. Of knowing. That after all of this, I may not be able to reach the true end.

Somewhere it is a gray day, and on the sidewalk outside the coffee shop, a dead robin in the gutter, a hand reaches out holding a note that will change everything.

Langer had believed in Silvina as the bringer of death and destruction, had welcomed that. Hellmouth Jack didn't care what Silvina had built. Just wanted it, even if it would never have been for him to use. And me? I didn't know if it was for me to use, either.

Odds are, someone will find me dead on that hillside. Odds are, the ark inside the mountain is most probably doomed, and Silvina, in the end, was just someone desperate and alone and delusional. Those are the odds.

But if she wasn't. But if it is not doomed. But if I were to rise, and if I were to rise as my own ark. Shedding light and matter. Generating the renewal beneath my skin. If I were to survive the fury and wonder of that, then I would come back into the world, my body the gospel of Silvina.

Where shall I wander if I am not left insensate here? What will spill forth from me and into the world? Spreading a message wherever I go, to whoever I meet. As long as I am able. As some new thing.

I've been stared at my whole life. What is a little more of that?

The beating of my heart. For now. The pity of it: that I may not know what happens next. Or even recognize it. And that, perhaps, after all that has happened, I don't deserve to.

But you might.

..   ..   ..

One hundred years.
    What is the world like now?
    What is the world like after the end of the world?
    Is there a hummingbird, a salamander?
    Is there a you?

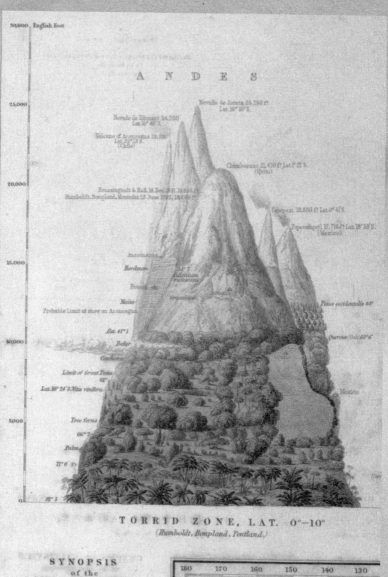

APPENDIX:

THE HELLMOUTH FILES

friendsofsilvina.com

TOP SECRET * P#158a: JACKSPLAT

Intercepted material prior to communication with Vilcapampa Enterprises. Asset Mesa detained and held for questioning and his team liquidated. Attempts to turn Mesa ongoing. Mesa report to Vilcapampa Enterprises follows this page; minimal intel value. Mention of strange woman does not correspond to SV's physical description.

Points of Special Interest re Project JACKSPLAT

- No additional materials discovered in the abandoned vehicle Mesa discovered outside of Quito, except for a torn page of salamander drawings crumpled up around used gum. (Sample included with Mesa note, next page; "meta" ref to his former analysis position with us?)
- Operative remains at large, whereabouts unknown. May have several passports and thus options. Physical description sent to border security, including airport security and port security, at all adjoining countries.
- Original files discovered by Mesa: whereabouts unknown. No Vilcapampa intercepts indicate receipt of original files.
- Other evidence (see doc P#158a-22) suggests that "Jack" has made contact with a cell of the terrorist group "Friends of Silvina".
- Deteriorating mental state of "Jack" corresponds to continued frustration re SV op. However, field psych opinion is this worsening condition does not lessen the danger posed by Jack to compromise national security, even if it does affect his ability to properly analyze incoming data.

Analysis

Although conceivable that the entire file is an attempt to redirect our attention in some way, the excerpt from a top-secret transcript and other materials are verifiable and factual, whether actually so or in the sense that they are consistent with subject's focus and state of mind.

Jack's continued fixation on SV and SV's so-called yet so far apocryphal "mega eco-op" remains a concern, perhaps primarily in a context of disinformation that could yet metastasize as significant security breaches via actions taken by the "Friends of Silvina". Especially as security conditions overall continue to deteriorate worldwide. (For example, our own freedom of operation in the relevant countries has been compromised by massive climate refugee movement, extreme civil unrest, and the breakdown of agriculture and infrastructure.)

To what extent we should continue to pursue JACKSPLAT over domestic internal security ops seems a relevant and increasingly urgent question. Please advise.

Gabriel Mesa <mesag@ascorp.com>
Dama De La Muerte <muerte1@corp2345.com>

Ref: "Jack Sprat," alias actual "Jim Lord"

Agente Reportando: Gabriel J. Mesa

C. Vilcapampa:

El auto estabá al lado de la carretera, con la puerta abierta del lado del
conductor. No parecía que hubiere ocurrido un accidente. El motor prendió al
primer intento. Nada en la guantera, en los rodamientos de las llantas, o en el
tapiz. Nada en la cajuela. El conductor parece haber huido de prisa; sin
embargo el aspecto meticuloso del interior del auto me hace sentir como si
alguien lo hubiere limpiado luego de que este se marchó. No puedo descartar que
el auto hubiese sido forzado a salir de la carretera, y el conductor raptado,
pero esto parece poco probable dado lo que conocemos de lo peligroso del sujeto.

Esto ocurrió a 125 kilómetros fuera de Quito. Un área remota, coordenadas
4.5804° N, 73.7564° W. Un sendero llevaba hacia los árboles, pero no pude
encontrar huellas recientes. El lodo, resultado de una lluvia reciente, hizo
difícil la búsqueda. Imágenes captadas por dron no revelaron nada útil y otro
vuelo por dron más tarde en el día tampoco mostró resultados.

Sin embargo, había una carpeta en la silla delantera del lado del pasajero.
Estaba fuertemente atada con ligas, que por las marcas nadie parecía haber
quitado en algún tiempo. Los contenidos no parecían ser datos, en la usanza
común, ni los resultados de una investigación, sino más bien como los recuerdos
de una investigación. Me parece, para serle franco, que los contenidos de la
carpeta tenían valor sentimental o personal para el conductor, y que el dejarla
atrás tenía para él un significado importante.

He hecho copias y le envío los originales con esta carta. Con gusto puedo
destruir las copias si usted así lo desea.

Sobre el tema central, de lo cual esto posiblemente fue una pista, la Mujer en
Llamas no ha sido vista en Ecuador en más de una semana. Hay rumores de
milagros en sitios remotos, pero como con tanta información que va de boca en
boca, los detalles se deforman y exageran hasta el punto de llegar a ser
inútiles. Yo personalmente no creo que la mujer existe.

Con gusto continúo la búsqueda tanto del conductor como de la mujer, pero me
parece que necesito más información, si es que usted está dispuesto a
compartirla. Por ejemplo, sé que al sujeto lo hemos estado llamando
"Bocadiablo" y ese es el alias que está utilizando acá, pero si usted conoce su
verdadero nombre creo que eso podría ayudarnos de alguna manera.

Sin poder obtener más contexto, estoy tanteando a oscuras. Además, la situación
política acá ha deteriorado. Entiendo que es el entorno en el cual todos
trabajamos ahora, pero en este caso ya no es seguro andar aquí por carretera.

Espero que este informe le haya sido de interés y quedo a la espera de su
respuesta.

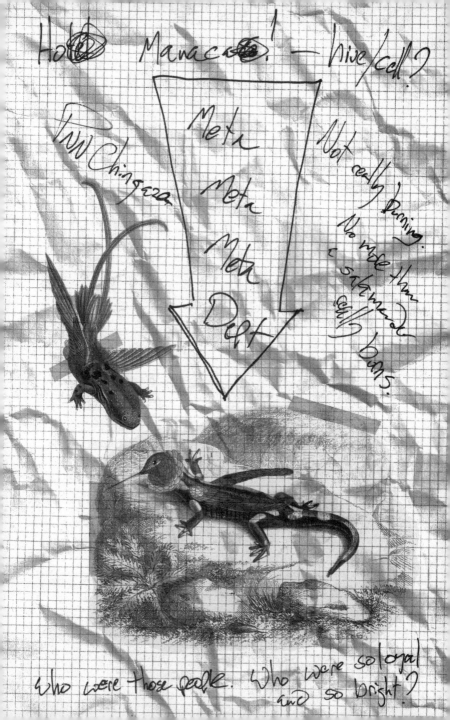

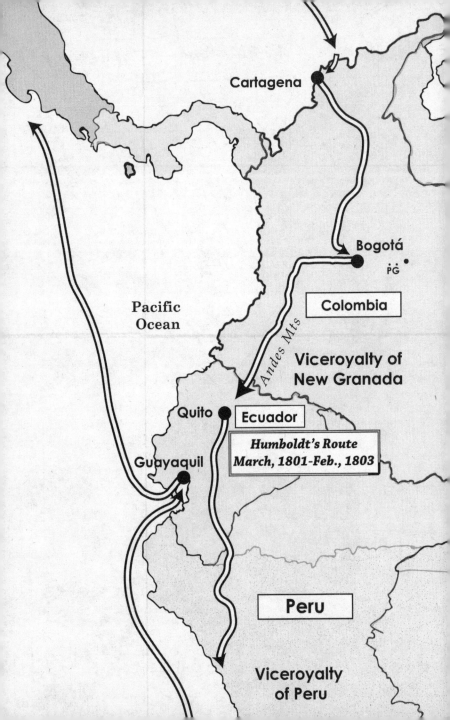

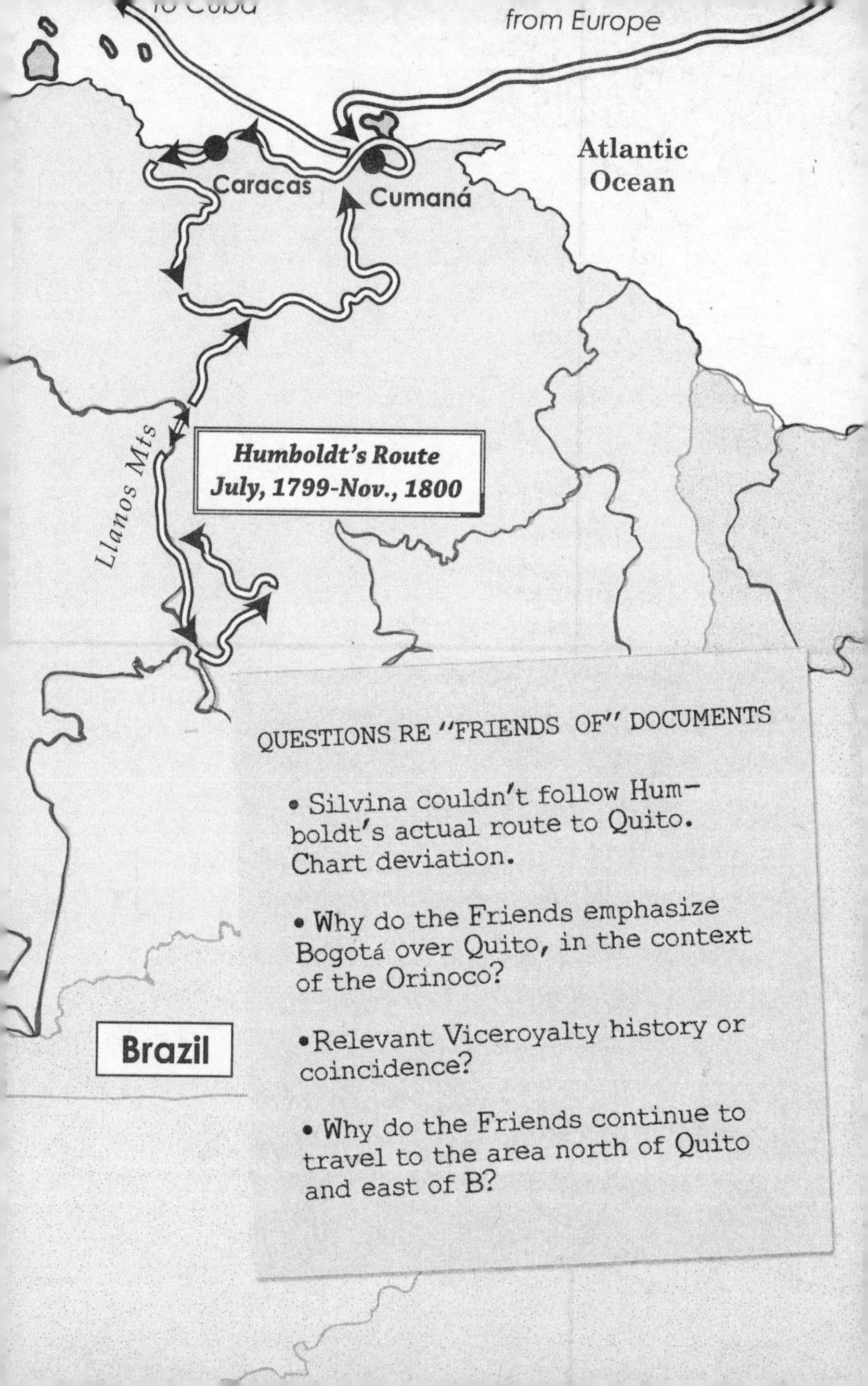

to Cuba

from Europe

Atlantic
Ocean

Caracas   Cumaná

*Humboldt's Route
July, 1799–Nov., 1800*

Llanos Mts

Brazil

QUESTIONS RE "FRIENDS OF" DOCUMENTS

• Silvina couldn't follow Humboldt's actual route to Quito. Chart deviation.

• Why do the Friends emphasize Bogotá over Quito, in the context of the Orinoco?

• Relevant Viceroyalty history or coincidence?

• Why do the Friends continue to travel to the area north of Quito and east of B?

Subject 2: It's a little meta. Or maybe just beta.

Subject 1: Meta beta theta creata.

Subject 2: You're silly when you're drunk.

Subject 1: You're drunk when you're drunk.

Agent: But it's a beautiful dream, don't you think? A hundred of these Shangri Las.

Subject 1: Maybe even one in Shangri La.

Subject 2: I like it. It could work. You could use each as an anchor for activism. For meeting.

Agent: You could build a kind of country within all these countries. One that cares about the things you care about.

Subject 1: Change the world.

Subject: Don't be sarcastic. This is serious.

Subject 1: No, I'm serious, Silvina. I promise. I promise I'm serious now.

Subject 2: Well, all right then—cheers to us.

Agent: To us.

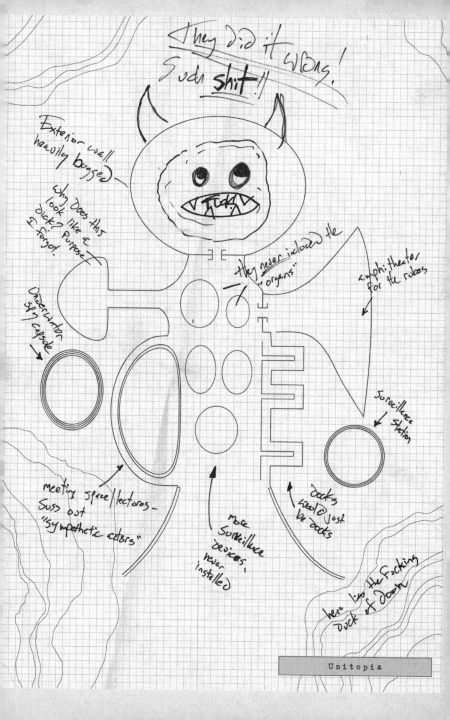

Unitopia

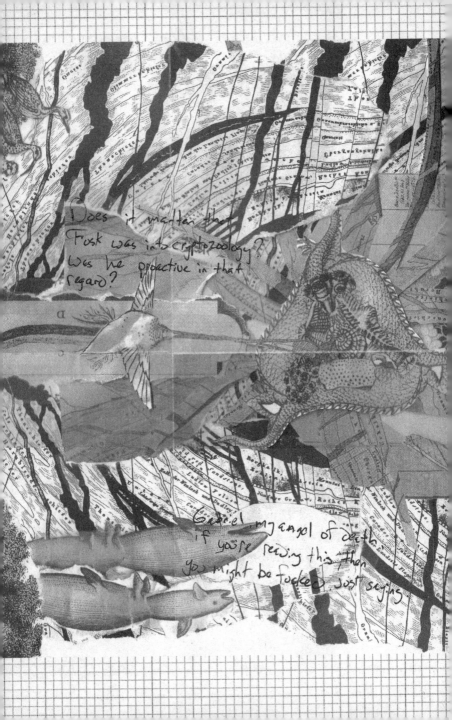

Does it matter that Frisk was into cryptozoology? Was he proactive in that regard?

Gabriel my angel of death if you're reading this then you might be fucked just saying

Silvina's plan was
Distributed, not concentrated.
Each (friend) has one piece?

where is of hammer I want of hammer where the FUCK

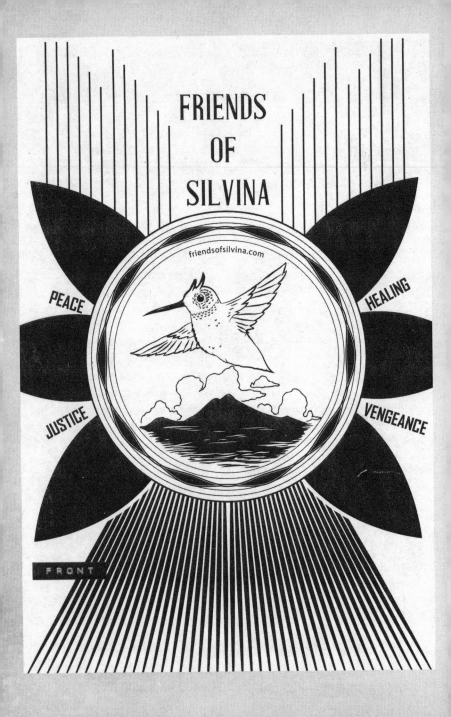

JOIN IN!

The Friends of Silvina invite you to the blessed moment: Silvina's resurrection is upon us in all ways and across all things. Gather as you know how, at the time that is the time. The world may be ending, but we are just beginning. The love and the devotion you have shown this cause, the blood and tears, will now be rewarded. But only if you remain true. Join, fight, make the world anew.

Los Amigos de Silvina les invitan al bendito momento: la resurrección de Silvina nos está alcanzando en todas maneras y a través de todas cosas. Reúnanse como todos ustedes saben, al momento que es el momento. Puede ser que el mundo se está terminando, pero nosotros apenas estamos comenzando. El amor y la devoción que ustedes han demostrado por esta causa, la sangre y las lágrimas, ahora serán recompensados, si se mantienen fieles. Asegúrense de checar por ojos que te espían y recuerden las reglas de enfrentamiento de Silvina. Únanse, luchen, hagan el mundo de nuevo. Busquen los números correctos.

BACK

STOP LOOKING

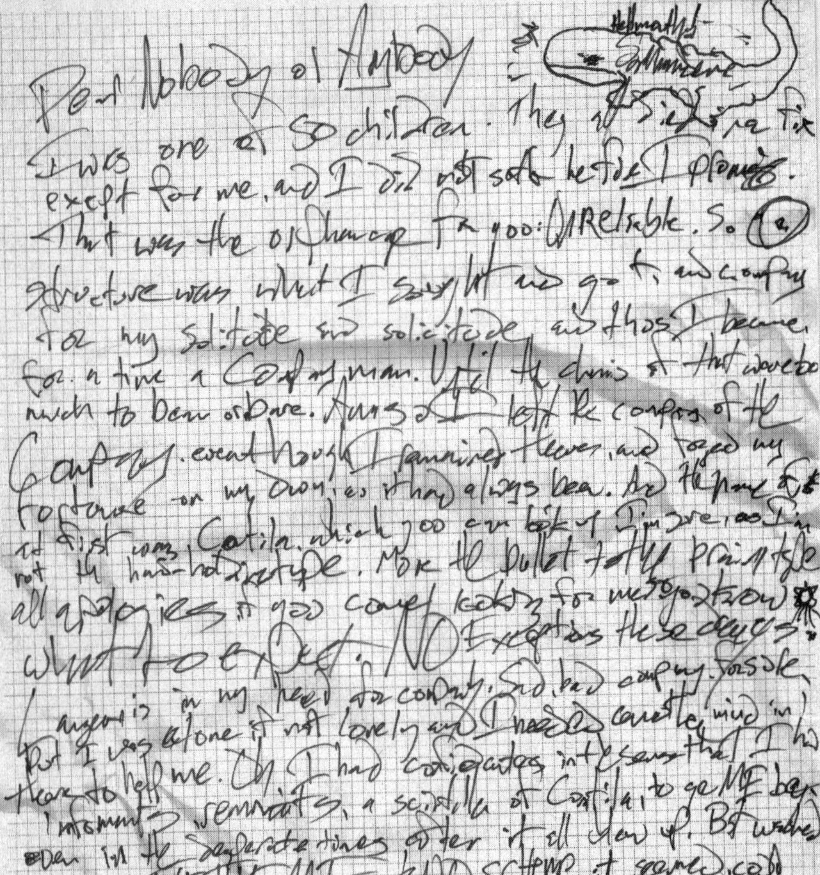

Typed transcript of handwritten JACKSPLAT rant.

Dear Nobody or Anybody:

I was one of 50 children. They all died in a fire except for me, and I did not set the fire, I promise. That was the orphanage for you: unreliable. So, structure was what I sought and got, and company for my solitude and solicitude and thus I became, for a time, a Company man. Until the chains of that were too much to bear or bare. And so I left the company of the Company, even though I remained there, and forged my fortune on my own, as it had always been. And the name of that, at first, was Contila, which you can look up, I'm sure, as I'm not the hand-holding type. More the bullet to the brain type, all apologies, if you come looking for me, so you know what to expect. No exceptions these days.

Langer in my head for company. Sad, bad company, for sure, but I was alone if not lonely and I needed another mind in there to help me. Oh, I had confidantes in the sense that I had informants, remnants, a scintilla of Contila, to get me by, even in the desperate times after it all blew up. But washed up was the theme and no scheme, it seemed, could undo it.

STOP LOOKING

I had bits of her journal recovered from the remains of a damp, singed houseboat. I had the paraphrase of her letter to Jilly Billy. I had the half-hearted research torn from the clutches of Jill's assistant. I had access still to transcripts of Contila wiretaps, interrogations, and more from back in the day, just dangling there from above, in the clouds.

I marvel, now, at the idiocy of my decision-making. The man who is drowning will clutch at the most insubstantial reed to save him, whether it bears his weight or not.

STOP LOOKING

It felt like punishment, I must admit. In her handwriting, the one I will not name for fear of bringing Friends. But when had she written it? By what alchemy did it appear on my café table in Buenos Aires a year after Jack and Jill went up a hill? Was it forgery to torment, or honest admonishment, demonishment, demolishment—meant to ward and warn, that a Company chap come to no harm? Senior Senor Vilcapampa I knew to be cold and no longer above ground, but his wife had as hard an edge. Did his wife not appreciate how close I was to their crypt-lair?

By then I had given the heave-ho to one form of transportation and put my back into another, such that by all rights I should be untraceable. Yet

STOP LOOKING

Langer was right about one thing. This world needs a reboot or just the right boot. And I could've been the one. I could've been that one, or some one.

STOP LOOKING

I rearrange the letters, think of rhymes, and it all comes up nonsense.

POTS KING LOO

LOOP STING OP

KING POOL TOP

Then I look back across Contila and so much else and it all comes up nonsense once again.

I was one of fifty, once. There was a kind of pitiful strength in numbers, even in getting a regular beat-down from the beat-up elder children. I can recall their wizened faces looking down at me as if in that moment they held some knowledge I needed, but all I really needed was a weapon. A flamethrower would've been nice, but unavailable by mail-order and not something a kid with few skills can make out of things he salvages from his bunk bed or the lunch room. Perhaps if I had saved enough breakfast cereal bar codes.

STOP LOOKING

I'll never stop looking; it's all I have left, I must admit. I'm the inquisitive type; I just can't stop whittling away through the wood rot. I can't stop plucking the eyes from any taxidermy I see, just to be sure no message awaits me the way it did Jill. Wild boar, stare boring through me.

Kangaroo, emu, insurance salesman. The last may have not been taxidermy, but the same result, given I didn't buy what he was selling. But there have been no missives conveyed, just that the high-step rapid retreat is hell on the knees and you might smash into something on your way and do further damage and wonder just how you got here.

STOP LOOKING

I suppose I should take some bankrupt pride in at least getting close, so very close, so damn close I can almost hold the prize in my fucking hand, smell it close, taste it close. Am I closer now? Am I warm, warmer, hotter, hottest? I never understood why she wouldn't create It closer to where she was born, but, then, I'm not sure I understood much about her except the passion she brought to her work.

And where did Jill end up, I wonder? And that again, I'll never know even if I never

STOP LOOKING

There's more to say, but I've run out of time and also of paper. But not of will. Where there's a will there's a way— and that way is on foot I fear. Follow if you trust me about the flamethrower. Otherwise, you might just forget about me. I done those terrible things, boss, I did, but she done worse. I think.

KING SOO LOST